The *Ghost* of Christmas *Pastel*

Cybil Lawson Mystery 1

Originally Published October 2024

Sarah Ickes

Cozy Mystery | Light-Hearted Traditional | Woman Sleuth

"Their faces were a mixture of hurt and betrayal, with a healthy side of revenge ready to seep out."

Thank you!

to Sherry, for reading this when time was short
and of the essence.

And to Val, who helped with the timing of a
certain clue.

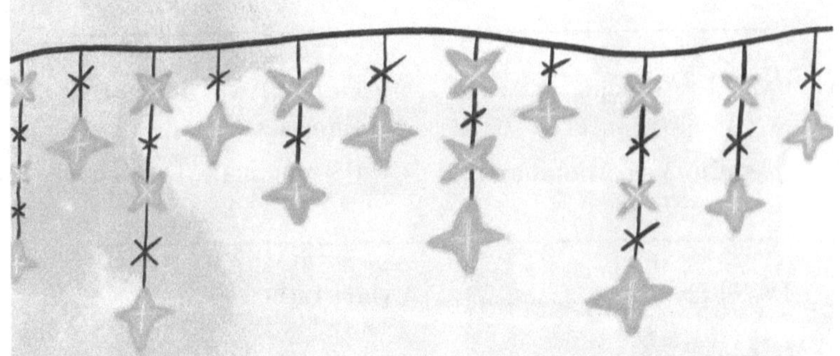

For G, who makes all things possible.

CHARACTERS

Cybil Lawson............................ works at Mark's Crafts and Art Supplies

Yasmin "Yas" Manahan.......... Cybil's roommate, best friend

David Lawson.......................... Cybil's father

Cynthia Lawson........................ Cybil's mother

Uncle Wiley.............................. Cybil's uncle, Cynthia's brother

---

Detective Phoenix Lawson..... Cybil's uncle, David's brother

Officer Tyrone Noel................. new cop on the force

Marjorie Stonewell................... choir director, church secretary

Marta Stonewell....................... middle sister, owns hair salon

Melody Dayton (Stonewell).... Oldest sister, Christine's step-mother

Christine Hieghner................... Melody's step-daughter, owner of local art gallery

Raven Hieghner....................... Christine's daughter, Marjorie's great-niece

CHARACTERS *continued...*

<u>Cybil's Co-Workers</u>

Grab a cup of hot cocoa and dive into a wintry world of murder and mayhem...

READ YOUR WAY

If you are looking for a more interactive way to ride along with Cybil in her first investigation, feel free to make copies of her notes and the character list to take down your own observations. See if you can deduce who the killer is before she does.

Interested in just reading the story?

That's perfectly fine as well. Enjoy this Chrismas-themed mystery any way you want.

If you really liked this story, please share it with your friends and post book reviews on any platforms you use. Tag my accounts on social media to share!

> Interested in making the craft Cybil does for her project at work? Check out the back of this book, or my website for the full set of instructions.

Discussion questions and media packets for this novel are also available on my website.

Cybil's NoteBook

and don't miss out on all the action!

<u>Murial Robertson Mysteries</u>
The Serpent's Star
Angled for Revenge
A Counterfeit of Death
An Ancient Poison (coming soon)

<u>Vectra Tillerman Adventures</u>
Written Wings
The Fall of Time (coming soon)

<u>Vectra and Murial Cross-Over</u>
The Nation's Grief (coming soon)

<u>A Family's Masterpiece Series</u>
A Family's Masterpiece (coming soon)

<u>Cybil Lawson Mysteries</u>
The Ghost of Christmas Pastel
In Plein Air Sight (coming soon)

<u>Twisted Short Tales</u>
A Year 4 Twisted Short Tales (coming soon)

DECEMBER 14ᵀᴴ

(around 9:00 pm)

There she was. Just lying in the snow. It was as though she had planned on making a snow angel on her stomach, instead of on her back. But the pain riddled on her face erased that possibility right out the window. Besides, who would want to play in the middle of a darkened street anyway?

Underneath a few inches of kicked up white fluff, her purple coat was as plain as day. Draped upon her very still body was the red dress she had worn to the dinner earlier in the evening, and while the black boots were disproportionately large on her feet, they were undeniably hers with the initials M.S. on the bottom of their soles. Her hair, which was dyed to eliminate the graying, was messy and in need of some decent brushing. However, that was something she no longer had to worry about.

Yasmin stood beside her friend, horrified at the discovery she had just made. Her hand clinched tighter around Cybil's arm, studying the marks running up the deceased's back, and leaned to the side in order to whisper in her ear. "Are those…"

"Yep. Grandma got ran over by a reindeer."

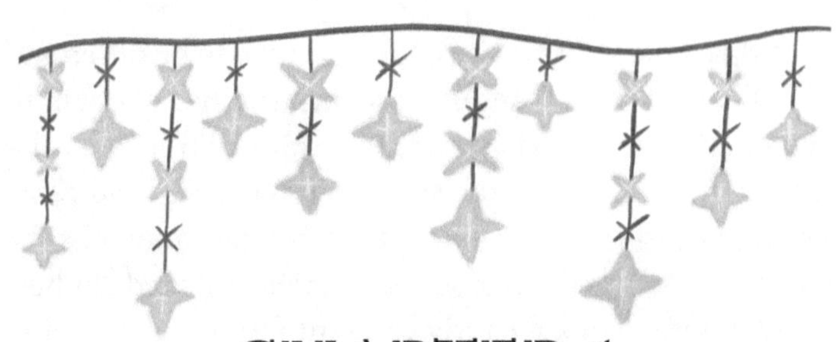

CHAPTER 1

Fourteen Days Ago...

Cybil Lawson gazed up at the night sky just as a bright, white line, pierced the dark, before vanishing completely. Quickly shutting her eyes closed, she made a silent wish and slowly peeked down at her phone. With a single tap of her finger, the digital clock showed it to be striking midnight and the date magically changed from November 30th to the first of December. A joyous smile spread across her face, and reflected the same contentment in her eyes, once they fully reopened. *I am determined to make this Christmas better than the last three years.*

She sat atop the window seat, in the make-shift living room, and returned her gaze upon the peaceful stars high above Robbyr's Cove. Things were finally coming together, after many weeks of worrying about how she was going to pay off her car's recent accident. Though it was not a major fix, the money it required could only be paid by an empty checking account. As a result, Cybil relied on the use of her roommate's vehicle for transport to and from work. But, with her new promotion to part-time manager at Mark's Crafts and Art Supplies, she was looking forward to receiving a higher wage, and longer holiday hours, to increase her weekly paycheck. "This Christmas is going to be different."

"What was that?" Inquired a curly-haired woman, in green pants and a red sweater. Her hair bounced as she danced in the kitchen to a song about a red-nosed reindeer, and nearly struck a potted plant off the counter as she spun around. Cybil shook her head as she watched her best friend happily stick a candy cane into two mugs, piping hot with fresh cocoa. The young woman then proceeded to cautiously scoop them up in her hands, before heading over to join Cybil by the frosted window.

"Nothing, Yas." She gave her roommate a perplexed look at the striped Christmas candy she was not fond of. "Yasmin, you know I like the *look* of peppermint, but not the *taste* of it."

"I just wanted you to try it." Her friend countered her sceptic stare with a toothy grin of her own. "You might be surprised, and find that you actually *do* like it."

"I highly doubt *that*." Cybil's hand wrapped around the handle of the reindeer head-shaped mug, and looked directly into its painted black eyes. *Well, it never hurts to try something new, right?* A gulp of hesitation could be loudly heard in her throat, as she failed to see the chocolate drink through the whipped cream. Crushed pieces of candy canes were sprinkled atop the fluffy white goodness, adding to her fears about the taste. "And you added crushed pieces as well."

"Had to be festive!" Yasmin lifted her mug to her mouth, and drank in the warm deliciousness that filled the senses. When she pulled the happy elf head away, she could feel the presence of cream on her chin. "I think I could use a napkin. Is it just on my chin?"

"Where *isn't* it, would be more like it." Cybil chuckled at the almost complete Santa Claus beard on Yas's face. While her friend dashed back to retrieve a towel from the kitchen, the perfectly twirled cream in her own mug, was begging to be played with as she waited for the drink to cool down. "Is this what you plan on making for the Annual church Christmas dinner?"

"Marjorie placed me in charge of drinks this year." Yas called from the sink, her mouth in mid-wipe under a dampened paper towel. "She said that after my disastrous job at bringing the salad last time, she was going to try to give me something 'simpler' to manage."

"Well…" Cybil didn't want to admit to her friend that she was terrible at making a salad, but since everyone in town now knew, there was no use in trying to keep it a secret any longer. "A Caesar salad is fine to have as a precursor to the main entrée, but at least that comes with parmesan cheese at certain places."

"Laugh it up, Cybil Lawson, laugh it up." Yas strode over quickly in her long legs, and jokingly slapped her friend in the shoulder. "But three different types of lettuce constitutes as a salad in my book."

"And where did the non-existent dressing fit in?" She was, of course, referring to the fact that Yas had forgotten to bring the *one* bottle of ranch she purchased to accompany the dismal mixture of lettuce. "Who did you blame it on again?" Cybil thought to herself for a brief moment, "ah, that's right. You blamed the pastor for making you leave the dressing on our counter."

"He startled me." She defended. "Driving by our porch, and seeing me put the light on for when you got off of work. Asking me if I wanted a ride, because you had my car and all. I believe it was in the garage for an oil change that day."

"Oh, yes. How horrible for a pastor to offer one of his flock a ride to the Annual Christmas Dinner." A smirk replaced her cynical look at the peppermint-tinted cocoa. "I must remember to ask him not to startle you again with such a kind gesture this year." She chuckled as Yasmin smacked her again.

"You will not. I was just nervous, tis all. I'm not as outgoing as you are. 'Shy' should have been my middle name instead of 'Holly.'" Yasmin returned to her elf mug, enjoying the soothing warmth against her tongue whilst her fingers toyed with a necklace, dangling just above the lip of her cable-knit sweater. In its beautiful rose gold metal, her middle name picked up on the small amount of light from above, a family memento she had come to cherish. "By the way, Marjorie assigned you to be in charge of cookie donations."

"WHAT?" Cybil's jaw almost dropped into the pile of cream now dissolving in her drink. "I don't recall volunteering this year." Her right eye squinted at the sudden tilt of her roommate's head. "*Yasmin?*"

"Huh?"

"Did you sign me up at your choir practice last night?"

"Perhaps…" Yasmin held the elf's cheerful face in front of her own. "Okay, I did."

"YASMIN MANAHAN! I have more hours at work this year, and I specifically told you that I was going to take a step back from volunteering this time."

"Yeah, you did say that. But…" Her voice faded off until Cybil demanded that she speak louder. "It is the easiest position to take on. You create a paper sign-up sheet, hang it up on the corkboard in the church's lobby, and wait for the signatures to faithfully appear. Everyone else is doing most of the work, you just have to organize the dessert table and ensure the cookies arrive on time."

"And that's supposed to be easy? Yas, if my memory is

right, Mrs. Tudball held that honor for the last ten years before passing away. And she offered to pick everyone's orders up from their houses, AND filled in with her own cookies when needed."

"So?"

"We're sharing your car until I have enough money to pay the garage for the work they did. And that is not going to happen until after Christmas. HOW IS THIS GOING TO WORK?!"

"We will figure something out. You worry too much." Yas leaned her head against the cold window, as her hazel eyes stared back at her in the glass. While outside, the street lamp flickered on and off, in desperate need to be changed by the township.

"You're right. The solution is simple. Quite simple, in fact. Just go back to Marjorie and explain to her that it was all a big mistake. That I can't do the job justice and…"

"Kind of too late for that."

Cybil did not care for the raised octave in her friend's voice, which usually occurred when the other shoe was about to drop. "I'm almost afraid to ask. What did you mean by that?"

"Marjorie was so delighted to have the volunteer list done, that she already handed the list to Pastor Lawrence so he can announce it in the morning, before the sermon." Cybil opened her mouth, about to speak out in another protest, but Yas beat her to it. "I know, I know. Can you blame me though? Tara Newston was going to put her hand in the air for the spot, and I could not let her get it. And Marjorie was NOT going to give it to me, under any circumstances, after the way she came down on my poor salad."

"Yas, I have a lot of training to do for my new position. With Christmas around the corner, and my mom gushing over the fact that her brother will be joining us for dinner this year, I'm under enough stress as it is. Adding onto the fact that I will *now* be handling the most important part of the Christmas dinner, for the church, my volcano is about to erupt on overload."

"Sorry, Cybil. Truly I am. But I also took note of how long your face got at the idea of not being able to help out at the dinner this year."

"That's because I'm not going to be able to attend. I'm the bottom manager on the ladder, and with everyone else having their vacation and holiday plans already approved, there is a slim chance of me getting off that night." Cybil balanced the untouched mug atop her knee, watching the crushed peppermint fall into the cocoa, the cream mostly consumed by the hot drink. Sadness lingered between the two friends, making the chilly outdoor air seem warmer, and more inviting, as it seeped through the single-pane window.

Living in a converted railroad station held an undeniably unique charm to it; however, it was also a bit problematic when it came to certain financial basics, such as the electric bill. The brick station's history, since 1908, was filled with tales of robbers and gangs jumping off a few miles down the track, in order to hide out in the town. Everyone's families could be traced back to criminals in varying degree, including that of murder in the first. Whether their ancestors actually did the deeds they were accused of was often a mystery in itself; due to the lack of records from the illiterate bandits. Even their town's own name of Robbyr's Cove, was a self-evident example in their lack of written education. A misspelled word, and the absence of a cove in the land-locked area, did not speak highly of their founders.

Still, the fun stories whispered about at children's bedtimes, maintained a level of fascination for the old place among the residents. Kids dared one another to creep up to the lonely lantern, hanging high over the back door, around Halloween night. Cybil enjoyed watching through a peep-hole they had installed to amuse herself by their yearly antics. The story told of a supposed ghostly spirit, of a mail thief, who was told to be trapped in the broken light, rusted into the base of the railroad lantern. And when the creak of the old metal could be heard, it was warned he was trying to break free from his tiny prison. Yasmin had offered to have someone fix the noisy light before, but, Cybil did not wish to ruin the laughs she got every October.

Not only did the tales of their outlaw in-laws spark imaginations of buried treasure hidden around the valley, the real-life story of the seven brothers also lived on in the local historical society's museum. Erwin, Quin, Stephen, Brian, Ned, Calvin, and John were not blood-brothers, but they were all connected through a major jewelry heist com-mitted in 1902. The oldest of the crew, Erwin, had not only been the mastermind of the successful operation, but he also happened to be Cybil's great-great grandfather. And while their story went down into legend, the jewels had never been found. *I wonder why my uncle is coming home for a visit?*

"Do you think that the jewelry heist origins of our town are true?" Cybil asked, breaking the mutual silence on the window bench, and snapping her thoughts back to the pres-ent.

"Why ask me? As Larry likes to continually point out while I'm working on Thursday evenings, I am not from 'round this here parts.'" Yasmin did her best to mimic the town's retired police chief, who frequented Ralph's Dry Bar and Grill every week, on the same day, for a game of pool.

"But that's the reason I'm asking you. For an outsider's opinion." Cybil playfully smiled at her friend. "In all seriousness though, do you think it could be real?"

"I don't know what to think. Sounds too much like a movie or an outlandish book plot to me. But, the classic saying is that you can't make up real life. So maybe the far-fetched stories are true." Yasmin took another sip from her cooling drink. "What brought this on all of a sudden? Your mom said you used to pretend to find the treasure as a kid, but I haven't seen you pick up the midnight flashlight and gravedigger's shovel lately."

"Well, my mom is *super* excited that her brother is coming home for Christmas this year. I mean…she is even making a double batch of every cookie recipe she normally bakes."

"Wow! The town won't be big enough to handle that load."

"I know, right? She made sure to tell me not to talk about anything to do with Robbyr's Cove's history. 'Not a peep' about it around my uncle when he arrives next week."

"Wait, is this the uncle who is a treasure hunter or something like that?"

"I think 'wannabe treasure-hunter' is a more appropriate title. As far as I know, he works as a janitor at a college, and does some research work for one of the professors on the side. He loves to read, so I would assume that having access to the library on a daily basis is a plus for him." Cybil brushed back a few strands of loose hair about to fall into the melted mush in her cup. "Apparently, he can get easily carried away when it comes to talking about the stolen jewels. It's just…"

"What?"

"I haven't seen him since he left town when I was twelve,

and all I can recall is his 'laboratory' that was literally the spare bedroom turned into a treasure seeker's workplace. It was filled with images, corkboards, clues, and blown-up scans of locations in town. Even had the classic red strings leading from one pin to another."

"You did tell me that he was a bit of a recluse. Maybe he should have gotten a hobby like model trains or miniature bookshelf scenes. I saw that they're becoming very popular in my online book club."

"Searching for the treasure was his hobby, and I had no issue with that, nor with the root beer soda dispenser he created in the closet."

"Man, did I miss out or what?"

"That machine did make the best root beers in town." For a brief moment, the nostalgic memory brought up a bittersweet smile for Cybil. Until she remembered what she heard earlier in the day, and it faded from her lips soon after. "I must admit, that I was also really looking forward to seeing him again. And one of the things I wanted to talk to him about was the jewels. Guess I can't resist my curious imagination when it comes to buried treasure. But when I was at the grocery store today, I overheard Bethany Quaker tell her daughter that the 'Crazy Custodian' was coming back to town."

"Mrs. Quaker is one to talk; with the amount of gossip going around about what she is growing in that *fancy* new greenhouse she put up at the end of summer. Besides, what does it matter what other people think?"

"Well, it got me thinking about the movies and tv shows we have seen where the crazy guy usually ends up being right. What if the treasures are buried within elaborate clues that the original gang set up to protect their bounty?"

"Are you sure you are talking about the same founders of the town who could not spell the word 'robber' correctly?" Yasmin studied her friend's sparkling eyes. "Don't tell me that you are thinking about quitting your day job in the hopes that some *phantom jewels* are going to pay off your garage bill."

"Fat chance at that happening." Cybil joked the matter off and decidedly changed the subject. "How are the questions going for the upcoming trivia night at Ralph's?" Yasmin rambled on about her concerns on whether the topics she had in mind would be too difficult, or too easy, but her friend's thoughts were not on the state flower of Montana. Instead, it was up in the clear night sky and her childhood fantasies of going on adventures like *Indiana Jones.*

CHAPTER 2

"Here." Brandi shoved a thick packet of papers at Cybil, who had just shut the door to her short locker in the break room. The papers almost hit her nose, momentarily blinding her from the unexpected way the assistant store manager made her daily greeting. Every evening, rain or shine, the thirty-something woman would end her shift with a worn out face and a passive disinterest. It was one of the things each new employee was warned about, in advance, during their initial tour of the blah-looking room. Even after three years of working as a cashier at the craft store, Cybil could hear the southern voice of a former manager telling her not to touch locker number forty-two, and to keep out of Brandi's way when her shift was over. It was one thing she had been able to accomplish for most of her time there, avoiding the moody monster…until now.

"Ah, what is this?" Cybil pulled the paper out from her face far enough to see the bolded words "Standard Operating Procedure" on the top of the packet.

"SOP. You are going to need to study it for when different situations arise. Look over it whenever you get a chance during your shift." A foreboding finger slashed upward in the air at Cybil. "And don't go working on it during your off time. It is against the law to require employees to do unpaid training such as that."

"Thanks for the advice. Where is Juliet? She's supposed to be guiding me through my first day."

"Juliet called off sick. So I have been reassigned to you."

"But you should have clocked out five minutes ago."

"Yep. That's what I told Matt. But apparently everyone else is maxed out in their hours for the week, and the district boss said 'no' to overtime just yet. They are still trying to cut back on extra payouts after the Covid mess." Brandi tied her long, straight hair into a pony tail at the back of her head. "So I am here till closing tonight."

"Okay." Cybil put on a fake smile in the hopes that her fellow manager could not see her disappointment.

"You don't have to pretend with me, Kid. I wish I could be at home right now and not here to train yet another hire for this position. But we have to make the best of it, so follow me." Brandi waited for Cybil to throw her brown vest on over her plain t-shirt, punch in her numbers on the time clock, and swiftly moved onto the sales floor. "Being a manager means that you are going to be the one person that people expect to have the answers to their problems. You won't have them right away, so don't be frustrated if you have to ask one of us for the first few weeks. Especially since you are starting at our busiest time of the year."

"Is it alright if I carry a notebook and pen around with me to take notes?"

Brandi shrugged her thin shoulders. "Sure. Doesn't bother me in the least." She placed her key in the door to the office, and swung it open for Cybil. Gesturing at the black rolling chair, Brandi offered for her to sit down, as they were going to dive into the security system. "You should already know the basics of this from your prior years here, but I am going to go over this anyway. There are cameras focused on the aisles with the highest priced goods and the items that are a known risk for being taken. We also have a camera that watches over the register and the front part of the store. The parking lot is not as well covered, but that area is managed by the mall's own company, so you shouldn't have to worry about any of that."

Cybil clicked her pen tip open and began to furiously write down the way to bring footage up from a previous day, how to select which camera to view on the monitor screen, and how to access the archived files for anything over two months old. "Alright, now that you have the crash course in our camera system, we are going to head into the vault room to do a run through on the how we will take down the registers at night."

"Brandi?" A broken voice came over the headset in the assistant manager's ear. The soft tone could only be Hazel, who worked in the framing department and was also a lover of Japanese Anime.

"Yeah?"

"I'm going to need some help in framing."

"On it." Brandi lifted her finger off the button to speak, just as Cybil confessed to having forgotten to grab a headset in the break room. "Come on back with me and I can explain a few things along the way." She made a large, circular sweeping motion with her hand in the direction of the door and exited the office. Cybil trailed her past numerous end caps while they cut through the yarn department, and rounded the customized ornaments display until the framing counter came into view.

Her eyes grew large at seeing who was waiting to be helped. "Uh, I'm going to use the restroom real quick. Be back in a flash." Cybil dashed behind the assistant store manager, keeping her hands up as a shield for her eyes, and made a beeline for the women's restrooms.

"Okay, but this would be a great time for you to get some of your training out of the way!" Brandi called after her.

Cybil banged the door open and rushed into the first available stall. She slid the lock into place and heavily leaned against the speckle-colored wall. *Marjorie.* It would not have mattered if the choir director had popped in for a framing job under any other circumstances. However, unknown to Yasmin, Cybil had already assured her boss that she would have open availability during the holiday season; even when he specifically asked her about the night for the Annual Christmas Dinner. If Marjorie announced to them about her "volunteering" to head up the cookie donations, things could get a little awkward. *Great! Just great! It's going to look like I lied to Matt.*

"Cybil?" Hazel hesitantly spoke into the bathroom.

"Yeah?"

"Brandi is asking for you. She says that this would be a good introduction into learning the framing end of the store."

"Could you do me a favor?" Her eyes squinted into the air, hopelessly wishing for Marjorie to go away because she forgot something, or left her reading glasses at home. Anything would have been better than standing at the counter and waiting for assistance to frame whatever she had in her hands.

"Ah, sure?" Hazel sounded curious.

"Tell her I went back home because I was sick, and not feeling well."

The door to the bathroom banged shut as Hazel walked up to the locked stall, and peered in through the crack between the door and the hinge. "You don't look sick to me."

"Hey!" Cybil flung herself around to see a brown eye staring at her in the open slit. "That is a little discomforting. You do realize that, right?"

"I knew you weren't sitting on the toilet. Your shoes were pointed the wrong way."

"Oh." Glancing down at her black sneakers, Cybil tilted her head in agreement. "Very perceptive of you."

"Come on. You don't want to make Brandi mad, today of all days especially."

Cybil reluctantly, and against every instinct in her body, clicked the lock open and swung the door outward to see her co-worker standing there in her black apron, small name badge, and her usual low space buns hairdo. Fashionable loose strands were purposefully separated from the rest of her jet black hair to dangle on either side of her face. A muted pink had been skillfully applied to her lips and on her eyelids, softening the slightly "goth" feel from her attire. "What's wrong? It's not like you to shy away from work."

"Never mind. I'll come out in a minute. Just need to wash my hands." She hoped her cheeks weren't blushing from the lie that slipped from her mouth. It may not have been the answer she wanted, but at least it would provide her with a few more seconds of procrastination. Hazel appeared satisfied with her answer, and headed back to the framing counter with the grace of a floating angel, much like her own personality. Often times, Cybil would find herself asking the heavens how a person could be so calm and patient with customers who were either annoyingly indecisive, tiresomely opinioned, or rude penny-pinchers. *I understand penny-pinching, but most of the time, the ones who are rude about it don't need to rub them together in order to pay.*

Sooner than she would have liked, the time for getting her hands cleaned was over and she was off to face the music of Marjorie Stonewell. Within two seconds flat, the middle-aged woman recognized Cybil's shy face and made sure everyone knew in her own loud style. "CYBIL LAWSON! How great to see you. We missed you at church this morning. I was simply elated when Yasmin told me that you would handle the cookie donations for the Christmas dinner. It is the best part of the meal, as you *well* know, and also the highest honor one can be bestowed for the event. To be honest, I was a little worried about who was going to take up the baton after Mrs. Tudball went to be with the Lord. But with you at the helm, I can rest assured that it is in good hands."

The reddest tomato in the whole state of Pennsylvania could not have matched the coloring on Cybil's cheeks. She nervously flashed a look Brandi's way and was surprised to find the woman's face as stoic as ever. Though, she wasn't sure why she was surprised. Brandi's emotions were not readable like a book, and in fact, she barely even broke into a partial grin since Cybil began working there. Rumors would circulate among the staff that she used to smile in school and then the fun was literally drained from her in college. "Overworked due to her science degree, and under the pressure of unpleasing parents, that's what did it," was another famous line. Too many fictional reasons had been fabricated with every new employee, and each one more absurd than the last. *I think we are up to alien abduction at this rate.*

"I had to be here at work this morning, and Marjorie, you are too kind." She gave the woman a beaming smile. "I will do my best to live up to Mrs. Tudball's big shoes."

"I figured you would, Deary. Because the whole dinner

revolves around it, I know I can count on you." A large grin caused her wrinkles to fade away for a moment, and seemed to erase five years off her age instantly. With chestnut brown hair being replaced by wisdom grey, Cybil was pretty sure that the woman would be moving up her monthly appointment at the beauty salon. Green eyes, mischievous in nature, were slightly dulled in comparison to the bright red lipstick and equally bright green scarf tied around her neck. Bow-wrapped present earrings, in traditional Christmas colors, shook by her ears as they stood out against the darkened coat she wore overtop a red shirt and pants.

"Well, you certainly are already embracing the festive spirit."

"Ooh, this is nothing. But thank-you. This year, I felt like I was seriously lacking a healthy dose of joy and good-will. It's been a little hard for me these past eleven months." Marjorie blinked back her watering eyes and dismissed the sudden sadness altogether. "Now then, I believe this lovely woman was about to help me get this piece framed."

Cybil finally brought herself to look upon the canvas print sitting on the counter, instead of the quick glances she got in during their conversation. Studying the artwork that came into the framing department was the best part. She enjoyed the stories the framers would share about their customers' masterpieces, and study what kinds of works people bought in...and were willing to pay to get framed. It was all a part of her grand plan to sell her own pieces to the public. But that dream would have to wait until another day far in the future. "I love the color scheme."

"My niece did the original work in pastels, but I ordered a print to be made up because I wanted to install this." Marjorie flipped a switch on a battery pack in her left hand. In the same instant, light sprang forth all over the blue and orange painting: inside the lamp posts, the cozy restaurant and even on the top star of the town's Christmas tree. "Looks great, doesn't it? It is almost like you can feel the magic of the season through her work. I have another print of a painting she did last year that I had done the same way. It hangs above the mantel in my living room on a timer. That way, it doesn't burn out the lights faster. They go off at 10:50 pm, sharp."

"The painting is quite lovely; especially the area of the frozen lake with the skating children on it. I'm sure her mother is quite proud of her."

"One would think so." A sigh filled the air for a split moment. "I told Christine that she needs to include a few of Raven's pastel pieces in the Christmas exhibit at her gallery. But you know how that goes with family members. They don't listen to you, unless someone else is speaking the exact same words." Marjorie flipped the lights off and laid the battery pack on the counter. "By the way, that reminds me. I have been meaning to talk to your uncle, Cybil. Not the crazy one in town for the holidays, no. The detective one. Was wondering if he was going to attend this year, to the Christmas Eve sermon, considering that this is the first time since…"

Cybil didn't have to hear the rest of the sentence Marjorie failed to finish speaking. It wasn't a secret that her aunt had passed away back in April, because half of the town attended her funeral. She was a well-beloved member of the community, despite being married to the only detective the town had on their payroll. No matter what circumstances arose, however, it seemed that there was nothing that could get in the way between her and her friends. For example, when Detective Lawson had to arrest Portia's husband for stealing Ralph's ultra-valuable, signed, basketball from the dry bar, she still kept up her volunteer breakfast work with Cybil's aunt. In fact, Portia chatted along with Aunt Petunia up till the day she passed. "Ah, I couldn't tell you. We don't really speak to him as of yet."

"That is such a shame." Marjorie flew her arms outward like a bird's wings and hurriedly walked around the counter to give her a hug. Cybil's eyes widened at the impending embrace, and she stopped breathing as a potent wave of perfume hit her nose. "Family riffs are the worst. They divide what should be the strongest unit of support on this planet."

"Right." Trying to sound sincere, Cybil redirected the emotional woman back onto the print she wished to have framed. Brandi showed her how to plug the measurements of the piece into the program on the computer, and how to type in the identification number of the style Marjorie had chosen. After the choir director picked a distressed black color from the Country Home Collection, Cybil had to restrain her face from displaying the shocking price tag at the bottom of the screen.

"Wait. Wait. I should have a coupon. At least, I saw it in my bag, this morning, before I left." Marjorie dug around in her red handbag for another five seconds before she vocally proclaimed her success at locating it, and pulled a mailed coupon from its messy contents. "Here. This should be valid still." She handed over a seventy percent off flier that Brandi punched into the system. At the new, lowered amount, Cybil still could not afford the price of such an exquisite choice.

"All set. Your total will be $381.67. How will you be paying for this today?" Brandi quickly scanned the barcode on the order she printed, selected the card option on the register, and waited for the credit card reader to work its magic. Cybil was surprised to find that the choir director didn't bat an eyelash at the quoted price. *That certainly is a lot of money to put into a frame job. Without even having glass cut, and a mat to fit the artwork. How much does she make as the church's secretary? Being the choir director is a volunteer position.* The telling beep of the machine informed everyone that the transaction had been completed, and Brandi headed into the work room with the print.

"It was very good to see you Cybil. If you want, I can handle putting the sign-up sheet on the bulletin board, so long as you haven't changed your phone number." She gave her a sugary smile.

"Ah…no, I haven't changed my number. Still the same." Cybil cautiously answered. When it came to talking to Marjorie, it was best to keep things simple and to the point. She was one of the main gossipers in town, and no one wanted to be caught in a lie with her ears in range. A bloodhound may have a good sniffer to track down scents, but her's was queen at uprooting false words.

"Fantastic! I will have it printed off tonight so it can be up first thing Monday morning. No time to waste in getting the food in order."

A small grin was all Cybil could muster to keep the feel-good vibes going, while she secretly hoped for the woman to just go away. Her wish was soon granted as Marjorie waved farewell from over her shoulder as she left, leaving Cybil to stand awkwardly alone behind the counter. Brandi and Hazel were in the work room, going over preparations for the completion of two orders due the following morning. But the sound of hushed voices piqued Cybil's interest and when she approached the threshold to the room, the whispers suddenly ceased. "Brandi, I can explain."

"I think you better."

"I did not volunteer to help with the cookie donations.

My best friend did, and…" The assistant store manager held her hand up in the air to stop her from saying another word.

"I'm not talking about the cookie donations. I'm referring to the hug you just got from Ms. Stonewell."

"What about it?" Cybil was all confused. Brandi's face remained stoic, but her voice had certainly changed to being more demanding.

"Ms. Stonewell doesn't hug. *ANYONE*. She used to work as a substitute science teacher for my eighth grade class, and we had a student who liked to hug all the people she met in the hallway. As soon as she tried to hug Ms. Stonewell, she was adamantly denied to touch her, and caused the student to cry."

"Maybe she didn't care for the student that much?"

Brandi solemnly shook her head. "I overheard her tell another teacher about the incident and how she 'kept her distance from everyone without discrimination.' If there is one thing I do know about that woman, it is that she means what she says. There is no misinterpreting her words."

Cybil's mouth remained mute. This new revelation was something that made the confusing occurrence that much more puzzling. *Why would she show so much kindness toward me? And why break a rule she was obviously a stickler for? The family riff wasn't new, and it was something Marjorie would have known about through her connection to Aunt Petunia. What was going on exactly?*

CHAPTER 3

Normally, Ralph's wasn't open on Sunday nights. But with Christmas right around the corner, many folks liked to take their visiting relatives there, and the local businesses wanted to have a space where their office parties could go. So that meant extra work nights around the holidays, and more tips from the incoming customers for the employees at the right time of the year.

As Cybil approached the entrance to Ralph's, a single Christmas wreath stared back at her on the door. The old ornaments, fading from years of outdoor service, gave her soul a welcomed warmth. It was nice to see some things stay the same as time ticked along, but the fraying and half-missing red bow, was in desperate need of an update. She reached for the door knob, complete with a reindeer hanger, and stepped inside to escape the cold air. It was blatantly obvious that Yasmin had been given access to the Christmas decorations again.

In the foyer to the bar, a table-top Christmas tree sat atop fake snow and was surrounded by miniature carolers singing to dogs and cats. A train, a little too large for scale, was coming into the station while three horse-drawn sleds were returning from the outskirts of "town." The neat display consumed the wide window sill, and continued onto a short table next to the wooden bench for customers waiting to be seated. Cybil walked around the mistletoe dangling from the archway, and slipped past the automated snowman like a pro. For years, she worked on mastering the ability to stealthy go by without the frozen friend shouting "Merry Christmas!" as everyone passed by its hidden sensor.

"Hey, stranger!" Yasmin continued wiping out a glass at the sink behind the long, wooden counter at the bar. Christmas lights were strung up on practically every surface, except for the tables considered to be the restaurant portion, and even a Santa hat had been perched on top a cardboard cutout of a famous basketball player. "Was about to go on break. Up for a root beer?"

"You got it." Cybil's butt plunked onto the nearest green-covered stool, and she snatched the TV remote up before the owner could get there first.

"Cybil…" He tried his usual sweet talk voice. "Can I please have the remote?"

"Uh…no." She smirked at him. "I want to see how the soccer match went first, and *then* you can have it back."

"I could just cancel my all-sports-access package. Then there wouldn't be a reason for you to steal the remote anymore."

"Admit it. You like fighting with me. It's part of my charm."

"Yeah, right! You thinking too highly of yourself, girlie." Ralph chuckled, wiping his hands on a red rag he had shoved through a belt loop on his pants. He was an older gentleman, about to reach his sixtieth birthday in June, and had an incredible talent for whipping up a flavorful steak in under five minutes. After successfully going through an AA program twenty years ago, he realized that he wanted to fill the void where the atmosphere of a bar had once been. That was when he came up with the idea of opening a dry bar, where his town-famous steaks were offered on the menu on select nights. "When you going to have your car back from the garage?"

"As soon as I scrape together enough dough to pay the bill, that's when."

"I can't image that your parents wouldn't mind helping you out, if you just asked them."

"How do you know that I didn't ask them already?"

"Because you are stubbornly independent. That's why. And if you had, that car would be sitting in her drive this very minute."

"For your information, Ralph, my parents are still on vacation and won't be back until Tuesday, my dad has misplaced the keys to the spare vehicle, and I turned down their offer of paying for half of the bill after I explained the situation."

"Cybil, you have family and friends who are willing to help. We all could use a little bit of that from time to time. Why not…" Ralph shook his head in defeat. "I don't even know *why* I am bothering with trying to persuade you."

"You got that right." Yasmin bluntly stated. "She seems bent on wreaking havoc on my schedule instead." She plopped her lunch down on the counter next to her friend, and opened the container eagerly. "I think her new goal is to see how much she can drive me crazy before the New Year arrives." Slowly crunching on her salad, Yasmin savored Ralph's homemade dressing that had two blue fair ribbons to its name. But as she glanced over at Cybil, she noticed the troubled look on her friend's face, and became worried it had something to do with next Saturday night. "You're still able to go with me to see the Christmas Carol, right?"

"Yeah, no issues there. Marjorie came into the store today, though. She wanted to have a print framed of an original painting her niece had done." Her friend urged her to continue by nodding her head as she stuffed another forkful into her mouth. "And she gave me a hug." At this point, Yasmin's mouth dropped open and a piece of south-western chicken almost rolled back out, making it obvious that Ralph had made the salad. "I know. Brandi told me her aversion to touching people, so I wasn't sure…in fact I'm still not sure…on what to make of it."

"She does care about the dinner, but not *that* much." Yasmin took a sip of her lemonade. "Brandi's right. Marjorie has never hugged *anyone* in public. Doesn't do it at church either, even after the service. Before tonight, I would have sworn that she wouldn't have hugged the pope if he ever visited, regardless of us not being Catholic."

"Marjorie said that the past eleven months has been hard for her. She almost choked up telling me that, in point of fact. Does that mean anything to you?"

"It's not like she blabs about her personal life to anyone, really. Other people's secrets, sure. But not her own. The most I've heard from her, is whenever she talks about Wavy Clips right before she goes to the hair salon, and about the Christmas dinner. Oh, and of course, her dog. She talks about him until he is in your dreams at night. Marjorie loves him to death."

Cybil returned her gaze to the television and the dis-appointing score rolling across the screen during the post-game report. "She also asked after my Uncle Phoenix."

"That's because they used to date in high school." Ralph piped in from the corner. "Way back in tenth grade as I recall, for the year anyway. She still holds a soft spot for him, even after your uncle married Petunia."

Cybil gave him a quizzical look. "Ralph, you never cease to surprise me. How well do you know Marjorie?"

The dry bar owner shrugged. "I only had a few classes at the same time with her. I can tell you the basic facts, but I wouldn't be going on a trivia show about the subject." He filled up a tall glass with orange soda, which was called 'Orange Ya Thirsty?' and handed it off to one of the other patrons. "Truth is, she has been a pretty private person since I've known her. I always thought she talked so much about others to keep them from asking questions into her own life."

"You think she has something to hide?"

"Most of us do. But while she probably does, I wouldn't think it to be scandalous like an affair or anything. She just loves books, and helping at the church."

"You make her out to be a saint by that description. And as one of her choir members, I can personally vouch that she isn't." Yasmin had her hand up in the air as though she was taking an oath right then and there.

"No one is perfect. Including the person who doesn't take criticism about her singing very well." Ralph narrowed his eyes in on his employee.

"Ha-ha." Yasmin kidded. "Maybe her life is rather dull? Perhaps that is her closely guarded secret."

"Whatever it is, it's not for any of us to concern ourselves with. More trouble than good comes out of nosing where it don't belong." Ralph's eyebrows rose upward, emphasizing the point to the two young women.

"Heard loud and clear, boss." Yas took another playful bite of her salad.

"So…" Cybil leaned her elbows on the counter, and batted her eyes in Ralph's direction. "Are you still up for donating a container of your Fabulous Golden Nuggets this year?”

“I couldn’t face Marjorie if I didn’t.” He chuckled.

CHAPTER 4

The sun shined straight across Cybil's face as a pillow smacked her awake. Dazed from the rude awakening, it took her a moment to fully realize what the loud beeping was in her ear. "Wake up already!" Yasmin shouted from the doorway. "Your alarm has gone off three times and woke *me* up."

"Right! Right! Sorry." Cybil shook her mind to clear the sleepiness away and chucked the flower-patterned pillow back at her roommate. "Forgot to mention that you have to drive me in this morning."

"WHAT?!"

"Yeah. One of the other managers asked me to switch shifts with her yesterday and I agreed because…"

"I get it. Good impression and all." Yas grunted into the air. "Great. And my back-up ride is fast asleep at this time. *As I should be.* You knew that this weekend was going to be tiring for me." Being as how Ralph lived about ten minutes away, he had volunteered his driving services for whenever Cybil's frequent car problems arose. However, he was one person that no one wanted to disturb in mid-slumber. The story of his mother almost getting clobbered by a right hook

28

when he was a seventh grader was warning enough.

"Sorry."

"What are we going to do when I have to go in?"

"Don't worry about it. I'll see who gets off at five with me and ask them for a lift."

"Are you sure?" Yasmin did not like leaving her friend out to dry like that, especially with a cold snap moving into the area that evening. "Remember that it is supposed to get into the freezing temps tonight."

"I got this." Cybil found herself wishing that her parents had not decided to try camping in the south after the Black Friday weekend. She had offered to stay at the house during their trip, but since her parents were in-between pets, they said that it was enough for her to stop over once in a while as their neighbor was already on alert for anything suspicious. *If only I knew where their car keys were, because they were obviously not on the hook by the microwave.* While the spare keyring to her parents' house was sitting on her bedside table, a copy of their car key was sadly not attached. It was supposed to have been done over six months back, but that was life at its best.

"When do your parents get back?"

"Tomorrow."

"Well, you get the first shower." Yas called from the kitchen, fixing herself up a single serve cup of coffee. She had given up trying to convert Cybil into a coffee drinker after having her unsuccessfully taste test numerous different flavors from both local and international sources.

It wasn't long until the porch light was flicked on and Cybil was locking up the door while Yasmin warmed her car in the side driveway. Her phone dinged a couple times in a row, causing her to pull it from her pocket and glance down at the screen. Text messages were coming in from various cookie donors with details such as their name, cookie type, and questions as to when they were needed or how they were going to be picked up. "Not now." She grumbled on her way to the car.

"Who's phone keeps going off?" Yasmin inquired after the fifth ding since they left their house. "Sounds as though someone is quite popular this morning."

"That would be me, unfortunately." Cybil switched her phone to silent. "It's a wave of incoming cookie donations already. And it hasn't even been a full day yet."

"That is Marjorie's Magic for you. She certainly has a loyal friend base when it comes to the holiday dinner."

"I guess. Or she is blackmailing them into giving me the cookies rather than their secrets being exposed." Cybil laughed. "Sorry. Sometimes I can't help that detective narrator voice from coming out."

"Like on…tune in tomorrow night to see if Franky killed Sabrina for her money, or because she was about to reveal his true identity to her police chief father." Yasmin echoed the deep and foreboding tone some true murder show hosts used to entice viewers into returning at the same time, on the same station.

"Exactly. Hey, I hope Marjorie brings her own cookies to the dinner so I won't have to deal with that terror of a dog she has."

"Gabriel? He's such a sweetheart. Com' on."

"No way is that dog a 'sweetheart.' Not to me at least." Cybil adamantly shook her head. "No sir. Uh-uh. I had to sew up one of my best pairs of pants after that little monster tried ripping one of my legs to shreds when she brought him into the store three weeks ago." She flashed her eyes and pursed her lips in an imitation of the choir director. "I'm so sorry, Cybil. My darling boy doesn't do that. He just doesn't.

I have no idea what has gotten into him."

"I haven't had any issues with that *wonderful* and *sweet* Jack Russell." Yasmin rubbed it in. "Besides, it could just be that he dislikes you."

"Thanks for that uplifting remark." Cybil flatly stated, unamused. "Keep your focus on the road, okay?"

CHAPTER 5

"Do you think you're starting to get a handle on how to close down the registers?" Brandi walked into the safe room as Cybil was weighing the bills on the scale. She typed in the number of ones from register five before looking up at the other manager. Juliet had been out with the flu for the past two days, and was dearly missed by the display of names scribbled on her get well card in the break room. However, it wasn't her that Cybil was feeling sorry for.

"Yep. I think I'm getting it alright." She smiled at the weary woman, trying to picture her as a spunky high schooler in the day. *I know they say that nothing is impossible, but that is pretty close to it when trying to imagine that.* "Register two is next and then its onto checking the bathrooms after John is done cleaning them."

"Great." Brandi quickly left and returned to the storage room where the trucks were unloaded, back at the dock. She buried her head into the binder of order numbers to finish filing a massive inventory discrepancy, but her ears still picked up on the fact that Cybil had followed her through the double doors. "What's on your mind?"

Cybil shyly stepped in, hoping she didn't appear as a

scared child to her. "Um…" She tried clearing her throat, like they did in the movies, which resulted in her coughing up half a lung instead. Now thoroughly embarrassed, Cybil figured it was the best time to ask. "I was wondering if you could cover a few minutes of my shift on the fourteenth."

"For what reason?" The assistant manager did not look up from the order sheet. "Did you hear about the number screw up from the last truck shipment? We only received three hundred embroidery floss skeins and the system input *five thousand* when Lola scanned the boxes with the gun."

"Yeah, I heard about that from Westley." Cybil braced herself for the denial she assumed would be coming, and asked her question at the speed of light. "I'm in charge of cookie donations for the Annual Christmas Dinner at my church and wanted to be there for the first ten minutes to ensure that my part is done. I would leave immediately after the ten minutes and get here about fifteen minutes late."

Brandi stopped sifting through the order sheets to look Cybil in the eye. She squinted, studying her facial expressions in an attempt to validate what she said. A hush fell over the room as Brandi uncomfortably stared until she opened her mouth to speak. "Would you like to have the night off and we can trade shifts entirely?"

"Seriously?" Cybil wasn't sure she had heard her correctly. "You truly mean it?"

"Yep. I'm not one for lying, nor am I for leading you on just for the heck of it."

"That would be fantastic! What shift do you want for me to cover for you?"

"Christmas Eve." Brandi peered over her nose at her co-worker. "The store is closing at 6:00 pm this year, instead of 5:00 pm, and my family celebrates on Christmas Eve as opposed to the actual day. Dinner is to be at 4:30 sharp at my house."

"It's a deal."

"Good. I'll switch it in the scheduling system and let Matt know." Brandi fiddled with the back end of her pen. "By the way, we got in the cinnamon pine cones this morning."

"That's a little late for them."

"Yep. Got stuck in transit. But, instead of finally getting in more of those chocolate countdown calendars…the ones we *actually* sell out of…these turned up as faithful as ever."

"Wonderful." Cybil sarcastically responded. "And here, the front end was hoping that they were going to skip this year." She thanked Brandi again as she left the storage room, dreading having to tell her parents about Christmas Eve and having to plug her nose up as soon as the box of pine cones was unleashed upon the store. Every year, the infernal things would show up in a large cardboard box atop a wooden pallet. Once the box was opened, the overwhelming scent of cinnamon would drench all inventory, and customers alike, within a twenty foot radius. The poor imitation scent of cinnamon would linger for days, sometimes weeks, and so would the absence of people and staff in the same vicinity.

"Hey Cybil." Westley walked up to her and practically scared her out of her wits. He instantly apologized for spooking her, adding that he thought she had seen him coming.

"It's not your fault, and I'm fine. What's up?"

"My mom asked me, to ask you, what flavor of cookie was not taken yet and if it was alright for me to bring them to work for you to have, saving you the trip to our house."

"Is there no one in this town who has already heard about me heading up the cookie donations?"

Westley's head slowly moved from side to side. "Regina told Nancy, who told Ethel, who told Luna, who then told my mom. I'm pretty sure the entire congregation knows at this rate."

"Lovely." She imagined a sign-up paper with fifty filled in lines and a stress level as high as the empire state building. *Hopefully Yasmin can make me an extra-extra-large hot chocolate that night.* "I'm going to have to text you later, Westley. Today, my phone has exploded with text messages, and the flavors kind of start running into one another in my brain after a while."

"No sweat, I get it. Shoot me a text whenever it's most convenient for you."

"Are you sure? I tend to be a night owl and it might be around 2:00 am when I have it figured out." She watched him bat the air with indifference.

"I'll see it in the morning when I wake up, no prob."

"Okay, thanks. Oh, and by the way…stinky pine cones coming in this evening." Cybil chuckled as he stuck his tongue out and pointed in his mouth to signal "ew, gross." He continued on up to the front registers, where Hazel was covering his fifteen minute break while Cybil returned to the safe and completed counting the money for register five's drawer.

Buzz. Buzz. Her phone vibrated against her leg. At first, the plan was to ignore the annoying sound and to act like it never happened. *Buzz. Buzz.* Cybil's curiosity prodded at the corners of her mind. *Buzz. Buzz.* "No. I am not going to look at it until after work is done. I am on the clock." *Buzz. Buzz.* She managed to get into the office and shut the door before she ripped her phone from her pocket. "What is going on?"

Her eyes scanned over the messages. Almost all of them

were from church members with questions pertaining to their food donations. Cybil's gaze got stuck on the very last text, coming in from Marjorie, herself.

This is going to be our best year yet.

CHAPTER 6

Three days later, Cybil had her planner filled with time slots of when she was supposed to pick cookies up from all the donors; and it looked like a fallen house of cards. Arrows pointed to days where the pick-up was actually scheduled, unable to handwrite any more into the space allocated for the correct date. White-out tape covered some mistakes three times that had to be changed due to a forgotten birthday party, a work-related event, and one person who's cooking class had been pushed back due to the teacher getting food poisoning. As she wrapped up talking to Mrs. Ashton about her Nutmeg Log cookies, Cybil allowed a sigh of relief to fill the air. "That was the last of them."

She glanced around at the railroad house she was enjoying all to herself. Yasmin was off doing some Christmas shopping, and the place was quieter than it had been since December began. Cybil had nothing against Christmas music, but after hearing *Santa Claus is Coming to Town* fifteen times in the last twenty-four hours, she was not opposed to a break. Each year, Yasmin would get a different jingle stuck in her head, and this year was Dean Martin's rendition of the timeless song. "Finally I can get myself something to eat for lunch."

Cybil had just enough time to put her fingers around the refrigerator door's handle when her phone buzzed against the counter again. "What is it now?" She picked it up to see the caller ID as being from Marjorie and begrudgingly answered the call. "Hi Marjorie. I have things well in hand on my end."

"That's great, Cybil. But I have even better news to share with you. I was over at Snip 'n Sheer, getting my hair fixed up from all this horrible wind lately, and ran into Payton, the owner of the new spa in town. She is having her grand opening in late February, and would like to donate two all-expense paid luxury packages to the church's dinner. When Begonia was giving her change back, she mentioned about our cookie tradition and Payton was simply delighted at the idea. So now, instead of her gift being the prize for guessing the number of marshmallows right, we are going to have a baking contest with the cookies."

"What?!" Cybil wasn't even going to ask why she was there instead of being at her favorite salon, Wavy Clips.

"Yep. We are going to have one batch where a judge tastes the cookies and announces the winner."

"But, Marjorie, the cookies are all different kinds and types. It would be worse than comparing apples to oranges."

"Oh come on! It will be fun. And that luxury package includes six hours in the natural salt cave, furnished with real pink Himalayan salt." Her voice seemed to ooze through the phone in a daydream.

"And who is going to be the judge?"

"That's the thing…"

"No, Marjorie. I am NOT going to be the judge."

"Where is your adventurous spirit, Cybil?"

"Must have gotten stuck back at the wrapping department in the North Pole. I'm drawing the line here. No! Why don't you be it?"

"But if I do, then my cookies will have to be disqualified from being in the running."

"Then you are going to have to get someone else. Did you ask Pastor Lawrence?"

"He bowed out immediately, citing that God doesn't choose favorites. What about your mom? She has a good sense of taste when it comes to food."

"That's not a bad idea. My parents returned from their camping trip on Tuesday." Cybil thought back to the long phone call conversation she had had with her mom, getting a full rundown on what happened on their vacation. It had been filled with bonfires, charcoaled marshmallows, and rain-soaked trails in two different southern states.

"Fantastic! I'm going to call her up and ask right now. Talk to you later." Marjorie immediately ended the conversation and Cybil didn't mind in the least. There was no doubt in her mind on what her mom's response was going to be, since she wasn't a fool when it came to the matters of women's baked goods.

"Am I allowed to have some food now?" Cybil asked the dead air, exasperated.

"Go right ahead." Yasmin's voice scared her to the bone, prompting her to jump off the ground and nearly shriek into the utter stillness.

"How did…how…" She took a moment to catch her escaped breath. "Without…me…"

"I guess I forgot to lock the door when I left, because it was open when I came back. You must not have heard me walk in, either, as you were having a near panic attack from whatever Marjorie was saying to you on the phone just now."

"That's one way to put it."

CHAPTER 7

As she walked into work the following afternoon, Cybil caught sight of Matt, the store manager, heading in her direction, and quickly changed course. He was famous for asking people to start their shifts early, if they arrived around ten minutes before, and she had been looking forward to enjoying a warmed up cinnamon roll for a few moments of peace. In an effort to ditch him, she nearly bumped into a cart with a demanding three year old in the seat, and watched her hope shatter like an ornament.

"Excuse me, Miss? Do you work here?" A nine-year-old girl blinked her large blue eyes at Cybil.

"I…ah…" She glanced over to see Matt staring at her from the side aisle. "I sure do. What can I help you with?" She sighed as the kids' mother asked where the snow globe water was located. Trying to keep her sassy comments in check, Cybil politely informed the woman that the item did not exist, and offered to look up a recipe online for mixing the ingredients together.

Five minutes, and three DIY crafting websites later, Cybil rushed to the employee room and flew over to the time clock on the computer. The sound of sarcasm in John's voice could not be mistaken. "Ooh, look who's late?"

"Lay off, John. Some lady asked me about our snow globe water and held me up. That's all."

"Snow globe water?" He was skeptical for good reason. "Okay, I know that I have heard some wacky questions in my day…like 'where is the plug adapter that comes with the Christmas Tree,' or 'do you sell appliances,' but snow globe water? Get real!"

"It was legit. I'm telling you the truth." Cybil managed to get her vest on in one swift motion and headed straight for the door. Her hand was about to grasp the knob, when it swung widely open and almost knocked her in the head. "What the…?"

"Oops, I'm sorry, Cybil." Matt gave her an apologetic look. "Just came in to tell you that I'd like to speak with you in the office."

"Yes, Sir. If I could explain…"

The store manager held his hand up to stop her from continuing. "You're not in trouble. In fact, I have a little task for you to do."

"Okay…" She wasn't quite sure what the tone of his voice implied. And after Yasmin volunteered her for cookie duty, a dreadful feeling began to brew on the walk to the office. *Please, don't be bad. Or time consuming. Please, be something good.*

As soon as the door closed shut, Matt handed her a short packet of paperwork he printed off from an email that morning. "Corporate wants all the stores to partner with a local business for the holidays. The basic idea is to help promote the community we live in, and really bring a nice focus back onto our neighbors and family during this month. At least, that's what the introductory paragraph states. Anyways, the task is simple. Create a craft by partnering up with a local business so that we can promote both us and them at the same time. Each store will then submit their final product into the district manager for a possible prize bonus for the store."

Cybil's eyes scanned over the paper and the short illustrations that accompanied it. "So…you want me to do this?"

"Yep. Since you are the most artsy staff member we have, I figured you would like to try your hand at it."

"Who do I have to partner with?"

"That is entirely your choice. However, do keep in mind that they need to have a reputable establishment and nothing hinky or out-of-sorts. It reflects on our business as much as it does on theirs."

"Yes, Sir."

"You don't have to call me that. Just Matt will suffice."

"Okay, Matt. Thanks. When do I need this done by?"

"That's the thing. You need to have this finished by the weekend."

"WHAT?!"

"Yeah. Brandi was supposed to have been checking up on the emails lately, and she got behind. I just saw it today, and it was sent out over a week ago."

"Great!" Cybil's face tried to hide her disappointment, seeing her ever-dooming Christmas holiday going down the drain. Sure, it sounded like a fun project, but she already had plans to attend a traveling theatre group's performance on Saturday night with Yas. The musical was a Steampunk Christmas Carol, and the Ghost of Christmas Past was a college friend, with a set of free tickets for them to see it.

"And don't worry. You'll get paid for this. Just clock your hours and I'll be sure to put them into the schedule. Since you are part-time, we should be able to make it work."

"Thanks." Cybil faked another smile, though her mind

was racing around in creative juices, thinking of the different businesses in town she could contact. There were many good shop owners that would be willing to work with her, she was certain of that, but then there was the ultimate goal of the project. What craft to make?

After Matt gave her a rundown of what happened during his shift, he handed off the clipboard checklist to Cybil and left for his truck on break. With a final wave out the door, Cybil walked back to talk to the framing manager, Betsy, and decided to pick her brain for an idea.

"Well," The short brunette gazed up at the ceiling, deep in thought from reading over the packet of information with Cybil. "That is a nice concept, and seeing such a generous one from a corporate business is nearly unheard of."

"But, what about the craft?"

"Maybe you could work with a local ceramic artist, and make an arrangement with our fake flowers? Do the classic Christmas colors, and perhaps a touch of the berries? Though, absolutely…and positively…"

"No glitter!" They announced in unison.

Glitter was the archenemy of all craft store employees. While the light, and sparkly, embellishment did do nicely to enhance a variety of crafts, unsupervised kids and college pranksters, enjoyed dumping complete jars of the stuff on the shelves and the floor. It was the hardest aisle to keep clean and it was a pest when it came to the framing department. Betsy liked to strongly warn any new employees to be extremely careful with what they placed on the framing counter. One pesky little dot of glitter could get into a framed piece and become an absolute nightmare in getting back out, even with an air compressor to clean the dirt away.

Cybil toyed with the thought in her mind, trying to envision what the final product might look like. Though it was a start, she wasn't really connecting to the proposed project, as though it was an unfinished puzzle still missing a piece. "Thanks for the…"

"Hey, Cybil?" Came a tenor voice over the headset, with a pair of squabbling customers in the background.

"Yeah?" She hesitantly replied, mouthing a question to Betsy as she waited for his response.

"Uh, we have a situation up here that needs a manager."

Both women immediately removed their headsets from their ears, squinting as the sharp notes of furious shouts could be heard right before he cut out the transmission.

"Donna called off, so Westley is cashiering tonight." Betsy informed her, answering Cybil's inaudible question from earlier. "Matt called around, but no one could come in. Or wanted too. It is Friday night, after all."

"By the sound of their hollering, Matt should take this."

Betsy shook her head. "He's on lunch. So, you're it."

"Cybil?" Westley's voice practically begged for her to come up.

"Coming." Cybil regrettably began to leave the framing counter, turning to ask one more thing of Betsy as she stepped onto the sales floor. "That doesn't even sound like Westley. Does he have a cold, or something?"

"Or something. He's not sure what it is, neither does his doctor. I wouldn't stand that close to him if I were you. According to him, it started up shortly after he got back from hunting in the woods."

Just Peachy! Cybil muttered in her head, speed-walking her way to the registers located at the front of the store. It was during moments like these, dreading the customers' complaints, that made the aisles seem not long enough. She could picture all the merchandise leaning into one another, whispering, and saying how doomed she was, and that they'd never see her again.

Much sooner than she would have cared for, Cybil reached the second register where the two women were hashing out a fierce argument of the silliest of sorts. They were pointing their freshly manicured fingernails at one another and shouting horrible, un-Christmas like threats whilst Westley stood there in a nauseated state. Though, at this point, Cybil wasn't sure if it was because he was sick, or from getting a headache listening to the fighting women. *It might be a combination of the two.*

"Ladies, how can I help?" She politely asked, clasping her hands together and evaluating the items on the counter. It was an array of Christmas décor, ranging from glittered ornaments to printed plasticware, and more. Resting against the checkout stand, was the tell-tale box of a Christmas tree, and a large, metal tree collar. *Watch it be over the last sugar plum fairy pen and notebook set.*

The older of the arguing customers spoke up first, her cherry red lips matching a festive pair of earrings and the stylish flats on her feet. "This woman has the Christmas tree I want to have for my daughter and son-in-law. And when I asked her for it, in the nicest way possible, she said 'no.' So, I pleaded for her to show a little bit of the holiday cheer, and allow me to buy my pair of newlyweds their first Christmas tree…" Her eyes nearly bugged out from her skull in frustration and anger as she spoke, "she raised her voice and practically screamed at me to go away."

"Ouuuu!" Younger, and with less makeup on her face, the blonde-haired customer glared a set of beady little eyes at the other woman. "I did no such thing. I was not screaming for you to go away. This is not screaming." She tensed her back and straightened her posture, becoming as tall as one can at being five foot four and a half. "THIS IS

SCREAMING!"

Cybil held her hands up in surrender, and quickly tried calming the blonde-haired woman down. "Please, please. Do we not have another tree?"

"No. At least, not under your tree displays over there." The red-lipped customer flatly stated, and promptly pointed at the "forest" of fake Christmas trees all blinking in white twinkles.

"Okay," Cybil reached into her vest pocket and produced a phone scanner, aiming it at the barcode on the tree's box. "Let's just check to see if we have any additional ones in our inventory."

"I already looked." Westley piped up, almost forgotten about in the sea of bickering. "We are supposed to have one in backstock. But…it's most likely in the shipping container by the dumpster."

"I'm going to go and take a look. Be right back." Cybil gracefully stepped away from the register, called Betsy up to the front to handle the oncoming line moving toward checkout, and headed straight for the employee room. She opened up the door to grab her coat, suddenly glancing down at the store keys jingling from the lanyard around her neck. There were only three in the key ring, and they were all to doors within in the building.

"Ah, Betsy…you have been to the back trailer before, right?"

"Well, not by myself. I know the key is in the office."

"Thanks." Cybil retraced her steps again, grabbed the key from the store manager's desk, returned to the back door, and walked across the unloading dock. She made her way over to the seasonal trailer storing the extra trees, and fidgeted with the lock until the metal door swung open. Her eyes scanned the boxes stacked up ten high, and began searching for the one their inventory said they had on hand.

After about five minutes of rummaging through the shipping container, and finding that none of the back stock was the right model number, she called in her unfortunate report to Westley and told him that she would come up in a few minutes. As Cybil began shutting everything back up, a shadowy figure caught her attention from behind the dumpster. Her neck went electric with goosebumps, sensing that she was being watched by an unknown person. She stood still for a moment, uncertain as to what would be her next move. *Do I calmly just walk back to the door, do I stay put, or do I try to find out who it is?* Brandi had already warned her that a teenager had been arrested for selling homegrown marijuana to fellow students behind the strip mall last month; making it pretty clear that the last option was the worst one to choose.

"Hey, Betsy," Cybil spoke into the headset. "I'm coming in. Guess this would be a good time for me to flush that clog out in the men's bathroom." It had been awhile since they talked about the code phrase in their monthly employee meetings, so she hoped that the manager remembered what it meant, and come searching for her.

Having the secret code had been a former employee's idea, when an elderly customer, with failing teeth and a busted leg, kept pressing on a cashier to go out with him. There had been no other customers in the area, and the managers were busy with their own tasks, so no one else was there to cut the man off. The employee had handled it well, by asking for a replacement in the headset so that she could use the bathroom. From then on, the phrase was repeated to each new person, mentioned at each meeting, and had a permanent sign on the corkboard in the breakroom.

That being said, with no other incident over the past

two years, it slowly slid to the back of people's minds, and the sign was more of a faded and curled up old paper now.

"Yeah, let me help with you that."

Cybil displayed a small sign of relief when she heard the pre-planned response. Maybe it sounded a little like a movie's spy plot, but it suddenly didn't seem silly in that moment. And as she waited for the other manager to appear, Cybil slowly moved back to the building, her eyes alert in all directions.

Just as the door flew open with Betsy in the threshold, the dark-covered figure dashed down the side of the mall and disappeared around a neighboring store's unloading ramp. Shivers went down Cybil's spine as she glanced over to see her co-worker's face frozen in shock. "You alright?"

"I am now. Thanks for coming." The two ladies shut the back door, ensuring that it was properly locked, before Betsy placed a comforting hand on her co-workers's shoulder.

"No problem. Did you get a good look at the guy?"

Cybil shook her head. "I did notice the way he walked, though. His legs might be very bow-legged, because the way he shuffles his stride is different than I've seen before."

"Do you know what he wanted?"

"Perhaps a Christmas tree?"

Trying to put the creepy encounter behind them, Betsy wished Cybil luck in dealing with the troublesome women at the front, and returned to her framing duties as she hummed to the jingle over the loud system.

"Ehh, can I have some help up here please?"

"On my way, Westley." It was hard to miss the squabbling behind his voice, of the two customers going at each other's throats once again, prompting Cybil to practically jog the rest of the way up. "Hey, what is going on here?"

The older woman's red lips were smirking with a sinister smile reaching into the corners of her wide cheeks. "She can't afford the tree!"

"It was marked on sale at 20% off. That's what the sign said!"

"The sale is for the ornaments and lit garland, Ma'am. Not for the trees." Cybil glanced over at her co-worker, who was now looking more green in the gills. "Look, I checked the back trailer, and we are out of this particular one. That being said," she managed to shut down the yelling that was about to ensue, "I saw that one of our nearby stores has a few and I will put a call into them for another one to be transferred here. Does that suit everyone?"

"That's fine with me." The older one reluctantly answered, still eyeing the blonde-haired customer with disdain. "But I will take my tree right now, if you don't mind!"

"She went to rip it from the other woman's grasp, and failed to do so as Westley removed the tree in the nick of time.

"She doesn't have a credit card, and with the tree not on sale, she can't afford it all." He explained to Cybil.

"Oh." Looking at the price, and calculating out the adjusted cost, Cybil utilized her new managerial power to discount the item, citing that it was the season for giving. The blonde-haired woman beamed in gratitude, and gladly paid for the merchandise as the other customer fumed.

Glaring daggers at Westley, the older woman almost spit onto the counter as she stammered out of the store. "Don't expect to have any dinner ready for you when your shift's over!"

Cybil's eyes enlarged with amazement and curiosity at the woman's interesting statement. She turned her attention to her co-worker, and watched Westley's paled face blush

from embarrassment.
        "She's my mother."

CHAPTER 8

Cybil parked her roommate's sedan next to the handicapped spot in the parking lot of Jeffrey's Greenery and Birdbaths. It was Saturday morning, and according to Matt, she had until Sunday night to get the project done for work, as the photos were due at the start of the week. If she wanted to still attend the musical that night with Yasmin, then she was going to have to get the project done as soon as possible.

"I still can't believe that Westley's mother acted like that." Yasmin was close to dosing off, already feeling the impending crash of morning fatigue coming on. With only three hours of sleep, she planned on taking an afternoon nap to ensure that she would be awake and alert for the show in the evening. "She's always so nice to everyone at church."

"Clearly, none of them have been between her and the perfect Christmas tree. I thought she looked familiar yesterday, but couldn't quite remember where. And I didn't know that she was Westley's mom."

"Well, you also tend to slink away as soon as everyone begins to leave and avoid the after-service conversations."

"I'm just shy. That's all."

"Shy? You? As I recall, you're the one who stood in front of your entire high school class, and gave them a financial presentation as part of your internship at the bank."

"All you have is my word for that, since we didn't even know each other back then."

Yasmin scoffed the air as they climbed out of the vehicle. "You don't lie. I already know that. What I don't know is why we're here."

"So you were sleeping on the way over!" Cybil accused her friend while approaching the front door, just as Westley nearly bumped into them with a few pieces of wood in his hands. "Whoa, there."

"Sorry, Cybil." He offered both of them a small, apologetic smile, and then adjusted his grip on the wooden chunks, securing the pieces against his stomach.

"At least you're looking better."

"Yeah. Guess it was the twenty-four-hour bug, or something like that." He quickly replaced his smile with a look of embarrassment as they stood in the entranceway. "I'm really sorry 'bout the way my mother acted yesterday."

"It's not your fault, Westley. You can't be held responsible for her actions." There were numerous times where Cybil had been criticized for reading too much into things, also known as "over-evaluating." However, the guilty look that swept across his gaze, was no figment of her imagination. It was real enough for both of the women to see.

"I suppose. Blame does have a funny way of being put on the wrong people though, huh? Well…I should be going. Carving a Christmas present for my sister. Jeffrey was kind enough to let me have these."

"Cool. See you on Monday." Cybil couldn't keep her mind from wondering if everything was alright with her co-worker. He was normally more cheerful, and relaxed around strangers, let alone people he normally talked with in town. She had never seen him so shifty and acting so secretively before. *But I suppose, some of it could be an after-effect of not feeling well.* "Yas, did you see that look on his face?"

"The one that screamed 'I'm in so much trouble' look?"

"Yep."

"Nope. Didn't see it all." A playful grin beamed on her lips. "He seemed a little nervous, if you ask me. But, then again, he only stops by on board game night at Ralph's. You deal with him more than I do. And you said he was pretty sick looking last night." As they walked into the large garden center, mostly filled with freshly cut Christmas trees and simple wreaths, Yasmin's attention was instantly glued to a cement angel statue. "That's beautiful! It would look great in our backyard."

"How do you plan on paying for it?" Cybil reminded her. "You already bought all of your gifts, by the way."

"I know." Yasmin straightened up with a pout on her face. "So, how you did you come up with this again? A customer was buying a bookend of an elf head, and Westley said that it would look better if it was a gnome?" She seemed to recall a few fragments of the story told to her during the car ride.

"It was right before we were going to close the store, and a customer was going to purchase an elf-headed wreath. Westley then mentioned how his cousin is turning their outdoor tree into a gnome with a few simple items, and I came up with this idea. By the way, I didn't know that Westley's family used to be lumberjacks in the woods off Mel's Point." Cybil beamed as her eyes picked up on the exact thing she was looking for, sitting on the floor in an aisle located five over from where they stood. "I talked to a woman by the name of Malfini earlier, and she sounded excited about the whole thing, including what I'm going to make with those tomato cages."

"But isn't this their lowest time of the year, for customers that is?" Yasmin yawned like the drama queen she normally kept packed away, except for when she was extremely tired or thirsty.

"Precisely. That's the point! We can help them advertise during their off-season to bring in more customers." She turned back to her friend, who was opening her mouth for yet another yawn. "Would you stop that?!"

"Can I help you?"

Cybil swung around to see an almost thirty-year-old woman, slender in build and standing extremely tall. Her jet black hair was braided and resting on the right side of her head, with a red bow near the bottom of the weave. A plain green apron masked her clean-cut clothes underneath, in a failed attempt to shed her former ballerina life from her appearance. "Are you Malfini?"

"I am indeed. Are you Cybil?"

"Guilty."

"I think your idea of crafting an evergreen gnome from tomato cages is wonderful by the way, and I already have some pulled for you. Let me grab them from the back, and we can get them removed out of inventory." She gracefully floated across the floor, leaving the two women standing in the middle of the outdoor Christmas décor.

"She did this on purpose, didn't she?" Cybil glanced over at the wire figure of a doe with lights running all over its body in a comforting candle-like glow. "I am such a sucker for Christmas deer."

"Check this out! What a cute little teddy bear!" Yasmin oohed and aahed over the small blow-up as though she was a toddler at a fair. That was, until she saw the price tag and nearly gave herself a heart attack. "He ain't *that* cute!"

Cybil chuckled at her friend's look of pure shock and quickly signaled to her that Malfini was coming back with the two tomato cages in hand. "They're perfect!"

"They'll work great for the project you have in mind. Oh, and you should stop on by Jeffrey's office to discuss what you're doing. I tried my best to explain, but I think it would sound better coming from you."

"Sure thing!"

"His office is against the far wall. Last time I checked, he was hip deep in paperwork and a break would do him some good." Malfini rushed off to answer the call from a cashier at the front of the store, just as Cybil and Yasmin made their way over to the well-organized wall of enlarged pottery. From where they stood, a light could be seen emanating from within the office and they decided to approach the entrance cautiously; a decision they were soon grateful for.

"What are you doing here?" Jeffrey's voice could be heard from behind the office door, seemingly shaken by the other person's presence.

"I came by to let you know that Marjorie is changing things up a little bit this year, at the Christmas dinner."

"And you could not have told me this in an email?"

"What I have to say next, should not be recorded. Anywhere. Rumor has it that there is going to be a prize awarded for the best cookie. And the prize is an all-expenses paid luxury spa day at that new, fancy place going in downtown."

"So? Marjorie will most likely make herself the judge. Why would this be of any concern to me?"

An inaudible shake of the other person's head, was only acknowledged by Jeffrey proclaiming "No!"

"That's right. Some other poor sap is going to be made

the judge. Because Marjorie is going to enter. And the rumor is that she is going to make them!"

"Impossible. I thought the recipe had been stolen five years ago?"

"Oh, no. She has it alright. But hasn't baked them in almost fifteen years. Perhaps she won't remember how to. Though, she has quite a mind for cookies."

Jeffrey went about thinking to himself, arms leaning on top of his desk in contemplation. "If she makes them, and they are as good as I recall…"

"She is a shoe-in for the win. Something has to be done about this." The female voice coughed in the chilly air. "Does it really have to be this cold in here?"

"Oh, let me shut the door and then we can discuss matters." Jeffrey's footsteps could be heard as he walked up to the green door Cybil and Yasmin were still hiding behind. As he reached for the knob, Cybil threw her fist up to the painted surface and knocked two times. Yasmin had to quickly cover her look of sheer panic and tried to blend in with her friend's ruse. "Oh, hello?"

"Hi. Sorry to barge in like this, but Malfini told us to clear a few things with you before we leave. Is this a bad time?" She blinked her eyes, hoping that he wasn't able to notice her curiosity in finding out the other person's identity.

"What is this pertaining to?" It took him a moment, seeing the out-of-season tomato cages between them. "Oh, are you Cybil Lawson?"

"Yes, Sir." She explained what the goal of her work project was, and that she would send him a picture of the final product as soon as it was completed.

"I think it sounds like a marvelous idea. And since Malfini really liked it when you talked with her, that is good enough for me. If I didn't trust her judgement, then I wouldn't have made her my manager."

After their good-byes, Jeffrey closed the gap and began talking to the unidentified woman again, their voices now muffled.

"Why did you alert him to our presence?" Yasmin asked.

"Because he was on his way over. And if he caught us before I said anything, it would look like we were spying or eavesdropping."

"But we were." Yasmin smiled at the cashier as they approached to pay for one of the natural wreaths hanging nearby. Both women remained hushed on the topic until safely back in the car. Once the doors were shut, Yasmin rambled on about being next on a hitman's list.

"We are not going to be on a hitman's list." Cybil laughed. "Why are you so scared about a gardener?"

"Because he is talking to Mrs. Norman about Marjorie, and doing something to keep her from winning the cookie contest. And he is from New York."

"Okay, first…how do you know Mrs. Norman's voice well enough to identify it? I heard her screaming in my ear yesterday, and couldn't vouch that it was definitely her voice in that office. Secondly, what has New York got to do with anything?"

"He may know the mob. Or the mafia."

"New York is a big state. Jeffrey may have come from a rural town where there is barely any crime." Cybil put the left turning signal on and waited for the light to turn green. "You haven't answered my other question, by the way."

"She has big trust issues when it comes to her husband, and he comes into Ralph's every Friday night. Like clock-work, she calls in about ten past seven to check in and see if he actually showed up, what all he had to drink, and if he has any company. After dealing with her monotonous questions for a number of years, I have gotten to recognize her voice within a few words."

"Wow. Well, those two seem to trust one another if they are discussing their plans for committing a shady deal."

"That's because they both signed up for a cooking class at the same time and were stationed at the table during the class. They began to hit it off as friends, when they realized both of them were from New York, acted in high school, and have a fondness for rare, tropical plants." Cybil just looked at her friend in bewilderment. "What? I don't go asking everyone about their personal lives. I work at a bar. Dry as it may be, it is still a social hangout. People talk to me, and I hear things."

"Hmmm. Says the woman who thinks she's not outgoing."

"Hey, look at the snow!" Yasmin pointed out the windshield, watching fresh snowflakes fall delicately from the clouded sky above them as she ignored Cybil. "Perhaps we will have a white Christmas this year."

CHAPTER 9

Cybil's phone alarm dinged into the air as she hurriedly placed the nose on her Christmas gnome tree for work. The collapsible dog bowl made for a great red-reindeer inspired accent against the woven garland on the tomato cage. It was attached with a simple carabiner clip, hidden underneath the draped fabric of his makeshift hat from plain t-shirts, and a little ball to dangle at the tip from the foam aisle. "Just in time."

"ARE YOU DONE YET?" Yas shouted from inside her bedroom. She was touching up her make-up and double-checking her hairdo in the wall mirror behind her door.

"YEP. TAKE A LOOK."

Emerging in a red sweater, black pants and boots, Yasmin adjusted her necklace to align in the middle of the sailor's cut around her neck. She blinked her glittering eyelids and congratulated her friend on a job well done. "I have to say…he is pretty adorable. And you can see what he is supposed to be."

"Thanks. A few quick snapshots, so I can text them to Matt, and then I can get ready to go."

"I'll be in the car." Yas clicked the outdoor light on and

was about to head out the door, when she caught sight of a shadowy figure standing across the street. His silhouette almost merged into the darkness of the metal mesh fence surrounding the power company's supply boxes. But his head moved slightly, causing her eyes to catch him in the dying light of day. "Ah, Cybil?"

"What is it?" She peered into the darkening landscape in time to see the man begin to walk off after gaining unwanted attention. "I wonder if that is the same man I saw at the loading docks yesterday."

"Come again?"

Cybil explained the odd encounter of the shadow figure looming near the dumpster at work, and Yasmin told her that she needed to contact the police.

"I might. But first, we have a performance to attend."

CHAPTER 10

Applause could be heard all throughout the auditorium at Robbyr's Cove's own downtown theater. The place was alive with yelps of success, and hollers for a job well done, as the cast from the performing troupe bowed in front of their audience. Cybil and Yasmin could not have been more thankful for the tickets to such a wonderful, and imaginative, rendition of the classic Christmas tale. It was a steampunk take, on the Christmas Carol, with gears and clocks and industrial machinery that added a fascinating artistic spin on the three ghosts of the holiday.

After the actors and actresses departed from the stage, both women exited to the front lobby, in order to meet up with their generous ex-classmate. Cybil pointed her out first to Yas, a thinner woman caught in the middle of a pack of future ghosts, all wearing plague doctor masks and black bodysuits with rotting wings. "Danica!"

The Ghost of Christmas Past, a white being in airy rags and a light-silver jet pack, turned around at the sound of her name, and propelled herself forward to join them. "Cybil! Yasmin! It's so great to see that you could make it. What did you think of the performance?"

"It was splendid! I was a little unsure at first, to tell you the truth, but it was professionally executed and nothing short of Broadway worthy!" Cybil patted her on the shoulder, and gave her a hug for extra measure.

"Oh, thanks! I'm not sure we deserve such high praise, but this group is really the best one I've been in. Everyone is really welcoming, and we work great together, and…well… it's like I found a home."

"That is truly wonderful to hear, Danica." Yasmin dropped the last of the popcorn into her mouth. "Would you like to share a slice of pizza with us tonight?"

"I wish I could, but we already have some food waiting in our dressing rooms, and we have to start packing the set up for the next stop." Her eyes beamed from seeing her friends standing there, all decked out to the nines. "It means a lot to me that you two came. Things haven't been the best between my parents and me for a quite some time, so I don't normally have people attending to see me."

"We wouldn't have missed this for the world, Danica. Besides, it's not every day that we get to see a steampunk adaptation, nor to know someone performing onstage!" Cybil handed her a small bouquet of flowers she had stowed away in her backpack. "You did fantastic!"

"Thanks! Hey, you two want to come back stage? To see the set in-person?"

"That would be great." Both women followed their ghostly friend back into the long corridor that ran to the side wings of the theater. It was mostly lit now, since the show was done for the night, but Cybil could imagine how creepy it would be when the entire space was pitch black. "How do you guys see anything during the performance?"

"It takes some getting used to, but we have low lights we keep toward the ground near the entrances, and our positions marked with tape in certain areas." A pocket watch dangled from Danica's tied belt, adding an eeriness to the deserted stage as the chain clinked when she walked. "We actually had an accident happen to our Tower of London during transport this week, and I was about to contact you to see if you could fix it when we arrived. But one of the other members had an artist contact in the area and she did a fairly nice job of it. You can't even see where the wood had been bashed in. And one of our trees was in need of repairs as well. She seemed pretty knowledgeable about them, in fact."

"That was nice to think of me, Danica, but I've been so busy lately, that was a good thing your crew member contacted her instead." Cybil gazed up at the towering representation of Big Ben, and the stairs they used to climb up and down throughout the show. The hut they used for the house, and the side rooms for the rest of the village, were all lined up on the opposite wing. "By the way, who was the artist who worked on the pieces?"

"Raven is her first name, but I don't know her last." Danica turned around with a glint of enthusiasm in her eye. "Do you want to see Mr. Marley's chains and ghostly cell?"

The car came to a gentle stop at a traffic light near the town square. Cybil peered over at the locked-up shops for the evening as she was forced to endure Yasmin singing to *Rock'n Around the Christmas Tree*. While her singing was very good, her friend had a tendency to get a little over excited about the holiday tune, and was dancing along to the beat while waiting for the red light to turn green. "Are you ever going to stop?"

"Nope. Just to irritate you!" Yasmin's mischievous grin was slid in between the lyrics with a skill Cybil would never be able to master. "By the way, don't forget that we are both going to Church early tomorrow, to go over the decorations and to finalize the details for the food."

"Sure. And right after that, I will be able to fly to the moon to bring back cheese for the sandwiches." A smirk spread wide on Cybil's face. "Face it, Yas, after the way Marjorie has been treating me with so much kindness, and in a bizarre friendly manner, I'm not sure that I want to see her again before the dinner."

"Oh come on! I wanted to see her hug you again. To see it with my *own eyes*. Then maybe, just maybe, I can start to believe that she is part human after all."

"She can't be all that bad if the church has had her running the choir all these years."

"You know my sentiments on that." Yas curtly responded as they made the turn onto their road.

"I'm sorry, Yas. I shouldn't have said that." Cybil brushed back her chestnut hair and quietly got out of the car once her friend parked the sedan in the driveway. "Do you want me to warm up some cinnamon rolls before we head to bed?"

"Yeah, that would taste good tonight." Yas pulled her jacket up to her ears to block out the whipping wind that began to hammer the front of the house. Despite having trellises on almost all sides of the boxed in porch, their vines were practically bare in the winter and the place was known for getting bad wind gusts swarming around the old building.

"And while they are being heated up in the microwave, we can discuss when you are going to tell the police about the shadowy figure." Yas clicked on the radio and placed her coat on the hanger. "Because you need to tell them."

"Tell them what exactly? That I saw a man near the dumpster at my work, and then saw another person on the other side of the road? It was so dark out, that it could have been anyone. I have no proof that it was the same person, nor do I have any proof as to what the man was doing." The microwave door swung open as Cybil placed one of the rolls inside and pushed the machine to start. "Why are we even discussing this?"

"Because its creepy, that's why." Yasmin pulled two forks from the blue drawers under the marble counters. "And we really should report it to the cops. I know that your uncle makes you nervous. But…"

"My uncle is the *very* reason why I'm *not* going to the station, and why I'm *not* going to call it in either." As the first dessert was ready to go, she threw the second one in and pushed harder on the start button. "And that's the end of it!"

CHAPTER 11

The next three days were as hectic as could be expected for a retail store in the month of December. Kids were running up and down the aisles as parents were walking in a zombified stupor in need of gifts and project supplies for their school assignments. Singing animatronics were a constant sound in the outdoor décor section, and the train buildings were lit up brighter than a clear night sky. It was crazy, and fun, with a few irritable customers in-between. Westley was proud to say that his mother was on speaking terms with him again, and the district manager loved the gnome idea that Cybil created for the DIY task Matt assigned. Everything was going at a steady pace, and it was soon time to begin the epic cookie pick-up relay.

Yasmin had secured travel to work by way of Ralph for the few days that Cybil was going to need to confiscate her vehicle. But when his phone call came in on Wednesday morning, Yas knocked on the door to her bedroom in a foreboding way. "I don't want to come out, do I?"

"Cybil, I am going to have to take my car back." Yas opened the door, not wishing to shout the entire message through the beige-painted wood. "Ralph got a call that one of the company parties that booked our back room, needs help in bringing supplies from their office. And I have to pick up some more cases of birch beer from the beverage distributor over in Howeston. Because…"

"Okay, okay, I get the picture." Cybil bolted up from the bed with her boots laced and knotted, nearly dressed for the day and the wintry conditions outside. "I am going to have to call my parents."

Given at how serious her mother took Christmas, Cybil didn't relish having to call her up and ask for the car. Her mother was bound to have errands to do with Uncle Wiley coming home the following day, but it was unfortunately unavoidable at this point.

"I'm so sorry, Cybil." Yas cast her friend a pouting face, receiving a tossed pillow in return. On the way to the bathroom, she could practically hear the shriek from her roommate's mom through the cell phone.

"What do you mean you need the car for the entire day?!" Cybil's mother nearly exploded in the phone's speaker.

"Just that, Mom. I have to borrow the car in order to collect all of the cookies for the dinner on Saturday. Today is the only day I have off of work, and I need to gather up as many of them as I can."

"But my brother is coming tomorrow, and I need to have everything looking perfect for his arrival. He hasn't been home in…"

"In fifteen years, I know." Cybil promised to make her cinnamon streusel cake for her uncle's first meal at the house as a trade, and was relieved when her mother agreed. "Thanks. I am going to have Yas drop me off there in about twenty minutes. See ya then." She signed off the phone, gathered her items, and hurried off to catch Yasmin about to leave out the front door.

About an hour later, Cybil was already heading onto her third stop at an elderly lady's home along the pleasant Swan Road. It was the nicest end of town, with glittering windows that seemed too clean to be real, and ornate landscaping maintained all twelve months out of the year. Each driveway had its personal street lamp and enameled number signs hanging from their black posts, and winter berries dotted the holly bushes marking the entrances off the main road. Number 359 was located on the right side, and Cybil drove her mother's blue hatchback up the snow-covered macadam.

Within moments, a woman wearing pink and green attire, and dressed in fur-lined winter boots, walked out from the garage to hand Cybil a container filled with sugar cookies. "Ms. Korman, I could have met you at the door, instead of having you come all this way out in the cold air."

"Fiddlesticks. I'm not decrepit. Besides, I wanted to ensure that nothing happened to them before they reached your car."

"What did you think could happen? Do you have a bear in the neighborhood I should be concerned about?"

"Well, no. Not really. Oh, never mind. I haven't any trouble with you thus far, so I'll take the chance. What the heck." Ms. Korman gave her a single nod of the head, and then promptly returned to the safe warmth of her house. Cybil was left dumbfounded at what the woman had just said, but her fingers were aching for the warmth inside the vehicle, and she returned without asking.

"What was that woman talking about?" She made sure that the cookies were safely stowed away in the passenger seat, and continued onto her next pick-up. What she didn't expect, was to be met with the same curt greeting from a woman in a dark blue suit and a white blouse. Her voice was as cold as the outdoor temperature, and the donors was beginning to look more and more hostile the longer she went about meeting everyone at their specified times. "I do believe I need to have a talk with Yasmin."

The phone rang twice before her friend responded through the speaker. "How are the cookie donations going?"

"They certainly are much warmer than the people who baked them."

"Come again?"

"Yas, why do I get a funny feeling that something happened at church on Sunday, when I wasn't there? If you want to find the locks not changed at the house, I suggest you talk, and fast!"

"Okay, so I know that you didn't show up because of not wanting to see Marjorie this past weekend, and I understood that. She was acting rather odd around you and all, but that also lead to some of the others speculating that you two are in on it together."

"IN ON WHAT TOGETHER?!"

"Rigging the cookie contest."

"I cannot believe this! This is exactly why I try to stay out of helping at certain events. Because of the drama, and some people read way too much into things."

"Tara was irritated that she didn't get the cookie donations, so when your mom turned it down, she was offered the judge role by Marjorie. Of course, Tara accepted, and since she has had her beady little eyes on wriggling in under Marjorie's wings for quite some time, a rumor started passing around that the entire contest was rigged, and you were purposefully trying to distance yourself from it all."

"Does Pastor Lawrence have any idea what is going on?"

"He does now." Yasmin gulped, staring at the pastor sitting at a bar stool in front of her.

"Alright. So…am I now going to be flogged and beaten with stones or something?"

"No. I thought I had squashed the rumor when I told everyone that I was the one who volunteered you, and that you hadn't actually wanted to help out this year due to your busy work schedule. The only *problem,* is that Marjorie overheard me telling them that, and her joy kind of deflated a bit."

"Am I in the doghouse with her now too? Thanks to *your* big mouth?"

"I'm sorry Cybil. I didn't mean for anything like this to happen. And I was going to tell you, but our work schedules haven't meshed lately and I just wanted you to be enjoying the holiday as much as you normally do, and…"

"Yeah, I get it Yas. I know you were trying to look out for me. But please, next time, don't volunteer me without asking first."

"I promise."

Cybil ended the call, gazing down at her "To-Do" List and the seven other stops she still had to complete that day. "Almost done. I'm almost done."

CHAPTER 12

Stir the water, oil, egg, and cake mix together until well blended. Cybil went about mixing the ingredients for the cinnamon streusel cake that was going to be needed after work. Today was the day her uncle was arriving in from Virginia, and she was a ball of twittering emotions. While she was happy that her uncle was going to visit, an unavoidable pit of hesitation would not leave her alone. *Why would he come home now, after fifteen years? He never wanted to visit us before. The most communication I've had with him is in the cards he would send me for my birthday. Oh, I hope he isn't sick and...*

RING! RING! Cybil sighed, closing her eyes and not daring to peek down at the brightened screen of her phone. RING! RING! She forced herself to look, and saw the caller ID as being from work. "Should I or shouldn't I?" Her hand reached over and clicked it to voicemail so she could return her focus onto making the streusel. RING! RING! The phone would not stay silent, and by the third phone call, Cybil regrettably answered it. "Hello?"

"Cybil, hey its Hazel. Am I glad I got ahold of you. We had a potluck yesterday, good thing it was your day off, but almost everyone got sick from the chicken salad. Can you come in early?"

"How much earlier?"

"Now would be great!"

Cybil pulled the phone away from her ear, wincing at the thought of abandoning her cinnamon dessert, the one she had promised to her mother, all so that she could go into work. Then, there was the other matter at hand that popped into her mind. "Ah, Hazel, who is going to close?"

"Funny you should mention that…" Hazel's short chuckles were a failed attempt at lightening the mood.

"So when you said everyone got sick, you meant *every-one*."

"Matt, Brandi, and yeah, it was Juliet's first day back from the flu. Betsy managed to escape without tasting it, so she came in early to cover, but when the phone began ringing off the hook with call-offs, she had to stay and…"

"Alright. But you owe me for this."

"I hear you loud and clear, Cybil. Thanks and I'll be seeing you real soon."

Cybil stared at the half-mixed batter sitting very sad on the counter, and overheard the oven's light blinking off at the right temperature from behind. She wanted to cry, to sit down and scream into the heavens that nothing was working out the way she had hoped it would. But that was not going to solve anything, and she was now on a deadline to get into work. "YASMIN!"

"What?" The sleepyhead stumbled her way out of her room in red pajamas, and a tangled mess of hair. "Are you making me something delicious to eat?" Her tongue smacked against the inside of her jaw at the sweet aroma of cinnamon wafting in the air.

"Actually, you're going to make it. I'll explain in a little bit, but I am also going to need your car keys."

CHAPTER 13

"Thanks again, Cybil." Hazel strolled by the cash register where her co-worker was taking a small break on a sitting stool. "Sorry that you have to take your break out here."

"Well, I did forget that the cashiers were part of 'everyone' in your statement." She immediately stood up at the sight of another family coming down with a cart filled of glittery decorations. "At least it will be safer for me to walk on the crosswalk tonight."

"Why's that?"

"Because I'm going to shine bright like a flashy diamond by 9:00 pm at this rate." *And I will be lucky if I make it over to my parents' house before everyone leaves, she muttered to herself.*

Hazel gave her a worried look. "Ah, Cybil, no one told you that our extended holiday hours began today?"

She blinked. "No…"

"We close at 10:00 pm now. Sorry, I thought you knew that."

"I am so dead."

By then, the family had reached the end of the roped line, and Cybil greeted them with a smile on her face. Hazel decided to stick around, until after the sale was completed, to see what her co-worker was talking about. When Cybil explained about the dinner that evening she was supposed to attend, Hazel actually sighed with relief. "Oh, good."

"Good? My mom is going to have me slaughtered for not showing up. Fortunately, Yasmin was able to get my dessert done and I have my dad coming to pick it up in a little while."

"Obviously it's not good, but it's better than what I feared you were going to say."

"How's that?"

"Betsy told me about the shadowy figure you saw lurking near the dumpster the other night. He has been back a few times since then."

"Are you sure it's the same person?"

"When I take the trash out from the framing department, he seems to be lurking just out of range. As soon as he sees that it's me, he hurries off."

"Do you think he is looking for me? Specifically?"

"Who knows? He could be the ghost of Stephen Longthorn, in search for his buried jewels after all these years."

"Don't tell me that you believe in those tales?"

"I know one thing. According to my aunt, she said that he vowed to return after the cemetery's gate cracked, and the bell would toll for three long strikes. You know, because of his last name."

"I remember reading the article online, right before Thanksgiving, Hazel. Yes, the cemetery gate cracked due to age, but the bell wasn't struck by any supernatural beings."

"It did ring out that night."

"Like it does every time the wind blows fierce around the tombstones. Honestly, you need to lay off of the scary stories for a change."

"You can be a skeptic all you want, but you can't ignore the fact that we hadn't had any issues until that gate cracked and the bell rang out."

"Or until I became a manager. Are you going to accuse me of being cursed now, also?"

"No. But that's not all Stephen's threat said. He also stated that when his ghost came back, it would be for the necklace he stole."

"Hazel, I think you are mixing him up with one of the other founders of our town."

"Nope. Stephen stole two items of great worth from a visiting duchess of the Netherlands. One was a brooch with the royal insignia proudly displayed in the middle of its setting. And the other was a necklace set with emeralds, rubies, and diamonds from exotic lands. They haven't been found to this day."

"You wouldn't be related to Stephen Longthorn, by any chance, would you?"

"According to our family tree, he happens to be a relative of mine, so yes. How did ya figure that one?"

"Because the only people to believe in those legends are the ones who can connect their ancestry to one of the founders. The rest of the townsfolk just dismiss it into legend and lore, where it rightfully belongs."

"Say what you will, to each their own. But I'd watch your back with that shadowy figure lingering about. Best if we walk out to our cars together tonight, after the store closes up. I know we do that anyhow, but I'll stick a little closer to you this time."

CHAPTER 14

Friday was filled with getting reamed out by cookie bakers, Cybil's own mom, and the customers at the store. As the clock rolled into 5:30 pm, she couldn't have gotten out of work fast enough, and parked at Ralph's, so that Yasmin could drive her home during her break. Despite there being plenty of sport recaps to sit through at the bar, Cybil had a major headache from it all and didn't listen to any of the announcers.

"Are you alright?" Yas swerved slightly to avoid a rabbit that popped out from the side embankment of the hill. There was construction going on in town, and the detour took them into the countryside for a short stint of the trip.

"I will be. Once I somehow manage to dispose of this headache."

"Is there something I can do to help?"

"You already are by taking me home instead of subjecting me to Mr. Norman's complaints about his football team and listing out every aspect they need to improve upon during the offseason." Cybil's thin-lined lips pushed up into a smile for a brief moment, as she felt another pulse behind her temple dragging her face back into a display of anguish.

"Besides, I haven't been sleeping the best as of late, and that usually ends up giving me one of these after a while."

"Oh, I found out something interesting tonight. Raven's family was in at the bar for dinner around 4:45 pm. They were there for almost fifteen minutes, when her mom got a phone call and then they rushed out the door."

"Did you find out why?"

"Nope. Not sure what it meant, considering that Christine…you remember Raven's mom…told their waiter they were there to celebrate both Raven's and Rex's birthdays. Given that they are only three days apart, I overheard that they get paired a lot together for parties."

"That's odd."

"A lot of people merge birthday celebrations together."

"No, not that. About them leaving so shortly after arriving."

"Christine seemed pretty upset with whoever was on the other end of the call. Apparently, from what their waiter could gather, the person was at their house and demanded to know where they were." Yas pulled into their driveway, suddenly slamming on the brakes and jolted Cybil awake from her half-dozy state of pain.

"What the…" She watched with fright at the back of a figure in dark clothing, standing in the middle of the paved drive. At seeing the luminous glow of headlights trained on him, the person whipped around and greeted the two women with a friendly smile.

"Hey, Yas!"

"Hi Rodger." Though she returned his smile with one of her own, it was quite clear that she had also been startled from seeing him looming under the cloak of darkness. "I forgot you were coming tonight to look at the leak in the pipes."

"That's alright. I was running a bit late from my other job, and I showed up only a few moments before you two did."

"Cybil, can you…"

"I got it." Cybil waved her friend off. "I can handle this while you get back to work." She gathered her things from the back seat and led Rodger Freedmon into the house. "Pardon the mess. We have been working non-stop this past week."

"Boy, you're telling me. I have been bopping all over town with family get-togethers and dinners all planned out. It tends to be a busy time for plumbers with all of the extra usage from the water pipes and the cooler temps freezing uninsulated ground lines."

"Lucky for us that ours is only a drip. I'll show you where it is." Cybil understood her roommate's philosophy behind being proactive with the maintenance of the building. They had a good relationship with the landlord; an elderly woman who trusted the two friends to keep the place in shape and was willing to repay the upkeep, so long as a receipt for the work was provided.

She opened the floor hatch near the back wall of the kitchen, revealing a set of stairs leading into the pitch black basement below. With a simple flick of a switch, three light-bulbs sprang to life and highlighted the dripping pipe in no time. Cybil slowly made her way down the steps and slightly lowered her head as they reached the issue at hand. "Yasmin worried that it might affect the water pressure if we didn't have it looked at right away."

"I don't believe that it will be all that dire, but it is better to be safe than sorry when it comes to these old things." Rodger gestured toward the copper pipes that were way past their prime. "This spring, we are going to have to take care of this, you know?”

"Until then, things are working out just fine the way they are." A small grin was all Cybil could offer at present. It was enough to think about the garage bill for her car, let alone for the piping to be redone. There was no need to worry about it being paid for by their landlord, but the extensive time it may take, would certainly require displacement from the house for a spell. That was for another day to worry and pace over though. "Are you okay then, Rodger? I have a strong headache I'm nursing and a couple of acetaminophen tablets are calling my name."

"Sure. No sweat." Rodger whistled at the sight of all the cookies safely stashed in their containers and labeled with sticky notes as to their type and the donor's names. "Are you going into business as a baker?"

"Oh, those? No." Cybil chuckled at the notion. "Those are for the Annual Christmas Dinner at the church this weekend."

"That's tomorrow? Wow, time does seem to fly."

"Huh, I guess it is tomorrow." Her brain still felt trapped in a fog. "I'm surprised that your sister didn't talk to you about it."

"Tara, well…um…we don't speak to each other much these days." Rodger cleared this throat and reached into his tool box to grab a wrench.

"Sorry to hear that."

"Don't be. Let's just say that I haven't been blinded to the fact that she is a bit of a jerk."

Cybil smirked to herself.

"I saw that." Rodger gave the newer washer a firm twist. "She is still my sister, don't get me wrong. But Tara clung more around our step-father than I did. His unfortunate, how should I say, characteristics, left a lasting impression on her. Everyone thinks he forced her to take his last name, being as how she was still in middle school when our mother married him."

"Let me guess, Tara actually wanted her name changed?"

"Bingo! We have ourselves a winner."

"Yeah, her attitude has pretty much stayed the same since high school. And I don't think it has improved any after Yasmin volunteered me to take on the cookie donations this year."

"Oh, I *heard* about that." Rodger laughed. "I think the whole neighborhood did as soon as she came home that night. My mother didn't care for the way I was smiling in the kitchen as she stormed off to her bedroom in a frenzy. I was there to install a new faucet in the sink. One with a price tag my mother would be all too happy to tell you about."

"Because she got a good deal?"

"Actually, quite the opposite. She's been more into material items since she got the inheritance from her second marriage, and she is not afraid to wield it around like a mighty hammer either. Tara has been bellyaching about Marjorie Stonewell for the last two years or so. If it isn't due to not moving up in the church choir, then its due to not being able to use her whole potential for something else. Personally, I feel as though she is just seeking whatever job she believes to be the most important, or attention grabbing. Before Marjorie's, she had her eyes set on becoming a secretary at the township building. Mother says that she has a constant desire to fit in, due to her being adopted and all. Even though I don't ever see her like that. She's just my sister. I don't care if she isn't blood."

At this point, despite having a still hurting head, Cybil was beginning to suspect that there was another motive for their plumber's willingness to chat so causally with her. It had moved beyond small chit-chat, and it wasn't like they were even remotely close to one another. "Ah, Rodger? No offense, but why are you telling me all of this?"

He pulled a rag from his pocket and used it to wipe off some oxidation chipping away near the washer. "I wanted you to warn your friend that my mother and sister are planning on making a large donation to the church, on the promise that she is kicked out of her position."

"By 'friend,' you mean…Yasmin?"

"No. I mean Marjorie Stonewell. Isn't she your friend?"

CHAPTER 15

"Get up sleepy head." Yasmin's voice managed to cut through the deep sleep Cybil had been in. "If you want me to help load all of the cookies into the car, then we need to do so now."

A moaning sound of protest erupted from her roommate's mouth, wishing nothing more than to remain under the warm blankets in her bed. It never seemed to fail whenever she was finally getting some decent sleep, some annoying alarm or Yasmin's voice, would rudely interrupt it. "Ten more minutes."

"Fine. But not a second over that. You hear? I'm practically beat already and there is no telling if I am going to be awake by then."

The sound of Yasmin's receding footsteps pleased Cybil's half-conscious brain, as she flipped to the other side of the bed and yawned into her pillow. She could have sworn that not more than thirty seconds had passed by the time she heard her friend calling for her again. "Alright. Alright. I'm getting up."

"How did it go with the pipes?"

"I've been meaning to talk to you about that." Cybil

groggily answered.

Yasmin rushed back and peered around the threshold with wide eyes. "Why? Is it worse than we thought?"

"What? No. No. Nothing that drastic. The receipt is on the counter, if you want to look over it. I'm talking about his sister, Tara."

"Oh, her. What about Miss Pretty Princess?"

"She is coming after Marjorie's job at the church."

"I can't say I'm surprised. But I don't believe she would be very good at taking over."

"Because she would have to actually work?"

"Precisely."

Cybil reiterated what Rodger had divulged to her and watched her friend's face go through a rollercoaster of expressions. When all was said and done, Yasmin had just one thing to say. "WHAT?!"

"I know, right? This whole thing is getting out of hand with everyone thinking that I'm good friends with Marjorie. I mean, doesn't anyone realize that she only hugged me once, two weeks ago, and not ever before? If we were so close to one another, than wouldn't it have shown more?"

"She has been acting rather odd lately. Like the last two practices were not normal. She usually begins the session with a short prayer, and she failed to do that twice in a row. Her conducting has been slacking too, as though she is very distracted by something else. But she doesn't talk to anyone about her personal life, and she has slowed down on chatting up the gossip as well."

"Perhaps she has a cold?"

"No. Her vocals sound on pitch as ever. We tried asking her various questions, to make sure it wasn't her state of mind, or any sudden depression. Nothing worked on getting the truth out of her, though. Marjorie insisted she was fine and that was that."

Cybil shook her head. "Whatever it is, we are not going to figure it out tonight. As if we even care; however harsh that may sound."

Yasmin threw the light switch for the basement, laying her sights on the cookies awaiting their judgement for taste and appearance. "They all look so delicious!"

"By the way, Rodger did say something about the basement not being the same size as the dimensions of the top level." Cybil pointed to the eastern wall foundation running perpendicular to the railroad tracks coming into town. "It is a number of feet short from the outer wall aboveground."

"Silvia told us that this place had been worked on over the course of its history. And that the basement wasn't this large to begin with. So that's probably what it is." Yasmin filled her arms with the first load of the delectable desserts. "Are you ready to fill the car or not?"

"I'm coming, I'm coming." Cybil reached down to stack two containers of sugar and oatmeal raisin cookies. "I will just be happy when these are at the church and out of my care. Thankfully, there are enough donations that I don't have to bake any."

"Who do you think is going to win?" Yasmin's eyes lit up with intrigue. "I mean, do you really believe what everyone is saying?"

"By everyone, I would assume you mean the rumor that Marjorie is making her family's famous cookies? The secret recipe that no one has seen since her mother died?"

"The very same." Yasmin nearly tripped on the top step coming out of the basement and gripped onto the cookies for dear life. "Whoa!"

"If anything happens to just one of these cookie batches, Yasmin, I will have to leave town." Cybil watched her footing once on the wooden floorboards, and moved swiftly over to the front door. "How cold is it out?"

"It's below freezing. You might want to bundle up your coat."

A blistering wind pounded the front porch as the two women brought out the first load of precious cargo. It was the sort of cold that tingled the nose and numbed the cheeks, all the while trying to dig into the bones of any person foolish enough to defy its wrath. Cybil shivered under the thick layers of insulated cloth, rushing back into the house in great haste. "You didn't say that Jack Frost was in the area."

"You also claim to love the cold weather and have no issue when the temperatures run below freezing." Her friend smirked.

"And that is certainly true. But not when I was warm in a soft and cozy bed, from which I was rudely awakened during the wee hours of the morning."

"Quit your complaining, and march down those stairs!" Yasmin demanded. "Judging by the size of the stash we have waiting for us, I say that we have three more rounds, easy."

"You wouldn't think that so many women would have the time to bake their cookies for the contest."

"Well, you mention a free spa-cation, and some women would even walk a tightrope. It's amazing what some people do for something that is considered free."

Cybil picked up a bin marked as double fudge bits and another two identified as snickerdoodle and gingerbread, respectively. "Do you think I should warn Marjorie about Tara and her mother? I remember what she was like when we were both in school, but she might have changed her ways?"

"I don't know. Marjorie has her ear to the ground so

much so, that I swear I would find groundhogs living inside her brain. That being said, however, Tara's mother is still as determined as you described her to be. Once she gets her eyes set on something, there is no stopping her."

"Wow. I didn't realize you knew her so well."

"Let's just say that our paths have crossed a few times at the bar." Yasmin didn't say another word the rest of the time it took them to haul the cookies into the car. She even declined Cybil's offer to make her some food for her usual after-work snack. All she muttered was "night," before closing the door to her bedroom, and drowning out the world by playing some Christmas music.

CHAPTER 16

Saturday morning came swiftly, whether Cybil was ready or not for the Christmas Dinner that evening. She yawned herself awake at ten o'clock, thankful to be able to sleep in after a week of openings and mid-shift; especially with the midnight caper. That was one thing they never prepared students for after graduation; that just because there was a diploma in your hand, didn't mean you could stop having to wake up before sunrise.

Cereal was the perfect choice for breakfast with the full day of helping at the church ahead. And within an hour, Cybil was ready to go as a special Christmas present dangled from her earlobes. She took a moment to watch the small pearls and fake emeralds shimmer in the bathroom's light. While they held a low monetary value, this pair of handmade jewelry was an early surprise from their landlord, Sylvia, and one that Cybil truly appreciated.

As she scooped the keys up from the side table, locked the door behind her, and drove out to the main road, Cybil inhaled a sigh of relief at the time listed on the dashboard. It was nice to leave on schedule once in a while, and having already discussed the sharing of the car the night before, it was determined that she should come back to pick Yasmin up around midday. Especially since her friend needed her beauty sleep, if she was going to attempt to style her hair in a waterfall braid. Someone at a hair salon would have been more experienced, but the idea was not to spend money, so Cybil was curious to see what Yasmin was going to end up looking like.

Traffic was rather normal for a Saturday afternoon. While shoppers were out busily buying up presents to wrap at the corporate store right off the interstate exit, the small businesses in town were getting prepped for the weekend right before Christmas. It was the evening that many people looked forward to, as there was always a big party at the square's veteran memorial, as well as a prayer of thanks to all the soldiers who paid the ultimate sacrifice. It was an event that the Lawson family was duty bound to attend, according to Cybil's mother, who always placed a white lily by her father's and cousin's names inscribed on the plaque. That was when the hot chocolate flowed and the bands were constantly playing until ten o'clock at night. No one complained, as everyone was out and about for a great time, and the businesses really prospered.

As the red light turned green, Cybil pressed on the gas and slowly made her way over to the church. There was no need to rush, nor did she wish to ruin someone's hard-earned chance at winning the contest. No sooner had the church's driveway come into view, then a burgundy sedan cut her off on the main road, forcing her to slam on the breaks. Her arm shot across the passenger side in an automatic reflex, to keep all of the stacked containers from tumbling onto the floor. The car proceeded to speed off down the road at an alarming rate, as a passenger in the back seat, slightly turned her head. Cybil was unable to see who it was, but an identity wouldn't have eased her anger at the rudeness of what just happened.

Thankfully, none of the food appeared worse for wear, and the car behind her drove off to the side to avoid rear-ending Yasmin's car. Cybil took a deep breath to calm her rattled nerves, and continued on her way over to the church coming up on the right side. It was a beautiful building that symbolized history in the modern world, and would have been considered as a quaint country church by many city people.

The red brick structure stood the test of time against the newer homes being built, or renovated, across the street. Where the cars parked in the unloading area was covered by an extended porch; which had been modified to facilitate a handicap ramp to the left of the original stairs. A small fountain was well maintained by the church's life-long janitor, though it was covered in plastic wrap for the winter months. Stained glass windows adorned the two circular openings in hand-carved wooden doors that had been donated by an expert craftsman in the late 1960s. Before the fire, the building consisted of one room that was for worship, eating, weddings, and everything else. Afterwards, the townsfolks raised enough funds to bring it back better than ever; which included a short steeple located by the doors and additional rooms for youth groups, classes, and special activities.

One of the youth group boys greeted Cybil as she pulled into the designated unloading area, and offered to help her bring in all of the food. It wasn't long for all of the containers to be emptied from the vehicle, and the smiling boy, now holding a few crinkled bills in his palms, instructed her on where to park her car. As volunteers were usually asked to reserve the front for the incoming members, this year came a few tweaks. It seemed as though someone thought the organizers of the Christmas Dinner should get a bonus for helping, and placed signs to mark the new section as such.

"Well, I'm not going to hit a gift horse in the mouth." Cybil muttered to herself. She braved the cold again and made sure to lock the car as she walked into the building. Her eyes moved from left to right, observing and taking in all of the wonderful decorations adding a nostalgic ambiance to the activity center.

Tired and worn out pews lined the walls, completely encircling the long tables and fancy collapsible chairs that had been put up by the teen youth groups. Small nativity scenes were carefully arranged as the centerpieces sitting on top of dark red runners and light blue cloth coverings. Even fresh cut evergreen branches, poinsettias, and a few sprigs of amaryllis were dotted along the runners, in short green glass vases. The plates were disposable, in order to cut down on the amount of dishes which needed to be cleaned up afterwards. But the place settings could not appear more put together if an event coordinator had designed it themselves.

Sylvia Johnson caught sight of Cybil standing in awe of the space and gracefully stepped over to join her. She had been in charge of having the dinner look spectacular for as many years as rock and roll was around, as she would tell fellow members. Her degree in art, and an eye for the little details, made her a great interior designer. "I see that my powers have not failed me yet."

"I highly doubt that you will ever lose your special touch." Cybil's grin quickly turned into a beaming smile as soon as her eyes spotted a fully decorated Christmas tree near the far wall. It was a tradition for the young kids to create an ornament each year, to be displayed upon its real branches, and then cataloged into a box to be stored within a designated section of the basement. Ornaments were housed there from every year since the second building was constructed in 1942, after all of the original ones from 1894 were destroyed in the fire. In fact, replicas of those very ornaments were dangling from another tree situated slightly behind the larger one. And that is when Cybil noticed the third tree. "Are you recreating the ghosts from *A Christmas Carol*?"

"Finally, someone gets the reference." The older woman gave a sigh of relief. "By the way some of our helpers were talking, you could have sworn that Charles Dickens was a foreign concept."

"I'm sure a few of them were joking, though, probably not all of them." Cybil gestured toward the kitchen with a swift motion of her hand. "I have all the cookies. Could you spare a volunteer, or two, to help me bring them in from the cart a boy loaded up for me?"

Sylvia called two young teens from their current job of stringing more lights up around the window sills, and re-assigned them to help Cybil sort out the desserts they were piling up near the front of the room. As soon as they got through them all, each cookie type had a corresponding label taped to the containers, to avoid possible allergies, and the name of the person who created them. "Alright. I guess my job is done so far. We can't remove the lids until later tonight, so they don't dry out, and I told Yasmin I would pick her up around two o'clock."

"We will be here. Oh, and I haven't forgotten about the check for the pipe work I owe you two. Yasmin texted me this morning with a picture of the receipt, and you will have the payment for it come Monday." Sylvia promised.

"I have no doubt in my mind. We know you're good for

it." Cybil gave her a warm smile as she departed. "Be back
in a flash!"

CHAPTER 17

Christmas music filled the space like a cheerful hug, whilst everyone chatted along with friends and family before sitting down to eat. One of the biggest topics of the night, besides what the new shopping center was going to offer, revolved around the cookie contest that was going to take place after dinner was served. It was a subject of great interest amongst most of the members, though it was instantly hushed into mere whispers as Pastor Lawrence meandered through the crowd. While some were doing that as a sign of respect to his wish of being excluded from the matter, others suspected him of favoring Marjorie from all of her work at the church.

He casually strolled up to Yasmin's beverage table to take a gander over the drinks he saw in almost everyone's hands. "Your hot chocolate appears to be a big hit."

"Thanks! Cybil was my guinea pig for the recipe. Would you care for a glass?"

"Don't mind if I do. I suppose the milk chocolate is the lighter of the two shades?"

"Yep. I wanted to have an option for both, seeing as how they are about equally popular in my opinion." Yas smiled.

"Would you like any peppermint sprinkled on top?"

"I'll pass. But thanks for the drink." The pastor swiftly moved onto another volunteer as he made his rounds in thanking them for donating their time.

"I told you I wasn't the only person in town who avoided peppermint at Christmas." Cybil whispered in her friend's ear. "Will you believe me now?"

"Two people is not an epidemic. So I guess I can cut my losses on this argument." She joked. "At least I have already received a number of positive comments on my contribution this year. Ol' Marjorie can eat dirt!" Yasmin got excited, practically jumping up with a little squeal, when Cybil warned her to stop.

"Shhhh. Don't look now, but she's coming this way."

"Cybil!" Marjorie exclaimed, looking over the young woman's classy dress of sleek black and a touch of gold above a cutout near the top of the chest. "You are looking so beautiful this evening. But I do feel that your outfit is a bit more suited for a funeral, than that of a festive Christmas Party."

"I do have a Christmas bangle on." Cybil presented her with a bracelet containing numerous bells in alternating colors of red, green, and gold. "And my earrings have green emeralds on them."

"And that is lovely." She smiled in a way that could have easily been considered a mockery or a façade of being genuine. "And Yasmin," Marjorie's voice switched to a higher pitch when she saw the cocoa glasses neatly organized on the table in front of her. "I hear that your drinks are a real smash this year."

Yasmin batted her eyelashes. "Would you like to try one for yourself?"

"Perhaps later." She turned around to find her niece's

family checking out the dessert table. "Ah, Raven!" The teenager whispered something to her mother and then joined them at the request of her great aunt. "This here is Cybil Lawson. She, and her friend Yasmin, live in that railroad station on Hedrick's Road."

"Hi." Raven raised her eyebrows, giving both the women a short wave of her hand.

"Yasmin, I believe that your hair could do with a little touch up." Marjorie criticized, using her finger as a pointer to emphasize the messy bun located at the back of the young woman's head.

A touch of pink embarrassment showed up on Yas's cheeks from the comment, and she immediately padded the bun to ensure no lose bobby pins were standing apart from her hair. "Thank you, Marjorie. But this is a style that many women wear."

"If you say so. Personally, I think you would have been better off with a French braid than that waterfall monstrosity that…"

Cybil cleared her throat in a signal to change the subject and directed the matter back onto Raven. "You did a great job at mending the set for the theater troupe that was performing last Saturday night. My old classmate portrayed one of the Christmas ghosts, so we were able to get a backstage tour of the sets." She smiled in an attempt to be warming to the teenager.

"Yeah. There were a few simple fixes that needed mending. Didn't take long to do, but I sure heard about it anyways. Excuse me." She whipped herself around in the floor-length Victorian red dress that made her appear older than what she actually was. As she did, a loose bobby pin fell to the ground, where Yasmin picked it up for her.

"That's a pretty scrunchie you have there." She commented on the thick hair tie wrapped around the neat bun on top of the young girl's head. It color coordinated with the rest of her stunning outfit.

"Thanks. My hair has a mind of its own. It's a challenge to keep it up most days." Raven rolled her eyes at the beckoning call of her mother and rushed back to see what the fuss was all about. They watched as Christine practically scolded her daughter for something inaudible to their ears.

Marjorie sighed. "All her mother pays attention to is her art gallery. I actually thought she had begun to give her daughter more attention as of late, because…well, anyways. Here I am, rambling on when I should be finding Pastor Lawrence to get this show on the road, as it were." She politely nodded to the two ladies before moving toward the front of the large space, where the Pastor was calmly sipping on his cup of hot chocolate.

"I heard that Raven isn't allowed to hang a single piece of art in her own mother's gallery." Yasmin leaned toward her friend in order to share the tidbit of gossip. "Officially, her mother sees it as favoritism."

"And unofficially?"

"Christine thinks her daughter isn't good enough."

"Yasmin, if I didn't know you any better, I'd say that Marjorie is wearing off on you."

"What a rotten thing to say! I just hate to see a kid with such talent be railroaded by her own parents." Yasmin's head tilted to the side, as her face went sour in disgust. "But it doesn't mean that being overly supportive is a good thing either."

Tara suddenly walked in like the queen of the prom, dressed in a slim gown with hand-stitched beading along the bottom trim. Her hair appeared to be have been done by one of the local salon, and her nails were just as flashy as her shoes. Next to her, stood her witch of a mother, who looked equally as dolled up with only a few more creases around her lips.

"When we were younger, it was rumored that her mother didn't smile in order to keep the lines from growing on her face." Cybil whispered. "But one would think she could afford a smile or two for this evening. It is Christmas, after all."

"I wonder where Rodger is?" Yas glanced about the room, surveying all of the attendees. "I would have thought those two would insist upon having him enter with them."

"He hasn't picked up a Bible since his girlfriend died two years ago." Cybil's mother spoke up from behind. "Which is more of an excuse than my own daughter has for not talking to me."

Cybil winced at the sound of her voice and hesitantly turned to see Cynthia Lawson glittering in a navy blue top and pants, with a periwinkle coat draping past her hips. Her earrings were simple, yet not lacking design, and it matched her necklace, bracelet and ring to round off the look. Curled brown hair reached to her shoulders in a wispy sort of way, as it bounced about her head as though gravity didn't exist. "Hi Mom."

"Cybil Lawson! I have called you persistently for the last twenty-four hours, after you hung up on me as I demanded to know why you failed to show up for dinner Thursday night. You had me about to show up on your front porch until Yas saw me at the gas station yesterday, and told me you were still breathing."

Yasmin caught the sideways look her friend gave her.

"I know, Mom, but I had to work late."

"Is that any reason for you to keep ignoring me?"

"You want the truth? I didn't feel like listening to

another lecture from you after yesterday morning. It was enough when you went into a drawn out speech on family being more important than working all the time. You didn't even let me explain that my co-workers had fallen ill from a potluck and literally had no one else to call in."

Cynthia stiffened her back whilst peering into her daughter's shifting eyes. "Well, perhaps your absence was not the only one felt at dinner that evening. Your Uncle Wiley ran late after dashing off to who-knows-where and then acted depressed most of the time he was sitting with us. Kept picking at his chicken and peas. It was just like when we were kids, and he received a bad test grade that our mother promised to discuss with our father."

"Sorry to hear that. Did he say why?"

"Not sure, exactly. He mumbled a few lines in regards to repeating history and then clammed up whenever either one of us asked. Personally, I was hoping that seeing you would help him come out of his shell to answer us." Her mother quickly sipped on a glass of water in her hands. Cybil had a sneaky suspicion that she wasn't telling her everything, but there was no use in arguing as Pastor Lawrence began clapping his hands to get their attention.

"I'm sorry to be breaking up all the lovely conversations in this room, but it is time to eat. Shall we say grace?"

CHAPTER 18

The food was as good as it was every year…fantastic. All of the ladies, and a few of the men, did a marvelous job at cooking mashed potatoes, baking macaroni and cheese, and sautéing mushrooms. Boats of gravy were endlessly flowing amongst the members, as well as the buttered bread and green beans. Platters of ham, chicken and stuffing were being passed down one side and then up the other by eager stomachs waiting for the bread and noodles to follow soon after. Being in PA, it was extremely hard to find anything that wasn't influenced by Pennsylvania Dutch cooking in their area. Like the pickled eggs, chicken corn soup, and shoofly pie making the rounds, Cybil could not see herself living anywhere else. There would be too many foods she would find herself missing.

"So, Cybil, which cookies are yours?" Her mother asked right before taking a forkful of stuffing.

"None, thankfully."

"Awww. Didn't you want a day at the new spa?" Her father joked.

"Ha-ha." Cybil knew he was picking on her, since he knew, as much as anyone she was friends with, that the spa was not her cup of tea.

"I heard that owner of the new place is from Chicago. Isn't that where you are from Yasmin?" One of the other members chewed on a slice of the honey ham she had on her plate.

"Many people are from there."

Clink-clink. All faces looked up to see Marjorie holding her glass up like an offering in one hand, and a knife in the other, as she stood behind the microphone stand. "The cookie contest will commence in twenty minutes." She flashed a mischievous grin.

Cybil tapped her napkin against her mouth and excused herself from the table. She had promised to help Marjorie prep a single cookie, from each batch, for the blind tasting, and it was better to get it done sooner rather than later. There were over twenty different cookies to pick from, and a tall glass of water sat at the ready next to the first contender. After Marjorie was delighted with the way everything looked, she chimed her voice loudly into the air, and handed the announcing over to the pastor. What happened next, was a complete surprise to everyone there.

The floor was suddenly overtaken by the presence of a nun walking in from a side classroom branching off of the main center. Upon the bridge of her nose, sat a pair of rounded glasses that resembled a larger version of the rosary beads dangling on the right side of her hip, and her face appeared to be of a woman in her late thirties. She spoke not a word between red lips, but stood in the shadows of the entranceway, awaiting to hear her holy name being called.

"When did we become Catholic?" Cybil's mother whispered to her husband. "She reminds me of that movie with the signing nuns and the gangsters going after a witness."

"Thank you Marjorie." Pastor Lawrence wiped his

brow nervously. "As most of you now know, this year is a little different from the previous ones, in the sense that our massive cookie exchange has been altered slightly. Before everyone comes up with their bags prepped to haul home all the goodies, we have a wonderful donation to award to the winner of our new cookie contest. Here to decide on who will be taking home an all-expenses paid trip to the new spa in town, will be Sister Bertrille."

Tara Newston's mouth dropped open, and her mother was about to shout out in protest, if it wasn't for Marjorie rushing over to where they were seated next to Mrs. Newston's cousin; who happened to be the largest used car salesman in the county. Their faces were a mixture of hurt and betrayal, with a healthy side of revenge ready to seep out. Pastor Lawrence cleared his throat when the nun gave him a sideways glance, and he continued on with his reading of the rules and announcing the start to her taste testing.

Yasmin poked Cybil in the shoulder blade, mouthed her a question, and then repeated it in a soft whisper after her friend didn't understand. "Did you know about this?"

"No. I had no idea."

"Looks like Tara and her mother didn't know either." Yasmin motioned her head in their direction just in time to see Mrs. Newston raise a threatening finger into the choir director's face. Tara sat there, nodding her head in agreement with her mother's words, before storming off into the kitchen in her toddler-like tantrum. "Something is weird about all of this."

Sister Bertrille gracefully, and methodically, took a bite from each of the samples presented to her in the line-up. Once she had tasted each of the flavors, and had given them a few seconds to sit on her tongue, she signaled that she had a winner. The tension filling the room was hard to miss, as it consumed the space faster than a wildfire, until the air weighed heavier than a mountain range. Each of the women held their breaths in anticipation of their name to be called, and each baker trained their eyes on the microphone with laser focus.

Two words, or a complete name to be exact, dashed all but one of the church members' dreams at claiming the prize. It was a silent room at the sound of "Marjorie Stonewell" being spoken by the pastor and the nun in near unison, which drew patchy applause and skeptical faces. Marjorie acted as though she was surprised beyond belief to have been chosen as the winner, and smiled from ear to ear in gratitude for the spa tickets.

"Wow. This is such an honor. Thank you, Sister, and to you Pastor Lawrence. And especially to Payton, who donated these ticket vouchers. I will be happily enjoying these with my great niece, Raven." The older woman's gaze fell upon the table section where her family was seated to dinner. In that moment, Christine nearly leapt up from the table to protest as her husband pulled her back down with his hand tightly gripping onto her arm. Pastor Lawrence quickly moved the show along by opening up the annual cookie exchange, or "cookie grab," as the locals had become fond of calling it.

Jeffrey, from the garden center, was the first person to run up to the container of cookies Marjorie had provided. He immediately picked one up and tried it to see if they were made from the famous recipe he remembered sampling as a child. Mrs. Norman was the second to join him at the same cookie spot, in order to taste them as well, and shared in his bewilderment.

"Are they as good as you remember them to be?" Marjorie asked, smirking in the corner of her lips.

"They're different." Was all Jeffrey allowed himself to say. They were different, indeed, but flavorful in a wonderful way with hints of vanilla and lavender that added a subtle perfume with the finely chopped rice crispies for a slight crunch in the texture. It was a heavenly combination and certainly praiseworthy if it belonged to anyone other than Marjorie. "It has a lighter feel to its overall flavor."

"It is the same recipe as my mother used to make."

"LIAR!" Mrs. Norman exclaimed. "This isn't the same. I distinctly remember tasting almonds when your mother made them."

"I believe you are mistaken. They are no different from when I remember eating them." Marjorie responded through clenched teeth. "Perhaps your taste buds are not what they used to be?"

"How dare you insinuate that I…"

"Ladies, ladies. Please." The pastor broke in, before it was about to turn ugly real fast. "Let us leave this be, shall we?"

Yasmin cast Cybil a curious look, as they watched Jeffrey's face fall lower than the foundation. Both women rushed up to the table to see if he was ill, but it was Yas who asked the business owner the question. "Are you alright?"

The man flashed his eyes up from his own sorrows in order to see Yasmin staring at him with kindness in her expression. "I suppose. Dreams are not lost in a night. Or so, I keep telling myself." His gaze hardened into a potent anger not easily read. It was unnerving to say the least.

"Pardon me, Jeffrey, but I would not have pegged you as one who went to spas." Cybil glanced at the candy-cane inspired sugar cookies one of the pre-school teachers had baked. Half the container was already emptied out as people zoomed around to shove cookies into their take-home bags, in spite of the trio standing in their way.

"What? Oh, I'm not. Excuse me." He shuffled his way passed a pair of twin girls counting out their hauls equally, while still filling their zip-lock bags with more delicious goodies.

"Odd reason for being so upset over losing." Cybil noted. *Or a lack of a reason, actually.*

"Considering he doesn't go to spas." Her friend pipped up. "Call me a loon, but I could swear that something else was wagering on this contest."

"You two are holding up the line." Cybil's mother flatly stated, showing the growing amount of people waiting for their turn at the dessert table.

"Sorry." Both women dodged out of the way and convened in the corner overlooking the kitchen.

"Something isn't right about the nun. If I could just put my finger on it." Cybil jumped out of the way as the other volunteers began cleaning off the tables.

"You mean besides the fact that she is supposed to be as judgement-free as our pastor?"

"Good point, but yes, besides that."

"Well, Tara and her mother might take their revenge out tonight with the daggers their eyes held."

"That may be, but it isn't our problem. However," Cybil pointed in the direction of the hot chocolate stand, "we have to start cleaning up here shortly."

"There you are." Pastor Lawrence's wife approached them, coming from the kitchen area. "Can we talk?"

CHAPTER 19

"Smile!" Cybil snapped a picture of a young couple sharing a molasses cookie together at the table. It looked as staged as it was in the photograph, but that is what the pastor's wife wanted, so that is what she got. The fact that no one had noticed the photographer was even missing, still baffled her. While the woman had said they were all caught up in chatting with everyone coming in, that story only went so far in Cybil's opinion. Sometimes, she despised people knowing her background in art.

Yasmin did not escape unscathed either. Across the room, she had been placed in charge of getting together the boxed meals the church handed out the next day for the house-bound senior citizens. Since Yas had experiences with parties and events at Ralph's, the pastor's wife felt that she could manage it without any issues. At least, that was the theory.

Chuckling to herself, Cybil watched from afar at the chaos ensuing outside the kitchen. A long table had been turned into the prepping station where volunteers dished out rationed leftovers into foam boxes for delivery. Yasmin's visible frustrations came from the scattered list of people whose names were marked as recipients, and politely asked a youth member to fetch her a highlighter and three colored markers. *Boy, I am so glad that I am not over there.*

The remaining hot chocolate was being devoured by the people milling about as Cybil continued to take pictures with her phone for the church's social media and website manager. Personally, she preferred to use her DSLR camera for event images, however, such abrupt notice created "make-it-work" moments such as these.

"The least you can do, is take my picture for the website!" Tara demanded when she saw Cybil aiming for a photograph of filled cookie bags. "I don't want all my hard work to be for nothing."

"Tara!" Her mother called, expecting her daughter to jump to her side. "Why would you give them that sort of satisfaction?"

"I want my face to go somewhere. You didn't want me going to get it professionally done this time, remember? I worked to look this gorgeous, and it is about to get photographed." Tara posed in her dress, striking a want-to-be model stance, and waited for Cybil to finish taking a few pictures.

"Thanks, Tara. I got them." She tried to sound more enthusiastic than she really was.

"You'd better have them. And I expect my photos to be plastered on the church's page by tomorrow afternoon." She whipped her head around before Cybil had a chance to tell her that it wasn't her decision.

"To think that I thought you were bad as a teenager." David Lawson spoke up from behind a bottle of soda.

"Aren't you glad you didn't have to deal with Miss Bossy Boots over there?" Cybil smiled at her father.

"Sure am. Then again, I wouldn't have tolerated her

behavior as much as her mother does. Though I believe she actually encourages it."

"That money well may be drying up, I hear." Cybil's mother chimed in, joining them after finishing a conversation with a fellow member. "That's what the rumor is, anyways."

"Interesting. Tara did say…" Cybil's attention was suddenly pulled by two sisters who wanted their picture taken as a memento of the evening. With one having flown in from England to see her younger sibling, how could she say no?

As soon as she snapped the image, and collected one of their phone numbers to text it to them later, a loud eruption sounded off near the kitchen. Cybil rushed over to see if everything was alright, and found herself witnessing a spat between Christine, Raven, and Marjorie. Marta and Melody, Marjorie's sisters, stayed out of the fight but continued to watch from the sidelines.

"I told you to STAY AWAY from my daughter!" Christine spat in Marjorie's face.

"Mom, I was just giving her a hot chocolate." Raven defended, standing in between the two bickering women.

"Do you have a problem with your daughter's kind gesture toward another human being? Or is it because I understand her better than you do, and you can't seem to grasp that fact?" Marjorie challenged.

"Why I ought to…" Christine slapped her in the face, much to the shock of everyone standing in the room.

"That's enough!" Melody ordered. She tapped her husband's hand, resting on the back handlebar of his wife's wheelchair.

"Christine, Melody's right. This isn't the time nor the place to be having this conversation."

"This is a church, is it not?!" She practically screamed as Yasmin hastily shut the doors and slid the panels closed on the open serving windows. "I thought you are supposed to come as you are!"

"Why don't you two take this someplace else?" Marta, Marjorie's younger sister, heavily suggested with arched eyebrows and a demanding tone of voice. "Dirty laundry should not be aired in public."

"I am allowed to publicly show my irritation with HER influence over MY child!"

"Well, perhaps you should pay her more attention then!" Marjorie jabbed back. "You can't seem to cope that Raven is a much better artist than you are!"

"Where is the popcorn when you need it?" Cybil's father whispered in her ear, thoroughly enjoying the reality television episode occurring right before him. "I was wondering when the party was about to get interesting."

Marta took a look behind her at the room of people starting to stare through the panel that was stuck open. She quickly shoved her relatives into one of the classrooms in the hall, scolding them along the way. Poor Raven was left standing there with a hot chocolate in her hands and cheeks as pink as a potbelly pig. The teen shifted uncomfortably on her feet until her brother, Rex, came over to check on her and dragged her toward the back of the kitchen. A hush still lingered in the large room for a heartbeat more, as everyone blinked at one another in surprise of the sudden outburst from a family not known for such display of emotion.

"Well, that certainly gives a whole new meaning to 'go tell it on the mountain.'" Cybil joked with her parents before they said their farewells and left for home. They normally helped with packing up and delivering the meals, but Mrs. Norman had offered to do it this time around. So, they took the opportunity to catch up on some Christmas movies and a bag of popcorn with their names on it.

"Cybil, how did the photos turn out?" The pastor's wife approached her from behind, quiet as a mouse and just as loud with her question. In a creepy way, it almost felt as though she was trying not to be overheard by any of the remaining volunteers.

"Really great. I think there are a number of images that will be perfect for the website and social media."

"Fantastic. If you can just send them to this email address, Rex can get to work on uploading them this next week." She handed Cybil a business card for the church.

"Yeah, I can do that. But, ah, first, I should blur out everyone's faces of who I didn't ask permission from."

"Come again?"

"In order to have these images out on a public format, I asked everyone for their consent, and while they all agreed without an issue, I wasn't able to ask everyone in the room. For those faces in the background, I can blur them out to protect their privacy."

"Oh, do you use one of those computer programs where you can do like a magic touch and all that fancy stuff?"

Cybil bit her tongue and reminded herself that the pastor's wife was not into electronics. "Yes, it does a variety of things like that."

"Well, Rex can do that. And if he doesn't, I'm sure that his sister, Raven, has a program that can. Just send the images to the address and we will take care of the rest." She forced a smile on her lips, batted her fake eyelashes a few extra times, and then thanked her for the help.

"You're welcome." Cybil mumbled while watching the older woman leave in purposeful strides. She was amazed to see how many steps it took her to go from one end of the room to the other, as though it was a personal challenge to complete it in as little as possible. Witnessing the woman pull out her smartphone, Cybil shook her head as she posted an image of the Christmas tree for the third time that day. *And she pretends not to understand. Oh, well.*

With the quietness returning to the emptying space once more, Cybil reserved a few seconds for herself by gazing up at the tall evergreen shining brightly in the dimly lit center. The ornaments were all special in their own unique way, and one of them might had been hers from years ago. Each one was tagged with its creator's name and the corresponding year it was done, written upon its small surface in some shape or form. All of the handmade decorations added a touch of nostalgia to its radiant display in a way difficult to fully describe.

"Look out!" A little boy hollered to his giddy sister plowing forward with her head turned back to face him. After she returned her focus to what was in front of her, the little girl skidded to a halt in a failed attempt to not crash into the beautiful tree.

Ornaments went flying in the air, though most were thankfully still attached to the branches by their hooks and ribbons. The little girl burst out in tears as glass broke behind her, causing Cybil to rush over to inspect the damage. A small ball was smashed beyond repair, and the painting of a winter landscape sat in ruins upon its tiny shards. "It's alright." She tried assuring the young child while taking a peek at the tag of who made it. "These things happen, and no one liked the creator of that one anyways."

A woman in her late twenties rounded the corner of the threshold to collect the girl, apologized for the mess and offered to pay for the damages. "There is no need for that." Marjorie stepped out from the closed door of the nearby classroom, with her great-niece and great-nephew in tow. "Accidents occur, and we have plenty of more ornaments to fill its spot. Raven, Rex, can you please visit the storage room in order to find a replacement?" She held out a pair of keys to the two teens, who took them reluctantly. "You know where it is, just pick another one out of the box marked 1998. Thank you."

Cybil watched everyone else disperse, leaving her alone with the choir director next to the tree in need of some patch work. That was, until Sylvia entered from the bathroom. "I heard a crash and wasn't sure I wanted to come back out. What happened?"

"Just a careless child knocking into the tree. But I shall leave you to fix its display." Marjorie ushered Cybil toward the back wall, where the tables had already been taken down by the youth group, who had moved onto collapsing the chairs. "I just wanted to thank you for taking the pictures tonight. I had informed Pastor Lawrence that Rebecca was not able to make it, but you know how it goes with bosses sometimes."

"No problem. But, do Raven and Rex have a ride home? I didn't see their mother come out with you three."

"Oh, they're fine. Rex has a car. Though, it was very nice of you to check in on them. It is more considerate than what their own mother would have done. She is so…" Marjorie silenced her words and shook her head out of pure frustration. She began to scratch her arm, with her red painted nails, over an area of skin that was irritated.

"I can relate." Cybil pointed to the rough patch Marjorie was attending to.

"Mine is not normally this bad. I even put a moisturizer on every morning and evening. Never had an issue with the brand until this last jar. I bet that the company changed their formula, but perhaps it is my allergies. After all, what can you expect when there are nuts in some of the cookies from the contest? And one of our members, who I have warned time and time again not to make it, made her banketstaaf like normal. Honestly, I think she purposefully makes that almond pastry just to spite me."

"Are you just allergic to almonds?"

"No. There are other things as well, but thankfully they are extremely rare for this area." Marjorie forced herself to stop scratching before she broke it open and started to bleed. "What Marta sees in Christine, I have no idea. She never showed an interest…"

"Marjorie?" Sylvia politely interrupted. "I can't seem to find one of the tablecloths that I had the kids fold up and place on the main table. Did you take it by happenchance?"

"No. Why would I take a dirty tablecloth? Are you sure you didn't just miscount?" Marjorie made her way over to the stack of folded fabric to assist Sylvia, while Cybil wandered into the kitchen to make herself useful with the dishes from the hot chocolate stand.

CHAPTER 20

Cybil's hands were beginning to prune from continuing to wash the cups Yasmin had used for her drinks. They were actually milkshake glasses one of the members had donated after retiring from owning a malt shop decades ago, but despite their age, the glasses looked nearly perfect just collecting dust in the cupboard. When her friend learned of them being there, she had it in her mind that they were going to be used no matter what, which was all fine and dandy; minus the end result of a mountain of cups to be washed by the person who didn't even dirty them. And the dishwasher had perfect timing on when to breakdown.

"Where is she?" Cybil mumbled under her breath. Her fingers were inside a folded over washcloth, laden with soap and hot water, as she finished up cleaning the twentieth cup. "She said it would only take a second to help Sylvia with her belongings. Only a second. Well, that second has come and gone at least thirty times over!"

Cynthia walked in with two turkey platters from the main room, and jumped in to help her daughter with the drying. "If you are talking to yourself, you are being kind of loud about it."

"Mom, what are you doing back here? I thought you and Dad went home to watch an old movie?"

"I forgot my favorite pair of glasses. Like always." She sighed at the blue-framed pair hanging from her shirt. "Was thinking of asking you for one of those Bluetooth tags for Christmas, so I can keep better track of them."

"Have you seen Yasmin? She was supposed to be back by now from helping Sylvia load her car with the borrowed decorations."

"Sorry, I didn't see her on the way in." Cynthia placed the cups upside down onto flour towels. "How many of these things are there?"

"According to Lawrence's wife, there are over thirty-five." Cybil was about to pull the "water into wine" apron off just as a frenzy of knocks could be heard at the back door. "Finally, maybe that's her!"

Through the middle window of the worn-out door, Cybil caught a glimpse of Yasmin waiting outside with a scared look painted across her face. "Where have you…" She stopped when she noticed her friend shivering, and not from the freezing temperatures of the night chill. Her eyes and cheeks were plastered in shock, as her voice stammered out inaudible words.

"What on Earth? Are you alright? What happened?" Cybil did a visual check of her friend, not seeing anything wrong or any evidence of a struggle. "Yasmin, speak to me."

Instead of trying to repeat her faded message, Yas latched onto her friend's arm and began to drag her outside. "Hey, wait a minute. I have to get my winter boots on if you are going to be taking me through the yard!"

All of the oversized boots were kept at the front entrance to the center, to avoid tracking in melting snow and salt, except for a few select members of the church staff, who had a key to the back exit. Cybil raced to the front, grabbed ahold of her boots, and then returned as quickly as she could, to find her mother trying to comfort Yas. Once her feet were inside her black and faux-fur lined boots, Cybil had her friend lead her over to what was so troubling. It was certainly not anything like she had expected to see. Given Yasmin's care for animals, the sight of a dead squirrel, or a trapped and injured fox, was what she figured her friend had discovered. But that was not the case at all.

There she was. Just lying in the snow. It was as though she had planned on making a snow angel on her stomach, instead of on her back. But the pain riddled on her face erased that possibility right out the window. Besides, who would want to play in the middle of a darkened street anyway?

Underneath a few inches of kicked up white fluff, her purple coat was as plain as day. Draped upon her very still body was the red dress she had worn to the dinner earlier in the evening, and while the black boots were disproportionately large on her feet, they were undeniably hers with the initials M.S. on the bottom of their soles. Her hair, which was dyed to eliminate the graying, was messy and in need of some decent brushing. However, that was something she no longer had to worry about.

Yasmin stood beside her friend, horrified at the discovery she had just made. Her hand clinched tighter around Cybil's arm, studying the marks running up the deceased's back, and leaned to the side in order to whisper in her ear. "Are those…"

"Yep. Grandma got ran over by a reindeer."

CHAPTER 21

Police lights illuminated the night like beacons for a runway at an airport. Cars were positioned to keep traffic from coming in on all sides of the three way intersection as the ambulance crew loaded her body into the back of the emergency vehicle. Photographs had been taken already, with statements being recorded by a few of the officers that normally worked with the town's only trained detective on the squad. The whole ordeal was nerve-racking, to say the least for Cybil. It wasn't so much finding the dead body that had her upset, since she had seen her first one at the age of seven, but it had more to deal with having to face the detective again.

His car rolled up in the falling snow with great ease in the new tires he had installed the week before. With a coffee in one hand, and a clicker in the right, his tall and lanky form walked briskly over to where the victim had previously been sprawled out in the middle of the road. He was careful not to step in any areas not documented, and began demanding as to why the body had already been removed from the scene without him being present.

"Because I instructed them to handle my sister with

respect and dignity, Phoenix." Marta piped up from where she was cradling Raven in her arms. The eldest sister, Melody, was also watching from afar with her husband and Christina, her step-daughter. For the most part, their faces wore the look of sadness one would expect from the family of the deceased. But after the public quarrel that occurred less than five hours prior, it was obvious their emotions ran deeper than the surface. "I thought it was wrong to have her out in the freezing air with the snow coming down like what it was a moment ago."

"Mrs. Warner…"

"Ms. Stonewell. I reversed that months ago."

"Ms. Stonewell, you are not in charge here. I am. And I will be the one to tell my fellow officers what to do when processing the scene." He turned his attention away just as one of his men picked up a small piece of jewelry and dropped it into an evidence bag.

"Why? My sister died while walking to her car. Isn't it obvious? Quite frankly, I don't know why they even called you in the first place."

"Then perhaps you would like to explain to me why there are hoof marks going up and down her back? Or the fact that there are wide ski marks in the snow down the other street? According to one of my officers, there is a recent car vacancy along the sidewalk down Graner Avenue, and it is conveniently located where the ski tracks begin."

"Because someone drove by and didn't care that my sister was lying dead in the road. That's why. They didn't even see her, probably. Too attached to their mobile device, I suspect."

The detective was about to say something in turn, but decided against it, and glanced over to see his niece starring directly at him. For a brief second, their eyes locked and buried feelings emerged from their sleeping crypts. Old pain spread over Cybil's face upon confronting him after fifteen years of silence. She dreaded the questions he was supposed to ask her, and the foreign territory of having to speak to him for longer than a single word. Though a younger version of herself would have raced out to hug her wonderful Uncle Phoenix, things had changed long ago.

His cell phone rang out with the same tone it had for years, and he flipped it open to talk to the caller. It was obviously something of great importance, as his eyes slightly widened and he quickly snapped it shut without saying much of anything with so many ears about. "Officer Mac-Neal, please take care of the family members and gather a statement from each of them as to their movements this evening."

Detective Lawson moved swiftly passed Cybil and Yasmin as though they were not even there, and whispered quietly into the ear of another officer just approaching the scene. His chestnut hair was becoming white from the snowflakes rapidly building on the top of his head, as he covered it with his hat. From his stature, Cybil would have guessed that he was into the chess club rather than the football team in college, though he held more of the presence of a leader than that of a follower. A strong jaw, and definitive nose, were telltale markers to the fact that he was not from the area, and the latter characteristic displayed a portion of his Italian heritage. He hastily pulled out a notepad and pen after hearing her uncle give him some words of advice, and made his way over to where the two young women were still shivering against the cold.

"Which one of you is a Miss Cybil?" His voice faltered on the last syllable, as if unsure he had said her name right.

"That would be me." She raised her hand in gesture. "I'm

Cybil Lawson."

"Cybil…Lawson?" The officer re-stammered, giving a sideways glance back the way her uncle had vanished. "As in Detective Lawson, Lawson?"

"That would be correct. The detective is my uncle." She watched his sudden display of awkwardness. "Did he forget to mention that little detail?"

"We didn't have a lot of time to converse." He cleared his throat and inquired into who the actual discoverer of the body was.

"I am." Yasmin voiced. "I was helping Sylvia, ah… Sylvia Johnson, with getting her decorations into her vehicle, when I noticed a body lying in the middle of the road. When I crept closer, I saw who it was and ran to get Cybil."

"And who called for the police to come?"

"My mother, Cynthia Lawson. She isn't here right now because she had to get home due to the outside temperature. Over the years, she has developed a condition toward the cold if she is out too long in it. But I can give you her phone number." Cybil reached into her pocket and pulled out a cell phone to retrieve the information for the officer.

"Did you not have your phone on you when your friend came to find you?"

"No. I left it in the kitchen by accident as I was fetching my snow boots from the front of the building." Cybil held up her mother's number shining brightly on her screen for him to see. "My mom handed me my phone when she came out to tell us that help was on the way."

"Thanks." He jotted down the nine digits and proceeded to ask them questions into their relationship with the victim. Cybil and Yasmin did their best in answering the officer, just as another cop strolled behind him with a mumbled joke that clearly was not well received. "I'm sorry, you were saying?"

"What did he say to you?" Cybil squinted, as though that made her hearing work twice as good.

"Nothing. Now, what were you telling me about…"

"You have the perfect name for this murder, Noel. The First Noel!" Another officer commented, before he was told to shut his mouth by a woman also in uniform.

"Your name is Noel?" Cybil asked, curious as to what was going on.

"It's pronounced Knoll."

"Let me guess, you haven't been here long, have you Officer…" She couldn't read his name through his overcoat.

"Noel. My last name is Noel."

"Ah, well Officer Noel, if those two get too rough on you, just remind them of the time they ran their father's tractor into the flagpole at the high school, and that the principal knew nothing about it because David Lawson fixed it for them. And if they want to keep it that way, they better wise up."

"How is the threat of an old high school principal going to keep them in line, exactly?"

"If you had ever met our old principle, then you would instantly know. Let's just say that the ol' hunter is still around and tends to hold onto grudges. Especially when someone messes with the flagpole his father installed and donated to the school with the treasure he dug up on the farm." Cybil padded her friend on the back, returning to the issue at hand. "We have been standing out here for a while now. Can we continue this conversation inside?"

"I would prefer to continue it out here, if that's alright with you? She can go inside until we are done." Officer Noel gestured toward the church for the all-too eager Yasmin to warm up from the night air. "About what time did you discover the body?"

"Yas came back to the kitchen around 8:50 pm. So perhaps, 9:00 pm? I was in the middle of washing dishes from our Annual Christmas Dinner, so the time was not my priority."

"And when was the last time you saw…"

"Marjorie Stonewell. She used to be our church's secretary and also our choir director. That woman was a dedicated member, who not only volunteered for everything, but also loved her job."

"That's a little unusual, don't you think? For a secretary to be also one of the attending members?"

"Marjorie was a headstrong woman, Officer Noel. Whenever she made her mind up, she was going to do just that. She was also the most qualified applicant the church board received when the position became open approximately twenty years back. At least, that's what my Mom told me."

He motioned to the family still braving the cold, and who had returned an even icier glare at him in turn. "And were they also at this Christmas dinner?"

"Yes, as everyone who overheard their heated argument can attest to as well."

"A heated argument? Could you describe that for me please?"

"As far as I remember, it was more between Christine and Marjorie over Raven, Christine's daughter. If you want more details, you better get it straight from the horse's mouth. But I'd warn you to keep your head down when the fists start flying in that family."

"Thanks." Officer Noel continued to finish scribbling down his last line of notes. "If you want to join your friend in the church, I will be along to ask for her statement in a moment."

"What did he say?" Cybil abruptly asked.

Officer Noel stopped, noticeably caught off guard by her question. "Who?"

"My uncle, Detective Lawson. What did he say to you?"

"I don't believe that it's my position to…"

"Officer Noel, if my uncle didn't wish to speak to me, you can just tell me so."

"The truth is…um, well…what I can tell you is that his decision to leave the scene was not based on your presence."

"He certainly had a funny way of showing it." Then it dawned on Cybil as to just who the deceased was. "Well, don't I feel like a heel. Perhaps he did still hold a soft spot for her after all."

"How's that?"

"Just the other night, I found out that my uncle used to date Marjorie back in high school. She still cared, in a manner of speaking, and he might have as well."

"Detective Lawson never mentioned anything about that to me. All he said was…" Officer Noel closed his lips up tight when he saw Cybil staring attentively back at him. "There is another urgent matter to attend too, and it couldn't wait."

Cybil rolled her lips together, trying to formulate the words to say without sounding too overbearing. "I saw the phone call, so I suppose I should believe you this time around. Just, let me know if I can be of any more help in your murder investigation."

"My what?" He looked perplexed at her, clearly churning their previous questions around in his brain. "I didn't mention anything about a murder."

"You didn't have too." Cybil gestured her head toward the scene that was being hastily covered and assessed as the snow began coming down in heavier flakes. "If you would like me to send you the pictures of the crime scene, just let me know."

"You took pictures of what exactly?"

Cybil showed him her phone and scrolled through a few photos she captured when the hoof marks and ski tracks were more visible in the snow.

"How did you know that it was already a crime scene at that point?"

"I'm not sure what all you have seen Officer Noel, but out here, not many people die with hoof marks running up their back. And the animal's tracks only start about two feet from the body. So unless Santa has a rogue reindeer making killer landings, that is pretty suspicious in my book."

Officer Noel blinked at her, trying to size her up and figure out just how deep in this crime she actually was. "You aren't a reporter, are you?"

"No, I'm happily not. Let's just say that I have been down this road before." Cybil pointed to the last image, where she was able to find the end of the animal tracks and the closed gate to a side alleyway in the background. "You might want to look behind this gate. I have a feeling that the killer exited through there, making it appear as though the elusive animal simply vanished."

"Are you into true crime podcasts or addicted to crime shows?"

"No. If there is an email address you can give me, I can send you the images."

Officer Noel slowly nodded his head. "You were a *Josie and the Pussycats* fan, weren't you?"

"If you must know, I was really into *Scooby Doo*. Though I fail to see how that is relevant."

"Just trying to figure out why you have already come up

with this theory and felt the need to take pictures when the woman could have died of natural causes."

Now, it was Cybil's turn to slowly nod her head. "Ah, you must have been into *Captain Caveman*."

"Because…?"

"You are just as annoying as he was. Look, if you don't want the photos, just say that and I will delete…"

"No, that is not necessary. I would like to have a copy of those." He went to reach for a card and handed it to her without even looking to see which police station was typed under his name.

"You're from New York?" Cybil's eyes widened, suddenly remembering Yasmin's concern of Jeffrey being connected to a hitman from the same state. She shook the silly, and fleeting, thought away just as Marta approached them with a disgruntled face and a chilled great-niece.

"If it is all the same to you, I think we should continue with the interviews inside the church, if the statements we gave to your fellow officers are not good enough." She extended her daggers of a look onto Cybil. "And I don't appreciate someone trying to play up my sister's demise as anything but what it is, all so she can pretend to be *Nancy Drew*."

"I apologize, Ma'am. Your family can go for now, and we will contact you if we have any further questions."

Marta arched a dangerously threatening brow his way, as she escorted the other members back to the church's parking lot.

"Excuse me?" A thinner man in his late fifties, with a fleece-lined ear-muffed baseball cap and blue overalls came up from behind. At his feet, stood a short half yorkie/half Chihuahua mix that was drowning in a pink winter coat. "I was told by the other officer that I had to talk to you in regards to what I saw."

"Certainly. You were a witness to what happened here?"

"I definitely saw something out of the usual. I was walking my wife's dog, Ella, down Berner Avenue, when a car came speeding around the corner with skis attached to its back wheels. At first, I figured it was just teens being wild and such. But when I got up here, I saw that young woman, and another, standing over a body in the snow. I told one of your fellow officers my statement, and she said I should tell you."

"Thanks, Mister?"

"Ed Blankenship. I'm just sorry it happened to a nice woman like Marjorie Stonewell. She was helping me to quit smoking with such kind words of encouragement and all." He smacked his lips, revealing a smidge of chewing gum between his lips. "Oh well. Have to head back to my farm. I'm sure you understand." With an abrupt turn on his heels, Ed wished Cybil a nice holiday season and left as Noel finished jotting down a few bullet points from their interesting conversation.

"Wait? I didn't see a farm on the way here. It's all houses."

"That's because Ed is referring to the chickens he tends too. Barely enough to count on two hands, but he likes to call their coop his 'farm' and provides them with top-of-the-line luxury." Cybil took note of the policeman's skeptical look. "I'm not lying."

"No, no. It is so bizarre that I actually believe it." Noel flipped his notebook shut and glanced around the area, staring up and down Garner Avenue. "Is there any place to eat that is open at this hour? Say within a ten minute drive?"

"Just The Corner Restaurant and Nickel of Time."

"Great. I would have been happy with one option, but two will work."

"The local warehouses work later into the nights closer to the holidays, trying to fulfill all of the online orders. So, both places stay open for the workers."

"Which one is the fastest?"

"Nickel of Time. Judy has a menu section dedicated to the grab-n-go mentality. There are bagged lunch options, such as turkey and ham, along with chicken sandwiches and soups."

"Sounds good to me."

"Oh, but I should warn you that if you choose the Nickel of Time, you can't tip using any dimes. Or pay with them, either."

"Come again?"

"Judy has a thing about dimes. She doesn't use them. Doesn't even have the bank rolls in her register's cash drawer. If she owes you ten cents in change, Judy will give you two nickels instead of a dime."

Noel shook his head. "I must say, that is a new one for me."

"Oh, then you will have to meet our town's most famous cat, Silver D."

"There is a cat in a restaurant?"

"Yes and no. Judy had a tunnel system installed in the dining room, that goes along all the walls and into Silver D's closed-in area. She even had clear acrylic sections placed in the design so the customers can see him walking around, and one at the window so he can bask in the sun. None of it extends into the kitchen or any area with food per regulations."

"That is a relief. Hmm," Noel thought over his two choices. "Which one has a decent burger?"

"Well, if I may, I highly recommend the chicken corn soup at Nickel of Time. It is top notch in flavor. And Judy makes a fabulous wet bottom shoofly pie."

"Chicken corn soup? Shoofly pie?" The man's face was plastered with a perplexed gaze, making Cybil chuckle at his lack of knowledge when it came to Pennsylvania Dutch food.

"I bet you haven't been here longer than a week."

"Three days, actually."

"Well, Officer Noel, welcome to Robbyr's Cove."

CHAPTER 22

Officer Noel stuffed a bite of chicken corn soup in his mouth before he went to ask Yasmin for her statement. They were the only ones still there, except for Pastor Lawrence, who stayed until he could shut the church up for the night. The two men began talking for a little bit, while Cybil helped her friend finish washing and drying the dishes. She glanced over at Yasmin, whose hands were shaking in the sudsy water.

"You don't have to finish these if you don't want to." Cybil tried to comfort her.

"That's alright. It's just…to think that she was murdered, makes all of this so much worse. I'd rather have something to do, as a distraction, than nothing at all. These need to get done anyhow." She gazed up at her friend with a seriousness in her eyes. "I'm really glad you were here to be with me tonight."

"Of course, girl!" Cybil reached over to give her a hug. "It's alright. We got this." She smiled at the counters mostly filled with drying milkshake glasses. "I will even let you put all thirty-nine glasses away yourself, if that will help you keep your mind off of this."

Yasmin suddenly jerked herself away from her friend. "Thirty-nine? Did you say thirty-nine?"

"Ah, yeah. I've counted twice now. Thirty-nine glasses."

"Cybil, there are supposed to be forty." Yasmin's lips shook nervously. "Why would someone have taken a cup?"

"Ladies," Officer Noel stepped into the kitchen with the pastor to this left. "Are you ready for us to continue?"

"We are." Cybil nodded her head encouragingly at Yas, and pulled a stool out for her to sit down on as she drained the last of the water from the sink.

"Okay, now according to one of the other officers, Mrs. Norman reported not seeing Marjorie Stonewell coming out the front of the church, so did you happen to see her exiting through the back?"

"I was out helping Sylvia Johnson with her decorations when I overheard a noise I couldn't identify. It might have been a car starting up, but it sounded odd. Then I saw the back end of a vehicle speeding down the Avenue, it had a busted taillight…I remember that…and then I stepped around the front of the building to see…see…Marjorie lying in the middle of the street."

"And that is when you went to find Ms. Lawson?"

Yasmin silently nodded, then her brows closed in over the bridge of her nose in thought. "I didn't see Mrs. Norman out the front of the church when I came around."

Officer Noel glanced over the notes taken by a fellow cop. "Says here that she was in the process of loading up the back of her car with leftovers to be taken to the seniors who couldn't make it this evening."

"She was supposed to be, but I was in the kitchen to ensure all the leftovers were packaged correctly for the trip. Mrs. Norman even made a point to say that she was going to park her vehicle near this back door in order to pack up the meals." Yas stared at her fingertips.

Cybil anticipated his next question, and decided it was best to answer it before he asked. "I entered the kitchen shortly after Yasmin disappeared to help Sylvia. Mrs. Norman didn't enter from the back while I was here, either."

"There are no tire tracks near the door to confirm her story. Though I did happen to see two minor indents in the shape of shoeprints to the right of the threshold as I entered." Officer Noel scratched out some quick words on a single line of his notepad.

"Marjorie, as well as some of the other church staff, are allowed to keep their boots at this entrance, while the rest of our members are instructed to leave their boots just inside the main doors to our building." Pastor Lawrence chimed in.

"But would she have left them outside?"

"No. She cared for her boots a great deal." Pastor Lawrence locked up a number of the cabinets as they talked.

"Oh my gosh!" Yasmin turned to face Cybil. "Her dog! Gabriel!"

"I'm sure one of her relatives will take care of him." She replied.

"Even so, I'll stop on over and check in on the poor animal." Pastor Lawrence offered. "That family, well… how should I put this…is not on the best of terms with one another."

"How will you get in? Marjorie doesn't leave a key under the mat or anything like that." Yas asked.

"I have a spare. She said that it gave her peace of mind, knowing that there was a copy with someone she trusted, in case she ever locked herself out or lost her own."

"Officer Noel? Are you ready for the rest of Yasmin's statement?" Cybil looked at him chewing on the last piece of a chunk of freshly-baked bread.

"There's more?" Her friend looked bewildered at her, unsure as to what she didn't say.

"The missing cup?"

"What missing cup?" The officer switched his glances between the two women in wonder, when Yas started to tell him about the wrong number of glasses left after the dinner.

"And you think this has some kind of bearing on the case?" Noel asked. "It may be that someone has a pair of sticky fingers."

"Regardless, it was still out of the ordinary, and we thought it was best to report it than to keep it a secret, right?" Cybil bumped her roommate in the back, forcing her into another silent head nod.

"Alright, well, yes, I do believe that you all have been very helpful in answering my questions this evening. If we need anything more from you, please write down your phone numbers for me." Officer Noel flipped his notebook to the last page, and handed them his pen. In turn, each of them did as he requested, grateful that there was finally hope of them returning home for the night.

CHAPTER 23

Cybil slammed the door shut behind her, as Yasmin migrated toward the kitchen in the old train station. Despite the fact that they were both pretty wiped out after the events of the evening, their minds could not slow down on going over everything they saw, were asked, answered, and observed. It was like a fast-forwarding movie being replayed in an endless loop while the audience members shouted for it to be stopped.

"It's odd." Cybil remarked as she kicked her snow boots off at the doorway.

"What? The indents of shoe prints sitting outside the back door?"

"Yeah. All of the spots were wet from staff members' shoes in the back hall. None of the them were dry, so the outside pair didn't belong to anyone working tonight."

"So?"

"Who did the other pair belong to? They had to have been placed there today, so perhaps they were used by the killer?"

"Maybe someone didn't know our policy, since there were a number of people invited by a relative to attend. They could have grabbed them before they left at any time during the dinner."

"But Sylvia is very strict on the back door being used only by the people in the kitchen, for fear of getting a lecture from Marjorie on attendance records for events. Not to mention safety for our members. And by the time that Officer Noel noticed them, they were probably too mangled to be of much help identifying their size and tread."

"Whatever the case, it's in the police's hands thankfully." Yasmin reached for her hot cocoa mix, and then decidedly put it back in the cupboard. "It seems kind of silly now."

"What does?"

"My beef with Marjorie."

"Oh, Yasmin, you can't go on thinking that you're a bad person because you didn't get along with her. Not many people did."

"You're right, but it still doesn't make me feel any better."

Cybil approached her friend with a wondrous idea of the biggest proportions. "How about you go and get some sleep? I'm going to make myself a sandwich before I head to bed, and then we can drift off into our dreams and push this nightmare far away."

CHAPTER 24

The next morning, Cybil returned to work with a darkened shadow above her head. As she walked into the employee room, Frances and John began whispering to one another, giving her suspicious looks behind her back. It caused an uneasy feeling to begin in the pit of her stomach, sensing their curiosity sitting in the air.

"If you have a question, best to spit it out then holding it in and bursting at the seams." Cybil turned around, fixing her vest whilst tapping down on the "enter" key of the time clock.

John cast a caution look at his co-worker. "Oh, we don't want to…"

"Ask me about the dead body I found last night? This isn't exactly a large room, John. I could hear you two whispering like church mice." Cybil shook her head. Before they left the church, Noel had warned her not to talk to anyone about the questions he asked and to wait until the corner officially identified the body. It seemed pretty dumb to wait for the obvious to be stated, but the woman's face was half-hidden in the snow and she wasn't the gossiping type of girl anyhow. That being said, it was a small town, and news

136

of it was probably racing through the rumor mill at twice the speed of lightning. *Still, I gave my word.*

"Well…yeah. I heard that a knife was sticking out the woman's back. And it was oozing with peanut butter on the handle."

"What?!" Cybil chuckled at the crazy notion, and the oddness of the peanut butter detail. "That is ridiculous. And completely untrue."

"So what did happen? People are saying it was Marjorie Stonewell who they found lying in the snow."

Cybil shook her head, declining to answer. "I promised to remain mum on the victim's identity until it has been officially released. And I wasn't even the one who saw the body first."

"Come on, Cybil. You're not a cop. You can tell us." Her other co-worker piped up.

"No, Frances. The family has the right to learn through the proper channels about the details surrounding the woman's death. Besides, it shouldn't take that long for the media to get ahold of the story."

"Well, we tried John." Frances finished her bagel and cleaned up the trash. "But I guess that means that Chassy was right."

Cybil sighed. "And what did Chassy say?"

"That once you became a manager, you wouldn't want to talk to us little peons on the low level."

"Please, Frances. Is that what you think this is? I am merely upholding a promise I made."

"To who?" Frances leaned forward, eyeing her like a vulture does prey.

"One of the cops."

"You mean Noel? Oh, I'm sorry its pronounced as *Knoll.*" The twenty-nine year old huffed, deliberately mispronouncing the man's name the first time. "Never pegged you for the blue side."

"Just because you've had a bad experience with the police, doesn't mean they are all like that. Besides, it isn't us against them. We all live in the same community."

"Go ahead. Spout your 'unity speech.' But leave me out of it!" The door slammed shut behind Frances as she returned to the sales floor.

John blinked. "She's just upset."

"You think?" Then it dawned on Cybil. "Isn't this the first Christmas Frances won't be with her father? Still no trial yet, huh?"

"Nope. The date got postponed." John slurped down the rest of his energy drink, though Cybil didn't see a need for the normally high-spirited man to have it. If anyone resembled a caffeinated squirrel, John would be it.

"Man, I can't imagine how her mom is coping."

Her coworker huffed. "That woman probably had a celebration when he was hauled off to jail. Don't think she rightly cares if he is innocent or not."

"How did Frances know that I was talking to Officer Noel last night? She doesn't go to church, doesn't live in the vicinity of where the tragedy took place, and the officer has only been in town for three days. Not to mention, how did she know how to say his name?"

John matched Cybil's stare. "If he was the one who busted your father, you would instantly recognize him at the supermarket."

"I forgot she was from New York. No wonder she has an ax to grind with him."

"He went undercover, and ended up dating her for a few weeks before the arrest was made. I would say that ax is pretty sharp indeed."

"Help needed at the front. Help needed at the front. Thank you." One of the new cashiers broadcasted over the loudspeakers.

"Yeah…Tonya doesn't have a working headset." John wiped up a brown mark on the table and opened the door for Cybil. "After you, My Lady."

"And they say that chivalry is dead." Cybil thanked him with a smile and hustled her way up to the registers, where an irate customer was already fuming.

Cybil tried hard to maintain her pleasant "customer service" face, dreading to hear what issue this woman had with the fake flowers on the counter. "What can I help you with?"

"You can start by labeling this plant correctly. This is not wisteria, but in fact, it is a lilac." After Cybil politely informed the woman that they have no control over warehouse packaging, the customer swiftly moved onto her next complaint. "Well, then maybe you ought to change your signs around then."

"Come again?"

"Lilacs are $2 cheaper than the wisteria. But since the tag is wrong, including that of the barcode, I am being charged the more expensive price."

"We can easily fix that." Cybil asked Tonya to step back, letting her into the tight space in order to type in her override codes. "There." She turned, beaming at the customer with her best fake of a smile. "Anything else I can help with, Ma'am?"

"As a matter of fact, there is!" The woman reached into her cart and pulled out a pair of earrings without any labels, box, or sticker barcode. "I found these on the floor, back in the decorating aisle and didn't see a price anywhere. But in your jewelry section…"

Cybil picked up the earrings from the customer, and

looked them over. "Um, I'm sorry Ma'am. Where did you find these?!" She couldn't believe it. They were identical to the pair of earrings that Sylvia had given her for Christmas. That isn't possible. "I don't believe these ones are for sale, Ma'am."

"And why not? They look just like that Jasper Gringer line you all are selling. Same silver and everything."

"No, Ma'am. This pair belongs to someone else."

"Are you refusing to sell these to me?"

"Yes, Ma'am. I am." Cybil took a firm stance, trying to be as kind about refusing the sale as possible. "These were dropped by someone, a customer, and are not just a product with lost packaging."

"I don't believe it!" The woman went off, ranting about how the store had been going to pot ever since her son left years ago. She whined that the frame she wanted would not be ready in time for Christmas, that the lazy employees refused to do their jobs, and that they were sold out of many of the items on her list. "After all, they say the customer is always right. So now, here you are…telling me that you are not going to sell me a product that does not have a…"

The door to the office could be heard opening, and then shutting, indicating that one of the other managers had entered the sales floor. Cybil looked over to see the top of the store manager's head above the aisle containing impulse merchandise, and tried shoving away her anxiety. "What seems to be the problem here?" He rounded the corner with a very stoic expression on his face. "Hello, Gladys."

"Hello Matt." The woman stood as hard as stone, and matched his gaze. She recounted what the issues were and ended with a threat of complaining to corporate.

"Well, you sure are old enough to make that kind of decision on your own. But I am not going to offer you any discounts, or any free product, to make it up to you." Matt motioned for Cybil to join him, as they walked back to the office for a briefing on an upcoming birthday party that was scheduled for Friday. Behind them, the woman continued on fuming about inconsequential things.

"Who is that woman?" Cybil asked her boss.

"Gladys Nightstone. A mother who thinks too highly of a worthless son. Personally, I think she knows what bum of a son she truly has, but it's too painful for her to admit it to herself." Matt unlocked the door with a small, bronze key, and ushered Cybil inside. "Make sure to pull all of the supplies for the birthday party. And the ones for the holiday craft coming up on Saturday. I realize it's a week away, but we have a lot of signees, and I want to be sure we are going to have enough supplies before they are sold out."

"Okay. Sure thing."

"Now, before we go over the supply list, there is something else I've been meaning to ask you."

Cybil simply looked on, uncertain as to what he was going to say.

"Who was the dead body outside the church last night?"

CHAPTER 25

Ralph was wiping out a tall glass per usual, when Cybil dropped in that night to find Yasmin surprisingly not there. "What do you mean she called off sick?"

"Just like I said. She messaged me on the phone, actually, to tell me that she wasn't coming in because of a stomach bug she picked up at the dinner yesterday." Ralph waved to a regular customer who had just walked in the door and was heading over to his normal chair. "Between you and me, she probably made the best move with all the rumors flying around about Marjorie's death. Even the online community social pages have Yas's name splattered all over them as being the one who found her body."

"Well at least they have their facts right on that much. I had a few co-workers who thought I was the one who discovered her in the road."

"Business has been fairly steady with people wanting to gossip with others about what they know or speculate." Ralph signaled with his finger for her to lean in closer. "Did you know that she might have even been murdered?"

"Who said anything about that?"

"Apparently one of the officers was discussing the matter

at the station when Crazy Jo was waiting to pay the fine for having his goat tied up to a fire hydrant again. They said that a light-brown haired woman, who was friends with the first person on the scene, made some accusations about it being a murder. She even claimed to have pictures of the crime scene on her phone to that new fella, who arrived in town three days ago."

Cybil felt like the butt end of a joke. "That's enough, Ralph. I can hear it in your voice that you figured out who the accuser was."

"Well, the pool of suspects wasn't vast. And I seem to recall a case you cracked for your uncle…"

"That was years ago, Ralph. Besides, I didn't crack it for him. I just stumbled upon the answer and got lucky in solving it. Alright?"

"Un-huh." The dry bar owner did not sound convinced. "Well, we will have to agree to disagree on that one. With that being said, however, I think your uncle will have his hands full with this case."

"He wasn't at the scene for more than five minutes last night, so I highly doubt he will be the one investigating it."

"Really?"

"He received a phone call and headed off without saying anything to me. Just whispered some instructions to another police officer, and then drove off. The same officer ended up being the one who did the questioning of all of us at the scene."

"Was there something you were expecting for your uncle to say?"

"Honestly, I'm not sure what I expected to happen."

"Well, I can guarantee that you didn't see this coming." Ralph's face was stuck in an expression of awe, prompting Cybil to turn around and see Detective Lawson standing

right behind her.
    "Hi Cybil."

CHAPTER 26

Cybil had spent countless minutes thinking about what she would say to her uncle, if he ever decided to start speaking to her again. But what ultimately spilled from her mouth, was too anti-climactic to be a good story. "Hi."

Detective Lawson moved swiftly past her to ask Ralph, who was on duty at the bar the previous night, ending the quick conversation she secretly hoped to have lasted just a tad longer.

"One of my employees. Why?" The business owner replied.

"John Ridley reported his reindeer, Rudolph, missing from his farm this evening."

"So why are you inquiring into last night, then?"

"Because the reindeer might have been missing since then, and we are double-checking all avenues of possible contact with the animal."

"You think I keep a barn filled with straw in the back storeroom?"

"Just answer the question, Ralph. Did anyone happen to mention seeing the reindeer today or yesterday at all?"

"Not that I recall. But I'll ask my employee when she

gets in."

"Thanks." He was about to leave when his niece piped up from her stool.

"Are you going to be handling Marjorie Stonewell's death?" Cybil's eyes remained glued to the shiny bar counter.

"At the moment, the cause has not been determined until the coroner is finished with her body."

"Publicly correct as always."

"That is all I am going to say on the matter." Detective Lawson exited through the door as fast as he could, determined to be at his next stop on schedule.

"Wonder why that reindeer would wish to leave such a comfy lifestyle at John's place?" Ralph wondered aloud. "It was like the palace of luxury over there."

"I saw John at work earlier today and he didn't say anything about a missing reindeer. So, he must have just discovered Rudolph's absence when he got home." Cybil was about to order a drink, when her phone started to rumble from an incoming call she didn't recognize. "Another scammer. I get tired of their harassment."

Ralph glimpsed down at the number registering as unknown and chuckled. "That's a New York area code. Most likely someone trying to make sure your car's warranty isn't out of date."

"That or…" Cybil hesitantly picked up her phone and answered it with an uncertain voice. She didn't want to be right that it was who she thought it could be. But as the male voice introduced himself on the other end, her suspicions had been confirmed. "Hello Officer Noel. What can I do for you?"

"Do you own a pair of handmade earrings with a single pearl and three small emerald-like beads that dangle above it?"

"As a matter of fact, I do. Why?"

"Can I meet you at your home to take a look at them this evening?"

"On a Sunday night?"

"Unfortunately so."

"I can meet you there in roughly thirty minutes. Will that suffice?"

"See you then."

Cybil hung up the call to stare blankly at the bar owner, who was concerned by the expression on her face.

"What's wrong? Does he think you have something to do with Marjorie's death?"

"I'm not sure, Ralph. But I have to go. You might want to start praying."

"For who?"

"The person who killed Marjorie Stonewell."

CHAPTER 27

Cybil drove up the icy drive in her friend's car almost at the same time as Officer Noel arrived. She had barely gotten a message to Yas about the impromptu guest showing up, when the cell tower went out and she had no idea if her friend received the text at all. But her curiosity was soon answered as Yasmin threw the door open at the sight of the two walking toward the porch. "Better get in with this winter weather playing havoc on everything. Just got a report on the television that some of the cell towers have gone down due to the harsh winds on the other side of the valley. Glad we still have the landline backup."

"I apologize for interrupting your evening, but I have to take a look at the earrings Sylvia Johnson gave you for Christmas." Officer Noel politely asked.

"Of course. Wait here." Cybil headed back to her bedroom to retrieve the handmade pair she knew to be one of a kind. That was, until her eyes came upon the second set at work that she brought home with her. After locating the originals on her stand, Cybil brought them out for the officer to see.

When she arrived back in the living room section of

their open plan design, she noticed Officer Noel taking a special interest at something on top of the console table, near the door. He seemed to be studying the items situated in a haphazard manner, and causally shifted his attention away at the sound of Cybil's footsteps coming back.

"Is anything wrong?" She peered over at the trinket tray with coins, a sticky note pad, jar of pens and pencils, pairs of sunglasses, and their handbags all messily arranged.

"No." He switched over to inspect the jewelry in her hands. "You have them both alright."

"What is this about?" Yasmin asked.

"We found an earring matching this pair at the scene, under a layer of fresh snow. We asked the pastor's wife, to see if she recognized it, and she said it belonged to Sylvia Johnson. But when I phoned Ms. Johnson, she informed me that she gave you her set as an early Christmas present."

"Yeah, Marjorie held a jewelry class last year for a number of the women in the church. Sylvia made these in class and as far as I knew, they're one of a kind. Until…"

Officer Noel's interest piqued. "Do you know something about this other earring?"

"Not exactly. But at work today, something odd happened. I work at Mark's Crafts and Art Supplies, and a female customer wanted to pay for some earrings that had no real packaging or price on them. When I took a look at the item, they were identical to these." She produced the second pair from her coat's pocket. "I've never seen a duplicate and the store doesn't sell them. That much, I do know."

"What is the significance? That other pair means that anyone could have the matching set to the one found by Marjorie." Yasmin pointed out. "And if they are readily available, then the other person could have replaced theirs already."

"That is if this has any bearing on the murder in the first place." Officer Noel jotted down a few lines. "But what you are telling me means that I can't rule anyone out just yet. Thank you ladies and have a good night." He abruptly left their house and radioed in to dispatch as to where he was off to next.

Cybil immediately pulled her cell out and dialed Sylvia, scolding herself for what she had just done. "Please pick up, pick up."

"What's wrong?" Yasmin went to hand her a sandwich, to which her friend quickly dismissed.

"I might have just landed Sylvia in the hot seat." She tapped her fingers on the counter until their landlord answered. "Sylvia?"

"Hi Cybil. Did the police come yet? I wanted to phone you, but I couldn't think of the best way to say it. You do have both earrings, right? That's what I told…an Officer Noel?"

"Yes, he was already over. Just left, as a matter of fact. Say, those earrings you gave me, they are one-of-a-kind, right?"

"Originals, made by yours truly. That's why I told him what he claimed couldn't be true."

"Sylvia, what if I told you that there was another set that matched the ones you created?"

"Where?"

"At Mark's Crafts."

"That's…it just isn't possible. We made those in that jewelry class Marjorie held last year."

"I told Officer Noel. But, Sylvia, I also told him about the other pair I found at work and that means you are not in the clear anymore."

"Because that proves there are duplicates and that I

could still have mine?" A weary sigh came from the other end of the line. "I do not understand any of this, Cybil. Why are they asking such questions when Marjorie died from natural causes? Or…was it…not so natural?"

"I'm pretty sure that she was murdered, Sylvia."

"But what motive would I have against Marjorie? My nephew would have a more likely reason for wanting her dead than I do."

"You did like his fiancée before Marjorie's hands got into their wedding plans."

"That was years ago. If I wanted to kill her, I could have done so a hundred times over without anyone noticing where or when. I visit the church often enough for all of the special banquets and vacation bible schools. Not to mention the weddings and funerals."

"I realize that, but Officer Noel isn't one of us and might try to size that bitter angle up to see if it fits." She refrained from bringing up about how Marjorie managed to lose Sylvia's mother's brooch upon borrowing it for the spring choir show, just a few months ago. And that was without mentioning a separate incident where Marjorie accidentally backed her sedan into the front fender of Sylvia's expensive sports car over the summer.

"Let him try, Cybil. I'll make him eat his words!"

"I bet you would." Cybil smiled on her end. "By the way, did you ever find out what happened to the missing table-cloth?"

"Nope. I guess that's another mystery."

With a cheery sign off, the conversation was over, and Cybil hung up the phone just as Yas did likewise after a brief talk with Pastor Lawrence. "It seems that he can't get ahold of anyone in the Stonewell family to see if Gabriel is being taken care of. He asked me if I would be willing to check in on him."

"I thought he was going to do that last night?"

"He did, and Raven said she took care of him for the evening, but her mother won't allow the dog to come home with them, and now he can't seem to reach anyone at the numbers he has. We will have to backtrack to her house after visiting him for the key, but it is for a good cause." She attempted a pout of pity.

"What is? To save a dog that despises me and to probably keep him from turning the house into his own private bathroom?"

"Precisely." She dangled the keys from her fingers. "Ready to cast off, Skipper?"

"Aye, aye, Captain." Cybil pulled her jacket up and turned off the lights behind them. Her attention stopped on the narrow console table as she walked out the door. Everything was in order, and the half-ripped sticky note showed that they still used paper memos instead of digital reminders like many others their age. *I wonder if that is what caught his interest. Maybe he was surprised to find that we still use paper?*

"Are you coming, Slowpoke?"

"You better not have eaten that sandwich you made for me."

"Are you kidding? And risk being killed by you?" Yasmin started off laughing at her own joke, but suddenly digressed in the light of recent events. "We better get going."

As they drove down the slick roads, Cybil studied the streetlamps filled with flame flickering bulbs. It provided a welcomed sense of nostalgia to a night feeling darkened with dread and finality. The more she thought over what happened at the dinner, the more unsettled her mind grew. Turning to catch her roommate's reaction in the faint glow of the approaching traffic light, Cybil ignored a wondering thought looming in the corners. "It was almost like the killer was mocking her in death."

"You keep saying that it's a murder, but the police haven't mentioned anything about that to the press."

"Well, come on, Yas! You saw the track marks on her back, hoof patterns that did a poor job at shifting the blame onto John's missing reindeer, Rudolph."

"Rudolph is gone?"

"That is what Detective Lawson said today at Ralph's. And before you ask, don't. I'd rather not discuss that disappointing encounter."

"I just hope that all of this is cleared up by the time my parents fly in on the 20th , so they can see the town as we know it to be. Not this gossip fest that Marjorie stirred up."

"I'm pretty sure she didn't mean for this to happen."

"No, but…do you think we should attend her funeral?"

"Let's focus on getting to her house in one piece, first. Then we can worry about formalities later." Cybil coughed into her gloved hand and took a sip of water from her bottle in the cup holder. "What's the plan when we get there, chief?"

"I guess I'll venture in with you behind me, since he has developed a severe dislike for you." Yasmin smiled and turned the radio up as the Christmas song began playing through the speakers. Her higher voice did not pair well with the original singer, but it was all in the name of joy; so did it really matter? Cybil shook her head before leaning it against the cold car window in contemplation. She had a gut feeling that this season was not going to be as happy and cheery as her high hopes led her to believe.

CHAPTER 28

After leaving the pastor's house, sitting catawampus to the church, Yasmin had Cybil hold onto the key for good measure, while she navigated the trippy roads with her new snow tires. They were both grateful for the deeper tread and traction they provided on the freezing roads, having gone by a few accidents waiting for tow trucks down other avenues.

Cybil looked up at Marjorie's house, now coming into view around the corner, when she noticed a beam of light shining around in the darkened windows. It was pointed and concentrated like a flashlight, and hurriedly dashed away, frantically moving about as though it was in a wild search for something in particular. Yasmin called 9-1-1 to report the suspected break-in, just as Cybil picked up the phone to call her mother for a different number, and told her friend to drive by without stopping. Their headlights were bound to scare off the intruder, and that was the last thing they wanted to do.

"Hello, Melody? This is Cybil Lawson. I'm sorry to be calling you so late, but I thought you should know that someone is inside your sister's house." She explained where they were, driving around the block to avoid alerting the burglar, and relayed to Yas that Melody was on her way.

"The police said that they would be sending someone by to check it out as well."

"So, I guess we just drive around until they arrive?" Cybil cast her friend a dubious look. "At least Melody is only seven minutes away."

"More like fifteen minutes of eternity. I'm not trying to be mean, but it takes her longer to get in the van with her wheelchair. The thief could be long gone by then."

"Well, unless you are secretly trained in the art of judo, I don't think it would be wise of us to go all commando on whoever is in there."

"You're right." Yasmin subjected herself to the reality of the situation. "But what if the thief tries to flee before anyone shows up?"

"Then we will attempt to keep he or she here. But in the meantime, quickly pull into the neighboring house's driveway, two down from Marjorie's. With the barren branches of those trees, we will have a good view from there and they shouldn't suspect any danger."

Watching the clock on the dashboard tick the minutes away was slower than observing drying paint. Cybil let out a sigh of relief when she saw a minivan turn into the driveway within three minutes and motioned for Yasmin that it was time to go. *That was certainly a lot faster than we anticipated.* They pulled up behind the silver vehicle just in time to see two ramps being extended to the ground from the side door. Melody's electric wheelchair came humming out and rode into the snow without any issues, as her step-daughter, Christine, jumped out of the driver's seat on the other side.

"There she is!" Christine pointed to the dotted light

frantically being turned off within the house. She didn't hesitate to race up the sidewalk running between the garage and the main building, to where a window was slid open, and managed to catch sight of her own daughter failing to flee the scene. "I caught her!"

Melody rolled up to find Raven's chest heaving from her doomed escape, the teenager staring at her mother with a glaring look. "Are you proud of what you have done? Why don't you scream it from the rooftops that you found your daughter breaking into a house? Huh?!"

"Alright. That's enough!" Melody ordered. She turned to see Cybil and Yasmin slowly walking up the drive with police lights coming down the road. "It appears as though we have caused enough trouble for one evening, without having to wake all the neighbors from their slumber."

When the police officer inquired into what was going on, Christine explained the whole episode to Raven's embarrassment. Since everything seemed to be in order, he logged the incident with dispatch, and continued on his way for the evening. Yasmin offered to open the house, properly, with the pastor's key, and everyone was pretty soon inside the single-story rancher. Gabriel greeted Raven with licks and spun in circles until his beady little eyes caught sight of Cybil bringing up the rear of the incoming guests. His happy-tempered expressions soon turned into deep stomach growls and short teeth being bared in her direction.

"What did you do to this dog?" Christine asked in puzzlement.

"Nothing that I can recall." Cybil held her hand up in surrender. "Perhaps if there was a treat that he liked, I could give it to him as a peace offering?"

"I'm afraid to say that his treat container is empty." Yasmin pointed to a plastic jar, covered in paw prints, and sealed with a twisted lid. Only crumbs barely coated the bottom of the container. "Melody, do you know what he eats?"

"Sorry, I don't. I have only been in this house once or twice before, as my sister preferred to visit me than the other way around. A part of me likes to think that she did so out of consideration to my condition. Although, I would sooner bet that it had more to do with keeping my wheel tracks out of her carpet." Melody rolled her eyes at the sound of more shouting coming from Christine searching for Raven, who managed to slip from her mother's grasp and run off.

"Ugh! That BRAT!" The art gallery owner sped her way down the hall to the right, swinging doors madly open as she shouted.

"TRY THE BASEMENT!" Melody harshly suggested. After her step-daughter headed down the stairs, she abruptly turned the direction of her wheel chair around and instructed the others to leave those two be. "Let's just say that Christine was not meant to be a doctor. Her bedside manner can be sharper than a cactus needle."

Yas remained silent, sharing an unspoken look with her best friend. As they calmly walked around Marjorie's living room, trailing after Melody's chair, Cybil's eyes went straight for the Christmas cards dangling from a piece of taunt twine. New clothespins held all of the lovely winter season images of landscapes, puppies, and book decorated trees. Pinned behind each of the bi-folded cards, was a piece of their respective envelopes with the sender's address and the stamp used to mail the card. "Whoa!" Her mouth dropped at the sight of seeing places such as Nashville TN, Denver CO, Lincoln DE, Chicago IL, Normal WI, Grand Rapids MI, San Antonio TX, and even two from Cachan, France and Magdeburg, Germany as well. "Marjorie sure did know a lot of people."

"Huh?" The deceased's sister wheeled herself across the wooden floorboards of an attached hall. "Oh, those. Marjorie was a part of an online 'Santa Exchange' club, you might say. But it was closer to pen pals than handing out gifts. Each year, she would sign up as soon as registration opened, and she would tell them how many cards she wanted to send, and receive, for the season."

"And the group is international?"

"Yes. In fact, Marjorie was so excited to have gotten a few from across the Atlantic, that she called me up to tell me." Melody offered a nearby snow and winter bird card a bittersweet smile. "It was something an online book site held every year, and it ended up becoming a tradition for her."

Cybil wasn't sure what to think about Marjorie's eldest sister. According to all accounts, it was Marjorie's fault Melody's legs became paralyzed when they were in high school. Everyone thought that the two sisters were at odds with one another, speaking only when in public to show face and nothing more. Yet here was a different side to the story. Melody appeared to be mourning in her own reserved manner, with no tears and no obvious emotion dictating her actions. However, the grief was real in her voice and eyes, while she continued to gaze upon the cards with a saddened fondness.

"If I may," Cybil cleared her throat, "I didn't realize that you were on such good terms with your sister?"

"We were never as much of rival enemies as the rumors made us out to be. But that did not mean we talked every day and where glued to the hip, as it were." Melody faced the younger woman, standing close to the fireplace and the nativity scene situated on top the mantel. "I forgave her for what happened all those years ago. It was an accident, plain and simple. I've tried to explain that to some of my friends, but to no avail. They believe me to be taking the high road, and still blame her for all I have gone through."

"And for the new wheel chair you are going to need because of your arthritis?" Yasmin chimed in, remembering the collection plate that went around that prior Sunday.

"Getting older is not for the faint of heart, Ms. Lawson. I have come to terms with my problems, as many others have it undoubtedly worse than I do." Melody gave her a gentle, but firm, stare for emphasis on the point she was about to make. "Officer Noel already spoke with me about my feelings toward my sister, and I understood the implications he was trying to delicately beat-around-the-bush with. Seeing as how my financial predicament appears as a good motive for killing Marjorie, I can assure you that I had nothing to do with her death. Her will is of no use to me."

Cybil's suspicions were turning in her mind at hearing what Melody had just said. She hadn't mentioned anything about Marjorie's will, and yet, this woman was telling a mostly strange person that she had no use for it. If she had been reading this in a novel, Cybil would certainly have marked it down as a clue. And the way she talked about her conversation with Officer Noel, certainly gave an insight into the police's thoughts.

Just as Cybil was about to ask her a question, however, Christine came busting into the living room with anger written in her eyes. "I can't seem to find Raven anywhere!"

"Did you check the basement, like I suggested?"

"Yes, and she isn't there."

"Perhaps she is in her smuggler's hole?" Melody patiently stated to her step-daughter.

"Her what?"

"You really don't pay attention to your own family, do you?" The old woman huffed. "The gap in the walls down in the basement, between the wash room and the reading nook. The 'smuggler's hole' was their nickname for it, given all the bootlegging lure about this house."

Cybil's interest was thoroughly piqued by now. "I'm sorry, but did you just say that there's a bootlegger's smuggling hole in the basement?"

"Sort of. I mean, who is to say either way? The house was originally built in 1901, and construction had been done to the place numerous times. Marjorie would have known its history far better than Marta or myself. However, I would wager that it is most likely the result of work that was done in the 70s, as opposed to anything of real significance. Regardless, Marjorie and Raven used to sneak off into the basement and pretend that they were making illegal alcohol while being on the run from the cops. Of course it was just root beer. My sister never took a sip of the real stuff in her entire life."

"Oh, yeah. That's a good thing to encourage in a young child. No wonder why Raven is the oddest of my children." Christine walked off, heading to the basement door once again; this time, with more sense of urgency.

"Says the one who doesn't even listen to her!" Melody yelled over her shoulder, sighing as her step-daughter dismissed her words with a hand wave. Shifting her attention back onto Cybil, the elderly woman's lips broke into a half grin. "She really does try her best. Though, parenting is not a skill in everyone."

"It is certainly not one of mine." Cybil gave her a half-smile. "Well, I guess Yasmin and I have better get going…"

"By the way, why were you coming here in the first place?" Melody asked in a rather curious voice, bordering on accusation.

"Pastor Lawrence couldn't get ahold of anyone, pertaining to the dog, Gabriel. He was worried about the little guy, and called Yasmin to check it out."

"You might as well take the little rascal, seeing as how none of us will be able to watch after him for the time being." Melody glowered up at her. "That being said, I didn't know you two had a key to the house."

"We don't. Pastor Lawrence allowed us to borrow his copy." Cybil was slowly picking up on the sense of a fishing expedition from the older woman, and warned herself to be careful treading into those waters. There was no telling what witty little trap she could be walking herself into.

"Well, he probably has my old phone number. It was changed not long ago." Melody abruptly swung her chair around and propelled herself down a long hallway on the opposite side of the dining room. She continued her way into a widened entrance to the right, turning into the kitchen with great ease and experience.

Yasmin came up on Cybil's left, to let her know that she gathered Gabriel's things, when a shriek of panic could be heard coming from Melody's direction. Concerned that something had happened to the eldest Stonewell sister, both women rushed in to find the woman in a shock of disbelief at a busted lock dangling from a cheap hinge. "It's gone!"

"What's gone?" Cybil asked.

"Our family recipe. The recipe for the cookies. It's gone!"

CHAPTER 29

Before long, Cybil and Yasmin found themselves facing a sea of red and blue flashing lights for the second night in a row. Officers marked crime scene tape around the property, and ushered the nosy neighbors back into their homes. Cybil shook her head and leaned against the window bench in the living room as she watched Officer Noel approach the front door. He stepped over the threshold and turned to his left to see both women looking sheepishly at the floor.

"I might have known that I was going to see you two again. Just not so soon."

"It wasn't our wish either." Cybil gestured to the hall behind them. "The robbery happened that way." She peeked over her shoulder and tipped her head for him to lean in a little closer so she could whisper what she was going to say next. "Pastor Lawrence tried to call her, and when I asked her about it, she said he most likely had an old number. But while standing here, I phoned the pastor to confirm, and he has her current information. He even told me that she gave it to him after her number was switched."

"And that proves what, exactly?"

"That she's lying about not getting a call."

"Or…that you are trying to divert suspicion from your-self. I checked with Mrs. Norman to confirm her story on loading the meals into her vehicle. She admits that she was at the back door during the time you said she wasn't."

"I swear she was nowhere near the back of the church at any point of that evening. I was in the kitchen, doing the dishes, after the meals were completed. You even said that there were no tire tracks to prove her claim over mine." Cybil placed her hands on her hips. "Why was she even packing all of the meals up that night? She could have easily gotten them the next morning, when they were scheduled to be delivered. Where was she going to keep all of them refrigerated?"

"Mrs. Norman told us that she has a chest freezer, in her garage, where she planned on storing them until the following morning. We also checked with the pastor's wife the following day, and she has corroborated Mrs. Norman's statement, saying that she opened the kitchen for Mrs. Norman and was told that it was to finish packing up the rest of what she didn't get in her car the previous evening."

"Fine. But when you speak with Melody, ask her about how many times she has been to this house. Only if you think it will help in your investigation though, and not be a distraction." She shifted her focus onto the floorboards underneath her feet, waiting for the officer to walk by to inspect the robbery claim in the kitchen. In doing so, her eyes accidently landed on a small, antique hair clip that had oddly fallen to the floor behind the couch and near the back leg of a side table. It was unlike any that she had ever seen in the retail stores, appearing to be older than the 21st century.

"What was that all about? Is he seriously taking Mrs. Norman's word over yours?" Yas whispered after Noel had left them alone.

"I'm not sure. He might have just been trying to rile me up to see how I reacted. Either way, it would be nice to have some solid proof that I was where I said I was. If only the security cameras worked at the church, and weren't just for show."

"You would have thought that the police would have checked this place out already. Or at least, roped it off with yellow tape."

"Our town doesn't have the resources to have a crime scene investigation unit on hand, so they probably sent in a request for help from someone in the city, who won't be in until tomorrow. Besides, it wasn't listed as a crime scene until today." Cybil looked about the room at the officers posted both on the outside and inside of the house, or the lack thereof.

"And we do not have the staff right now, because of another investigation at the moment." Detective Lawson stepped in with the next gust of wind, catching Cybil off guard to his presence.

"One that is clearly meant for specific ears only. I checked the local news as I was trying to fall asleep last night, and if I had to wager a guess, it has something to do with the Mayor's missing car."

"You know my position when it comes to an active investigation. I don't discuss the matter."

"You don't have too. Leaving a crime scene the way you did, that would have only happened if pressure was coming from the top."

"Were you two the first on the scene again?"

"Unfortunately." Cybil directed him to where the kitchen was. "Officer Noel is that way."

"But I'm telling you, the entire basement worth of items is missing! There are scuff marks on the floor and spots of mud left by the only two boxes down there!" Raven shouted at her mother, who was clearly not listening on purpose. The two Hieghners had been arguing with one another since Christine discovered her daughter downstairs like Melody had suggested. During the phone calls to emergency services, their bickering had reached the maximum level of noise and Melody ordered them to take it into another room. However, with the opening of a bedroom door by the teen's own doing, meant that everyone had to endure their squabbling again.

"How can you be sure that Marjorie did not just move the items? She could have sold them or given them away. It's not like you lived here with her." Christine argued.

"She would not have done that. Those were special to her family, and some of the items dated back to the early 1800s. Most of them came from the 1920s, though."

"You are not an expert at antiques."

"Neither are you! Selling knock-offs as originals is not very reputable, is it?!" Raven countered. She had her arms crossed in front of her chest to match with the defensive nature she exhibited around her mother.

"Excuse me," Detective Lawson interrupted, "did I hear you right that there has been more than one robbery at this residence?"

"There has indeed." Raven dramatically pointed to the stairs leading to the basement. "Almost all of the boxes, filled with Stonewell family heirlooms, are missing."

"Detective, if I were you, I would just ignore what my daughter says. She has a tendency to imagine things that aren't there, and..."

Cybil's uncle proceeded to check out Raven's story by inspecting the well-lit bottom level of the house. He glanced over the scuff marks she had talked about, and the patches of mud that did not plant themselves in the midst of the otherwise cleaned room.

Christine left her hands rest upon her hips, shouting from the top floor. "Like I said, Detective, she likes to make up stories, of which I mostly pay no attention to, mind you, and…"

"Ma'am, I am not you, and better for it apparently. Elsewise, another crime would have gone without being reported. Now, if you excuse us," Detective Lawson ushered Raven over toward the kitchen where Officer Noel was in the middle of getting Melody's statement.

Yasmin looked over at her friend with worry as Cybil's uncle walked straight past without even giving her a sideways glance. "Are you alright?"

"Yeah. I'm just tired." Cybil gave her a short smile as her phone dinged again, alerting her to another text message from her mother. "Did you get through to Ralph on the party you forgot was happening tomorrow?"

"No. And he should still be up. It's not his day off, the bar is open our regular hours tonight, and he is attached to his phone like a teenager. Called into work and they said they haven't seen him in over two hours."

Cybil's eyes moved up from the nativity scene on the mantel to the Christmas painting hanging above it. Just like the one the choir director dropped off to have framed, a string of lights had been placed in each of the stars dotting the peaceful night sky. "Ralph went to school with Marjorie."

Yas lifted her gaze up from her phone, in mid-text to her boss. "What are you saying?"

"Nothing, really. Just a thought."

"It's a thought that you can forget about. There is nothing remotely connecting Ralph with a motive to harm Marjorie."

"That we know of." Cybil looked at her friend with the tilt of her head.

CHAPTER 30

"Something is not adding up."

"You're telling me. The other side of traffic had two green lights by now, and we are still stuck on red." Yasmin tapped her thumbs against the steering wheel impatiently.

"No, not that. I mean about the robbery of the recipe card." Cybil's tongue licked her top lip in thought. "Melody told me that she had only been in that house once or twice before. But she skillfully picked the entrance to the kitchen that was large enough for her wheelchair to make it in."

"The other side is smaller?"

Cybil nodded. "It isn't as wide as the threshold from the hallway into the kitchen. Now, most houses have a connecting point between the kitchen and the dining room, so if someone was searching for a kitchen in a house, whose layout they were unfamiliar with, logic would suggest that they would head to the dining room. If she had, then Melody would have been forced to turn around and try the other route. Instead, however, she went straight for the entrance she knew would have been big enough for her to enter."

"I thought she told you she'd only visited the house once

or twice before?" Yas gratefully pressed down on the gas pedal as the light turned green.

"She did. Which confirms my theory that she is definitely lying."

"Not trying to rain on your parade, but is that really news? Those sisters are famous for twisting words and truth around."

"Still doesn't make it right. She isn't telling us the whole story; that much I am certain of."

"Speaking of keeping secrets, I noticed that you didn't tell Officer Noel, or your uncle, about the fact that Melody and Christine showed up way earlier than they should of, if they were coming from Melody's place. Remember when I had to drive over there once, to drop off a couple of gallons of Ralph's special Strawberry Bubble Fizz for a party last year? There is no way they could have made it to Marjorie's faster than a solid seven minutes. And that is only if Melody is ready to go right then and there."

"I noticed. But you also heard Officer Noel back at the house. He might start suspecting me of having a hand at Marjorie's death if I keep offering him my two cents."

"What are the odds that Marjorie, who hasn't baked her family's recipe in how long, decides to bake it all of sudden, and then gets killed before the recipe is stolen?"

"On the slim chance that the two events aren't related, I would say they were weirdly timed." Cybil abruptly reached for her phone and clicked on a contact.

"What are you doing?"

"Calling someone who would know a thing or two about the Stonewells." Cybil waited for her mother to pick up on the other end, before diving straight into the questions toiling around in her mind. Within a few minutes, riding along in the back seat, Gabriel decided to voice his opinions of the phone call, and Cynthia immediately asked why she could hear a dog barking behind her daughter's voice. "We are temporarily taking care of Gabriel for now. No time to explain. Thanks."

"What is it?" Yas slowed down as the snow blew across the street.

"I thought I was misremembering for a moment, but I'm not. After Marjorie's parents died, she moved into the house they grew up in. They had moved right before her sister's accident, and remained at that location until their deaths three years ago."

"Ooooh. The plot thickens! That would coincide with what Melody told us about her sister knowing the history of the house, and its prohibition past. So at least that part appears to be true. But I must say, that the deeper you go, the more lies she seems to be caught in." Yas turned the wheel to make a right. "Certainly moves her up on the list of suspects. She would have known about the safe in the kitchen, which isn't a common place to stash a combination door just to keep valuables secure."

"Or in this case, a highly sought after cookie recipe. Seems like a strange thing to steal, doesn't it? It's not as though we are dealing with industrial espionage, or anything. Right?"

"Not that I recall." Yasmin glanced up in the review mirror and saw Gabriel laying his head upon his paws as the lure of sleep became too inviting for him to stay awake. "Ah, don't worry little boy. We will have you in your new home in no time."

"Gabriel!" Cybil's head spun around. "That dog would bark its head off if an intruder was even touching the thresh-old to the house. So whoever stole the recipe card, had to have been a friend of Marjorie's or someone Gabriel knew."

"That narrows the field, but still leaves us with a lot of possibilities. I would start with Raven, since we caught her red-handed in the house after the recipe went missing." Yas made the final turn into their own driveway.

"I don't think she did it." Cybil opened the door and grabbed a bag of dog toys from the back seat.

"And why not?"

"I just have a feeling."

CHAPTER 31

Cybil called off of work the following day, having barely slept all night due to the robbery, the terror of Gabriel running around the house, and her own mind not wanting to shut down for the evening. There were too many factors that weren't meshing, and try as she could, her curiosity was winning the fight. *Well, perhaps if I cook us up some breakfast.* She quietly moved beside the couch where her roommate was fast asleep with Gabriel in her arms. There was no telling at what hour of the morning those two had dosed off, but it was heartwarming to see the dog enjoying some company. *As long as he doesn't eat any more of my clothing, then we are all good.*

She reached for the eggs, bacon, and ham steaks from the top shelf of the fridge and turned the gas stove on by the twist of a knob. Prepping the skillet for the first round of bacon, Cybil wasn't surprised to see both Yasmin's and Gabriel's' noses going at full bore. They each popped up from their slumber with sleepy eyes and zombie-like steps to find where the tantalizing smell was coming from.

"Is that bacon?" Her roommate was smacking her lips together in mouthwatering anticipation.

"It's nice to see that bacon still does the trick." Cybil smiled just as the doorbell rang. "Tell you what, go and see who it is while I flip these so they don't burn."

"Deal." Yas sped over to the door, and immediately stopped upon opening it. "Ah, Cybil? You might want to come here and check this out."

Her friend looked up from grabbing the milk out of the fridge, and saw Yas standing in the threshold with a puzzled expression plastered on her face. The chilly air was seeping in through the crack she kept open with her hand. "What is it? Is something wrong?"

"Just come over here and take a look at the package left for us." Yas waited for Cybil to come over, and watched her mirror her own state of confusion.

Sitting on top of a reindeer shaped doormat, cheerfully welcoming guests to their humble abode, was a circular fish tank fixated to a wooden base. It was adorned to look like a snow globe, with a decorated Christmas tree nestled between teal rocks and the side of the glass. A small jar of fish food had been tied to a folded piece of paper underneath the mysterious drop-off, adding to the unique gift.

Cybil shrugged her shoulders. "Well, I guess we could venture out on a limb and say that it can't be a bomb." She glanced over at Yas's unamused look and cleared her throat. "I'll get it." Reaching down to pick up the strange present, she suddenly felt the rapid poking and prodding from her friend's hands. "What?"

Yasmin whispered in her ear to look up, as they both witnessed a man dressed in dark clothing watch them from across the street, in the shadows of small evergreen trees. A car rolled on by nearly at the exact same time, and when their view was clear again, the man had vanished. Cybil hurriedly rushed the goldfish inside while her roommate slammed the door shut and bolted it tight. "Do you think that could be the killer?"

"If it is, then why would he come after us? We don't know his identity, so there is no need to risk being caught in order to spy on our house. Besides, the police are the ones solving Marjorie's death, not us." Cybil pulled the note out from the bottom, and read the message aloud. "I am sorry that this comes late to you, as I would have preferred dropping this little guy off yesterday. However, my job did not allow me to do as such, though I do not think that Norris is worse for wear. I remember how Marjorie said you had a fondness for goldfish, as they are the only pets your mother allows you to have. My hope is for him to bring you some level of comfort during this difficult time in your life. Perhaps at some point, I will have the courage for us to meet face to face, but until that time, just know that there is a guardian angel watching over you."

Yasmin's face was frozen in shock. "Wow. So who… Cybil!" She madly pointed to a shadowy figure moving about in the trees opposite the road. "He's still there." The smaller arborvitaes didn't do as well of a job at concealing him as the evergreens had done. He continued to shift behind them until the two women crept up to the glass for a better look, no longer listening to the sound of the sizzling skillet on the stove. No sooner had their faces pressed up against the cold surface, then a bus passed across the glass pane and the man disappeared from their sights again. "Do you think…that…that he could be the one from…" She instantly leapt up and attended to the bacon in the nick of time, upon smelling smoke billowing into the air.

"How am I supposed to know? All I caught was a glimpse of a man dressed entirely in black, in the shadow of trees. Did you catch anything more than that?"

"No. But what are the odds that two shadowy figures are watching you?"

"With my luck, I don't want to think about it." Cybil returned to the goldfish bubbling along in the circular tank. "Regardless of where he came from, it's not the fish's fault that he is here."

"I thought you had a dog when you were younger?"

"I did. Not to mention a cat and a few other animals." Cybil studied the message a little closer, sighting a smudge of chocolate icing on the back of the paper.

"My parents weren't into goldfish. Perhaps the person made a mistake?"

"Could be. He might have been delivered to the wrong house."

"What are you going to do with him? We don't even know who the fish is really for." Yas gazed into the bowl to see a pair of wide eyes staring back at her.

"Well, first I'm going to feed the little guy. Second, I am going to buy him a larger tank to swim around in."

CHAPTER 32

Later that same afternoon, Yasmin was off in another dog toy aisle of the pet store as Cybil walked around the fish tanks in search of the right-sized glass container. Being a little concerned at how much it was going to cost, she called in a favor to her parents and asked for a little Christmas money in advance. When she explained about her unexpected gift, altering the story a bit to conceal the possible stalker, they were more than willing to help her out.

Twisting the bills in-between her fingers, Cybil looked up and down the rows of tanks organized by size and brand. She allowed her eyes to peruse over the fifty gallon options, wondering who would want to have to clean it, before she reached the smaller units and remembered that she was going to need a filtration system.

"Can I help you?" One of the employees asked.

Cybil was about to inquire into which one he would recommend, when her phone rang in her pocket. She halted, tempted to ignore it because it was most likely a telemarketer, but looked down anyways and realized she had to answer it upon seeing the caller ID. "I'm good but thanks."

Yasmin walked over with a cart half full of supplies and

overheard part of Cybil's conversation on the phone, fearing that their afternoon was going to take a turn for the worst. She saw the irritation being displayed on Cybil's face. Once the phone call was over, Yas was reluctant to ask. "What's wrong now?"

"Betsy, the framing manager, told me that Marjorie's frame came in and asked me what she wanted me to do about it. I told her to complete the order since it was already paid for, which is what Matt told her to do as well. However, she did bring up the point that the only phone number attached to the order belongs to Marjorie, and it's not exactly like she can pick it up."

"You called off of work, remember? Showing up there today is not a good idea."

"Betsy is going to take it out to her car, under Matt's approval, and give it to me in the parking lot so that we can drop it off with Raven."

"Raven?"

"Yeah. She is the one who painted the original piece that Marjorie had a print made from. I know that it's just a copy, but she might want to have it nonetheless."

"What if she doesn't?"

"Then I guess we are just going to have to drop it off at Marjorie's house. You still have the pastor's key?"

"No. Melody heavily suggested for me to return it to her last night. Since her sister died, it was to eliminate any chances of someone else coming into the house, per her words."

"Or to keep other items from going missing under her watch. The way that family acts, I wouldn't put it past them to be after something her sister hid from the others." Cybil took a moment to look down at the covered cart bottom, and cast her friend a look without saying anything.

"What? Gabriel is going through a lot right now, and tips have been better at work, so I can afford a little splurge on him. I'm just glad that Marjorie had a crate his size. Elsewise, I don't know whether there would be a house left for us to go back to. That's why I made sure to grab some chewing toys while we're here." Yasmin's face spread out in a wide smile. "Did you pick out a tank yet?"

Cybil shook her head, sighed to herself and returned back to the task at hand. It was not even fifteen minutes later, when she had purchased a five gallon circular tank, with a filter system, and more teal stones to match the ones Norris already had. She was loading it into Yasmin's car just as her text alert went off with a message from Betsy, announcing when she would be able to pick up the print. "Well, we have half an hour to burn before our meeting."

"Want to try out the new fast food joint off the intersection at the mall's entrance? I hear they have a mean spicy chicken sandwich and a heavenly chocolate cake for dessert." Yasmin already had visions of the scrumptious food dancing through her head.

"Sure. As long as they have non-spicy versions too."

"You are no fun." Yas joked. They both dived into her car for the warmth, while the cold wind blew all around the parked vehicles. Snow lined the lanes and spaces due to plows stacking it into mounds on the outskirts of the mall's parking lot. The trees, devoid of any leaves, were beautifully coated with soft lines of white and the whole landscape seemed to sing a Christmas song of its own making. "Are you excited for Christmas?"

"I don't know." Cybil preferred to keep her emotions about the holidays to herself, so she decided to change the topic of conversation. "Officer Noel was really interested in our console table by the door last night."

"Oh he was?"

"Yeah. You didn't notice him looking over the area with our sunglasses, sticky notes and other things?"

"Not really. I stared mostly at my phone while he was there. It was a little awkward having a cop in the house. And there was a neat cat video on my social media, so that had me entertained."

"He tried to sound like nothing was up when I asked, but he was clearly studying the table top. The only thing I found different was a half torn sticky note. But I haven't written anything on there lately. Have you?"

"Don't know what you're talking about." Yasmin purposefully diverted onto something else. "Ah, we're here. Want to go inside where it is warmer?"

"Sounds good to me." Cybil heard the defensive tone in her friend's voice and wasn't liking it. There was certainly more behind Yas's short reply, but for now, it was not the time to bicker over a piece of missing paper. It was too cold to worry, for starters, and the sights of food bags leaving in people's hands was making her stomach growl in envy.

A text from Ralph came in on her phone as she exited the vehicle, and Cybil took the time to read over the short message from the bar owner. She couldn't help but feel attacked from the words he sent her, listing the complaints his patrons were saying about her and the cookie contest. After relaying the issues to Yas, she instantly typed up a quick reply.

"It's just idle gossip, Cybil. Don't listen to it. Ralph's warning you, tis all." Yas locked up the car with her key fob.

"I'm not mad at Ralph, he's only the messenger. But I can't believe that those people are saying it serves Marjorie right for rigging the contest. And that I might be next for being in cahoots with her." Cybil shrugged her shoulders.

"It's not like this was a national competition with a million dollars at stake."

"You know how people like to talk and spread rumors, regardless of whether it's true or not. Marjorie rubbed a lot of them the wrong way from time to time. So its natural they would want to shade her death in their favor. I'm sure Officer Noel would agree with me when I say that people have been killed for less." Yas stopped to help her friend up a slippery patch of the sidewalk.

"They always seem to say that, but no one ever tells you what the least amount was that someone was killed for. Did you ever realize that?"

"Hasn't really crossed my mind." Yasmin made sure they were out of the icy area before letting go of Cybil's arm. Over the years, she had grown accustomed to leading her balance-troubled roommate through many slick walkways, and had been fortunate enough not to fall more than once.

Another customer held the door open for the two ladies as they entered the building, and it wasn't until they reached the ordering kiosks, did they realize that the garden center's owner was waiting for his food right beside them. Cybil was the first to say "hi" and then shamefully apologized for not getting him the image of their joint business project yet. "I have been so busy, which is not an excuse, but I just plumb forgot."

"It's alright, Cybil. Christmas has a funny way of doing that to people. I swear it goes by faster every year." Jeffrey looked down at his wristwatch and fiddled with the thin receipt paper in his hands. "Apparently time moves quicker almost everywhere else but here."

"That's why we are over at the kiosks. I'd rather order through a real person, but the line…" She pointed to the sixteen men and women standing in front of the two cashiers rapidly tapping on their screens with specialized requests.

"I'm sorry that your cookie didn't win the contest." Yas spoke up from the other side of the double screen. "Personally, your coconut ones were my pick."

"Well, it is what it is. At least I am still alive, so perhaps I was better off not winning."

"Do you think someone targeted Marjorie because her recipe won?" Cybil selected a burger without pickles and onions. "Seems pretty drastic for a spa trip."

"There was more riding on the win than a mere luxury day at the new spa." Jeffrey glanced up as the number ahead of his was called over the loudspeaker.

"Like what?" Cybil hadn't been aware of anything else riding on the contest. At least, it wasn't general knowledge.

"Never mind. I shouldn't have said anything."

"No. Jeffrey, if there was something else going on in the background, such as an underhanded bet, I need to know. It's bad enough I have a number of the church members thinking that I was in cahoots with Marjorie in rigging the contest. Let alone what they are going to say about me being one of the first on the scene."

"Well, is it true?" Jeffrey pulled his jacket straighter after two kids ran into him.

"It most certainly is not! I only picked up the cookies because that was what I was tasked with doing. There was no conspiracy on my part, and everything stayed cool and dry in the basement at my house. Marjorie brought her own to the dinner and I assembled the rest of them on the table."

"Let's just say that I lost out on a pretty big deal because of her win." His number was announced from a young food prepper, prompting him to pick up his order and go to leave.

But Cybil was not deterred that easily. "What deal?"

"Ask the nun. She is staying at the Clifford's Bed and

Breakfast." He gripped hard onto the paper bag in his hand as he shuffled his way out the door. Cybil was left in a fog of confusion as to what he was talking about while her screen kept blinking for her to continue ordering or risk losing the food in her cart already.

"The nun? What has a nun got to do with any of this?" Yasmin poked her friend in the shoulder. "You need to pay for your food, girl."

"Yeah, I will." Cybil was more determined to find out just what was going on with what was supposed to have been a simple cookie contest for the church members. "And after Betsy gives us Marjorie's painting, I'm dropping you off with Gabriel and having a chat with a certain woman of the cloth."

CHAPTER 33

"May I help you?" The receptionist at Clifford's Bed and Breakfast smiled from behind large glasses attached to a handmade chain, draped around her elongated neck. A sweet aroma of her perfume wafted into the air with considerable potency, which made Cybil wonder if the older woman's nose was starting to go bad.

"Ah, yes. I am looking for one of your guests who happens to be a nun?"

"That could be Sister Bertrille."

Cybil bit her tongue in an attempt to keep her sarcasm back. *How many nuns could be staying here at once?* "I believe she's the one. Where might I find her?"

"In the café. She went in there about ten minutes ago."

"Thanks." Walking around the corner, Cybil moved into a small-scale dining room in what used to be the pride and joy for one of the richest families in the state. No longer did the grand mahogany table extend the entire length of the spacious area, nor did it even exist in the house any more. Instead, the same room had been altered to host over twelve café-sized tables, crafted from walnut, and draped in a light cream fabric. It wasn't difficult to spot the black and white dressed woman sipping on a coffee, as she read a page of the local newspaper, and Cybil wasted no time in joining her by the checkout counter. The last thing she wanted was for a voice in her mind to plant some doubt and cause her to abort her plans.

Seeing the presence of a young woman approaching her, the nun calmly raised her eyes up from the article she was reading on Marjorie Stonewell's death. "What may I do for you, My Child?"

"If you could spare a few minutes, I would like to ask you some questions."

"About faith?"

"No. In regards to the cookie contest at my church last Saturday. I believe you were the judge?"

"I am not sure of what I could tell you, but do sit down." She graciously motioned to the empty chair opposite of her.

To double-check her previous suspicions, Cybil glanced down at the nun's rosary beads dangling from her left hip as she took her seat. "What I need to discuss with you, may be better suited for a private conversation where no other ears can listen in."

"If you are seeking spiritual guidance, then might I suggest…"

"I am seeking guidance in the form of cookie recipes and underhanded dealings." Cybil interjected, staring the nun down with a set of steadfast eyes. "I believe I am speaking to the right person on the matter, after someone told me to speak with you and where you were staying."

"Might I ask who sent you?"

"That all depends if I have the right person or not." Cybil arched her brows, unwavering in her determination to find out some answers. She had dealt with unfounded rumors in her college days, and refused to allow herself to become a victim like the other girl did. "I just want to know the facts so the other church members don't go around accusing me of rigging the contest so Marjorie could win. I have enough issues without these rumors going around about me."

Sister Bertrille's lips nearly disappeared into an extremely thin line as she debated on what to do. Finally, she decided that it was best to come clean, and offered to escort Cybil into the old library. The converted study was empty, as people were using the on-site gym to get in their daily routines, just down the hall. However, Sister Bertrille closed the door as an added precaution. Both women sat across from one another again, this time in the more comfortable wingback chairs that were recently re-upholstered. "I'm guessing that Jeffrey was the man who told you about me."

"Let's just say that I'm not revealing their identity to protect them."

"Relax. I'm not from the mafia or anything. I work for Grinder Mills Foods. I believe you have heard of them?"

"Yeah, you're right on that. So what is an employee of one of the biggest snack companies in the country, doing in Robbyr's Cove?"

"Pretty simple, really. Our company is always looking for the next best product to put out on the shelves. The competition is ferocious in my line of work, so I figured on taking a risk in order for us to get ahead for a change. With Kropper's Munchies punching out the latest trends for the past year or more, my boss was eager for any new idea that might make a dent in their sales. So when I talked about these wonderful cookies I used to have as a kid, he asked me to look into acquiring the recipe."

"I'm guessing there is something in it for you if you seal

up the deal. A promotion, perhaps? Elsewise, why would you risk impersonating a nun in order to buy a cookie recipe? Seems like a pretty desperate act."

"So maybe there is a larger reward than just doing my job for the company. What's it matter? The point is that I came down to be the judge for the contest and decided that Marjorie was the winner. I was going to offer her a buyout option with Grinder Mills, but she died before I had a chance to ask."

"Who was it that asked you to fill in as the judge? According to everyone at the dinner, Tara was supposed to be the taste tester until you stepped into the room."

"There was a last minute switch in the casting."

"Was it Jeffrey who asked you to come down?"

"He tell you that?"

"He didn't have too. Being as how he knew your real identity, it was a logical guess."

"It could have easily been Marjorie who called me up." The nun leaned forward in the chair, staring down Cybil. "Why not ask if she was the one?"

"She could have. But Marjorie wasn't a fan of Catholicism, so its highly doubtful that she would have called a church or monastery in order to obtain a cookie judge."

"You have some good hunches, I'll give you that. Jeffrey and I went to school together in New York. For years, he has been working on a new cookie recipe in the hopes that it will take him places and make lots of money. His family comes from bakers, you see, and when he failed in pastry school, well, they weren't easy on him. So, I promised him that if his cookie so much as placed in the top two, at four different cookie competitions within one year, I would take the recipe to my boss and see what he thought. Nothing against Jeffrey, he's a good guy and all, but he does not have a lot of instincts when it comes to dough and baking."

"How much money are we talking about in this deal for Marjorie's recipe?"

"Depends on how much my boss is willing to pay. Small end would be in the six figures."

Cybil's eyes nearly bugged out. *That would certainly be a good motive for murder if others found out about this imposter nun, and why she's really in town.* "Isn't that a little high for a single recipe?"

"If the cookies were as good as I remember them being, then it would be an investment well spent."

"Wait, if you both grew up in New York, then how did you know about the Stonewell's family cookies?"

"I had an aunt here that my parents would visit during the summer on vacation."

"Are you and Jeffrey related?"

"He's my cousin. And with Jeffrey, he believes that should be enough for me to take his recipes to my boss. But I can't jeopardize my position like that. It's not like he is my mother, who actually knew how to bake."

"One final question." Cybil also shifted her butt toward the end of the seat, sensing that their conversation was coming to an end. She didn't want to have to awkwardly try to get out of the sunken cushions like her grandmother would at her parents' house. "Why are you answering all of my questions without keeping anything back? I expected a little bit of a fight from you on some of them."

"Oh, I didn't do this for free. If you happen to come across the cookie recipe card, I would be much obliged if you contacted me, or passed the word onto whoever else might have it. The offer still stands on the table."

"Well, thank you for the chat. I feel a little better knowing that if the ladies at the church try to pass judgement on me, I have a little ammo to fight back on." Cybil went to leave the room when the fake Sister Bertrille stopped her.

"Tell me, what threw your suspicions onto me that I wasn't a real nun?"

"Most nuns have their rosary beads on the right side of their waist, not on the left." She pointed to the beads swaying as the woman rose from the chair.

"That wasn't the same recipe that Marjorie used for the cookies." The fake Sister Bertrille suddenly stated.

"It wasn't?"

"I know she said that it was when Jeffrey and that other woman questioned her about it, but I distinctively remember there being an almond flavor in the cookie. Now, don't get me wrong, the cookie was still very good, and much better than Jeffrey's coconut ones he has been trying to perfect for years. But there was no almond flavor and a subtle hint of lemon that I swear didn't used to be there."

"No offense, but a memory from that long ago has a way of playing tricks on the mind sometimes."

"That's what all my professors tried to tell me in collage. But that is also the same reason I have the job that I do, and they don't."

Cybil was tempted to walk out the door that very minute. In fact, her hand was already latched onto the 19th century knob, about to turn it open, when a thought struck her. "What if I told you that I knew where the recipe was and could lay hands on it this evening?"

"My first inclination is to call you a liar. Marjorie was a close-guarded person by all accounts. A blabbermouth when it came to gossip, sure, but her own life was shrouded in privacy. Jeffrey filled me in on all the details. However, you do seem to have a knack for picking up on the smaller innuendos. So let's say I believe you, and like I already stated, the deal still stands. But you would have to bring it to me by tomorrow afternoon. That's when my return flight to New York is scheduled."

Cybil remained silent as she opened the door and actually exited into the hall this time. Her ears picked up on the final detail the woman spouted out from the room, as she walked toward the lobby.

"And that includes it being on the recipe card with her ancestor's stamp."

CHAPTER 34

The gallery was nestled in the older part of town, help-ing to add to its charm from the exterior. But that was where the historical flare ended. Once inside, the off-white walls forced the customer to stare at the paintings adorning them, bringing sole attention to the featured artists of the current show. Seeing as how it was the holiday season, Christine had chosen winter as the theme. That was as much as Cybil could make out, considering a number of the pieces were more abstract than realistic interpretations of nature and snowy landscapes.

Soft music played throughout the enlarged space to add holiday vibes in the air as a few people gazed upon the works. Raven was standing behind the front counter with a bored look painted on her face while she sketched in an artist journal at the desk. As she looked up to see Cybil walking toward her, the teenager quickly shuffled her drawing supplies into a drawer and tried a weak attempt at a smile. "Hi. Can I help you?"

"Maybe." Cybil pulled the canvas-wrapped print up to where Raven could see it and gently placed the framed work on top of the long, white counter. She began to unravel the kraft paper that had been shielding it from the weather and managed to get her fingers caught up in the tape.

"If you are going to ask if we will hang your artwork up in the gallery…"

"No. Not that. I'm not exactly sure how to quite say this…except for getting straight to the point. Your Aunt Marjorie had a print made up from one of your pieces, and she brought it into the art store to get framed. The frame arrived and her order was completed, but we didn't know who else to give this too."

Raven curiously helped her to open the package and looked upon the scene with a neutral expression when all was revealed. "Let me guess. She fixed it for timed lights?" Her finger felt along the sides of the frame until she found the button to switch the twinkling glow on. "That was one of her things. She said that art was a beacon of light from the artist, and that it should be displayed as such." The tiniest bit of a smile could be seen in the corners of her mouth.

"Yep. She told me that she had this done to another print of yours, and I think I saw it hanging up on the mantel last night. I believe she said that the timer helps to ensure the lights don't burn out as fast."

"That's the reason she told me. They would shine from around 5:00 pm to 10:50 pm. That way she could go to sleep without having to worry about forgetting to turn them off."

"Sounds very responsible of her."

"She was always trying to do the right thing, even when others didn't. But, there were times when what she chose to do, didn't really go down well with the other members. I'm kind of surprised that it took someone this long, you know?"

"Are you referring to something she did while being the church secretary?"

Raven nodded her head. "Last summer, the church was looking into relandscaping the area surrounding the main assembly hall. Since Mr. Jeffrey is a member, my aunt asked him to take a gander around the plants and see what he envisioned for the space; while staying under a budget outlined by the pastor. Once the plan was approved through the board, Mr. Jeffrey was just waiting for the official go-ahead to buy the plants. About two weeks later, Aunt Marjorie told me that he came busting through broiling mad and shouting at the top of his lungs at her. He found out that she had taken his plans and purchased the plants herself."

"Why on Earth did she do that?"

"Because my aunt discovered a markup difference between the prices listed per plant, and the cost from the supplier. Man, did that calm his jets real fast when she laid it out for him. Said that if he was going to bring it up to the pastor, then she was going to reveal his padding of the quote. Since then, he has been keeping his mouth shut. Aunt Marjorie had one of the boys from the trailer park do the job instead, so he could save up for a car."

"Wow! I didn't know about that. I mean, I remember that the job was finished and looked great, but not on how it all went down."

"And he is only one of the members my aunt had something to lord over with. She used to say that while the you should help others in need, you still have to watch out for yourself too."

Cybil gave her a comforting smile. "I'm sorry for your loss, Raven. It sounded like you two were really close."

"Tighter than most." The girl glanced up to see her mother making long strides in her direction. "And way more than I am with my mom."

"RAVEN! I told you a hundred times, not to mix the

international ship outs with the domestic ones." Christine angrily stated, ignoring Cybil for the moment. "They get processed differently because the international packages have to go through customs."

"I did what you told me to do. It's not my fault that your shipping manager messed them up again."

The teen's mom was near fumes as her face grew red from the pressure building within. "I bet you were listening to your out-of-date radio when I specifically instructed you to put the papers in the green folder, and not in the purple."

"It's called a crystal set." Raven coolly retorted.

Christine's mouth opened as though she was about to continue fighting until it dawned on her as to Cybil's presence. Her perfectly sculpted face bore into the younger woman and straight across the street. "Is there anything we can do for you?" Her voice would have chilled the snow. Mrs. Hieghner then immediately took notice of the canvas print on the counter, bringing her defenses automatically up to battle-ready mode. "Take that piece of trash out of this gallery. I do not care for artists trying to hock their work at my gallery without having first gone through the proper procedures."

"But I…"

A hand was thrust into Cybil's face. "Not another word. You are lucky I don't call the cops right now. Grab your 'art' and get out of my gallery."

Cybil had no other choice but to obey the demanding woman's wishes. Picking up the piece from the counter, she looked over to see Raven slowly nod her head with a limp grin on her lips. There were no words uttered between them as she walked out of the older building, feeling more depressed than before. The door to the car even fought her for a minute while she tried to swing it open and load the painting into the back seat once again. And at the sound of the latch finally releasing, Cybil's phone rang out another text message alert.

Yas: Can you pick up some groceries on the way back?

Just as she was in the middle of sending a response, Cybil happened to glance up as the vehicle in front of hers pulled away from the curb. Two spots up, sat the same purple car that almost collided into her on the day of the dinner. Curiosity wriggled around in Cybil's mind, causing her to bring the camera up on her device, and snap a picture of the license plate.

The wind was beginning to increase its intensity along the streets, causing her to witness a strong gust race through the stores' canopies, upturn a few chairs, and knock over a café table or two in its wake. "Whoa. I believe that's my cue to scoot."

Cybil jumped into the driver's side, finished the return text to Yasmin, and started the car. Her hands turned the wheel enough to inch out of the parking spot, about to rejoin the traffic on Main Street. That was until she caught sight of an argument going down between Raven and her brother Rex on the sidewalk. The teenager must have exited the gallery right after Cybil had, and the talk they were having was not a happy one. Raven's hands flew to the back of her head in frustration at whatever Rex was telling her, and it was clear that something had not gone right by the sound of their flaring tempers. However, that wasn't the most shocking part of the whole ordeal.

Mrs. Norman, Westley's mother, came strolling up the sidewalk with a mound of cash concealed in the palm of her gloved hand. In the middle of the two teens' argument, she passed it off to Rex in a sly move. Faster than saying "Bob's your uncle," the middle-aged woman was casually walking by Cybil's passenger window without making anyone the wiser as to what just happened. Two blinks of the eye would have missed the handoff.

What is going on here?

CHAPTER 35

"There you are!" Yasmin called out from the front door to the railroad house. She was clearly excited about something, and was practically jumping up and down as she called Cybil to come in as quickly as she could. "I've been trying to get a hold of you for the past half hour."

"Sorry. The roads were a little slick and I didn't want to send another vehicle into the garage."

"Cybil, look!" Yas madly pointed the remote to the television screen, and cranked up the volume so that the news reporter's voice could be heard throughout the entire building. "That nun who was at the church dinner is dead. She's been murdered!"

"Murdered?!" Cybil stared on in horror, not seeing anything on the news of what her roommate was talking about. "Are you sure?"

"They made the announcement about thirty minutes ago, but I think they're going to shoot back to the live footage here shortly. If not, I have it recorded on the DVR."

The pleasant scene of children playing at the park after the last snowfall was suddenly cut short by the station, as the face of the nightly news anchor returned to the screen.

"We interrupt with some breaking news. It appears that the murder of a hotel guest at Clifford's Bed and Breakfast occurred earlier today. Again, our anonymous sources have confirmed that the victim, was in fact, a nun named Sister Bertrille. Police are currently in the hunt for the last person to have talked with the Sister, and according to the receptionist, she is a young woman around the age of twenty-five. She has brown hair, wore a dark green winter coat, and has a mole on the side of her face."

"Oh no." Cybil's stomach fell to the floor in worry and panic.

"Besides the supposed mole on your face, I knew it had to be you. What happened?!"

"It was probably a piece of dirt in her glasses. But, Yasmin, I swear I didn't have anything to do with this. She was alive when I left. Honest."

A round of knocking pounded at the front door, ending their conversation as a male voice shouted in from the exterior. "This is the police! Open up! We need to talk with you!"

Yasmin hunched over to place a hand on her friend's shoulder, who was now sitting in the couch as low as the cushions allowed. "Do you want to hide in the basement? I'll tell them that you went south for the winter."

"No, it's best to leave them in." Cybil practically whined on the inside. She was about to ask what else could go wrong, but didn't want to jinx it. Another barrage of pounding on the door sounded out, to which Gabriel did not care for, and Cybil nodded to Yas, who hesitatingly obliged their orders. "What can we do for you, Officer Noel?"

"We have a few questions to ask of your friend, Ms. Lawson." Noel stared pointedly at Cybil, still wedged into the couch behind Yasmin, without saying anything else. His official tone rattled her to the bone, despite the knowledge that she did nothing wrong. Ever since she was a kid, she didn't like to get into trouble and was considered to be a brown-noser by some of her classmates up until high school graduation. To this day, her anxiety would go up anywhere a security officer was nearby, due to a misunderstanding on a museum field trip years ago.

"And what would they be?" She tried to act confident in both voice and posture, climbing up to a full standing position.

"It is in regards to a Sister Bertrille staying at the Bed and Breakfast down Mulberry Street. Have you heard of it?"

"Like many other people in town. It's one of the oldest buildings in Robbyr's Cove."

"Were you there this afternoon?"

"Yes, as a matter of fact. I was there to visit the good Sister."

"And did you?"

"I did. And she was very much alive when I left her about 4:30 pm."

"You act as though something has happened to her."

"Yasmin showed it to me on the television just a few minutes before you arrived. The news picked it up as a breaking story."

"What was the reasoning for your visit?"

"How did she die?"

"Ms. Lawson, I believe you are fully aware of how this goes. Now, why were you at the Bed and Breakfast with Sister Bertrille?"

"To ask her why she posed as a nun, and acted as a judge for the cookie contest at the church dinner Saturday evening."

Officer Noel managed to let a small indication of surprise slip on his otherwise stoic face. "What gave you the idea that she isn't…wasn't…a nun?"

"She wore her rosary beads on the wrong side of her hip, for starters, and then Mr. Jeffrey, who owns the garden center, said that I was to talk to her if I wanted to know what was going on in the background of the contest. There was clearly more at stake than the spa trip everyone thought to be the grand prize." Cybil filled them in on the details that the nun imposter had given her. After it was all said and done, Yasmin was the first to speak up.

"But you don't have the recipe, nor a clue as to where it is. Why say that?"

"It was a test. I wanted to see her reaction, and if she already knew that the recipe had been stolen. Clearly she did, because she said that the deal was still on the table for whoever wanted to sell it to her."

"We managed to keep that much hidden from the press, and would appreciate it if you two continued to keep your mouths shut on the matter of the stolen recipe." Officer Noel finished scribbling down some notes in his pad.

"Did you find a connection between the two deaths?" Cybil couldn't help herself from asking. The timing was certainly very interesting, to say the least, and that went without mentioning the contest and the winning cookie.

"You mean, besides the fact that you keep showing up?"

"Yes, besides that." She gulped.

"At this time, there has been no evidence discovered that can positively link the two incidents. So don't go drawing lines where there is nothing to connect."

"But I think there is. Just as I was leaving the fake nun in the library, she called out to me that she wanted the original recipe that contains their grandmother's stamp on the card."

"It is too early to tell whether or not they are the same

killer. But I suppose you are telling me this because she would have to have seen the card in order to describe it in such detail. You're thinking that she is the one who stole it from Marjorie's house and is putting a front on?"

"She could easily switch her story up at her job, and claim the money for herself, to go along with the promotion she was offered."

Officer Noel stopped writing, and gave her a curious look, clearly intrigued in this line of thinking. "Alright. I'll indulge you for a minute. Suppose she was the one who stole the card last night. How did she get in? That window was a little small for her to climb through, and there were no other apparent signs of a break in."

"She could have borrowed…" Cybil admitted her defeat. The imposter nun did say that she visited an aunt here during the summers of her childhood. She could have seen the stamp at any point of her life, and if her memory was as good as she claimed it was, then a description like that would have been easy to recall. "I'm not sure."

"Did she happen to mention her real name to you by chance? Or did you see any form of ID?"

"No. She had already answered all the questions I asked, so it's not like I was going to push for that information." Cybil brought herself to sit back down in an effort to stop slightly swaying from frazzled nerves. "But she did tell me that Mr. Jeffrey is her cousin, and she had family she visited in the area when she was younger."

"We'll check with Jeffrey and see if he can provide us with his cousin's real name." Officer Noel nodded to a fellow cop remaining steadfast by the door. "By the way, does this phone number ring a bell with either of you?" He rattled off the ten digits written in his notes. Based on the area code, Cybil thought that it sounded like the beginning of Yasmin's number, but the rest didn't sound familiar.

"Nope, not to me." Yas was quick to respond and Cybil echoed the same.

"Okay. That's all I have for now, but you two shouldn't make any plans on leaving town for the holidays."

"We aren't suspects, are we?" Yas's body tensed up while she fidgeted with her fingers.

"I wouldn't go so far as to say that. We just need to know where you are for any additional questions we may have. You have my phone number, so you can call or text me if you remember anything else." Officer Noel flipped his notepad closed and proceeded back to the door, stopping to look over at the console table again as he exited the house. Once the latch was shut, an eerie silence fell upon the living room. It remained undisturbed for a few short seconds until Gabriel's barking resounded from the crate Yasmin had put him in.

"I'm coming, puppy." Yas hurried over in an eagerness to not only move about, but to attend to the crying dog as a distraction for her mind. "It's alright." She opened the crate and allowed him to roam at free will, barely catching him in time before he relieved himself on the floor. Her fingers quickly snapped on the leash and they braved the chilly wind by way of the back door, leaving Cybil to stare after them in contemplation.

She turned her head to the snow falling outside of the window across from the couch. Her phone's weather app had dinged to alert her of the potential for up to an inch overnight, but that wasn't what caught her attention. *Why was Officer Noel so fascinated by the console table?* It was the second time he looked down at the collection of things gathered near the trinket dish, and she still had the feeling it had something to do with the torn off sticky note.

Cybil used the time alone to inspect the remaining sticky pad, and found the torn bit removed. A clean note was now left, causing her to wonder what had been previously on it. Her first instinct was to grab a pencil and rub the lead over to see if the imprint showed anything, however, the pad also felt much thinner than before. *I bet Yasmin removed a number of them to erase any trace of the message. But why though? What was so important?*

As she looked up from the narrow table, Yasmin re-entered from the back with Gabriel rushing inside. His legs strained against the leash, desperately wanting to reach the electric fireplace underneath the television. Her roommate bent over to free the little guy, allowing him to make his way over and curl up in the warmth of the pulsating orange glow. "It certainly has gotten colder out."

"Yasmin, what did you write down on this sticky note?" Cybil held up the item in question for her to see.

"Nothing that warrants mentioning."

"YAS! What is the big secret?! What did you jot down?"

"I wrote a meaningless piece of information that I ended up giving to someone else. Alright?" Yasmin stormed off toward her bedroom, announcing that she was going to turn in, and slammed the door behind her.

Gabriel looked over at Cybil with a glare in his beady eyes as he replaced his head onto the soft side of his bed, soaking up the heat. For whatever undisclosed reason, that dog really did seem to hate her. But the fact that he didn't even bark after the police walked into the house, changed her previous theory of the intruder having to be someone he trusted. If Gabriel was not into barking unless it was something he highly disliked, then the thief could have been anyone breaking into Marjorie's house. *Correction, the person must have entered with a key.* And that included

Yasmin's boss, who weirdly ignored his phone in the minutes after discovering the open window.

"What?" She directly addressed the canine still giving her a detestable look. "It's not my fault that she chose to go to bed and leave you out of your crate for the night." Cybil's eyes narrowed in on the dog. "You better not destroy this house by the time I wake up in the morning."

CHAPTER 36

Cybil gazed upon the train village display at work. Tiny mailmen were delivering last minute packages to the kids anxiously awaiting on the porches of their homes. Carolers sang out in silent song next to the little white church with classic stained glass windows as snow freshly fell onto the green evergreens of the tree farm. Down Main Street, an old soda pop shop was decked out in holiday attire for all the excited patrons inside, while sleigh rides were being held on the fake cobblestone roads with blankets on their laps and hot cocoa in their hands. Santa's workshop glowed with nostalgic charm at the top of the hill where a reindeer stable sat as miniature elves went about their chores feeding the animals.

Seeing the stables brought back the all-too-real scenario for her co-worker, John. He forced himself back to work that morning after looking tirelessly for Rudolph the previous day. His eyes were barely awake as he walked about the store, trying to bring product forward on the shelves and tidy up after messy kids. Cybil wished there was more she could do to help locate the missing reindeer. Not just to lift his spirits, but also because he told her what Rudolph's absence would mean to the Children Hospital's Christmas Party on the 24th. She had no idea that his family had been going there dressed as Santa for the past twenty years, each time with a reindeer who would do sleigh rides for the kids.

"Do you have any more items to put away?" John sleepily asked. If it wasn't for the fact that he used all of his sick time to extend his summer vacations, Cybil knew that he would be out in the woods in search of his beloved animal. But instead, he was restocking discarded product and fluffing flowered garland in the seasonal aisles while worry plagued his mind.

"No. Hey, John, why don't you go and take a short nap in the employee room? I won't tell Matt, who still has twenty minutes to go on his lunch."

"That's very thoughtful, Cybil. But if I sit down to catch up on a little bit of sleep, I'm afraid that you wouldn't be able to wake me again."

"Then at least tell me that you are not driving yourself home after work."

"I have my cousin coming to pick me up."

"Good. Because you look like a sickened tree. One good gust of wind and you're on the ground."

"My daughter told me to back down a little on the worrying and fretting, but I can't help it. Rudolph is my best friend and…if I wouldn't have eaten so much turkey last night, and checked on him like I normally do, I would have noticed his absence sooner. I might have even caught them in the act." He silently scolded himself. "I know it makes me so tired when I have that much, but nothing like this has ever happened before."

"So you really think he was stolen?"

"What else could it be? I double-checked all my fencing and the barn. Nothing was out of place." John stared at the miniature reindeer standing next to an elf feeding him. "I hope that he's alright."

"I'm sure he's fine, John. You need to stop blaming yourself and just focus your efforts on finding him."

"Cybil?" Betsy called in the headset.

"Yeah?"

"There's a man here to see you. His name is Mr. Jeffrey."

A perplexed look spread across Cybil's face. There was no reason for Jeffrey to be asking for her since the joint project was over, and she had sent the images to him after their fast food encounter. "What does he want?"

"To speak to you." Betsy's voice was partially overpowered by the forceful shouting in the background.

"Alright, I'm coming." Cybil cautiously approached the framing department from a hidden route, uncertain as to what she was stepping into. Right before she turned out from an aisle with her cart of returns, Cybil pressed on the headset and whispered into the mic. "Is everything okay, Betsy?" The raised voice was now gone, being replaced with an eerie silence that felt more foreboding than promising.

"For now."

Cybil gulped, drew up her courage, and then peaked around the bend. Jeffrey was leaning heavily against the counter as his fingers tapped impatiently on his arms, crossed in front of his chest. She rolled the clicking wheels of the cart forward and managed to put a smile on her face. "Mr. Jeffrey, what can I do for you?"

"What did she tell you?" He was not beating around the bush.

"Who?"

"Don't give me that. You know full well who I'm talking about." Jeffrey was visibly trying to control his frustration. "I saw the news last night. You went there after I told you to go, and then she ends up dead." He took a step closer to her, causing Cybil to move backwards. "What did she say to you?!"

"Mr. Jeffrey, I have no idea what you may or may not have heard, but your cousin was very much alive when I left her yesterday." She flashed a glance over at Betsy, whose hand was already on the phone and preparing to dial 9-1-1.

"She told you about our deal, didn't she? A deal that is flat lined because of you!" His nostrils flared out as he spouted off in her face. "I shouldn't have said anything to either of you. Just when things were finally looking up for me, everything has slipped through my fingers again!"

"Wait, who else did you tell?"

Jeffrey slapped the counter out of anger. "Where is it? Huh? The recipe for the cookies, where is it?!"

"I don't have it." Cybil caught sight of some nearby customers starting to gawk in their direction.

"Yeah, right! No way did Suzie…" The man felt his phone vibrating in his pants pocket and glanced down to see that the call was from his store manager. "Thanks to you, I'm being questioned by the police now. With her gone, my only shot at getting out of the plant business is that recipe card. If you find it, you call me immediately."

"And why exactly would I do that?"

"So I don't hand you over to the police as the prime suspect in her death." Mr. Jeffrey went to leave, his feet storming against the tiled floor.

"You were right." Cybil stated, catching his curiosity enough for him to turn back around.

"How is that?"

"Your cousin agreed with you that the cookies Marjorie made were not the ones you remembered eating growing up."

"I knew it!" A glimmer of confidence showed in the midst of his anger-filled eyes, staring into the far-off space behind the framing counter. "There was no almond flavor. Marjorie lied! Seems like her old school nickname was a sham after all." Jeffrey abruptly turned his attention back onto Cybil. "Contact me only if it's stamped in the corner with her grandmother's mark. Okay?"

"So, you've actually seen the card before?"

The garden center owner chuckled. "Are you kidding? That family guarded it as though it were gold. I only heard that the stamp was on the corner from a reliable source." Jeffrey clapped his hands together. "We're through here." He casually walked back to the front of the store and exited like nothing was wrong.

"Cybil, what have you gotten yourself into?" Betsy worriedly asked her co-worker, and friend. She placed the phone back in the landline holder, thankful that she didn't have to call the police.

"Apparently, stuck in a glass bowl, as much as my surprise goldfish is."

"Come again?" Betsy listened attentively to Cybil's story of the mysterious gift being found on her porch and the shadowy figure being seen from across the street. "Oh my gosh! Girl, you really need to report this to the authorities."

"I think they have enough on their plate at the moment without my gift-giving phantom. Besides, this person hasn't acted in a violent way towards me. Call me crazy, Betsy, but I feel like whoever it is just wants to communicate. Perhaps they're too shy or scared to talk with me face to face?"

"Well, I'm tired of seeing him out there." She pointed to the back door leading to the dumpster and the trailers filled with Christmas trees.

"You've seen him too?"

"Periodically, and only at night. I didn't want to raise the alarm with you, for the reason being that he scatters off when he sees me. One night, I managed to catch a glimpse of the side of his face, but not much more." Betsy looked Cybil straight in the eye. "I think he runs off because I'm not you."

"Then I doubt he's a homeless man; which was one of the possibilities running through my head. But after the fish delivery and his frequent visits…" Cybil's train of thought was cut short by the cashier in the headset, asking for a tree on behalf of a customer at the front.

"You stay here while I tend to the tree. No use sending you out there in case the man comes back." Betsy grabbed the keys dangling on a lanyard around her neck and dodged into the employee room to grab her coat. "Matt gave me a copy of the key so we wouldn't have to keep running up to the office."

"Are you sure you want to go? You said he only visits at night, and it's not one o'clock yet. I'm quite capable of doing this myself."

"That's true. But after Jeffrey came bursting in with his guns a'blazing after you, do you really want to take that chance? I shop at his garden center for my plants, and never would have pegged him as a man with such a temper. He's usually so mild-mannered." Betsy pulled her zipper up and walked over to the door. "It's bad enough having two murders to solve in this town within forty-eight hours of one another, but to hear that Jeffrey's cousin now died is too upsetting to wrap my head around."

Cybil made a mental note to inform her co-worker that the second murder and Jeffrey's cousin were one in the same, once they closed up the store for the night. *Since the deceased's family, or part of it anyway, was in the know, I wouldn't be doing any harm in letting Betsy in on the secret. She doesn't do much on social media either, so there really isn't a risk of sensitive information being leaked.* While she had planned on waiting for her co-worker to return, a simple request for help from the front end caused her to alter her timing a bit when the customer's name came through over the headset; Tara Newston.

CHAPTER 37

It was customary for one employee to watch the other walk out to the shipping container and back, ensuring that they were safe in the same area where the tractor trailers made their delivers. However, that scenario didn't involve Tara Newston, and her demanding ways, making a raucous at the registers.

Cybil took a deep breath as she came upon the line of customers beginning to form behind the complaining young woman. According to her wristwatch, the store manager still had five minutes on his lunch break in the comfy seats of his truck, which meant that it was up to her to calm down the over-dramatic princess. *Why is the day moving so slowly?*

Tara was in an uproar by the cashier. Her hands were flying in the air to go with her commanding voice and furious tone she loved to lord over people. "Why isn't my tree here yet?! I paid for it and I want to see it right now!"

"I'm sorry, Miss. Our manager is getting the tree for you as we speak and…"

"Hi Tara," Cybil interjected. "What can I do for you?"

The young woman's eyes seethed at the sight of Yasmin's

friend daring to offer her assistance. "I doubt you can do anything for me. I'm waiting for a tree, a long-overdue tree at that, and now I want to see the manager on duty about the incompetence of this store."

A small, and yet mischievous, smile could be seen on the corners of Cybil's face. "I am the manager, Tara. What seems to be the problem?"

"You?" Tara scoffed in disbelief. "You are the store manager?"

"No. But I am the manager in charge while he's at lunch."

"Fine. Then I demand a partial refund of my order."

"On what grounds?"

"On the basis that you are purposefully taking a chunk of my day out by forcing me to wait for your slow workers." Tara glared at the cashier wanting to hide in a deep hole somewhere else. "I haven't heard you call once for the die cutting machine I purchased."

She could tell that her co-worker, a newbie at that, was doing all she could to hold back her frustration from spilling out at Ms. Newston. "I was about to."

"Which color?" Cybil tried to give the employee a bit of support in her words and expression.

"The color of royalty, of course." Tara answered, despite Cybil not even looking at her when she asked.

"Green with envy it is." Cybil half-muttered to herself.

"What was that?" Tara's left eyebrow rose upward in warning.

"Purple, I'm guessing?" Cybil pretended to be polite with her response. When it came to customers like this one, sometimes it was hard to bite the tongue and not feed them a dose of their own medicine.

"Duh. No wonder this place is going down the drain." Tara placed her hands on her hips and tapped her foot against the floor. "Well, I haven't got all day."

Betsy soon announced her return in the headset, and immediately made her way up to the front with the tree in question. At Cybil's request, she jumped onto another register to help get the customers through faster. The line's growth was not showing any signs of slowing down, as it appeared that everyone had decided to check out at the same time. Just as Matt walked through the entrance way, Cybil disappeared into the office to select the right machine for Tara.

"Is that Tara Newston out there?" He hurried through the office door and shut it before the spoiled woman noticed him.

"Unfortunately."

"That would explain the long line. Alright. She's going to want you to handle the machine for her, I would imagine. So you finish up with her and I will jump on register one."

"Sounds good to me." Cybil lied. In all reality, she was hoping that he was going to volunteer himself to help the drama queen instead of delegating it to her. "By the way, she said she wanted to speak to the store manager."

"I'm sure she does. But I'm also sure that whatever you do will be good enough for me." He punched into the time clock on the computer. "Is John still on the sales floor?"

"He was grabbing a few lanterns from the top shelves for a customer, last I saw." Cybil made a fast exit and grabbed a cart from the corral by the front doors. She used it to follow Tara out of the store with the die cutter, and allowed Ms. Newston to guide the Christmas tree herself. When they arrived at the young woman's vehicle, it was not at all what Cybil had pictured in her mind for the spoiled woman.

Tara hit a button on her key fob, and the back door of her blue minivan popped open. As it rose, Cybil caught sight of a saying adhered to the window, saying "Don't test thee." Time 24:7.

"Interesting quote you have." Cybil gently placed the cutting machine next to a box of clear glass bottles. There was a faint scent of alcohol emitting from them, but that was common practice when cleaning and sterilizing for projects.

"Thanks. I got it from an artist listed on one of those handmade marketplace sites. When I realized that it was done on a die cutter, I decided I had to have one myself. That way, I can make different colors with the same saying and deck out my stuff in it." She smiled with a proud beam on her face. "I even have an order for one just like it."

"That's good." Cybil shoved the tree in next, and kept an eye alert for any possible surfaces she didn't want to end up scratching. What should have been an easy task was made much more difficult by the presence of an anti-slip mat, which did its job extremely well. Tara just kept right on chatting right along, and ignored the struggling employee attempting to move the tree toward the folded-down middle seats.

"Yep. Mrs. Norman asked for one when she noticed it at the Christmas dinner. That's what my brother tells me at least, but I haven't been able to get in touch with her as of yet."

"I didn't see your brother there that night."

"Well, he didn't actually go into the church. He just drove my minivan back there to rescue my headphones from the snow. I dropped them on the way out and hadn't noticed until after we arrived home. When I mentioned they were missing, he practically jumped at the opportunity to locate them." Tara sighed. "And to think, that if his van wouldn't have been at the garage, he wouldn't have asked to use my vehicle and I wouldn't have gotten my first sale."

"What about his truck?"

"Oh, a friend of his had to borrow it. Came over to pick it up while we were eating." Tara let out a heavy sigh. "Are you finished yet?"

"Almost." Cybil shut the door for her. "I suppose you will be applying for Marjorie's position when it's posted at the church?"

"Depends on whether they hire Jeffrey to be the new choir director or not, like its rumored to be. Both he and Mrs. Norman applied at the same time your little friend did last year. Miraculously, they all withdrew their applications not long after. One can merely speculate as to why."

"Didn't you also apply?"

Tara checked the time on her phone and gave a gasp. "I am going to be so late for my pedicure."

"Well, you are all good to go." Cybil announced, thankful to be done, and even more grateful for the tip Tara unwittingly gave her.

"Oh, I know I'm good. But you can go now." Tara waved her off and rushed into the driver's seat. "I'm so late!"

Cybil ran into the store, happy for the warmth to ward off any frostbite from the cold chill lingering outside. She pushed the cart back where it belonged and wished John well on finding Rudolph as he passed by her on his way out. *Lucky for him he only had a partial shift to do today.*

Three hours later, Cybil was finally able to take her last fifteen minute break and she used the time to message Yasmin for Rodger Freedmon's phone number. It took her a few tries at convincing her roommate that nothing needed worked on at their place, and it was just for asking him a few questions after Tara's earlier visit to the store. After her friend texted her the number, Cybil tapped on it and made the call.

"Hello, Rodger's Handy Work at your service."

"Hi Rodger, it's Cybil Lawson. Do you have a few minutes to talk?"

"Yeah, Cybil. What's up? Is the pipe holding alright?"

"Doing just great, thanks. Um, your sister was in at the craft store today and she mentioned something to me about getting an order for the saying on the back of her minivan."

"Don't tell me you want one. I mean, if you want, I can pass the message along, but I didn't think it was your style."

"No, no. It isn't." Cybil's eyes scanned the room as if there was another person listening in on her conversation, despite the fact that she was alone in the employee room. "My question is…well, it was my understanding that you weren't going to attend the dinner?"

"I didn't."

"Oh, I'm sorry. Tara said you borrowed her minivan and I thought…"

"I went there to recover my sister's headphones. She lost them on the way home and I offered to go back. That's when Mrs. Norman commented on the sticker."

"Around what time was that?"

"I guess it would be around 9:00 pm. Why?"

"And Mrs. Norman was out in the parking lot, right? She didn't have her car stopped near the backdoor to the kitchen?"

"No. She was in her car, talking on the phone and almost in tears at one point in the conversation. That's when she noticed me walking through the white snow, hunched over, in search for the white headphones Tara dropped. Mrs.

Norman asked if I needed help and I told her what happened."

"Did you end up finding your sister's headphones?"

"Heck no! A needle would have been easier to spot. I just called it a night and bought her a new pair at the store. She didn't even notice the difference. Why all the questions?"

"I…" Cybil was stopped short as a male voice interrupted her from Rodger's side of the phone call. The slightly muffled words were a little hard to distinguish, but the message came through loud and clear.

"Are you Rodger Freedmon?"

"Yes."

"We have a few questions for you, Sir. Starting off with why a neighbor saw your van parked at 157 Arnold Road the night of December 14th."

"Ah…Cybil, I have to go…"

"Is that Cybil Lawson?" An inaudible shake of Rodger's head gave the officer his answer.

The next voice Cybil heard on the phone, was that of Officer Noel's. "Ms. Lawson, you are coming dangerously close to the definition of interfering with a police investigation."

"Asking my plumber about the pipe in my house is none of your business."

"You can stick to that story all you want, but from now on, I suggest you confine all questions about the case to me."

"Understood." Cybil hung up with an anti-climactic push of the red button on her phone's screen. It didn't sound the same, nor have the same impact, when it wasn't a rotary or princess phone. Nonetheless, her curiosity was spinning in double time after hearing what Officer Noel had just said. *His van was supposed to be at the garage that night.*

"Hey, Cybil, are you back from break yet?" Matt asked

in the headset. "We could use another pair of hands on the registers."

"I'm on my way!"

CHAPTER 38

As Cybil waved thanks to Betsy for dropping her off at Ralph's, the night sky didn't seem so glooming. Her conscience felt better with the knowledge that there was another person's testimony that could corroborate her's against what Mrs. Norman had told the police. Cybil hadn't done anything wrong, but it wasn't like Officer Noel had dealt with her before. Having a piece of evidence to back up her claim felt liberating, if the time came that she should need it. However, all that went away when she saw Yasmin's face the moment she walked through the doors to the bar.

Since college, the two women developed a friendship that suggested they had known each other since they were five-years-old. The true number of years was more akin to less than ten, though neither one really kept count. That meant when the slightest thing was bothering them, it was noticed faster than a squirrel stealing corn kernels. Cybil instantly knew Yas wasn't happy with one of the customers and signaled to her with a thumbs up where the man couldn't see. A simple nod was all she needed to put their plan into action.

Heading toward the bathrooms, near the entrance to

the kitchen, Cybil pulled her phone out and called the bar's counter. She hid her hand between the wall and her butt as she watched Yas pick up the phone and start talking to fake customer looking to schedule a work party. Eventually tired of waiting for her to finish the pretend conversation, the annoying customer went to find himself a seat at a table and left the area mumbling under his breath. Cybil then quickly slid into the newly emptied stool before anyone else could. "You're welcome, my lady."

"Thanks for the rescue. He kept going on and on about his apple tree farm and how he swears a pair of rabbits have it out for him."

"Sounds serious. We better alert the officials to protect him."

"I don't think the cops would want to be within twenty miles of this place tonight."

"How come?"

"Most of the gossip is about how the whole world is going to pot, in reference to the murdered nun. And if I were you, I wouldn't go talking about it with so many people around. They are still saying that she is with the holy order." Yasmin raised a word of caution. "I also happen to have a piece of information for you that hasn't made it to the news yet, if you're interested."

"Do tell."

Both Yas and Cybil leaned in to whisper their coded messages to one another, while Yas wiped the same area of the counter in countless circles. It was their own blend that was known to no one else, and was a byproduct of watching a secret agents miniseries on the television years prior. "We received our weekly delivery of food, and the driver that hauls in our meats, recognized her from the television. He said that she used to work for the company you mentioned, but that she was fired from there six months ago. And he knows her from delivering cheese to a bakery three hours away from here."

"Plot twist!" Cybil's eyes widened, intrigued by the new details. "So she could have been trying to steal the recipe to use it at the bakery?"

"I looked it up, and according to the state's business filings, she is listed as the owner of the bakery. But if she was paying her bills like she was for our delivery man, then she was in the red, big time."

"Maybe…she wanted the recipe to sell it for herself? That certainly does put a different angle on her motives, and it coincides with the fact that she was on a tight schedule. If her books were that bad." Cybil ordered a small "Heard It Through the Grapevine" shake, and filled her friend in on hot-tempered Jeffrey's visit to the store.

"Cybil, you have to be more careful."

"What do you want me to do? I didn't visit the woman with the expectation that she was going to die shortly afterwards. Nor did I think that her cousin was going to come into my work like a fire-breathing dragon on steroids."

"Ooh, do my ears deceive me? Or are you two little nosy busybodies whispering?" Ralph whipped around the corner. "Must mean that you have juicy gossip going on. Elsewise, you wouldn't be speaking your alien language to one another."

"In point of fact, Ralph, you are the man I wanted to see." Cybil winked at Yas, letting her know that they would continue their talk at a later time. "How did Marjorie get her nickname in school?"

"You mean 'One-Face?'"

"Isn't that rude?" Yas filled a tall glass of purple soda and slid it down to a man five seats away.

"It was actually a compliment, in some people's opinions. See, she was so truthful and didn't say any lies, unlike her sisters, that the boys called her 'One-Face' instead of 'Two-Faced.' It kind of stuck from an early age in elementary school. Why? Did they print it in her obituary or something? I haven't seen it if they did."

"Actually, there hasn't been any discussion of a service, final arrangements, or anything like that yet." Pastor Lawrence joined them from the outside, after shuffling the snow from his boots and hanging his jacket up on the rack. "Apparently they can't even find a will and the lawyer is away on vacation to visit with family."

"Pastor Lawrence, should you really be discussing this with us?" Yasmin asked.

"Perhaps not. However, when I went by to see if they needed any help in getting the process started, Melody informed me that they would be making the arrangements when they are good and ready. It is up to her decision, being the eldest, and I am to keep my nose out of it until they have decided on what to do. How did she put it? 'If I wish to pay my respects, I can do so after the will has been read.'" He clasped his hands together and rubbed them to bring feeling back into his fingers.

"That family is strange, I'll say that." Cybil asked for a "Thristy Cowboy" after she finished the shake. The drink was just a root beer with a splash of vanilla and spice, but it always complimented a pulled pork sandwich rather nicely.

"Marjorie told me that they had a tough upbringing, and after Melody's fall, they never were the same again." Pastor Lawrence smiled at them. "Sometimes, things happen to help us appreciate what we have."

"Amen." Ralph handed him his usual Florida Classic, an orange soda mixed with lemon sorbet and a twist of lime added on the top rim of the glass.

Cybil sipped down on her drink, trying to summon enough courage to ask the bar owner her next question. She didn't like asking him where he was when they discovered Raven in her great-aunt's house, but it gnawed in the back of her mind that he didn't answer his phone. "Hey, Ralph, were you here Sunday night after I left?"

"Yeah. Where else would I be?"

"Are you having phone issues?"

"Not that I know of."

"Then why couldn't Yas get ahold of you that night?"

"When?"

"Around ten o'clock. I believe."

"Not sure. You must have gotten me when I was in the bathroom or cleaning the stove top." His eyes shifted to a customer at the end of the long counter and he excused himself in order to check on their drink.

Cybil decided that it was best to leave it be and asked Yasmin if she was ready to go. Her friend found her coat and scarf amongst the employee racks, and joined her in the parking lot where the air was as still as a statue. "He is avoiding telling me the truth."

"I realize that, Sherlock. But what else can we do? This whole nightmare just won't end." Yas got the car running and started driving back to the house. "I'm getting really nervous about my parents coming in on the twenty-third. Maybe I should tell them to postpone their visit until next year?"

"That's six days away. You do that, and they are guaranteed to come, if only to check up on you. No, that will make them more nervous and worried than anything else."

"Speaking of parents, how come you were alright with borrowing cash from your parents to use on a fish tank, but not on having your car fixed? I mean, you are my best friend and all, however, this is getting a little old real fast."

"Well…" Cybil's left eye squinted. "Let's just say that they don't know the full extent of the damage done to my car. And I don't want them to know either."

Yasmin huffed into the air, casting her friend a look of disapproval.

"You don't tell your parents everything either. I mean, don't they still think you work at the card shop in town because you're afraid of them finding out that you work at a bar? Regardless whether it is dry or not."

"After my brother, a lot of things changed for my family. So it's best to let it alone and to continue the charade, for my mother's sake." Yas glanced over in Cybil's direction. "By the way, I called the art gallery today to speak with Raven about Gabriel. She was there, and we talked, but she can't take him in on the account of her mother."

"That's just great. What are we going to do with him? It's not right having to keep him cooped up in a crate while we're gone, since we aren't home much as it is. At least with staggered shifts, there is someone home within five hours. And, that also leaves us having to tell Sylvia about our new roommate."

"Not anymore." She saw Cybil's eyes widen out of curiosity within the glow of the street lamps. "Sylvia stopped by to handle the bill from Rodger and apologized for her tardiness. Well, you can guess what happened next with Gabriel barking for attention. I explained the situation, and she understands. In fact, she actually got along with Gabriel right from the start."

"WHAT?" Cybil's jaw dropped to the floor.

"Yep. Sylvia has also agreed to watch him for us."

"I don't believe it!"

"Well, believe it. Gabriel is no longer at our place and you do not have to worry about him trying to kill you in your sleep." Yas's face broke into a large smile on that last part.

"Hey! It was a legitimate concern for me. You saw the way his eyes would stare into my very soul, watching me like a vulture does prey."

"You're right. He did seem to highly dislike you for some reason. But there's more. When I asked Raven about trying to take Gabriel in, she said that her mom only allows her to keep goldfish."

Cybil about jolted out of her seat. "That's who Norris was for!"

"And I think you might want to take a look at a man named Martin Stonewell, as a possible identity for your shadowy figure."

"Stonewell? Don't tell me that Marjorie, Melody and Marta have a brother?"

"Don't ask me how I know, because it's a long story."

"Why do you suspect him?"

"Call it a hunch. The point is, I think it's time you told the police about him."

"Can it wait until morning? I'm bushed from today's shift and there is a slice of apple pie calling my name in the fridge."

"Alright. Tomorrow morning, then. But you *need* to report it."

Cybil didn't care for the tones of caution tainting her friend's words. "Yas, what are you not telling me?"

"All I'm saying is that you shouldn't dawdle with speaking up on this."

CHAPTER 39

The clock struck one in the afternoon just as knocking could be heard at the front door. "Coming!" Cybil hurriedly shoved a bunch of printed articles and research notes under her laptop. She rushed over and peeked through the hole in the middle of the wood to find Officer Noel patiently waiting on the porch in a thick winter coat. Her hand turned the knob as she welcomed him inside. "I promise I haven't found any more dead bodies."

"A good afternoon to you too. While I like to hear the sound of that, the reason for my visit today is actually to ensure that *you* are safe."

Cybil hung her head. "Yasmin call you?"

"No, it wasn't her. The woman said she works with you at Mark's Crafts and Art Supplies."

"Betsy." Cybil scolded herself for not seeing that one coming. "She came to you about the shadowy figure who keeps appearing near the dumpster at night."

"According to her, he has even left you presents."

"Just one so far." She pointed to the fish tank on the kitchen counter. "It's so cold by the windows, we thought he might be the warmest there."

"Any possible idea who he could be? The shadowy figure, I mean. Not the goldfish."

"Martin Stonewell."

"The deceased's brother?"

"Yep. Yasmin suggested that it could be him after a conversation she had with Raven Hieghner. It all starts to fit into place when you consider the fact that he most likely thinks I'm her."

"Excuse me?"

"It's all because Marjorie hugged me. She *never* does that, apparently, and for an unknown reason, she gave me a hug that has shattered all minds in this area. But he was there that day; at the craft store when she brought in this canvas print to get framed. It would make sense that he followed her into the store, and then tried to get in touch with me from the outside." Cybil gestured toward the wintery scene hanging between the two bedroom doors.

"Do you have any proof that Martin was in the store to see this 'supposed hug?'"

"I don't, but the art store does. It's technically my day off. That being said, however, I already went over there and checked into the security cameras from that day. There was a man dressed all in black walking past the fine art aisle at the right time, and you have to go by that aisle to reach the framing department." Cybil handed him a sticky note with the time marked down, along with the date. "You can see it for yourself." She then redirected his attention back to the framed print on the wall. "I tried giving it to Raven when Betsy completed the order, but her mother intervened. And since Marjorie's house has been designated a crime scene due to the robbery, I didn't want to even *attempt* to drop it off there. Do you happen to have any news on finding Marjorie's will, perhaps? Because I would like to give it to whoever her beneficiary is."

"I'm sure it's going to make the gossip rounds eventually, so I might as well just say it. The lawyer who drew up her will was contacted by the family and he flew back immediately, given the unnatural circumstances surrounding his client's death. As I have been informed by a family member, the beneficiary for all her earthly belongings is the church."

"Nothing goes to her family members?!"

"Each of them have been given a few separately listed items. Apparently that was done to ensure that they could not contest the will in court."

Cybil was speechless. She never considered that Marjorie would do such a thing. The woman seemed to like doing things on the older-fashioned side, which wasn't a problem for Cybil. Some things were better conducted in the more traditional way. However, to leave most of her possessions to the church appeared quite callous on Marjorie's part. "Isn't that a bit odd?"

"Not when she worked, lived, and breathed her secretarial job there. It was probably seen as a thank you for allowing her to serve at the church for so many years. Or perhaps she liked the idea of giving it all in a charitable manner? I can't speak for her decision on the matter." Officer Noel observed the art print with a studious eye. "At least that will make it easier for you to give it to the new owner. Getting back to Martin Stonewell, why does he want to talk with you, or…eh…Raven?"

"I'm not sure on that, for the time being. When I have more of my research completed, I'll have a better idea."

"Research? What research?"

Cybil shyly moved her laptop and showed him the articles she had printed off underneath.

"You do realize that you are not the investigator?"

"I do know that. Just…allow me to look into the matter for another hour or two, and I might have an answer for ya."

"As long as it stays in paper form, and does not involve any questioning of people or following anyone in a vehicle." Officer Noel instructed, much to Cybil's delight.

"You got it."

CHAPTER 40

Cybil watched Silver D brush his fur up against the acrylic walls of his cat walk next to the window. Seeing all of the people bustling back and forth from their shopping exploits, was more of a bother to him than anything else. He enjoyed the slow pace of summer afternoons and the warmth of the sunlight that would invite him into a comforting nap. When the winter clouds rolled in to stay, he only came into the diner whenever his cat toys bored him.

A waitress sat down a plate of the day's special in front of Cybil's seat. "Silver D seems to like you."

"Only when he wants some attention." Cybil smiled and thanked the server before she stared down at her cell phone for the third time in the last five minutes. Officer Noel was supposed to meet up with her during his lunch hour, and the clock was telling her he was twenty minutes overdue. *He was even the one who picked this location.*

She almost gave up when a police car suddenly pulled into the parking lot. Cybil managed to get a few bites of her sandwich in, before Noel entered The Nickel of Time.

"Sorry I'm late. Was caught up in some traffic on the way back from the city." He glanced down at the food on her plate. "What's that?"

"BBQ. Coal region BBQ to be precise. It's like Sloppy Joe, for the sandwich. The bowl is filled with Amish macaroni salad, and the kettle-cooked chips are made from…"

"Can I get you something hun?" The waitress placed a menu in front of him, and tapped the button end of her pen against the notepad she held in the other hand.

"Ah, whatever she ordered will suffice."

"Coming right up."

"So, why were you in the city?" Cybil took a swallow of water from her cup.

"To retrieve evidence in the case from the lab. Dropped it off at the station on my way over."

"Which case?"

"You know I can't discuss either one with you."

"But you could give me a hint. Inadvertently, of course."

"Nice try. But I'm not falling for it. You are probably familiar with it being…"

"Off-limits." Cybil pulled a printed photo from a manila folder on her lap. "So let's discuss the subject of Martin Stonewell then."

"Alright. Why do you think that he is stalking you?"

"For starters, I want to confirm that the information I have from his arrest record is correct." She showed him what she managed to dig up from the digital archives on Illinois's online database, after sourcing out article details that he was arrested in Chicago.

"That's right. He was arrested for trying to sell stolen goods in Illinois."

"Raven is an artist. Could he be looking to get ahold of her in regards to stolen works of art? Her mother owns a gallery and her daughter works there on a daily basis. And I overheard Christine going off on Raven for a mistake with the international orders. She claimed that it wasn't her fault, but with regular traffic going overseas, that would be the perfect avenue to export stolen goods."

"Good theory, but if he saw you at the art and crafts store, then he would have obviously seen that you were not at the art gallery. His plans could have changed."

"Point taken. So…maybe he just wants to reconnect with his family? He was sent to prison for fifteen years. Isn't that an awfully long time for what he did?"

"That's because the papers don't have the full story." The waitress dropped a drink off at Officer Noel's place, with two lemon wedges on the lip of the cup. "He was offered a deal in exchange for providing the police with the whereabouts on his boss. The deal was never made because he refused to speak and since his boss was the accomplice on the job, Martin took the penalty for both of their crimes."

"I guess it's possible that the only reason for his elusiveness is that he wants to reconnect with the family." Cybil placed her folder off to the side, not feeling that it was necessary to show Noel all of the local articles she discovered, because he most likely had access to them at the station. Besides, she didn't want to admit that the extra time she used up, didn't prove to be very helpful. "That would be why he is so focused on talking with Raven."

"Because she would be the most open to chatting with him?" Officer Noel took a sip from his drink just as the plate with his food showed up. "If you're right, and Martin believes you to be Raven, then we better catch him before he does something we all regret. Your uncle contacted the local parole officer and discovered that Martin did apply to move back home for the reason of trying to keep away from his prior connections; which was part of his parole stipulation."

"I'm guessing that he isn't in violation of it, considering

you didn't say that."

"He's currently in good standings and checks in every week around the same time on Mondays."

"Is that where you plan on asking him about all of this?"

"That's the idea. But if you see Martin again between now and then, let me know. I don't care what time of day or night it is, you got it?"

"Are you actually concerned for me? So far, he hasn't displayed any aggressive behavior."

"Not specifically for you, but for my job. I just moved here and if the detective's niece got killed under my watch, I would see pink slips in my future." Officer Noel gestured to the meal with his fork. "And I am starting to get hooked on this Pennsylvanian Dugan food."

"That's Pennsylvania Dutch." Cybil corrected with a grin.

CHAPTER 41

Officer Noel swept the last of his Kaiser roll along the plate, ensuring that there was the least amount of food and sauce remaining for the dishwasher to clean up. Compared to Buffalo wings and New York Pizza, they were in separate food leagues. But there was an undeniably earthy feel to what made up PA's regional eats, according to Cybil. And it was a surprising change to see Plain Folk going down the older highways in their horse and buggies.

One of the things he never thought about, was the wide range of adornments the buggies would feature. So far, he saw chrome-fitted mud flaps, highly reflective orange tri-angles fastened square in the back, and even a pro-football team's flag draped like a cape. It certainly was a sight to behold, and he had already been warned not to take photos of them as a sign of respect to their way of life. Tractors, cows, and hay-bales coming through town was not unfa-miliar to Noel, but he had long considered that world to be in his review mirror. That is until he shot and killed his first man on the beat, and the homesick longing for the country life came roaring back.

He could still remember his old partner telling him to

stick it out and that everything would be alright in the end; "It's tough for everyone on that first kill. No one means for it to happen, and no one wishes for it either. But in a life or death situation, anything can go wrong." Noel was cleared to go back on full duty after an internal investigation had been conducted, and he planned on doing just that. However, the hauntings didn't cease as the days turned into weeks, resulting in him turning in his badge. *Funny how life takes us on different paths then what we originally set out to do.*

From the moment this job posting came across his laptop's screen, it seemed to be a sign that his path in law enforcement wasn't over just yet. There remained a tingling thought, roaming around in the back reaches of his mind, that wouldn't quit nagging at him to stop hiding from himself. Working in a home improvement store certainly had its moments, but it couldn't fulfill what the badge meant to him and what being a cop stood for. While every job had a few bad apples, with loud voices that tried tainting it for the rest of them, Noel wasn't about to let them keep him from fulfilling a promise to his sister.

"Would you like some more water, hun?" The waitress repeated a second time. She watched him rise from the stupor of staring into the ice-filled glass, and smiled a toothy grin at him. "You alright?"

"Yeah. The food just left me speechless." Officer Noel replied and stretched his arms to wake himself up. His lunch would soon be over and he was to report to Detective Lawson on how the man's hunches had been correct. Knowing very little, in terms of the family feud between the detective and his niece, Noel didn't wish to cross a line by asking for any of the specifics. Cybil appeared to be an intelligent human being who didn't want to harm anyone, adding to his conflictions over the real reason he had agreed to the meeting in the first place. After his last, and only job, doing undercover work, he swore he wouldn't do it again due to the bitterness of betrayal it left in his mouth. And while it wasn't exactly like he was posing as a different person, it didn't seem right to secretly use her information against herself.

He left a few dollars tip on the table, got up from the chair to pay his bill, and was ready to leave the restaurant, when his phone went off. Officer Noel looked down to see Cybil's number flashing across the screen and immediately picked it up since she hadn't been gone more than fifteen minutes. Assuming that it was to double-check that none of her belongings were there, he was quite surprised to hear a man's voice telling her to remain calm and to listen to what he had to say.

Noel rushed out to his car which was parked in front of the door, and radioed for backup. The closest car was stationed thirty minutes on the other side of town, as Detective Lawson was still on the case of the mayor's missing vehicle. While the face value of the sports car was a considerable amount, the real prize had been stowed away in the glove compartment. As noted in the case file, his wife had requested that her half-a-million dollar necklace be placed inside the house, but he had forgotten after dropping her off at the airport. He promised the police department more funding if they found it before she came back home, just in time for Christmas. And the chief was more than willing to oblige since he didn't care for Marjorie in the first place, regardless of Detective Lawson's objections.

As he waited for a response, the same male voice could be heard echoing down the bricked walls of an alley to the left of the restaurant. Officer Noel proceeded with caution toward the narrow lane, lowering the volume on his phone as he approached the corner.

"I'm running out of time. You hear? They're going to fire me and send me back to jail."

"If you're innocent, they are not going to take you away. You can still reconcile with your family." Cybil's voice rang out strong with a slight waver in the last few syllables. "I will even go with you as support, so you can tell the police the truth."

"The minute they see my past record, they're not going to believe me."

"Yes, they will. The ones I know there are honest and uphold the law. Just drop the knife and we can go there together."

Well, the honest part feels a little farce at the moment, Noel thought.

"There is no chance at getting Melody and Marta to talk to me ever again. Not without Marjorie. She always stood up for me, with our parents and anyone else who doubted me. It used to be just the two of us against the world, and she loved me so much so, that she broke one of her most principled rules in order to save me. Me, of all people."

Martin Stonewell, Officer Noel mumbled in his mind. *Cybil had been right.*

"We do what we have to for family. That's just human nature. And Great Aunt Marjorie wouldn't have wished our first encounter to be like this, Uncle Martin." Cybil lied.

"She said you understood what it's like to be on the outside looking in. My sister, I trusted her, and she trusted you too, Raven."

Officer Noel turned the volume off on his hand radio to ensure silence while inching his way into the alley. His hand moved to his hip where his gun was resting in the holster. As he drew his weapon, angling it toward the ground, he sidestepped two cups lying on the somewhat-visible pavement and walked over a Styrofoam container near scattered fries. All in all, the miniature street was a lot cleaner than one would have anticipated. Noel only hoped that the crunching of the snow wouldn't give himself away. From where he could see, Martin appeared to be holding a knife blade in Cybil's direction, though he didn't look to be making a lunge or a threatening advance toward her.

"Uncle Martin, let's go to the police and get ahead of this. What do you say?" Cybil continued with the façade that she hoped would keep her alive for a little longer. Since her back was to the alley, there was no telling if anyone was within range of seeing what was going down. Inside her mind, an inner voice was desperately praying for someone to rescue her. Martin Stonewell was no fool and managed to keep his distance too far away for the young woman to try either a sneak attack or to run back the way she came. "I believe you. Isn't that enough?"

"Not for the state." He pressed his thumb into the handle of the blade even harder, clearly having an inner battle over what he was doing. Martin couldn't see an option to get out of the mess he felt victim too, and it was showing on his face.

"Thank you for the fish you gave me."

A tiny smidge of a smile broke his otherwise serious face. "Norris. I named him after one of your favorite people. Marjorie told me about him."

"And the fish food was a nice touch. Uncle Martin, do you want to see Norris? We can go there in my car and see him back at the house. I even bought him some more rocks for the tank."

Officer Noel reached the edge of the building across the alley from Nickel of Time. He slowly peered at the scene unfolding in the middle of a small lot filled with parked cars and tried to figure out a path to get a better angle. There was still no sign of any other cops coming in to assist, making the decision even harder for him and the flashbacks that surfaced. *This town was supposed to have less crime when I moved here.*

From what he could see, Martin Stonewell appeared to have a good amount of separation between himself and who he believed to be his niece. With only a knife visible in the threatening man's hands, it was unclear if he had any other weapons on his person, but there was no telling how much longer Martin was going to stand there before someone else entered the lot and caught him off guard. Officer Noel counted to three in his head, ready to swivel out and point his gun at the target, aiming to wound in the arm or hand for the first shot. Just as he came out, however, a loud thud to the pavement reverberated off the walls and he stood staring at a beefy-looking kid holding Martin down on the ground.

The knife had been knocked away during the surprise attack from behind, giving Cybil the opportunity to snatch it up and keep Martin from being able to use it. She sighed with relief at the teenager who looked up and asked if she was alright. Officer Noel replaced his service weapon and walked up with his handcuffs to arrest the ex-con. "That was a pretty good tackle. You play football, by chance?"

"Wrestling." The teen grinned.

After Cybil found out the kid's name was Herald, she personally thanked him. "Where did you come from? I didn't even hear you make a sound."

"I was waiting in the car for my little sister to get done at ballet practice, and listened to the request for backup on the police frequency." Herald shyly glanced over at Officer Noel as he held the Stonewell brother as still as he could.

"Please don't take my ham radio license away."

"Don't worry about it. Now, if you use it to chat with us without an emergency reason, then we'll be around."

Sirens blazed into the air as two cars came rushing up from the main street, signaling that backup finally arrived. Cybil shook her head in disbelief. "About time they showed up."

"Dispatch said they were at some place called Mitsy's Farm?"

"Well, that is a good jag from here. But I'm just glad that Herald was listening in."

Noel handed Martin off to a fellow officer to be taken to the station, and informed Cybil that she was going to need to give them her statement. Herald talked with Noel while waiting for his sister, and it wasn't until one of the other officers completed their questioning of Cybil, did she ask him how he knew to come down the alleyway.

"You called me; which was a smart move on your part. I could hear Martin's voice in the background talking to you."

"I didn't call you. My phone was in my bag." She reached into the mini backpack slung on her shoulder and grabbed ahold of her phone. Cybil read over her past calls to find that his number was on the top of the list. "I guess it butt-dialed, in a way." Glancing up at the cloudy sky above, she whispered a special thanks to the Man Upstairs and politely asked Officer Noel if she could go home now.

CHAPTER 42

The following morning started off on a different note entirely. Waking up to the annoying sound of her phone's alarm, brought an unusual smile to Cybil's face. As the sun shone brightly in the very blue sky, it was already promising to be a great day filled with some normality for a change. Ten o'clock spread across the phone's screen in bold numbers, letting her know that she had to be up and ready in thirty minutes before heading off to work.

She reached up toward the ceiling to stretch out her arms and instantly recoiled to the warmth under her cozy bed spread. Curling up like a cat in a sun patch by a warming window, Cybil felt lazy and was thoroughly enjoying the present moment until her phone began ringing incessantly. The caller ID stated it was from her mother, though she didn't need a smartphone to tell her that. "Good Morning, Mom."

"Cybil, is both the doorbell and your hearing broken? I have been ringing and knocking on this dang door for ten minutes in this blasted cold." Cynthia Lawson scolded at her daughter.

"The doorbell doesn't always work right when the temperature gets below freezing, and I was sound asleep until just now. But I'll be right there." Cybil hung up the call and wondered why Yasmin hadn't come in to wake her up. Her roommate was the lighter sleeper between the two of them, meaning that she had unwillingly volunteered to manage the door. "Yasmin?" She called into the living room. Not a peep came from her friend's bedroom, so Cybil gently knocked on the door and announced her intrusion. To her surprise, Yasmin's bed wasn't slept in.

More pounding ensued on the front door, and she hurriedly answered it to find her mother shivering in a large blue parka, aching to reach warmer surroundings. "I have been trying to get ahold of you. Is Yas here?"

"No. I just checked and her bed wasn't slept in. That isn't like her."

"The police are looking for her, Cybil."

"What happened?"

"Last night, when I explained to your father about the episode with Martin Stonewell, that you told me about on the phone, he tuned the old radio to the police frequency. Remember how he used to listen in his study, checking up on his brother from time to time? Well, he secretly still does. Anyways, he overheard a few of the officers going over to Ralph's to pick up a suspect. They described Yasmin and said there was an arrest warrant out for her."

"Mom, I thought Dad was supposed to get rid of that scanner after the police chief warned him about hacking into their channel?" Cybil gave her mom a concerned look as she thought back to the accident that garnered their attention in the first place.

It was a Sunday afternoon and her father had been listening to the radio more than usual that weekend. He was tired from doing so much overtime at work, that he fell asleep at the desk with his hand pressing down on the talk button. The office couldn't understand why they could hear snoring in their encrypted frequency and immediately investigated into the situation. Fortunately for David, it was his brother's day off and the Chief agreed to keep quiet about the issue if her father promised to get rid of the equipment.

"He promised that it would never happen again and he did get rid of the microphone." Cynthia defended. "Besides, if he had thrown the radio away, then we wouldn't have been able to warn Yasmin in advance."

"You warned her at Ralph's?"

"Yep. Ralph told us that she ran out the back door and didn't reappear all night long. I was only hoping that she had come straight back home. But when I did a drive by, I noticed her car was missing."

"What time was that?"

"Around one a.m."

"I can't believe you did that. Now she is going to look even more guilty by running away. And why are they going after her? This whole thing is absolutely absurd."

"But that's what I told her on the phone. We were just giving her a heads-up, and told her *not* to run. That there was no need to worry, because we know she didn't do anything wrong, and we could help her get a lawyer. It wasn't until they reported her absence from the bar that I telephoned Ralph, and he told us what happened."

"Alright. Let me go get ready and then we'll head on over to Sylvia's. I think I know where she might be."

"I already checked with her and Yas isn't there."

"That's what she thinks. I'll explain in the car."

Cybil walked passed the kitchen counter on her way to the bathroom for a quick shower, when something from across the road caught her attention through the one window. She took a step backward and eyed the semi-hidden vehicle behind the row of trees near the power station's drive. It was parked almost precisely where they last spotted Martin Stonewell on the day he delivered Norris. "Were you being followed when you came here?"

"No. I saw the police car on the way over; probably on a stake out for Yasmin."

"That's comforting." Cybil finished the fastest shower she ever had, and got dressed in nearly fifteen minutes flat. She ran the brush through her wet hair five times, snapped on her wristwatch, and slid two bangles on the other wrist. They were like comfort blankets she liked to have close to her when trouble was on the horizon, and it was certainly looking that way now. "Are you ready to go?"

"Yep. We're going to have to take the long way if you want to lose your 'friends' over there." Cynthia motioned to the waiting cops with a tilt of her head.

"Kinda figured that." Cybil zipped up her coat and dashed off behind her mom to the car waiting in the driveway. The sedan roared to life as Cynthia turned the key, backing onto the road as the heater flashed on to the temperature she liked. "Do you have to boil us alive?"

"I don't have it set THAT high." Her mother defended. "So, why did Yasmin run if she is innocent?"

"Because she has a fear of jail cells. Her brother was captured by the police when she was younger, and he died in the cell at the hands of another man who was also in holding."

"Oh my gosh! You never said anything to me about that. If I'd have known…"

"Yas doesn't like to talk about it and she made me swear not to tell anyone else, including you and Dad. When I found out, I told her about our family's history in the police department, but she said that it was fine. She also said that we shouldn't expect her to visit, if we ever found ourselves on the inside of the station."

"Well, she is the one we might be visiting if this keeps up. And you think she is at Sylvia's without your landlord knowing it?"

"Sylvia has a guest house on the property that has been abandoned for over a decade. The boards are falling apart, and there isn't much in the means of furniture anymore, but it is a nice hiding spot in the woods. It also comes equipped with a forgotten entrance you can take a car into that not many people know about."

"I've lived here all my life and didn't know anything like that existed."

"It's a small place that was used by her ancestor's horse farriers, since it was originally built beside a horse stable. Then, it was changed into a small chapel after a swindler stole a large amount of their money around 1910. Her cousin stayed in it for a while when her divorce left her bankrupt and then Sylvia rented it out as a stay-over spot for hikers taking the Appalachian Trail."

"Ms. Johnson told you all of this?"

Cybil shrugged. "She was in a talkative mood one day, and spilled the beans about the structure. Yas and I were curious, so we drove around the woods near the back of her property line and managed to find it off a deserted lane, still running up to the main road." She looked in the rear-view mirror to see the car still following them. "Turn at Elderberry Drive, and take Lander Road, so we can use the second turn off and that should get rid of them."

"Here's hoping you're right." Cynthia took a few more turns in both left and right directions, until they came upon the back entrance to Sylvia's land. Giving her daughter the lead on where they were going, the two women kept their eyes peeled for the old entrance. "Thankfully there was no fresh snow last night to make my tire tracks stand out."

"Yeah, but it's not as if this is the interstate highway." Cybil suddenly pointed to the section where she saw some faint traces of tracks leading into the woods. "Drop me off here."

"Drop you *off*?"

"We can't afford them spotting the newer set of tracks going down the lane. It appears that Yas tried to hide them with some branches, see? And if the cops are looking for your vehicle now, it will be a good decoy for you to keep going back toward town."

"I understand that much. I just worry about your safety after what happened yesterday."

"Martin is locked up. I'll be fine, and you know where I am in case of anything else." Cybil gave her mom one last smile before climbing out of the car and started walking to where the dilapidated house leaned precariously to one side. It wasn't until she was halfway there, that she remembered it being in season for deer hunting and hoped no hunters crossed her path. Sylvia would periodically give her permission out to a few people from time to time, and there was no telling if any were amongst the trees at the present.

Luckily, the building was right where Cybil remembered it being and Yas's car was parked behind a wall of bushes protecting the northern side of the house. "Yasmin?" She called out softly into the frosty air. "Yasmin? It's Cybil."

"In here." Yasmin motioned for her friend to join her. "You alone, right? I didn't see anyone else with you."

"As far as I know. My mom dropped me off at the entrance to the lane and I did the best I could to disguise my footprints as I came up." She reached out and gave her roommate a genuine hug. "What's going on, girl? Why are the police searching for you?"

"Because I saw Marjorie the day she died. Earlier in the afternoon, when you were at the church delivering the cookies."

"But I had the car, so…she stopped by our house?"

Yasmin shyly nodded her head.

Cybil flipped through her memory bank. "That's how she knew what your hair was supposed to look like, rather then what it turned out to be. I wondered why she made that comment. But whatever happened, couldn't have been all that bad, because neither one of you showed any signs of a fight or a struggle. And she died after the party. But you were…" Her eyes widened in shock at the terrible thought circling her mind.

"The one who found her dead. Yes, and there is more…"

"Of which we would love to hear all about, down at the station." Officer Noel swung the door open, standing in a near complete silhouette against the sunlight pouring in.

Yasmin's face froze in panic as she tried fleeing out the back way, only to be stopped by another cop standing guard. The man immediately grabbed her arm, yanked it behind her, and placed a pair of handcuffs on the young woman. As the officer began reciting the Miranda Rights, Cybil swung around to face Officer Noel with anger blazing in her eyes.

"What are you arresting her for?"

"We're just bringing her in for questioning."

"That's a lie! You don't remind a citizen of their legal rights just to ask questions over a cup of tasteless coffee!"

"Cybil?!" Yas's fear was painted on her face, completely clashing with her smiling elf t-shirt. "I didn't do anything, I promise."

"That may be. However, we have a few questions that need answering in regards to the murder of Marjorie Stonewell." Noel held the front door open with his hand, and followed the other officer outside. "One of them being why you lied to us in your statement about not speaking with her on the day she was murdered, until the party that evening."

"It's alright, Yas. I'll get a lawyer to meet you there." Cybil locked eyes with her best friend, trying to soothe her scared nerves. "Listen to me. Yas." She waited until she knew her friend's full attention was on her. "You are going to be alright."

CHAPTER 43

"When can I see her?" Cybil leaned partially over the counter to where Regina Longe was typing on a desktop computer. A smug look was plastered across her red lips, spoiling her otherwise Snow White inspired attire. "Regina!"

"I have no idea what you are talking about, Ms. Lawson. Potential murder suspects are only permitted to see their lawyer."

"This is insane." Cybil huffed into the air within the lobby of the police station. It had been dazzled up with some red and green streamers, and had three "Merry Christmas" signs hanging from the walls, but there was no mistaking this place for a jolly party scene. "Yasmin is no killer. And I really need to see her, Regina."

"No." She went to stand, and gently placed her hands on the desk again. "Why don't you ask your uncle, if it's so important?"

"You know perfectly well why." She spat out at Tara Newston's best friend, and overall princess to her daddy's successful donut shop chain across the entire state. The jokes were plentiful in certain social circles, with the daughter of donuts working at a police station. Though Regina didn't really need the job, however, getting the juicy gossip was a major bonus and she liked working with the crush of her dreams who wanted nothing to do with her. Cybil only felt bad for the one cop, Lester, and what all he had to put up with while working at the same place as her sugar highness did.

"I guess you are going to have to deal without visiting your roommate then." Regina blew on her nails as if they were freshly painted before returning to the report she had been typing up.

But Cybil wasn't through trying just yet. "My father is getting in touch with a lawyer friend of his and when they arrive, you have better let us in! You don't seem to understand. I have to see her!"

"What is going on out here?" Officer Noel stepped up to the counter, barely looking Cybil in the eye as he kept his focus on the receptionist.

"She wants to see Yasmin Manahan." There was no doubt that Regina was thoroughly enjoying the whole thing. Even her voice oozed of payback from something that occurred in high school.

Noel looked at Cybil, and what he said next, was not what either of the women expected to hear him say. "Ms. Lawson, you may go in."

Regina blinked her eyes in disbelief, as her mouth fell to the floor in shock and dismay. "But…that isn't policy, Sir. It's not like she is a family member, or a lawyer."

"We are going to allow it this time."

"How do you…" The receptionist blinked her long lashes, "Does Detective Lawson agree with this?"

"He would if he were here today." Noel politely ushered Cybil behind the counter and into the hall where their interrogation rooms were located.

"I suppose I should thank you for this." She whispered in the empty space.

"None is due. After seeing the report on what happened to her brother, we thought it was best to keep her in the employee room until her lawyer arrived. But perhaps a familiar face might do her some good right about now."

"That is surprisingly thoughtful of you. What's the catch?"

"Let's not go making mountains out of molehills. If you want to use the interview room for some privacy, we'll bring her over then."

"Please tell me that this is all one big mistake, and you're not charging her with Marjorie's death."

"Perhaps she should tell you that herself." Officer Noel opened the door and let Cybil enter a room painted in grey, with a singular table and two chairs. It certainly felt more serious and isolating than what the televisions made it out to be, though she managed to calm herself down long enough to take a seat. After a minute or two, Yasmin came through the door to join her with a weary look on her face.

"CYBIL!" Her best friend rushed up and wrapped her arms around her roommate. "Did you get a lawyer?"

"Yes and no. My father's friend is out of town for a few days, and will be back the day after tomorrow. Apparently it is the time for vacation if you practice law."

"Great. What am I supposed to do until then?"

"He is contacting another friend of his that was in need of a criminal lawyer last year, and see if he's available. There is nothing to worry about." Cybil forced a smile on her face, attempting to bring a slim line of hope to the situation. "Yas, what was Officer Noel talking about when he mentioned you seeing Marjorie on the day of the party? Is it what you

251

were going to tell me at the old farriers' house?"

Her friend's gaze fell to the table, clutching onto Cybil's arm in a desperate need for comfort and support. "That torn sticky pad you asked me about was a phone number I had written down because Marjorie insisted that I take a note." She looked at her friend, hesitating on what was to come next. "I told you before about how I'm scared of jails because of what happened to my brother. But what I left out was the reason we were in the police station." Yasmin took a pause to steady herself. "It's because I had also been arrested, with him."

Cybil's jaw dropped wide like a drawbridge gate, though she kept silent and allowed Yas to tell the story in her own time. "I was ten, and he was eighteen. My parents were both at work, and he was supposed to watch me for an hour or two until they got off, and came home to make supper. Instead of helping me with my homework, Ezra took me in his car to an abandoned parking garage where his friends were distilling alcohol. And that is when one of the kids died from it."

"Oh my gosh!"

"That is why they killed my brother in the holding cell. Because he was going to tell the cops everything he knew, and take the deal they promised to the first boy who talked. I was ushered back to see him, apparently telling the cops that I would only speak with my brother whenever they asked me questions like who I was and where my parents were. That was when we walked in and saw what was going on. He was lying on the floor as one of the officers tried giving him CPR. But it was too late. My parents arrived and were devastated. I wasn't formally charged; since I was a minor and didn't partake in anything of what they were doing. They also found no evidence that went against my story."

"So what does this have to do with Marjorie's death?"

"My brother's friend, the one who died that night, was killed from the alcohol they made because it turned out to be poisonous. Some people call it wood alcohol." Yasmin stared straight into Cybil's face. "And that is what killed Marjorie as well."

CHAPTER 44

"Hang on a second. They talked to you? Without your lawyer?!" Cybil was visibly upset, and for good reason.

"No, they didn't. But I did get a chance to overhear a woman in nurse scrubs as they brought me in. She said that Marjorie died from toxic liquor. And she specifically mentioned wood alcohol." Yasmin seemed to be defeated, sitting sad in her seat with a face matching the gloom of the walls around them. "Apparently someone mentioned to Officer Noel that I knew about Martin Stonewell."

"I'm so sorry about that, Yas. How was I supposed to know that it was only going to cement your guilt?"

"I guess you could make up for it by telling me what our next move is, Watson?"

"Watson? How am I Watson?"

"Because I feel like I've been feeding you all the scoops lately, and that would categorize me as Sherlock."

"Okay Smarty-pants, but what has all of this got to do with the phone number you wrote down?"

"Marjorie had come over and asked me to write the number on a note for me not to forget. I wanted to know why before I did, but she remained adamant that I jot it down while she talked. It wasn't until afterwards that she revealed it went to a prison where her brother was serving time. He was supposed to be out in a few days and wanted to reconcile with what happened in the past. I wasn't sure what she was getting at, until she said that Martin Stonewell was in the same cell as Ezra. He saw my brother die and did nothing to stop it. Part of him felt responsible and he wanted to make amends to my parents and I."

"Did you agree with that?"

"Marjorie remembered me talking about their visit this Christmas and asked us to consider hearing her brother out. I refused on the spot and shoved the phone number into her pocket when she wouldn't take it back otherwise. There was no way I was going to bombard my parents, out-of-the-blue, with something like that. Especially at this time of the year. I told Marjorie all of this, and more. She ended up leaving in a grumpy mood and muttering something under her breath I couldn't quite hear."

Cybil thought back to the night of the dinner and shook her head. "That's why Officer Noel had us write down our phone numbers. To provide him with a writing sample." She gave her friend a look of encouragement. "So what do you know about wood alcohol? Other than being arrested at the age of ten with your brother."

"Methanol is another name for it. I mean, it's fairly easy to make, if you know how to, and it's *really* lethal stuff. There was a big stink about it during prohibition, where a lot of people were killed by being sold the wrong type of liquor. Not one of our government's finest moments, as they ended up being the cause of so many deaths that way."

"I think that mistake has plenty of company on the list." Cybil shot a look at the watch on her wrist with the bangles. It wasn't a smart watch, or anything fancifully designed with gemstones. But rather, it was a useful watch plated in rose gold for just a touch of feminine glam. Many people liked to tease her that she was living in the past, but that didn't bother her in the least. "It's been half an hour. My dad said he would call within fifteen, if the other guy could take on your case."

"Cybil, what am I going to do?"

She had never seen her friend so scared before, and wished there was a line or phrase that would make it all better. "Well, at least you won't have to worry about making your own food."

"And that's uplifting?" Yas whimpered. "Hi Mom and Dad. Welcome to Robbyr's Cove. Oh, and by the way, I've been arrested for murder. We can wish each other a Merry Christmas through the prison bars."

"I don't understand something. If you were a minor, and they never charged you, then how did they know that you had a past with wood alcohol?"

"Because Marjorie knew about the incident. She probably has some piece of evidence that was lying around her house."

"Okay, you lost me."

"Marjorie approached me after choir practice the one night, last summer, when she was being asked to step down from her position, and told me that if I wanted to keep singing, then I should withdraw my application immediately. Elsewise, I would find my dirt posted on the bulletin board. Anonymously, of course."

"Why that selfish and pig-headed…"

"Cool your jets, girl. It's sweet and all, you wanting to stick up for me. But you can't re-kill a corpse and I was glad she kept the job. I mean, that post was all she had and it wasn't her idea to step down in the first place. She was defending what she loved to do. While I didn't care for the cutthroat way she went about it, I respected the fact that she still cared for her job after all the years she served as choir director. A lot of others would have been burned out and walked away long ago."

"Yas, you just gave me an idea."

"I did?"

"You weren't the only one who applied for the position. There were three others, right?"

"Yeah. They all backed out as well. After she probably threatened them with their own pasts."

"So what if she has done that before? Or again, even? Someone was invading her space and targeting something she deeply cared about. That gives lots of people motive to want to have her dead. Not just you."

"I get what you're saying, but Cybil, they obviously know about my past. Not to mention that Marjorie knew it, and her threat against me. They know that she was killed by a poisonous form of alcohol, and…"

A few knocks came at the door, putting a premature ending to their conversation as Officer Noel informed Cybil that her father had arrived and was waiting in the lobby. She thanked him, and turned to give her roommate one final hug. "We are going to get you out of this, Yasmin."

"Cybil, I just…"

"Answer me this one question. Did you kill Marjorie?"

"No."

"Then you have nothing to worry about."

CHAPTER 45

"She has every reason to worry." Cybil's father shook his phone in the air, feeling defeated at not being able to locate a lawyer who was able to take her case. "That means that the judge is going to appoint her an attorney, and there is no way I am going to allow Matthew Donahue Mallidew III to be picked."

"Ugh. I can still here his awful jingle in my head. 'The lawyer whose name rhymes, is also the one who stops crime.'" Cybil stared at the clean counter of the receptionist's desk, where her eye was instantly drawn to the floral Christmas wreath propped up on an easel. "There might be some hope yet."

"How's that? Are the Evergreen's branches going to swing in and save the day?"

"Weren't you the one who told me a while back that Mrs. Norman's cousin is a lawyer with a prestigious law firm?"

"Yeah, in New York. But he may not do criminal charges, and he may not even have a license to practice law in Pennsylvania."

"This is the season for miracles." Cybil smiled at her

father, who was already flipping through his contacts to find the Normans' number just as Noel walked up behind her. Having found what he was looking for, David Lawson dodged outside for a better cell signal.

"Ah, Cybil. Yasmin has a request." His voice coming out of seemingly nowhere, gave her a fright as she turned around to see him standing about three feet away.

"Are you trying to give me a heart attack?" She scolded and re-straightened her shirt. "What does she want me to do?"

"Contact her parents and let them know that she can't come to the phone right now."

"Can I see her phone so I can get their number?"

"I can't authorize that. It's being processed as evidence."

"Let me guess…you are attempting to access its GPS tracker to see where she was at the time of the murder?" She gathered she'd hit the mark when his face remained as stoic as ever. "I can help you on that one. Because Yasmin left her phone in her bag during the dinner, it would not give you an accurate reading on her location. Besides, I don't think it would give you any more of a precise location than that general area. Or are you trying to look at the text messages she may or may not have sent to Marjorie?"

"You might not want to say anything more near your uncle, if your goal is to save your friend."

Cybil didn't think she had heard him right. "I thought you said my uncle wasn't here?"

"He isn't."

"Then how would I have spoken around him? We've barely talked in years and the most he ever said to me was at Ralph's."

"All I'm saying is that…"

"Look, Yasmin did not commit the murder, I know

that." Cybil's face turned sour in a matter of seconds, as soon as she saw a tall figure slink out from a door beside the interrogation room, where she had just left her friend. Even under a full moon, she would have recognized that silhouette anywhere. "Uncle Phoenix!" She called out, glaring through Noel with razor sharp daggers for eyes. "I heard you were not here today. Must be some false rumor going around."

Detective Lawson glanced over his shoulder, giving her no more than a small fraction of his time. "And that rumor was true. Just dropped in to grab a few items and I'm on my way out the door."

Cybil felt disgusted in herself for having taken Officer Noel's word. "You knew he was there while I chatted with Yasmin, didn't you? That was why you said…" She didn't need to finish the sentence.

"Nothing he heard could be used in a court of law. He made his intentions perfectly clear to me when I asked what he was doing here. It really *is* supposed to be his day off, Ms. Lawson." Officer Noel stood his ground.

"Doesn't matter! He listened in on a private conversation that gave him fuel to light the fire. Oh, sure. He will make sure that everything is done by the book, but that is only because he listened in on an unprivileged talk, handing him what to look for on a silver platter."

"Cybil, we are only doing our jobs, regardless of where the evidence takes us." Detective Lawson answered from behind Noel, surprising the daylights out of his niece. "A fact you are well aware of." He left out the back way just as his brother returned inside from calling the Normans.

Noel purposefully stepped in Cybil's path after her uncle was gone. "Look, I can't discuss the case, obviously. However, I can have a quick chat with you that might prove to be beneficial for all concerned parties, tonight. Are you working then?"

"After what you just did to me? Twice? I'm not feeling very charitable right now."

"It will be worth your while. That, I can assure you."

Cybil studied his face, wondering if she should believe him or not. *But Yasmin needs help.* "Fine. Meet me at Ralph's around seven o'clock."

CHAPTER 46

Cybil couldn't help but feel like she was back in high school with a backpack between her legs and a water bottle tightly clutched in her hand, as her father drove her back to her house. The majority of the time, he kept going off about how his brother should have been handling the case instead of some newbie from out-of-state, all the while keeping in rhythm to the song blasting from the radio. The singer may have been rock'n around the Christmas tree, but it wasn't improving either of *their* moods.

"I'm sure that Officer Noel is a capable cop." Cybil nearly choked on the last few syllables. Here she was, defending his abilities and actions to her father after it was Noel's own decisions that made the sting even worse. Though, it was Yasmin's fault for not coming clean in the first place and it seemed reasonable enough to have a different officer investigate Marjorie's death, given the past history between her and Detective Lawson. But since it was so long ago, would it have really mattered now? And who was taking the lead into the fake nun's death? Were they actually connected? *Surely they had to be,* Cybil thought to herself.

"The Chief told me the same line when I asked him

about Officer Noel's qualifications. Apparently he was in the process of becoming a detective with his prior force and he ended up working a few homicides back in New York. So his credentials were higher than everyone else here. They assigned him to my brother, who was supposedly given another case that is of a more 'top priority.'" David Lawson made air quotes with his fingers at the end of his statement, before drifting into his thoughts again. "How there is anything higher than a murder, I have no idea. But it could have to deal with the mayor's car being stolen. He certainly likes to throw his weight around when it benefits him personally."

"I have a feeling that's what it is."

"Well, I've also heard that he has been advised, countless times, to install cameras in the garage where he keeps that fancy sports car of his. But do you think he listens to reason? Probably believes that no one would dare steal from him in a smaller town. That crimes like that are just for city life." Cybil's father turned the radio up when the song changed to singing about walking in a winter wonderland. "I wonder if Officer Noel used to work in New York City?"

"Regardless, this isn't exactly uplifting my spirits at all." Cybil's face sagged into her hand, with her elbow perched on the door.

"Sorry, Kiddo." Her father slowed down for the upcoming red light at the traffic intersection. "Is there anything I can do that would bring a smile to that lovely face of yours?"

A small grin chuckled its way between her cheeks for a brief second. "Not unless you have any information that can get Yasmin off the hook."

"Well, maybe that handyman can tell you something. I think his first name is Rodger?"

"Rodger Freedmon? I already spoke to him, and he said

that he was at the dinner in search of his sister's earphones she dropped in the parking lot. He was the one who also told me that Mrs. Norman was having an upsetting conversation on the phone in her car, around the time she claims to have been at the back of the church picking up the leftovers."

"He wasn't looking for any earphones when I saw him."

Cybil's head popped up like a prairie dog. "What was he doing?"

"Peering through the window of the church at the dinner, as far as I could reckon."

"When?"

"Oh, it was right before your mother and I arrived, so perhaps 5:45 pm? We like to use the one side entrance because there are spots closer by and it's less to walk on this bummed knee of mine."

"Did anyone else happen to see him there?"

"Maybe. But I don't know for sure, because it's not as heavily used as the main entrance."

"Rodger told me he was only at the dinner after his sister came home. He lied about being there earlier, and he probably had a good reason to keep that a secret." Cybil's flame of hope was resurging. "When I was on the phone with him, I didn't get to ask all my questions because the police showed up and cut our conversation short."

"Speaking of vehicles…" David pointed to the minivan sitting in the drive to the converted railroad house. "Where you expecting anyone?"

"Not that I was aware of." Cybil's mood switched with the wind, easily shifting back to one of dread and hesitation. "Who do you suppose? I mean, it doesn't look like…wait… hang on…" She leaned forward in the truck and squinted her eyes at the license plate under the greying sky far above. "Is that Melody's van? It could be the one Christine was driving on the night Marjorie's house was robbed."

"I guess there's only one way to find out."

"Drive off and see who leaves a nasty-gram on the front door?"

"No. To park and get out of the truck."

"I was afraid you were going to say that." Cybil swallowed the lump of worry sitting near her throat. "And what if it isn't who we think it is?" She gripped onto the latch as her father turned the engine off.

"Then we run back to the truck, drive like mad and call 9-1-1. Or your old high school principal. Really, it's a toss-up." David's shoes crunched on the semi-hardened snow while climbing down from the driver's seat. He cautiously approached the back of the van, peering around to see if anyone was standing out in the soft beam of the porch light.

"Finally! Apologies for having my husband park weirdly in the drive, but it was the best way for the ramp to extend over the stairs, in order for me to get out." Melody's thin lips smiled, causing half of her wrinkles to disappear. "I would much prefer if we talked inside. The temperature is quite nippy out here."

Cybil's eyes blinked in disbelief. The railroad house was not wheelchair friendly, so going in through the door might be a little problematic. "No offense, but I'm not sure the door will be wide enough for your wheelchair."

"We already took care of measuring the width and I should be able to barely slide on through. Thank you for your concern, though."

A suspicious feeling made its way up Cybil's back as she opened the house and stepped inside to remove her coat. She turned the electric fireplace on, watched in amazement to see Melody slip past the threshold, just as she had promised she could, and offered everyone something to drink once the door was shut. While she poured herself a cup of milk at the kitchen counter, an unsettling presence would not rest in the far reaches of her mind. "So, is there a reason for your visit?" The words were out of her mouth faster than her brain was thinking, resulting in the question sounding more curt than quizative. "I mean, to what do I owe this surprise visit?"

"About the robbery that occurred in my sister's house, the one that you and your friend reported to Christine and myself?"

"Yes, what about it?"

"I want my sister's possessions returned." Melody went for the cutthroat approach, which evidently, did not sit well with her husband.

"What my wife is trying to ask is…"

"I'm through with niceties. If we wouldn't have waited in the cold for so long, than I would have followed through with what we had agreed upon!" She snapped back at him, watching him clam shut like a shy puppy.

"You could have just called ahead to see if I was even here." Cybil defended, even though she knew the woman's shouts hadn't been directed at her.

"I did. Multiple times. However, there was no reply."

"I had my cell phone with me today and I have no missed calls."

"Not your cell phone, the landline. I obviously couldn't have asked your mother, she would have blabbed to you and it was the only number associated to this address, online."

"That has been disconnected for over two years now." Cybil shook her head and decided it was best to drop the matter. "What stuff of your sister's are you referring to?"

"The items Raven said are missing from the basement.

Our family's heirlooms from centuries gone by. Those *irreplaceable* items were stashed in those boxes, and I want them returned to their rightful owners as soon as possible."

"That would be the church then." Cybil recalled Officer Noel telling her. "Marjorie's will promised her belongings would go to the church."

Melody's face withered from any trace of kindness left, leaving a stone wall of contempt behind. "How do you know that? If that lawyer talked, I WILL see his license revoked by the bar."

"Odd that you never accused me of looking at her will in the house, amongst the things you say I stole. One could only think that the rumors are true."

"What rumors?"

Cybil could tell she had her tasting the bait dangling in the air, and chose her moment to strike. "I thought it weird that no one in her family had an original version of the will. Since her lawyer was the only one in possession of the real will, and considering the fact that most lawyers keep mere office copies, that would suggest that there are a lot of issues running deep in your family. Elsewise, why wouldn't Marjorie have given you or Marta a copy to have upon her death? And for that matter, why didn't *she* have one stashed away in her own house? Say, in the safe hidden inside the kitchen cupboard?"

Melody was boiling mad from what she viewed as an insulting attack. "You have a lot of nerve!"

"Says the woman who wheels herself into MY house and demands for me to return items I NEVER saw before and certainly DID NOT steal!" Her eyes matched that of Melody's anger-filled glare. These were unfamiliar waters Cybil was navigating through, but she felt like a fire had been lit from within and Yas's life was on the line now, adding to her momentum. "I haven't the faintest idea what you're talking about. I have none of your items, nor do I know where they have gone."

"I told Mrs. Norman it wasn't true!" Melody spat out. "You were only lying that you had the recipe card!"

"But the card wasn't kept with the other things. You said so yourself when you found the safe opened in the kitchen of a house you grew up in, by the way. A place you are very knowledgeable about, and has a layout you remember quite well. Much better, in fact, than what you had me believing at first. Between lying to me about how many times you've been in the house, and arriving there much faster than physically possible, I'd say that you like to spin tales in order to hide your own guilt."

"Just because I told you a few fibs, doesn't mean I killed my sister."

"How do I know that you didn't have Christine steal it for you? And then she could have dispatched with Marjorie in that fight at the dinner. Marta had them continue their argument behind closed doors, so perhaps you two are working together and were going to split the money once the recipe sold."

"That lump of lard?" Melody practically laughed. "She isn't blood, and that is the way she sees it. Christine only drives me around when I offer to pay her in cash on the same day."

"How come you showed up at Marjorie's faster than you should have? By our calculations, it would take a solid seven minutes to arrive from your house. But your minivan pulled into your sister's drive in only three. Unless…" Cybil kept a smirk back from spreading across her face, but it remained noticeable in her eyes. "You were already searching for Raven."

"I'm done talking. Either you return my family's belongings or I'm going to the police and demand that charges be brought against you and Yasmin for trespassing, at the very least."

"Go right ahead. We had permission by the Pastor, with a key to the property, and since the church now owns everything, except for the few items allotted to you and the others, you have no grounds. What do you get in the will by chance?" Cybil couldn't help herself at this rate, it was becoming too much fun in seeing the older woman's blood boil after all of her high and mighty attitude had washed away.

"I only want what is mine. Bring my mother's brooch to me tomorrow morning, or I WILL be filing theft charges."

Cybil's father took the next stance, towering over Melody, and having heard quite enough of her mudslinging towards his daughter. "I suggest you get out, now!" He gladly held the door open for them both, pretending not to notice her husband trying to apologize on the way out. "And don't come back!"

"I was wondering when you were going to step in." Cybil took a sip of her drink and plunked herself down on the couch as her father slammed the door for the ultimate effect.

"It was your fight, not mine. If I handle all of your issues, then you would never learn or grow. Besides, you seemed to have things well under control. I just decided that she was overdue for an exit, stage right."

"Stage left, actually."

"If you say so." David checked his watch, tapping on its lens while giving his daughter the eye. "You don't have long to do what you wanted to before you have to meet up with Officer Noel."

"Alright, alright." Cybil ran to use the bathroom, shouting over her shoulder as she dashed. "Could you feed Norris, please?"

"Who's Norris?"

CHAPTER 47

Cybil slid the keys to her father's truck into the outside pocket of her jacket with a smile brimming from ear to ear. Though she had dropped her father off at her parents' house roughly thirty minutes ago, she could still see him standing there, fully burdened with grocery bags, and issuing her a warning to stay safe right before the bags broke in his hands. Her mother heard the commotion and came out to help, just as Cybil drove away to escape an explanation. *I haven't even been able to visit with Uncle Wiley yet,* she thought to herself. Part of her wanted to call him up, she had his number from a card a few years ago, but Cybil couldn't bring herself to do that. *He was the one who left, not me. I'm still waiting for him to make the first move. And it's odd that Mom hasn't spoken much to me about him since his homecoming dinner.*

Her stomach started to feel queasy from all of the nervous ideas floating around in her brain. The jumbled ball of worry, panic, and of course fear, had her throat going warm and leading toward nausea. *No, no, everything is going to be alright and I'm not throwing up in Dad's truck. He will skewer me alive.* Cybil forced herself to take a few deep breaths and to focus on the Christmas hymn coming through the speakers. She was back to feeling like her usual self just in time to be pulling into the nearly packed parking lot of the dry bar and saw something she didn't quite expect to see.

Ralph's was buzzing with a business party in full swing at the back of the bar. Holly jolly music poured from additional Bluetooth speakers with the channels all set to a Yule Log playlist that cycled through a repetitive video of a traditional fire. Shimmery garland was practically hung everywhere there was a clear spot, causing Cybil to wonder if someone had actually snuck some real alcohol in with them. Especially when she looked over at Ralph, and his face instantly convinced her that it wasn't his idea.

"What happened?" She asked.

"If your officer friend, over there, wouldn't have called to tell me that Yasmin wasn't coming into work, then I would have thought it was her. But believe it or not, one of the staff members at the party in the back, is REALLY into decorating." His eyes widened appropriately with sarcasm. "Besides, your friend knows I don't like stuff that shimmers."

"I didn't think anyone could outmatch Yas, but apparently so. And I don't have an officer friend, Ralph."

The older man shrugged his shoulder in the direction of a booth in the far left corner. "He said he is here to see you. Thought you might be going on a date and didn't tell me." He snickered.

Cybil squinted her eyes at Officer Noel perusing over the menu. "Well, he may be here to see me, but he is NO friend of mine. And we are going to need a steak, Ralph."

"You got it." He smiled as his eyebrows raised up, knowing full well what that tone of voice meant when Cybil used it. "Should I add a side of popcorn to that order? I wouldn't want to miss the showdown."

"Ha-Ha."

"Haven't seen a good fight in this place since Joe left for Michigan five years back. Been getting too peaceful 'round here for my liking." Ralph went all western as he spoke, sticking a toothpick in his mouth as though it was a cigar. "Go kindly on the tables and chairs now, ya hear?"

Cybil rolled her eyes and walked over to join Noel at the booth, eager to get the meeting done with so she could move onto more important leads. After the way she fell prey to a pair of his traps, an automatic defensive mode kicked in this time. *I am not going to be played as a fool again.* "Alright, so what is it you wanted to tell me? I don't chew the fat very well, so we best get down to business."

He casually looked up from the menu sheet. "If you ask me the right questions, I can provide hints."

"Great. A game show. Okay…how do you know what happened to Yasmin when she was ten-years-old? She was never booked, and even if there would have been some old police notes packed away in some dusty old box, how did you know where and when to look?"

"Ask Marta."

"Is she the reason you discovered it in the first place?"

"Ask Marta."

"Fine. Was Marjorie killed by wood alcohol?"

"I think a trip to Robbyr's Cove Museum would be a nice stop. I certainly found it rather enlightening." Noel hungrily bit into a chicken wing appetizer a waitress place on the table between them. "Are you going to order anything?"

"I'm good. This isn't a social call." Cybil held her resolve against a weak stomach that was aching for a nibble of the saucy food in front of her. "I'm surprised that you have already paid a visit to our town's historical building, when you have only been in Robbyr's Cove for a week."

"Your uncle suggested that it might help me to understand the town a bit more, since he is still dealing with the mayor's car theft." He saw the unyielding sternness in her face. "Look, I get that your father has been questioning my ability to lead this investigation due to the fact that I don't have a detective's shield. But I can assure you that it's being handled with the upmost care and devotion to putting the right killer behind bars."

"Does that mean that you're still considering other suspects?"

"Of course." Officer Noel thanked the waitress for plunking his steak onto the table.

"And I guess I might be one of them?"

He took a moment to chew the medium-well T-Bone cut, fresh from the kitchen, and allowed the flavors to hit his taste buds. Noel then proceeded to take a drink of water before deciding to ask a question burning in the back of his mind. "What is it between you and your uncle?"

"A family rift. Why?"

"Let's just say that he seems very keen on not coming across your path, nor that of your father's."

"I'm sure you have seen your fair share of family disputes. Ours is a dime a dozen. Now, if you have nothing more to say to me, I'll be on my way." Cybil went to rise from her seat, but Noel stopped her with a short plead.

"The purpose of this meet up was not to antagonize you by any means."

"So far we haven't talked very much." She watched his stoic expression and gathered a hunch. "You asked me here to see what new information I've uncovered, is that it?"

"Well, if you were an informant, I could give you a little information in turn, but only if nothing is held back."

She stood still for a split moment, trying to decide if it was worth taking him up on his offer. The burns of being used rang in her head without fail and she stared at the ceiling in contemplation. *Do I really have a choice?* Cybil retook her seat and divulged all she learned from Melody's recent visit to her house, her conversation with Tara and Rodger, and what her father had told her in the car ride home.

"That would explain the extra footprints dead-ending at the window. And the lack of tire marks in the yard by the back door."

"I did tell you that she wasn't there by the way. And you probably already found out about Rodger being at the dinner from questioning him about his van."

"Just speaking out loud. However, he did confess to us that he was there earlier in the evening and then returned to find his sister's headphones. He used her minivan to keep the pretense up that a friend had borrowed his truck for the evening, which gave him an alibi if anyone should have remembered seeing him, like your father."

"Did he happen to tell you why? I mean, why go to all that trouble to cover up the fact that he was there?"

"He says that he missed going, and wanted to see his sister and mother enter the dinner together. Tara was apparently all excited to be judging the cookie contest, which he wanted to watch her take part in. I must say, for a sister that is one selfish brat, he certainly treats her better than she deserves."

"I think he takes pity on her." Cybil remembered what Rodger had told her about his rocky relationship with Tara. It was a sour note she could relate all too well to.

"But Melody's attitude is rather concerning. I wonder what could be so valuable in those boxes that were stolen from Marjorie's basement?"

"Could be anything worth money. If she was right, that the items are from centuries past, someone might have a handsome nest egg they're hoarding." Cybil's stomach continued to growl as he wiped up the juices with a torn piece of bread. "Melody did mention to me about her mother's brooch, so perhaps there's a stash of expensive jewelry amongst the items? Did she have any cameras hidden on her property that could tell us?"

"Nope."

"What was the time of death?"

"Around the time you two discovered her body."

"But, that doesn't make any sense." Cybil thought back to what Melody had said about her sister and alcohol. It could have been a lie, like the rest of her words, but she believed this one to be true of the devout choir director. "Marjorie doesn't touch real alcohol and there wasn't any at the dinner." Then it clicked in her head, and the gloom of dread resurfaced. "You think that Yas spiked a dark cocoa hot chocolate drink and gave it to Marjorie?"

"Partially correct. Except for the fact that the medical examiner said that the levels shown in the tests were higher than what was found in her stomach contents. After taking a look at an itchy patch of skin on her forearm, she discovered that there was already a buildup in her body and the hot chocolate was used as a detonator to…how did she say…something to do with the previous acid levels."

"Her skin cream. Marjorie said that she had been having some issues with the last batches, and blamed the company for changing their formula." Cybil rested her arms on the table. "But Yas hasn't been in Marjorie's house. How would she have planted the wood alcohol in her cream?"

"Multiple choir members have concurred that Marjorie took it with her to practice on occasion, and constantly during colder weather."

"How long are you going to be keeping Yasmin in custody?"

"I heard that her lawyer was on his way when I left the station, but there might be some delay due to bad weather north of us. Your father is adamant that she receives his services as opposed to having the judge assign one."

"There is a very good reason for that. If you ask anyone living in town, you'll get the picture. I really don't understand how he stays in business."

"Whoever your father retained, apparently he is related to Mrs. Norman? Asked us if Mr. Norman was associated at all in the case before agreeing to represent Yasmin."

"Interesting. Like it would be a conflict of interest if he was connected to the case." Cybil started putting the pieces together. "I think I know what Mrs. Norman's phone call was about in her van in the parking lot. And if I'm right, and Marjorie found out about it, then Mrs. Norman would have had a strong motive to want her dead." Suddenly looking behind her shoulder, Cybil asked Noel why there were no people sitting in the booth beside them.

"I asked Ralph to leave those seats empty unless necessary, so we could talk with less prying ears." Noel finished his water. "Care to enlighten me with your theory? I have one figured out, but just to compare notes?"

"I will, after you fulfill your end of the bargain."

"Ask Marta about the journal. Then, we can talk further."

CHAPTER 48

The following morning, Cybil was already up and ready to go by the time her phone alarm went off. She was determined to have a chat with Marta, and to learn something more about the journal Officer Noel mentioned, while conducting a small test of her own making. If Melody was so adamant to get her hands on the cookie recipe, and the boxes of things missing from the house, then perhaps her sister would be as well. Taking the risk of irritating another Stonewell was not what Cybil considered fun, nor a good excuse to call off of work two days in a row. But she couldn't stop thinking about Yasmin having to spend the night at the police station. *And her parents are due to arrive in three days!*

Within one ring, the other end of the line was picked up by the Snip 'n Sheer manager, Begonia Oilphant, as the lady proudly declared in the phone's speaker. Her voice held a light, southern accent in her words, and added to the charming hospitality she gave off. *No wonder she is working at a hair salon.* "Ah, hi, I was looking to schedule an appointment for this afternoon."

After being disappointedly informed that they were

all booked, Begonia did mention about a recent opening for the next morning, which Cybil happily accepted and gladly gave her name for the reservation. Then a sudden "oooooooo" came over the phone from the perky manager, who instantly asked if she had indeed found Marjorie Stonewell in the snow, with a marshmallow fork in her back. "No, there was no fork."

"I told my sister she was wrong, and showed her all the newspaper headlines having fun with altering those Christmas songs; like Marjorie Got Ran Over By a Reindeer, Merry Murder, and God Rest Ye Dead Director. Well, she just said that you can't trust the main reporters because of fraudulent news, and tried convincing me that a man publishing articles under the pen name Birdman is more accurate."

"I think your sister might want to switch…" The manager abruptly cut Cybil off as a female's voice could be heard shouting in the background, and the line clicked dead just as she was about to finish her statement. "Hello? Hello?" She shook her head, wondering what could have made a gossipmonger zip her mouth up from a prime source of information. There was no doubt in her mind, based on the woman's tone of eagerness, that she rather enjoyed a good dish of secrets to spice up her job's mundane chores. But there was the possibility that Marta had overheard her employee, and shut the conversation down before it got out of hand. "No telling how many women have pestered her with details and plagued her with wasted condolences by now."

According to her father yesterday, who was passing along tidbits from her mother, Marta was the youngest of the three Stonewell sisters and was the one who held onto grudges for far too long. It was often speculated that she was going to try a career in singing right after high school, but she never did leave town. The reason wasn't shared with anyone outside of the immediate family, but that didn't stop the town's rumor mill from imagining as to why. Though many of the conjured theories were unreliable at best, there was one with a little more merit than the others. *Time for a museum visit. And I know just the tour guide to help me.*

CHAPTER 49

Cybil waved to grab Uncle Wiley's attention from the sidewalk leading up to the door of the Victorian House the town used for their historical society. His brilliant smile was something she still wished to bottle up and save for a rainy day, but she had to shove her personal feelings aside for this reunion. "I see you came in style." She pointed to the *Rolls Royce* gliding gracefully through the snow-covered drive as the chauffeur rejoined onto the main road.

"An old friend who wanted to catch up on a few of life's trivial questions." He wrapped her up in his arms for one of his famous "bear hugs" and walked up to the old front door in a familiar way. His gloved hands touched the original banister out of nostalgic remembrance, and stopped just short of gripping onto the door handle, frosted from the chill. Glancing about the porch, in need of repairs for next spring, Uncle Wiley breathed in the sharp December air and looked down at his niece with tears in his eyes. "I haven't stepped foot in this place since I left over a decade ago."

"Oh, if this is going to stir up some bad memories or anything…"

"No, no, no. Nothing like that, Cybil. It's just, well…it's

just that some of my happiest memories have been here. Working at the museum, I mean. I hope that they have been keeping it up well; whoever the new caretakers are."

"From what I hear, they truly have. The porch is scheduled to be fixed after the snow is gone, and a new exhibit will be installed in April." Cybil showed him the paper announcement pinned to the outside bulletin board. She brushed away a small amount of snow clinging to the plastic protective sheet, and read over the typed message. "Due to the generosity of an anonymous donor, we will be able to open up the third floor, with a whole new exploration into the Prohibition era."

"That really would be something. To see this house fully restored and all its room filled with historical treasures." Uncle Wiley's face beamed with a fatherly type of pride.

"Then, maybe we should go in and see for ourselves?" Cybil grinned, trying to mask her eagerness to warm herself inside the building, as opposed to freezing in the winter breeze. Her uncle dipped his head to her, and escorted his niece into the Robbyr's Cove Historical Society.

Nothing had changed since the time her uncle had worked the floors as the custodian. The reception desk was as old as the house, stained and well-maintained by the woman sitting behind its oak wood. A carpet runner extended the length of the short foyer, in the same green and orange coloring that was left behind from the previous owners. It smelled musty like old books, as plenty of them could be found in the research room to the right, and in the converted study on the second floor. Overall, the place resembled that of a quaint hotel as opposed to a modern day museum one would find in the cities.

"May I help you?" A stout woman, in her early seventies, greeted them in a friendly invitation. "We are serving up some hot cocoa and home-made sugar cookies in the study upstairs. And I believe that the Shakespearean Troupe is done with their practice, so you don't have to wear any earplugs to enjoy the fireplace."

"I take it that you are not a fan of his works?" Cybil picked up a pen and signed their names in the register book.

"Let's just say that I respect his skill of literature, but he is not a favorite of mine." The woman leaned closer to the counter's top, lowering her voice to a whisper. "And when you fail to make MacBeth's murder scene more interesting than paint drying, well…"

"That good, huh?"

"The man who started the troupe should have paid better attention in class. Because the internet can only do so much of the leg work for you; regardless of what they all claim AI can do." She rolled her eyes, and held up her hands in surrender. "I digress. Surely you have come here to look at our wonderful exhibits, than to hear me banter on about my ex-students."

"Actually…"

"Gretta Drake!" Wiley cut Cybil off, and blinked at the woman who was squinting her eyes through rounded spectacles. "You used to teach eleventh grade English at the high school."

"Why, yes I did." Ms. Drake remained silent for a pause, before asking if she had taught Cybil's uncle in school.

"You started working here the last year I was the custodian."

Ms. Drake's eyes lit up. "You're Wiley! Wow. It's been a long time. Henry told us that you were the best employee he had. He was in charge of this place till about five years ago, when my brother and I took over."

"Yeah, I was just talking to him about that on the way

here." Uncle Wiley winked at Cybil as he picked up a but- terscotch drop candy from a vintage glass container on the counter. "I can see that this museum is in good hands."

The sound of footsteps pounding down the stairs, hushed all conversation, while the Shakespearean troupe went to leave. It surprised Cybil to find that Mrs. Norman and Mr. Jeffrey were amongst the members, and she flashed them both a cheerful smile as they approached the first floor. Neither one of them appeared pleased in the least at seeing her there, and the argument echoing off the walls, made their ears cringe from the angry voices.

"I told you that your line wasn't right!" A man in brown hair descended first, shouting over his shoulder at the other tall man throwing his arms up out of frustration.

"Fine! Alright! You were right, and I was wrong! That is why I wanted to double-check with Marta before I was to speak tonight, but alas, she is not here AGAIN!"

The door slammed shut, causing the three remaining people to wince at the sound of the old hinges shrieking in pain. "Who are those two?" Cybil asked. "I recognize Mrs. Norman and Mr. Jeffrey, but not the others."

"I'm not sure. They moved to Robbyr's Cove about seven months ago, and joined the group on the second meeting." Ms. Drake's face brightened up with a sudden idea. "Say, would you two like to get a preview of the third floor exhibit?!"

"If that wouldn't get you into trouble with your brother." Wiley walked over to where an old flask from the 1700s was sitting on the same shelf he used to dust on a weekly basis.

"Are you kidding? My brother is better with documents and accounting, than with people and decorating skills. That is where I come in! We do make a great team together." Ms. Drake grabbed a key ring from inside the top right drawer and led them up two flights of creaky stairs. "We are going to have to repaint some of the rooms, of course, as they definitely show their age in certain areas. However, most of the furniture was well wrapped and looks as good as the first day they were built. I suppose we have you to thank for that, Mr. Hansen."

"I can't take all the credit for it, but I guess a little wouldn't hurt."

Cybil shook away the surprise at hearing her mother's maiden name for the first time in so long, and then smirked at her Uncle's failed attempts at making small talk. He was certainly more suited to cramped research tables and musty shelves of books with deceased authors. "So, Ms. Drake, does Marta normally miss her meetings with the Shakespearean Troupe?"

"No. In fact, she usually arrives earlier than the rest, and sets up scones and tea in the room. That makes two meetings in a row that she hasn't attended. Though, I tend not to judge, with the passing of her sister and all."

"But I was under the impression that they weren't very close."

"Well, even relatives we find to be distant, can still affect us in unexpected ways with their deaths. Her sister began going to her salon to get her hair done, you know. About eleven months ago."

"Really? What happened to being loyal to Wavy Chops? I remember my friend telling me that she talked it up right before having an appointment there every month."

"Who knows. The only thing Marjorie didn't tell anyone was her own personal life." Ms. Drake unlocked the door and waved them onto the floor that very few people had ever seen. "It's going to be so nice to see this entire house opened up. We are even going to have an opening party and food being catered!" She nearly skipped in the air from the excitement of it all. "Sorry, I tend to get carried away when it comes to talking about history and teaching."

"No need to apologize. History is one of my favorite subjects." Cybil glanced around at the crates that were partially unboxed. Various items from the 1920s were scattered about in a chaotic organization. Beautifully preserved hats lined a collapsible table, along with dresses, brooches and necklaces that would have dazzled at parties. Scarves were draped on a hat rack nearby, and were numbered by jewelry tags gently placed around their pretty fabrics. On the other table, books from the time period were catalogued beside a do-it-yourself still with glass bottles and dusty charts. "Is that Robbyr's Cove?"

"Yep! The little dots mark where supposed bootleggers camped out with their stills. Apparently the donor's family had ties to the local ring, and was possibly even the leader." Ms. Drake gently pulled the fragile paper out from underneath a large theater poster of *The Lodger: A Story of London Fog*. "There were three in the woods to the north, and four in the woods to the south of town."

"What is that mark there?" Cybil pointed to a faded black dot, that had been slightly smudged out where someone attempted to erase it.

"Not sure. Could be one where they meant to start up camp, but then it went wrong." The former teacher moved her glasses, examining the speck even further. "That would have been right where the abandoned tree house is now. The one Ol' Shaffer had installed for his spoiled rotten boy. He never did seem to make much use of it."

Cybil inched closer to the map, about to ask another question, when a small, antique hair clip caught her attention. She picked up the short card it was attached to, with a defunct company's name printed in faded green on the beige paper. "An electric hair curler with no heat?"

"Yes. They were advertised to women in the 1920s as a cheaper solution than to go to a hairdresser. That particular business swore that fifty million of their hair curlers were being used in the public." Ms. Drake motioned to the empty slits in the card and highlighted the fact that there was one missing from the simple packaging. "It was customarily sold as a pair."

A lightbulb went off in Cybil's brain. She had seen a hair clip identical to this one in Marjorie's house, when it was discovered that the cookie recipe had been stolen; along with Stonewell family's belongings.

"Is this really a certificate for flying over the capital?" Uncle Wiley broke in on his niece's silent discovery, by gesturing to the paper resting near the corner of the table.

"It is, indeed. We even have an old brochure that their employees would hand out at popular tourist venues and to tour guides. See?" Ms. Drake brought a pale blue and shag-carpet orange tri-fold up from behind a number of family pictures. "Imagine a whole business venture that was dedicated to training, piloting, and marketing flying trips over the capital of our country. The land, where the planes were built, used to be a race track, and later became a major airport near Washington D.C."

While Cybil did enjoy hearing fun tidbits of history, it was oddly the name on the certificate that caught her attention more than the airport's tales. *Stonewell? Chester Stonewell?* Her lips wanted to scream out in prideful joy that she had found the missing boxes from Marjorie's basement. But her instincts told her that it was a very bad idea to do just that. There was no telling how much Ms. Drake was involved with Marjorie's death, and they had no clue as to where her brother was at the current moment. He could be lurking in a side hallway for all she knew, listening in on their conversation like a stalker.

"Wow! This is all truly fascinating, but Uncle Wiley, we must be moving on through some of the other exhibits if we are to reach our lunch reservations by three thirty." She flashed him a sweet smile, and winked as he gave her a look of confusion.

"Ah, that's right. How could I have forgotten?" He cast Ms. Drake a charming grin. "I must say, this head would have been left on my dresser if it wasn't screwed onto this fat neck of mine." Chuckling the matter off, Cybil and her uncle thanked their nice guide for the exclusive preview, before returning to the first floor and heading into another room.

As soon as they were out of earshot, Uncle Wiley whispered in his niece's ear. "So, where are our dinner plans, Secret Agent?"

"I'll explain later." Cybil glanced over her shoulder to see Ms. Drake's elusive brother in the hallway, talking to his sister and pointing at them in the old chart room. The older woman's infectious smile was soon replaced by blushing cheeks and an embarrassed half-grin as they talked.

"I think we have been made."

"What now?"

"We better head out." Cybil poked her uncle in the arm. "Follow my lead."

They briefly stopped in front of a clock hanging on the wall by the hidden entrance to the old dining room, and Cybil asked her uncle to retell the story about how it got a bullet hole in its beautiful wood carvings. She used the opportunity to casually watch the brother and sister duo fight in the reception area. From where they were standing, she couldn't quite hear what was being discussed, as their voices remained low. But when the woman's brother angrily sailed his hands through the air, he nearly toppled the candy jar before stomping his way up the stairs.

Uncle Wiley kept on talking without fail and didn't even ask when Cybil grabbed ahold of his arm and dragged him up to the counter where Ms. Drake was in visible shock and worry.

"Ms. Drake, are you alright?" Cybil asked, both out of curiosity and out of genuine concern for the older woman.

"Oh, thank you dear, but I will be. My brother was just telling me some very distressing news. Apparently, you were the one to find Marjorie in the snow?"

"Actually, it was my friend Yas who did. It certainly was not a highlight of the holiday season for me, though. Frankly, I will be happy when the New Year rings in. All anyone seems to want to know, is what happened when I found her in the snow, in her blue coat. So at least, she went out in comfort, I guess." Cybil put on a façade of sadness and glanced over at her uncle, wondering if she would take the bait. "That is why Uncle Wiley brought me here. To help cheer me up by stepping back in time for a spell."

"Oh, yes. It is quite an escape in this house." The woman feigned a shadow of her former smile. "But, having known that Marjorie passed in her favorite purple coat, is more than nothing, I guess. You must have been close to her to know that."

"Between you and me, I barely knew her. I just over-heard that it was her favorite by one of her other relatives." After bidding their farewells, Cybil waited until they were both safely inside her father's truck, to start explaining what was going on.

"I'm assuming that we don't have dinner reservations?" Uncle Wiley's suspicious look turned a little mischievous.

"No. But we can." Cybil got the engine to roar to life and began driving on the way back to her place. "I think that it's possible Ms. Drake and her brother are involved in Marjorie's death."

"Oh my, do tell."

"Well, when I was in Marjorie's house a few days ago…don't ask me why…I noticed a singular hair clip on the ground in her living room. It looked just like the one attached to the old electric hair curler card I saw on the third floor. I also mentioned finding Marjorie in a blue coat, and Ms. Drake corrected it to a purple coat without even noticing. Now, she couldn't have seen that on the news or anywhere else, because that was a detail the police sealed up from the press."

"So you don't believe that the anonymous donor was Marjorie? I read the certificate too, remember?"

"Marjorie's niece had said that the basement used to have a lot of stuff in boxes. But when Detective Lawson went down to take a look, the room was practically empty. Scuff marks could be seen at various points along the floor, with a few specks of mud by one of the remaining boxes."

"So her niece thinks they were stolen?"

"Raven swore that Marjorie wouldn't have given them away." Cybil came to a stop at a red light just as small snowflakes began to fall. "Presumably, if the stuff being held in the third floor of the museum is Marjorie's, then how did Ms. Drake and her brother get the items after she died? The only person to have a spare key was Pastor Lawrence, that I know of."

"Marjorie didn't have a spare under a fake rock or the doormat?"

"One of the police officers checked over the entire front porch Sunday night, and there wasn't so much as a wear mark signifying that one was missing."

"She could have given them the donation before she died. You said it was already boxed up, and you only have the niece's word for most of it."

"That's true." The gears in her mind churned while driving down Bolster Road. "Who else would you give a spare to? Someone who you would trust or need to…," a lightbulb suddenly sparked behind her eyes, "fix things in your house while you were away. I wonder if Rodger Freedmon has a key to her house? He has done work for a lot of different people and the police questioned him as to why his van was seen in her driveway the night of the murder."

"You think that the Drakes stole the items on the night Marjorie died?"

"Why not? It seems only logical when you realize that there is a garage a mere mile down the road that Rodger's van might have been parked at. And if it was, then Marjorie's key could have been on the ring, and then if anyone would have seen them in the driveway, it would have looked like Rodger was there fixing another frozen pipe issue. But ironically, he was outside the Christmas dinner, watching through a window to see his sister and mother walk in and then returned later to search for his sister's missing headphones." Cybil felt pleased with herself. "That sounds like a great plot for a book. Doesn't it?"

"Sorry to burst your bubble, but Ms. Drake and her brother are both in their seventies. All that clothing and jewelry, not to mention the hats, paperwork, and the artwork, would weigh too much for them to haul all of that out."

"Rodger has a dolly, because I've seen it. It could have been in his van when they high-jacked it. You saw how passionate Ms. Drake was about opening all of the floors to the public, and expanding the exhibits there at the museum. Let's face it, Uncle Wiley. While the museum is great, nothing has been added in such a long time and it's in desperate need of new interest to bring in the visitors. The Shakespearean Troupe probably helps to keep the place in the black with some sort of rental agreement, but the cars have been sparse at best. The last entry in the register book was over two weeks ago."

"Hold on there, Detective. I spot a small flaw in their thinking. How did they know that Marjorie was dead?"

"They could have been the ones to kill her. Say she was going to donate the items in the boxes, that's how they knew about them in the first place, and then backed out at the last minute. With Marjorie out of the way…"

"Were they at the dinner?"

"No. But they didn't have to be. Marjorie was killed with poison."

"I'm not going to ask how you know that."

"Wood alcohol, to be precise."

Her uncle's face glazed over. "Pretty nasty way to go. But, most of that stuff has been banned from all processes and manufactured goods nowadays. The killer would have to have known how to extract it from its natural source, or have access to an extremely old supply. Not to mention that it is supposed to be very bitter to the taste. In order to mask its flavor, the killer would have to use…"

"Something to mask it like dark chocolate?" Cybil gave her uncle an uneasy look. "Yas ran the beverages that night and dark cocoa hot chocolate was on the menu."

"Your parents told me about your friend's predicament. How's she holding up?"

"She's okay for now. But there is something else still bothering me about the stuff we saw in those boxes. That brochure seemed familiar, the one for flying over Washington D.C."

"In what way?"

"I'm not sure. Maybe it was the colors? But I did just see some artwork on my social media account with planes in the paintings. So maybe that was it." Cybil took another turn, stayed to the left side of the upcoming fork in the road, and pulled into the parking lot of her uncle's favorite pizza shop.

He beamed at the neon sign, still boasting the orange and green words of Guido's Half Slice Pizzeria. "You remembered."

"Sure do. Guido's son owns the place now, but his father likes to help out from time to time." Cybil counted the money in her wallet, hoping that she had enough to pay for both their meals.

"Don't worry about it, girl. This is my treat."

"Thanks Uncle Wiley."

"Oh, but I didn't say that I'd do it for free." A mischievous smile spread out wide between his chubby cheeks. "But I will pay for the food if you show me your house, or should I say, the converted railroad station."

"I suppose we can make that happen." She flashed him back a cheery smile of her own.

CHAPTER 50

"What's that?" Cybil's uncle pointed at a framed drawing of four men and two women on the wall in the living room. Their clothing agreed with the year recorded next to the artist's initials, dating the line work back to the 1880s in the sketch of a shop situated behind the six people in front. "Did you do this?"

"If I was over a hundred years old, I would have. That is a genuine piece of American history right there."

"Where did you find it?" His interest heightened as his face closed in to examine it further.

"From the backyard. I was digging a hole to start laying a foundation for our home-made fountain when I unearthed a small rectangle of bricks covering over an old cigar box. That drawing had been folded up inside, tucked away with a few ticket stubs."

"Buried in the yard?"

"Yeah. There wasn't much inside the box. Just this drawing and the three train ticket stubs, like I just said. Why?"

Her uncle's eyes remained transfixed on the faces that had been carefully crafted to include their individual features. "The man in the middle, in the mustache and the bowler hat…" Uncle Wiley's voice faded into his silent thoughts, prompting Cybil to become even more curious about his suspensefulness.

"Uncle Wiley, what is it?"

He suddenly spun around and asked her if there was any additional writing on the back of the drawing, detailing further identification as to who the subjects were. When Cybil shook her head, he returned to the art piece as abrupt as before. "I cannot be mistaken. No, I have to be right, I have to be. But, how can I verify it if there is no way to prove it?"

"Uncle Wiley, you are starting to sound like an annoying riddle. What are you talking about?"

Her uncle's eyes held the utmost mixed look of urgency and seriousness she had ever seen. "Cybil, what I am about to tell you cannot go any further. Not until I am certain that I am right. Do you understand?" His niece nodded in agreement and impatiently waited for him to continue. "I'm pretty sure that the man in the middle is Erwin Lawson. Your ancestor and the leader of the bandits who founded this town."

CHAPTER 51

Cybil didn't know what to think, and blinked her eyes to make sure she was not in a dream. "Ah…great-great-grand-father Erwin?" She watched her uncle nod his head in agreement. "You're crazy. The most well-known fact about him was his massive camera shyness, so to speak; except for the fact that he did work at this train station. Besides, this artwork was completed over a decade before he came to this area."

"So? The oral descriptions we have of him, fit that man perfectly. And there!" Uncle Wiley placed his finger on the glass where another male figure was prominently penciled in. "I bet you that that man is Quin."

"That's preposterous. Truly, it is." Cybil played with her hair, trying to figure out what to do. She didn't know her uncle all that well anymore and had no idea how he would react to her asking for him to leave. Her mother had warned her that he had an obsessive nature when it came to the family treasure, having a few connections to the Lawsons in other ways. *Being a reader or a writer would naturally lead to an over-active imagination, right?* But the way his face lit up after noticing the drawing was beginning to freak her out.

"Where are the ticket stubs?" He hastily asked. "Did you also frame them? Scrapbook them? Please don't tell me that you threw them out. Of course you wouldn't have done that." Her uncle rambled on. "My sister said that you are fascinated by local history and a find like that would have been treasured, not seen as trash as others might have done."

"I meant to frame them." Cybil hesitantly answered, pausing as she tried to study his face. "Life got in the way, so I hid them in a safe place." She stepped into her bedroom and approached the side table rather slowly, in an effort to delay showing them to him. "But I don't remember offhand, where I put them. Why don't I take a quick look and give you a call at another time?" A short grin managed to form on her lips as she glanced down at her cell phone. "Wow! It's that late already? I have a few things to do before Yasmin is released and I also have an early morning shift tomorrow."

"Right, right." Uncle Wiley recomposed himself and cleared his throat. "Best be heading off as well, I suppose." He went to leave her bedroom, stopping to lean in closer and pushed his glasses up the bridge of his nose. "But if I were a betting man, I would stake my house that one of those ticket stubs is from Kalamazoo, Michigan."

"Uncle Wiley, if you don't mind me asking, why did you come back home for Christmas? I mean, you haven't visited in fifteen years." She watched him shift most of his weight to his left leg.

"I'm guessing you don't know about how I left the museum, then." Wiley cleared his throat and scratched a sudden itch at the back of his neck. "There was a misunderstanding one night, and a woman thought that I was the one who robbed her in the parking lot at the museum. Even though I wasn't, and there was no evidence connecting me to the crime, I had no corroborating witness to confirm my alibi. The police didn't think my treasure-hunting cork-boards were reliable enough, you see. And there was heat coming down from the mayor at the time. So I decided it would be easier to go away in the middle of the night."

"You didn't answer my question." Cybil had a sinking feeling in the pit of her stomach. "Uncle Wiley, please don't take offense at my next question, and I would feel silly if it was anyone else but you, however…did you come back because of the Stephen Longthorn lore? A co-worker of mine was talking about the bell ringing out…" She couldn't tell if he was listening to her or not, as his eyes fixated on the drawing once again.

Her uncle remained mute and he dared not look at her, for fear of the outrage she was about to lay upon him.

"Uncle Wiley? Please tell me that you did not come back just for a folktale about some missing treasure."

"I can't lie to you, girl."

"REALLY?!" Her sharp-noted voice was like a rag-ged-edged blade through his chest. "I'm guessing my mom already knew because she warned me not to bring any of it up around you."

"If she did, then it's because she has known me her entire life. I never actually outright told her."

"I can't believe this. And here I was thinking that you came back to see us, and me, after all this time. I was so naive."

Uncle Wiley twisted back around to face her. "But I did miss you, Cybil, and thought of you often while I was away. I sent you a card every year, didn't I?"

"Even disowned children can receive cards from their parents." Cybil's eyes were growing hard toward him. "I bet you wouldn't have even recognized me if I hadn't introduced myself as your niece at the Historical Society."

"No. That isn't so. I saw you. I would recognize you in a crowded room. Like when I knew it was you the other night, because of the way your eyes sparkled in that black dress you wore. Even when you were a kid, your face had a special gift to light up the room whenever you smiled. It was as though you reflected the sun's beautiful rays in your cheeks." But her uncle's charm was not working on her anymore.

"When did you see me in a black dress?"

"Eh…at the dinner party your mother threw on the night I arrived in town."

"But I had to work that night and missed the dinner." Cybil squinted at him, watching her uncle scramble for a new lie to save him. "The only place you would have seen me in that dress was at the church during the Christmas Dinner."

"I can explain."

"Oh you better! I didn't see you there all evening. But I did see a shadowy figure across the street." Cybil was beginning to think that maybe she did have two stalkers. "When did you get into town?"

"What?"

"When did you actually arrive in town? Not when you told my mother, but when you physically stepped foot into Robbyr's Cove?"

"That Thursday night, December 12th. Why?"

"Why didn't you want to come to the dinner?"

"Because I wanted to stay in for the night."

"No. Don't feed me another lie. What was the real reason you didn't want to go to the dinner?"

"That's a personal matter that is none of your business."

"I think it's time for you to leave." Cybil suddenly stated, feeling more hurt and betrayed than ever before. "Now." She watched as he made his way through the living room and out the front door, after she handed him her father's truck keys to get home. A huge sigh of relief escaped her mouth whilst she leaned against the back of the door, waiting to hear him turn out of the driveway.

CHAPTER 52

Cybil couldn't keep the tears from streaming down her face. She was trying so desperately to keep her chin up and her eyes focused on making the best of what was left of Christmas this year. And yet, it seemed to be imploding from the inside out everywhere she looked. Nothing was going right, and to have discovered her uncle's true reason for coming home had been another blow to her already weary heart. It was bad enough that her best friend was waiting for a lawyer, but to learn that her childhood hero, the one she stood up for when all others called him a loon and a nut job, stung more than anything else did. Her phone was already dialing as she held it up to her ear. "Mom?"

Spilling her thoughts over the phone consumed most of the following hour. She talked and talked, finally releasing all of the mounting stress and frustration the past weeks had bottled up inside. For the first solid twenty minutes, her mother remained silent and allowed her daughter to just let it all out. When she was ready to take a breath, Cynthia broke into the conversation. "Honey, that's exactly why I didn't want you to discuss the topic with him. I knew there was no stopping you from visiting him when you were younger, but after he left, which did come as a shock to me as well, I could only think of protecting you. So I stopped mentioning his name altogether to help you move on as time ticked by. Although, you can't be upset with him for not telling you about Marjorie. She turned him down multiple times to go out on a date. He was so embarrassed and that's why he decided not to come to the Church on Saturday."

"Wait…what do you mean about Marjorie? I didn't say anything about her. And he asked her out on a date?"

"Marjorie was the woman who mistook him as the robber in the parking lot at the Historical Society. He asked her to go out with him a few times in school, and then a couple more after graduation. So when she accused him of robbing her in the parking lot, it hit him a little harder than he let anyone believe, and just quietly moved away one night."

"If it wasn't Uncle Wiley, then why did she say that it was him?"

"Heck if I know. And the real person was never caught. When Wiley vanished, they swept the whole thing under the rug and forgot about it."

"But you would think that she'd have recognized him after they went to school together and all, right? Although, I just told him today that he probably wouldn't have recognized his own niece if I hadn't…" Cybil stopped herself as another lightbulb dinged in her mind. "Said who I was."

"Ah Cybil, are you okay?"

"Did they ever suspect anyone other than Uncle Wiley in the parking lot?"

"Officially, no."

"What about Marjorie's brother, Martin?"

"He did have a history with getting caught when he was

younger, but Marjorie said that he was on the other side of town when it occurred. Now that you mention it, though, I suppose the last time anyone saw him in the area was right around that robbery attempt. I don't recall hearing anything more about Martin until he showed up holding that knife at you the other day."

"Thanks for the info, Mom, but I have got to go now. Talk to you real soon." Cybil quickly ended the phone call in order to text Officer Noel.

We need to talk whenever you get a chance.

CHAPTER 53

The ringing of her phone brought her out of a deep sleep as her head was lying on top of her arms, resting on the desk in her bedroom. Various articles were strewn about the once clear surface, and were a product of her not being able to quiet her mind after the recent revelation. That was until she went cross-eyed and rested them for a minute, which turned into a nap of an hour or two. "Hello?"

"Cybil? Its Officer Noel. You said we needed to talk?"

"Yeah." She blinked her eyes awake and yawned into the crisp air, wondering what happened to the heater. "I think I have another suspect for you."

"Who?"

"Wiley Hansen. My uncle. Are you game for meeting up at Ralph's again?"

"Is he serving up his steaks tonight?"

"I might be able to put in a good word for you. Do we have a deal?"

"Sure. What time?"

CHAPTER 54

"Okay, you got me down here." Officer Noel announced as he strolled up to the table they sat at before. "You realize that I'm supposed to be watching…"

Cybil anticipated what he was going to say next and handed him the remote to the closest television. "The baseball channel is 245. Ralph and I have our own private war over who controls the stations in this place."

"I see." Noel pushed the buttons to the correct station, and then ordered one of the owner's delicious steaks. "So, why do you think that your uncle could be a suspect?"

"After having a chat with my mom, she told me something I never knew about her brother. So I did a little rereading over the research I conducted on Martin, and picked up on a singular article that talked about the robbery incident of Marjorie Stonewell." Cybil brought out her folder again, and passed him a specific piece of printed paper.

"This says it was written by the Birdman."

"Yeah, I got it off of his rather *interesting* website because I had too. I think the story was buried a bit because of who was involved, but my mom was the one who confirmed it really did happen. In his article, he refers to an incident on a hot evening in middle of summer when Marjorie Stonewell was robbed in the parking lot of the Historical Society. As you read a little further on, it also mentions the knife that was found at the scene, and that description is the same as the one Martin used to hold up another boy, from the same school, in *this* article." She handed him another paper, and he perused over both write-ups.

"Looks familiar."

"It was given to him by his grandfather. *And* was the same knife he used on me a few days ago."

"Alright. So what's the point?"

"For starters, I'm not saying that my Uncle Wiley robbed her back then. But he had asked her out many times on a date before, and she probably saw him as a nuisance. Say her brother needs money, and figures that in a darkened lot, she isn't going to recognize him if his face is covered and he disguises his voice. That is, until she sees the knife he drops in his escape and instantly knows who it was after he runs off. She was killing two birds with one stone; protect her brother and family from public shame, while getting rid of the problem in her life called Wiley."

"Why would Martin steal from his own sister?"

"To make sure that no one else gets hurt and she can't get into trouble for giving him more money if it was 'stolen' from her. At this point in time, he is practically disowned by his parents already for all the trouble he caused with the police and newspaper articles. I'm sure you know that their father was a prominent businessman and hated bad publicity."

"That's a pretty good theory, however, I'm not quite sure how this helps us in the current case."

"The phone number you claim Yasmin wrote goes to the prison that Martin was incarcerated at. Yas told me that

Marjorie forced her to write it down because she wanted to help him amend his ways for what happened to Ezra."

"We haven't found any evidence, or proof, that Marjorie stayed in contact with her brother within the last month or so."

"I think you do and just don't realize it. Use the note he left for me with the goldfish as a writing sample for the Christmas cards hanging in Marjorie's living room." Cybil offered it to him in a zippered plastic bag. "If I'm right, then it should match one of them dangling from the strings by those clothespins. A card was marked from Chicago right beside the one that came in from Normal, Wisconsin."

Officer Noel remained speechless for a brief moment, clearly surprised at her attention to detail. "You remember that from only being in her house once?"

"Well, a place called Normal isn't exactly, 'normal.'"

"Fair point. So you think that your uncle killed Marjorie because she rejected him one final time?"

"And he is blaming the perfect fall guy, Martin Stonewell, who is the reason for him leaving in the first place. My uncle used to work as the custodian at the museum, and currently works at a college where he has access to all the research books for a professor he helps. He certainly has the knowledge and is beyond capable of mixing together the deadly drink. And…I'm pretty sure I saw him lurking about when we discovered Marjorie's body."

"You have a pretty compelling theory, I'll give you that. Except for one thing; Martin confessed to being the shadowy figure you saw across the street that night. He said he had to work and by the time he made it there to meet up with Marjorie, she was already dead with you two ladies standing over her."

"Was he the reason she was heading over there? It didn't

make sense to me that her sisters were convinced she was walking to her car when the parking lot had plenty of spaces available."

Officer Noel nodded as his steak arrived. "He was supposed to have already been there, to have a more public reunion with his family right after the dinner ended. According to Martin, Marjorie believed it would go smoother in the presence of others because her relatives like to maintain their outward appearances. But he was late, and he figures that she went to find him when she died, planting her in the middle of the road."

"Could the poison have been a delayed reaction, which then occurred hours later?"

"We thought of that, and asked everyone if they had seen her earlier in the day. A few of the youth group boys said they spoke with her throughout the morning into the afternoon. Christine said that her family was at home until they left for the party, and her sisters swear they didn't see her until that evening. You know what happened with Yas's statement. Martin's whereabouts are accounted for by his manager, who has been briefed on the stealing situation at work that another employee tried to pin on the ex-con. Hence his whole desperate episode with you."

"Did you check to see if I was right on Mrs. Norman's phone call?"

"Her lawyer, of course, isn't talking, and we weren't able to reach her today. However, the other officers are going to try again tomorrow. Did you get a chance to talk with the person from our last conversation?"

"Not yet. But I plan on doing that tomorrow."

CHAPTER 55

"Good Morning!" Begonia Oilphant had the type of joyous expression that lit up a room even if it was midnight under a new moon. Her eyes shined, sparkling like the snow outside and like the makeup brushed over her cheeks. If Cybil had to wager a guess at who the woman's favorite character in the Nutcracker would be, she would have obviously picked the sugar plum fairy. "Are you here for your appointment?"

"I am. Cybil Lawson for 9:30?"

"Ahh! I was hoping you would show."

"Okay…"

"Well, lately people have been making appointments, but then canceling at the last minute or not showing up at all. Each one is different, and they are all new customers, so I'm starting to think that it's just some kids pulling pranks again." The woman tapped her fingers on the desktop's screen and asked for Cybil to wait in the seated area until being called. As she walked up to the magazine table, Begonia quickly dashed behind the separating wall to speak to the hairdressers when the sound of clicking high heels echoed throughout the building. Cybil only had enough time to skim read the headline of the local paper stating that "Police Have Suspect, Not Santa Claus," before Marta Stonewell turned the corner in a wicked pivot on two inch heels. It was said that she needed the extra height to make her feel tall, and considering she came up to Begonia's shoulders with the shoes she had on, it appeared to be true.

"Ms. Lawson, you are becoming quite a familiar face with my family. Are you looking to become one of us? Because if you are, I would highly discourage such a notion." Her square rimmed glasses sat high on the bridge of her nose, giving her an artisty-look with the attitude of a defensive tiger.

"I'm just looking to get a haircut, is all." Cybil did her best not to show her immediate intimidation of the woman with red nails, red lips, and wearing blood-red vengeance for perfume.

"I got her, Begonia. Give the next appointment to Laura." Marta motioned for Cybil to follow her to the farthest station from the front, which was also closer to the office for the owner's ease of convenience. "Have a seat."

A gulp nearly got stuck in Cybil's throat from the way she made the offer sound like "drop dead." She was pleasantly surprised, however, to find that the cushioned chair was actually more comfortable than others she had been in, but it wasn't as though she regularly scheduled her hair for a trim. The large mirror, in front, reflected the rest of the six stations in the beauty parlor. It was stylized in a more modern ambiance than what the exterior of the building had suggested, though traces of the original décor peeked out from behind the remodeling. "I'm not in the market for anything fancy, just a short trim to help with my splint ends please."

"But of course. You're main objective is ask me questions, isn't that right?" Marta pumped the chair up slightly, grabbed her comb and began to assess the condition of Cybil's hair. "I even hear that you might have the elusive cookie recipe card that everyone's after."

"I also heard the rumor."

"A rumor you started." Marta whispered in her customer's ear. "Either you are very clever, or very stupid. Only time will tell us which it is."

"Marjorie told my friend how good it was here, so that's why I came." Cybil's gut was beginning to churn with mixed feelings about this bad idea now. Out of the three sisters, Marjorie was looking like the nicest out of the bunch, and look what happened to her.

"My sister didn't come here that often. Only once or twice within the last year or so." The woman's own grey-tinged curls bounced around her face as she swayed from side to side, measuring out the distance of Cybil's hair. "Besides, if it were me, I wouldn't visit the family of the person my friend has been accused of murdering."

"But Yasmin isn't the killer!"

"What else would I expect you to believe?" Marta's lashes blinked, rubbing against the lens in her glasses. "She is your long-time best friend. It's only natural for you to defend someone who's childhood hero was a mouse in red shorts."

That did it! Not the cut to the enterprising mouse company, but to the fact that this hair salon owner knew something Yas kept mostly hidden from others. She wasn't the type of person to go blabbing everything to everyone, so how did Marta know? *It has to be all in that journal Officer Noel was talking about, and if that's the case, then what other dirty little secrets did this woman have?* "What else did you learn in Marjorie's journal?"

"I'm sure I don't know what you're referring too." She held a pair of scissors dangerously close to Cybil's right temple.

"Someone told me that Marjorie had a journal with all the secrets she unearthed on people. And I was also told that you have it."

"Let's say, hypothetically, that I supposedly did. What would you want it for?"

"To find out who really killed your sister."

"That wish list is probably a mile long as least, Honey."

"All the more reason to go over its pages and determine the people with the most amount of motive. I have some of the clues, but there's still more to decipher yet."

"That would be one word for it." Marta stopped snipping at Cybil's tired ends, sighing into the air as though a weight was falling from her shoulders. "Are you really into *just* saving your friend from going to jail?"

"Yes." She turned to look straight into the glasses of the hairdresser. "I'm not into smearing others with their past."

Marta stared at her for a long minute, trying to size up her words and if their meanings were genuine. A pause in her work soon transitioned to her taking a trip into the office and grabbing a hold of something on the thicker side in a brown covering. She asked for Cybil to join her, waiting for the young woman to pass through the threshold before closing the door to make sure no one else could see in. "What I'm about to show you, is not in my possession. Do you understand?"

Cybil nodded.

"I told the police that it was stolen from my place, but that I had copies made of some of the pages. It was enough for them to cast doubts on various people my sister had uncovered dirt on. But I wanted to reserve the right to solve a number of the pages myself, in case there was damaging words in our family's name."

"If I'm not crossing a line here, why would Marjorie have written poorly about her own family?"

"What I'm going to tell you next, is a secret that will die in your casket with you, ya hear?" The hairdresser's face bore a level of fear into Cybil that was hard to picture coming from the short woman. "And you are being told this because I don't think your friend did it either. But this goes no further."

Cybil nodded again, this time with added apprehension.

"Everyone in town believes that our great-great-grandmother came up with the recipe for those cookies they can't seem to get enough of. But during a family's Christmas party, one of our relatives had a few too many drinks and let it slip that she may not have been the one who came up with it. In fact, our great-great-grandmother may have stolen the recipe from another woman, after discovering her dead."

"WHAT?!"

"Many of our relatives thought that he was sputtering nonsense until our grandmother passed away and she left behind a number of letters in which the other woman and our ancestor corresponded back and forth on a cookie recipe that she was making. It was our ancestor who said she would be willing to taste test the cookies for her, and found her friend dead upon arriving. After realizing the cookies were delicious, and that her friend had no other family, she stole the recipe and claimed she created it."

"Is that why you stopped making them, and passed along the rumor that someone had broken in and stole the card years ago?" Cybil thought back to the conversation she overheard between Jeffrey and Mrs. Norman when she picked up the tomato cages.

"That was Marjorie's idea when she found the supposed letters while cleaning in the basement. She said that she burned the originals, and hid the information in secret code within this journal. But eleven months ago, when my sister started coming here after the other salon, who's name I dare not mention, messed up her coloring, we began talking more again. Then, one afternoon a few weeks ago, she gave me this."

The leather book was worn with age and the pages had begun yellowing from the oils of human skin, but the words were written as clear as day. Hundreds of notes on events, dates, and sources of information were compiled within the binding, giving a documented history of the town in a way Cybil never imagined. She flipped through fifteen pages until landing upon the first hidden message, consuming multiple sheets of paper.

Letters were bunched into groups of two, with the first of the pair always capitalized. However, they appeared to be separated into words of some kind as backward slashes marked the beginning and end of larger sections. Cybil had seen various forms of code originating back to the Greek and Roman era through online videos and television mini-series; though this was unlike anything she had come across before.

"I did a brief search on my computer, but it didn't come up with much; just a few sketchy website suggestions and images that shouldn't even be on a public setting." Marta excused herself for a moment as Begonia called her name from the front desk through a pager-like setup. Cybil hadn't even realized that the apron cape was still draped over her chest from getting her hair cut, ignoring it for the wonderful treasure trove the book contained. She was already getting a tingling sensation in her brain at what the code might be, but it would require more time to examine it and she didn't feel comfortable looking over its pages at the hair salon.

When Marta returned, she quickly scooped the journal into a plastic grocery bag and handed it to Cybil. "Pastor Lawrence is here and I need to speak with him on giving my sister a proper burial. Will you promise me to do your best to ensure its secrets are kept confidential?"

"I promise." Cybil tried to mask her enthusiasm at being handed what was most likely the clinching clue she had been searching for. "May I ask one question, though? Why trust me when we have barely spoken before?"

"My sister hugged you, Cybil. And for her many flaws and faults, she really did try to do her best in life. One time, she even told me that she thought of herself as the cause for everyone's pain within our family. Marjorie was a reserved person and for her to show that kind of care for you, well, that speaks volumes to me. If she trusted you, then so can I."

CHAPTER 56

The cold air blowing against the side of the Snip n' Sheer, was enough to freeze water instantly and that included Cybil's wet hair. She had been grateful for not asking Marta to style her head in anything other than a regular trim, since her appointment was cut short and there were more pressing matters to attend too. Clutching the book in her hands, Cybil made a beeline straight for her mother's car to stash the prized object under a blanket on the back seat, grateful for the loaner as Cynthia used her husband's truck for the day. *One would think that the police could have released Yas's car after discovering there was no evidence inside it.* As Cybil made her way to the driver's side of the vehicle, her eyes caught sight of a woman bundled up in a thick winter coat, rushing into the hair salon. *Mrs. Norman?*

On one side, she had an inclination to run back into the building to tell the woman that the police had more questions to ask of her, but that would not have been a good idea. Shaking the feeling away, Cybil jumped into the car and carefully pulled onto the road, heading for home. Today was her normally scheduled day off, but with her recent call offs into work, Matt had her phone ringing like a maraca. She muted the sound and continued to ignore him as the wind whipped about town in a mad frenzy, pushing people on the sidewalks and bouncing cars as though they were toys. The radio came in and out with the tides of the air, mocking the weatherman who was reporting tomorrow's forecast to be calmer and slightly warmer than it was currently.

With a quick pit stop for gas, Cybil was back on her way home once more and refused to stop anywhere until the book was safely tucked in a drawer at her house. What she wasn't expecting was to find Yasmin's car in the driveway and the interior light pouring out the windows. Excitement was building inside her chest as Cybil rushed up the stairs and unlocked the door to find her best friend fast asleep on the couch. Christmas ornaments were scattered about the floor like a mine field and she instantly shouted out, "You're home!"

"Ehh, what?" A dopy Yasmin raised her head just enough to see what the commotion was about. "Cybil?"

"No, it's a pink flamingo. Who else?" Cybil's smile beamed from ear to ear. "When did they release you?"

"About two hours ago, but your father posted bail last night, considering it's a weekend. I tried calling you, but it went straight to voicemail. Did you ignore it or something?"

"Oops! I bet I thought you were one of Matt's calls. He has been ringing my phone all morning."

"I think I know why." Her friend held up a bookmarked internet search on her phone, and watched Cybil's jaw fall open like a drawbridge. The headline was painfully clear and simple: Is Lawson Above the Law?

"Oh no." Her cheeks took on an embarrassing shade of pink as she took Yasmin's phone and scrolled through the article published late the previous evening. According to the journalist, the receptionist at the bed and breakfast remembered seeing the Detective's niece asking after Sister Bertrille, whose real identity was now being released as Suzie Gundersaw. "…spoke with us earlier today and can attest to the fact that Cybil Lawson may have been the last person to see Sister Bertrille alive before she died from being poisoned with an unknown substance. Considering she is the niece of our town's only qualified detective, could there be some blind eyes looking another way? In this article…" Cybil was so hot from anger, she nearly sweated underneath the coat she was about to shed. "Article my butt! This is someone's opinion!"

"Regardless, it has a lot of shares and you know the temperament of some people who only read the headlines."

"Yeah. Those are the people I try to avoid." Cybil placed the book on the oversized foot rest they also used as a part-time table for wrapping gifts and eating dinner. "With that aside, however, I do believe we are another step closer to finding out who helped Marjorie walk the staircase to heaven."

"You've been aching to tell me that bad line, haven't you?"

Cybil's face playfully showed that she was a little hurt by her friend's remark. "I thought it was at least a *little* bit funny." She sat her handbag down on the console table and filled in her sleepy roommate on everything her investigation had uncovered thus far. From meeting up with her uncle at the Historical Society, to talking over a steak with Officer Noel at Ralph's, and finally ending off with her latest encounter with Marta Stonewell, Yasmin blinked her eyes attempting to comprehend it all.

"Did you get any sleep while I was gone?"

"Apparently more than you have. I'm guessing it wasn't the most comfortable in a cell?"

"Try nerve-racking, fear pounding in my ears, and memory flashbacks I'd rather send to the bottom of the Mariana Trench."

"I'm truly sorry to hear that." Suddenly, the excitement Cybil was feeling seemed selfish and kind of silly. While it was neat to have the brown version of an infamous "little black book" in her possession, the gravity of the situation stung more than she anticipated. This wasn't some mystery where Nancy, Bess and George worked on a case file for her lawyer father. The stakes were real for the true person shielding themselves behind her roommate. "I'm guessing that's why there is this 'overload' on seasonal decorating?"

"I figured it would help me settle down, but I underestimated the coziness of our couch."

"Don't we all." She tried to sound more comforting. "Hey, do you want to help me decipher a secret code?"

"I guess?"

"Great. Flip open Marjorie's journal to the fifteenth page, and grab us both some paper and pens or pencils. I'll get the drinks and the music." Instrumental melodies of modern pop songs were more Cybil's speed when it came to tuning out the world and concentrating on studying, or trying to solve a coded message; while Yas normally preferred listening to the original pop songs themselves.

"How did you manage to get a hold of this?"

"Believe it or not, Marta actually handed it to me with the request that we seal our lips and do our best to ensure it doesn't reach the wrong people."

"Do the backslashes mark the end of one word and the beginning of another?"

"That's what I was thinking." Cybil selected a playlist from her phone, brought the flavored waters over, and sat down beside her friend. "But I also believe I know what kind of code she used. If I'm right, that is. Do you remember what Marjorie taught when she worked for the school district?"

Yasmin squinched her lips and stared above her head to think. "She was a substitute for a while, that much I recall. Ooh, ooh, wait. I remember she said something about handling the science department, with reading on occasion."

"Perfect! That's what I thought." Cybil could barely contain herself. "Do you see these groupings of two letters and how the first letter is also capitalized? I know the spaces are kind of hard to see, but they're there, and sometimes the letters are capitalized back to back." She pointed to a specific section in one of the lines.

C Ar P Al/Ca O B/Li H Ar

"I kind of see it. And there are pairs of letters that repeat, so that would suggest it's an actual message and not just ramblings."

"What if I showed them to you in a different light?" Cybil woke her laptop up from the side table and did an online search for a visual chart of the periodic table of elements. "Do they start looking more familiar now?"

Yasmin's eyes widened when she made the same connection running through her friend's brain. "They're elemental symbols! But what would the key be to poorly written chemical makeups that don't exist?"

"Each element has a corresponding number assigned to it on the table. And one of the oldest and most well-known ciphers is…"

"The Caesar Cipher!"

"Bingo! We just have to hope that she didn't shift the numbers in the alphabet, keeping with A being equivalent to one. And after a quick perusal, I don't recall seeing number twenty-seven, Cobalt, anywhere, so that's a good sign."

It didn't take Yasmin long to write the entire alphabet running down the left side of her paper, assigning them all numbers, and then jotting their corresponding element beside them. "Look, Cybil."

C Ar P Al/Ca O B/Li H Ar
FROM/THE/CAR

Both women stared at one another in joy. "It works!"

CHAPTER 57

While figuring out the code was relatively easy for Cybil, translating all of the encrypted entries was another thing entirely. Two hours later resulted in three flavored waters tossed in the recyclables, ten sugar cookies gone from the jar, and four printer papers filled with words detailing Marjorie's own life story. Between the both of them, they were able to have half of the entries sorted out, and took a breather to admire what all they accomplished.

"Just when you think you know a person…" Yasmin shook her head. "I would never have guessed that Marjorie killed someone in a vehicle accident. No one in town has any idea because it happened when visiting with relatives in another state. The woman was around Marjorie's age at the time, which should have been in her twenties by my calculations."

"Yeah, and her parents used Marta's college fund to pay for her sister's new ride." Cybil read off from her end. "As far as Marta was told. But instead, most of it went to pay off the lawyer bill when the other woman's family sued. Not to mention the hush money to keep it out of the press."

"No wonder her sisters didn't get along with her.

Between Melody's fall from the ladder and Marta's college dreams being crushed, Marjorie looked like the golden child they never would be."

"Maybe this is why Marjorie wanted Marta to have her journal. So she could finally understand what truly went on." Cybil finished the last sugar cookie on her plate. "Do you want to take a lunch break and then get back into it?"

"I'll stay here to work. Why don't you go down to the deli on Main and pick us up some sandwiches?"

"Deal."

The drive to the deli was both pleasant and electrifying at the same time. Cybil's brain was hyped up from the tales they had read in Marjorie's journal while the peaceful landscape brought a surreal calm to her nerves. She had to keep reminding herself to stay focused on the road instead of daydreaming of who the killer might be. Before she knew it, the deli was in view and Cybil used the parking garage around the back to park more safely.

Her feet were barely in the elevator when a female voice called out from behind. "Hold the door!"

Cybil placed her hand over the threshold so Mrs. Norman could slip inside, her chest heaving from running to make it in time. "Are you alright?"

"Yeah. Catching my breath, is all."

Cybil glanced over at her co-worker's mother, choosing to remain silent because Noel didn't tell her if they had a chance to speak with Mrs. Norman that day. No music was playing through the broken speakers, building the awkward feeling in Cybil's gut and increasing her internal pleas for them not to get stuck together between levels. A few shifts of her feet upon the smooth floor only added soft scuffs into the air and did little to ease the looming awkwardness.

"You work with my son, don't you?" Mrs. Norman

looked at her with a sense of puzzlement. At first, Cybil wasn't sure how to respond. It was possible that she had forgotten about the whole Christmas tree incident at the craft store, but then there was the other option that she was faking the innocent act.

"Westley. Yeah."

"I knew I recognized you from somewhere." She answered in an absentminded fashion. "I reckon you're the one whose been helping the Stonewells with the passing of Marjorie."

"That's one way of putting it."

"And have the police talked to you many times?"

"Well, they had a lot of questions, if that's what you mean."

"I suppose it is. But now they are trying to reach me again and I guess it has something to do with her death. Maybe for my alibi at the time."

"If you didn't lie, then there's nothing to worry about, right?"

"But that's just it. I did lie. There is no way I'm going to tell them the truth. I have a reputation to keep in this town. And that gossiper at the paper will eat me alive if she were to find out."

Mrs. Norman's eyes were glassed over in a daze, to the point where Cybil wondered if she was spaced out on drugs or was smoking marijuana. Smell was not the strongest of her five senses from both allergies and a previous sickness, so it would have to be really potent for Cybil to pick up on the aroma. "Mrs. Norman, are you really alright?"

Just then, the elevator dinged open much to the pleasant surprise of the woman standing beside Cybil. "Ah, my stop. Thanks for holding the door again."

She watched Westley's mother stroll out of the elevator and head toward the town square for the shopping district. Cybil immediately grabbed her phone and called her co-worker. When he didn't answer, she called the craft store and asked for him directly, ignoring Brandi's attempt at making small talk on where she has been the last few days. "Westley, I just had an odd conversation with your mother and…"

"Did she seem unfocused and staring into the distance?"

"Uh, yeah. That about sums it up."

"*Oh great.* Okay, where are you?"

"She just got off of the elevator in the town's parking garage and headed over to the shopping district."

"Alright. Stay with her and I'll be right over." Westley ended the call, leaving Cybil listening to dead air on her phone.

"Okay…what am I supposed to do? Become a stalker?" She shoved the cell phone into her jacket's pocket and dashed down the sidewalk after Mrs. Norman, who was already across the street and walking in the direction of the retro thrift store, Past Trends Refreshed. Waiting for the crosswalk light, which was taking forever to switch back, she contemplated taking her chances with the oncoming traffic, but that was bound to end in a mess. No sooner had the light turned, however, then Mrs. Norman entered the store and left Cybil's line of sight. "Okay, okay…" Her mutterings were half-hidden under her breath as she tried steadying herself. Westley never said what the problem was, nor how to handle a situation if it arose, so she was certainly entering some uncharted territory with a cloud of doubt resting overhead.

"Mrs. Norman, are you finding everything okay?" The owner of the shop asked her regular customer, who visited nearly every week almost like clockwork.

"I'm sorry, but I seem to have forgotten where the scarves are located?"

"At the back right corner, next to the door for the roof."

"Thank you." The woman blankly proceeded in the direction with Cybil now on her heels in panic. She flashed a smile at the woman behind the counter and purposefully changed to the other side of the clothing rack.

"Imagine bumping into you again, Mrs. Norman." Cybil grabbed her attention. "I mean, we hardly ever see one another and then twice in the same day. Maybe I should mark it in the calendar. Huh?"

"Perhaps. But then you might want to burn it before that memory becomes too painful to deal with." Her face was as stoic as before, though her choice of words was sounding more troublesome as she spoke. For the next ten minutes, Cybil did her best to keep the woman occupied on the weather, knitting, and anything else she could think of that had the least amount of chance striking a wrong cord. It wasn't easy to keep the conversation going when it was running into a circle, making her extremely grateful when she saw Westley hopping out of his car in front of the store. He didn't even take the time to attempt parallel parking, but rather settled for pulling the car as close to the sidewalk as he could before setting the blinking hazard lights on.

"Mom!" His voice seemed to break through her stupor a little bit. "What are you doing here?"

"My sister will need a new scarf to keep her warm this winter. It gets so cold up north."

"I know, I know. But, hey, listen. Why don't you come with me and we can drop by your favorite fast food spot, and then we can watch some of your favorite shows? Does that sound like fun?"

"But Lacy needs…"

"There is still time to get her one. And in fact, don't you remember? You picked up a scarf for her last week."

"I did?" Mrs. Norman followed her son out the door without any hassle or fuss, and he mouthed his thanks to Cybil as they passed by. The whole episode was like straight out of a warped television show and there was no telling what all was going through the poor woman's mind. At least she now knew why the police hadn't been able to talk with her.

Compared to what happened in Past Trends Refreshed, the rest of her small venture into town was pretty average. It wasn't until she was loading up the car, did her phone ring and the caller ID showed it to be Westley on the other end. "Hey, how is your mom doing?"

"Sleeping now. I gave her some sedative pills the doctor prescribed for her. Thanks for not letting her out of your sight back there. I owe you big time for that."

"No problem. Really." She smiled despite him not being able to see it. "What happened? If it's not too personal to ask. I just never saw anyone space out like that before."

"It hasn't happened since I was little. But it occurs when she is off her medication, like she was today. I asked her if she wanted me to stay…and I should have, even in the face of her trying to convince me that everything was alright."

"Westley, is there anything I can help with?"

"That's really kind of you, Cybil. However, I'm not sure what help I can even provide. To make a long story short, my mom thinks my dad walked out on her. Just took his clothes, hopped in his car, and left. I've talked with her about it, because he did leave a note and all, but…she was already in the process of getting a divorce started. Apparently our cousin from New York is helping her out."

"Westley, I'm so sorry to hear that."

"She won't listen to anyone right now, especially to me. I tried to tell her that dad went to hang out with his friends in North Carolina like he usually does. Every year he goes, and she has an argument with him over it. Truth is, she has been jealous of Dad's car for as long as I can remember. But lately, he has been taking more weekends down south and she has become suspicious. Nothing anyone says will change her mind. And when she gets all flustered, she doesn't always take her pills. She even paid a teen by the name of Rex to do a little spying for her with a camera."

"Would a visit from an old high school friend help? I can call my mom and see if she can spare a few minutes."

"That would be great, actually. It might be the remedy she needs. I mean, his note stated that he had to go this time, there was no other choice, and he has threatened to leave before, but that hasn't been for two years now. I really do think that he's coming back."

"I'll give my mom your number so you two can work out a time and we'll see if we can't crack through that thick head of her's, alright? In the meantime, I hope things get better for you and your parents." Cybil hung up and dialed her mother, who agreed without hesitation.

"Sure thing. Message me Westley's number and I'll call him straight away."

"Hey, Mom. There was something else I also wanted to ask. In Mrs. Norman's spaced-out-state, she kept mentioning a woman by the name of Lacy?"

"Lacy was her younger sister, who used to visit their cousin's family in New York. One time, she didn't make it back home and died in a car crash along a back road leading up to the state border line. There was an accident clogging up the main highway, so she opted to take the alternative route and…"

"Do you happen to know who the other woman was that killed her?"

"No one did. All I can tell you is that she was a minor and the records are sealed up. However…"

"What?"

"I always suspected that the family had some money, or were well-to-do, who were involved in the crash. Mrs. Norman's parents were on the poorer side and didn't have extra money to splurge on a college education, nor was a scholarship likely in her future. But after the funeral, they suddenly had the money to pay for their daughter's college degree and enough to buy themselves a much-needed new car."

Cybil wasn't sure what to say to that, except that her mother's suspicions sounded like they held a bit of merit to them. She said her farewells, and ended the call, plopping her phone on the front passenger's seat. The time was flying by so fast, that it hardly seemed to have already been two hours from whence she left the house. But as soon as she sat behind the wheel, Yasmin was texting her questions about where the food was and including a bunch of hungry emojis.

CHAPTER 58

Cybil walked into the house, arms filled with sandwiches, chips, and drinks, when she saw Yasmin nearly pop out of her skin. "What did you find?"

"A bombshell!"

"Well, don't bury the lead! Tell me!"

"According to the letters, Marjorie discovered amongst the family's heirlooms, the cookie recipe doesn't belong to their family!"

"You mean the rumors are true?!" Cybil raced over to see the translated entries her friend had been compiling together. "Holy cow! That's why Melody demanded that I return the items to her. They want to hide the evidence that will cause a big news scandal."

"Those cookies made their grandmother, and mother, the most famous bakers in town. I mean, to find out that those cookies are not rightfully theirs would smear their names in mud, and they couldn't legally sell the recipe either."

"Does she know who the real creator of the recipe was?"

"I'm just getting there. She conducted a search online, through an ancestry tree place, and believed she found a living relative. But I have to solve the next section to figure it out."

Cybil divided the food onto plates and grabbed the drinks she purchased. "You are not going to believe what just happened to me while I was in town." She filled her in on Mrs. Norman, what her mother said, and what Westley revealed.

"That explains why she was crying in the van and didn't tell anyone about her phone call. It was probably to her lawyer."

"Which also answers the question as to why her cousin said it would be in a conflict of interest if her husband was involved in the case against you." Cybil bit into the turkey, lettuce and tomato sandwich she always ordered on honey wheat bread. "And what if Marjorie was the one to kill her sister?"

"The car accident took place in New York, didn't it? Your mom said it happened on a road leading up to the state line."

"With the case zippered shut due to the person being underaged, however, it's going to be hard to find out unless she has it detailed in that journal." Cybil shook her head. "I'm still more concerned on those letters that Marjorie supposedly burned. They're a direct connection to their family's secret, and could be the motive behind her death. I mean, what if she made contact with the living relative, and then they realized how much that recipe was worth? Melody could certainly use that money for herself."

"Okay, let's go over what we know and see how many suspects we have so far." Yas suggested as she chewed on her ham and swiss sandwich with a toasted pretzel bun. "Do you want us to construct a murder board? Like they do on TV?"

"No. Are you kidding? Someone is libel to see it while

passing one of these windows and we don't need to put more of a target on our backs then we already are. Besides, if we write it down in a notebook, it is a lot easier to conceal if the police decide to make another unannounced visit." Cybil pulled out her paper and pen, and began writing people's names down the left-hand side of an unused paper.

"You really included your parents?" Yas gave her the eye.

"Hey, I'm just jotting everyone down at this point. Then I will go into eliminating those who don't have any motive."

"Alright, so…obviously Mr. Jeffrey had motive with Marjorie using his plans for the landscaping and then stopping him from making a quick buck off the church. And then there's the fact that he wanted to win so his cousin would endorse his recipe to her boss at the company."

"A company she no longer worked for." Cybil reminded. "Though we don't know if Jeffrey knew that or if she was trying to double-cross him."

"Tara certainly wanted Marjorie's job, and her mother even tried to use a little financial leverage to pressure the change to happen. If I remember correctly, there was some talk that they were the ones attempting to force her out of the job. What if Tara decided that she was too untouchable and took matters into her own hands? She is so used to getting whatever she wants, maybe it went all the way to her brain?" Yas suggested.

"And I also noticed there being clear alcohol bottles in the back of Tara's minivan."

"Could your Uncle Wiley be capable of murdering her? I know you like him and all, but some people just snap when they get rejected by the one they care about. He might have even asked her out again the night he showed up late to his homecoming dinner at your parents' house. But she did accuse him of stealing from her in the parking lot all those years ago, and if she rejected him *again*...then that could have been the breaking point for him."

"Honestly, I'm not sure. But let's not forget about Christine, Rex and Raven. Not to mention Melody, her husband, and Marta."

"There are a lot of hostilities swirling around in that hornet's nest. You might as well put double circles around both of Marjorie's sisters, especially after you said that Marta has been running late to practice for the past two times. When do they normally meet up to talk about Shakespeare?"

"It's floats around, per the flyer outside the bulletin board of the Historical Society. But one of their meetings fell on the night of the dinner, so that means that Marta had left the party at some point and then returned, if she was late and did show up that evening like Ms. Drake claims." Cybil's blank page was filling up fast.

"And don't forget that Mrs. Norman also applied for the choir director position at the same time as I did. With her life so upside down, and her med use in question, she might have committed the crime and not remember it. Between Mr. Jeffrey and herself, they could be working together."

Cybil looked over at her friend in wonder. "What about Rodger? Do you believe he has a motive? Tara could have him wrapped around her little finger yet. And Sylvia has a very weak reason, but it's still there nonetheless."

"Have you taken anyone off the list?" Yas asked, as both women stared over the web of scribbles and notes with arrows pointing to other connections.

"Not really." *But it wouldn't be much of a mystery if we did, huh?* Cybil thought to herself, pondering what they might be missing. "Yas, call Rodger and ask him for a recommendation for a good mechanic."

Her roommate's eyes lit up in worry. "Is there something wrong with my car?"

"No, your car is perfectly fine. But Tara said that his van was in the shop, and I'm curious to find out whether my one theory is true or not."

Yasmin picked up her cell and asked Rodger, who was more than willing to point them in the direction of his buddy's garage, located a mile away from the Historical Society.

Cybil smiled from ear to ear. "Perfect. Now we need to have a little chat with an old English teacher and her brother."

CHAPTER 59

Rather than driving back to the building, and risk getting caught by Ms. Drake's brother, Cybil decided to take a different approach. She dialed the number listed on their website and waited for the older woman to pick up the phone.

"Thank you for calling the Robbyr's Cove Historical Society. How may I help you?"

"Ms. Drake. It's so good to talk with you again. This is Cybil Lawson." She added a little dose of charm to her words.

"Ah, Ms. Lawson. Nice to hear from you. Did your uncle leave town already? A question has come up in regards to our heating system, and I would like to ask him about it before he heads home."

"No, he didn't leave yet. He's staying with my parents until the day after Christmas. I can tell him that you asked and send him on over to take a look."

"Marvelous. Is there anything I can do for you today?"

"I was wondering if you could answer a question for me."

"I'll do my best."

"The other day, when you gave my uncle and myself a preview of the upcoming exhibit, I was curious as to who the donor was."

"They wish to remain anonymous and we are obliged to honor their desires."

"Ms. Drake, it was Marjorie Stonewell, wasn't it?"

"I don't believe so." Her voice was beginning to sound unsure.

"Both my uncle and I saw the name Chester Stonewell on a piece of paper among the boxes."

"She may have donated the items. But it was her wish to…"

"At what part is stealing items from a dead woman's house considered donating?" Cybil surprised even herself for going that direct with her question.

"I'm afraid I have to go now. I just heard someone walk through the door and…"

"If you hang up on me now, I'll call the cops." She listened for a heartbeat, hoping that the woman wasn't going to see if Cybil was bluffing.

"What do you want?" Ms. Drake's voice sighed from her end of the line.

"We know you took Rodger Freedmon's van from his buddy's garage down the road, and used it to take all of those boxes from Marjorie's basement the night she died. Witnesses place his van in her driveway, but it couldn't have been Rodger, who was spying at the Christmas Dinner in his other vehicle. Tara even confirmed that his van was in the shop." Cybil could hear the woman's breathing suddenly go into panic mode. "It was you and your brother, wasn't it?"

"She was going to donate the items anyway. And when we heard she died, well, my brother and I know how wicked that family can be. We used to be their neighbors for a year.

So we figured it was now or never, before the will was discovered and the division of her assets went to those greedy people." Ms. Drake paused to wipe her forehead. "Marjorie was in talks with us over donating the entire collection she had, after she thoroughly checked it for any more letters of some kind."

"Did she find any?"

"Couldn't say. Marjorie told us that she would call when she was ready to hand the boxes over, but never did."

"Ms. Drake, you are going to have to search through the items and see if there are any letters sent between her great-great-grandmother and a friend over anything to deal with cooking or baking. It could be part of the reason she was murdered."

"Oh dear, oh dear. You're not going to turn us in, are you? We just want to help preserve history and this museum is overdue for a new exhibit. The collection we have hasn't had an addition in sooo long, and attendance has been wavering because of it. My brother and I meant no harm to anyone."

"That's up to you, on whether you call the police or not. Right now, I have something else to ask you. When did you arrive at the house that night?"

"I think around eleven, or about ten minutes past. There were no lights on inside, except for a night light in the kitchen as we passed it in search for the entrance to the basement." Ms. Drake hastily answered. "We didn't touch anything else in the house. Just the items that were marked to be donated in black marker on the side."

"How did you know that Marjorie died in the first place?"

"We…that is to say…my brother and I were on our way home, when the police sirens and flashing lights caught our attention. That's when Ed Blankenship, the guy with his dog and the chickens, told us who it was and my brother hatched up this scheme. He thought we should make the most of the opportunity by getting there before the cops arrived." She paused for a moment. "Having seen Rodger's van at the garage, we sneaked up and found the doors unlocked and the key behind the visor above the driver's side. We were originally going to bust our way in, but I tried a window to no avail and then that's when I suggested that we try the keys. Out of dumb luck, one of them opened her front door. I swear, that's the truth of it."

"Do you believe her?" Yasmin asked, as she went about translating another page of encoded text, whilst Cybil finished up on the phone and stared at the refrigerator in thought.

"Yeah, I do."

"I wonder if she will call the police."

Cybil shrugged. "Doesn't really matter if she does or not. I talked with Officer Noel about their possible involvement, and I wouldn't be surprised if they are confirming the same details right about now. Once Rodger confirmed the garage his van was at, it doesn't take a genius to draw the lines between those dots."

"Better not say that to your uncle." Yas chuckled as she rubbed her eyes. "I might be going blind from all of this detecting work. Want to take a break by watching a Christmas movie for a little bit, and then we can have it play in the background while we work?"

"As long as I get to make the drinks."

CHAPTER 60

The ending credits began scrolling up from the bottom of the flat screen as Yasmin stuffed her face full of more popcorn. For the past twenty minutes, the wind beat the sides of the house like a baseball bat and their eerie howls echoed through the glass windows fogged from the falling temperatures. Cybil yawned into the palm of her hand and finished off the last of her chocolate covered pretzels. Above the television, sat the analog clock, who's hands informed the two women that it was well past seven o'clock in the evening and they had only managed to decode an additional page.

"My turn to pick." Cybil snatched the remote from her friend's hand and switched to a different streaming service for a claymation classic from the *Rankin and Bass* company. "But first, I'm going to the bathroom."

She shed her blanket layers and walked across the cold floorboards in her soft slippers, whispering thanks to her mother for gifting them to her as a birthday present. The plushy insides weren't as hot like sherpa-lined ones, but provided a nice bit of warmth for her toes. Everything seemed to be looking a bit brighter in the last few hours, until the sound of shattering glass broke into her thoughts.

Cybil raced out of the bathroom to find Yasmin huddled behind the kitchen counter and telling the 9-1-1 operator about what she saw. Her roommate's eyes were frantic with worry as she pointed to the brick in the middle of the living room floor. Shards of glass and clay debris were scattered next to the Christmas tree to the right of the television. At first, Cybil presumed that an ornament was the cause for all the damage littering the small rug. But when she followed the path of the brick back to the smashed window, she couldn't hold back the anger bubbling inside. It was the remains of her sculptured head from a high school project lying on the ground, with the nose to the neck still standing on the table like an Egyptian artifact. "THAT'S IT! SOMEONE IS GOING TO PAY FOR THAT! I'LL KILL THEM MYSELF!"

"What? Oh, that's the sound of my roommate wanting to curse the sky for a broken art project. No, no. We aren't hurt in anyway. Shaken to the core, maybe, but physically intact." Yasmin cupped her hand over the end of the phone, to continue talking with the operator, when the sound of a car revving its engine roared to life and Cybil raced to the front door. With the darkened street, however, no license plate number could be seen, nor could any identifying features other than it was a darkened four door sedan.

"They got away!" Cybil's hand slammed the door shut out of frustration and immediately picked up her phone to call her dad.

"Uh, I'm already on the phone with 9-1-1." Yas reminded. "Who are you calling?"

"Someone who can help us barricade that window."

CHAPTER 61

"Do you have any kind of security cameras?" The police officer asked Yasmin as he jotted down a note in the pad he was holding.

"Only one for the back yard, but it was fried during the last power outage. We were meaning to update it in the spring…just didn't get around to it this year."

"And neither of you saw the person's face or the car they were driving?"

Again, Yas stammered the same response of "no," and glanced over at Cybil helping her father with the window.

David Lawson hammered a few nails through the plywood and into the wooden window frame still holding onto six large shards of glass. There was definitely evidence of past spray-painted projects outlined on the wood he had dug out from the garage, but that was nothing compared to the large spider web dangling from the top corner. He asked his daughter for the vacuum cleaner to suck it up, and was secretly grateful that his wife wasn't there to witness it. "Thanks Kiddo. Now, do you have your bags prepped and ready to go?"

"Not yet." Cybil wasn't sure she agreed with her father's

suggestion of spending the night at her parent's house. While it was quite unsettling to have the window shattered, and her art project brushed into a trash heap on the floor, there were worse things that could have happened. Besides, if someone was truly after them, wouldn't it be better to safeguard the place by staying put instead of putting her parents in danger? And there was no reason for the vandals to risk returning on the same night. *Don't be such a hard head, girl. Listen to your dad and go stuff a bag with some clothes.*

"I realize you don't want to seem afraid by whoever did this, Cybil. Though that is highly commendable, it would be a lot safer at our house for the time being." David motioned to both women experiencing the last minutes of shock on their faces. "And we can set up the couch bed in the living room."

"What are we going to tell Mom?" Cybil questioned. "I don't want to hear her give me a lecture or anything tonight."

"That's inevitable with her." He cast her a caring smile. "You know she will find out sooner or later, so it's best to bite the bullet, as it were, and deal with it."

Cybil felt the warmth of her father's encouraging hand on her shoulder, and couldn't help but release a small grin in turn. She reluctantly made her way back to her bedroom, to gather her things, just as Yasmin knocked on her door. The noise scared her already frayed nerves, causing Cybil to jump from the sound.

"Sorry. Didn't mean to startle you. The officer would like a word."

"Okay. Be out in a minute." Clutching her warmest sweater between her hands, the softness of the fabric acted like a comforting blanket to the confused emotions rolling around her mind. She should be scared more than anything else, but her thoughts were too relentless for that. They churned away in the forefront of her head with possible motives as to why someone would do such a thing. It could have been vandals, or juvenile delinquents…plain and simple. But after everything going on as of late, the window smashing was more likely part of Marjorie's death.

"Cybil?" Yasmin brought her back to the present. "Are you alright?"

"Yeah, I'm fine. Been thinking too much today." She gave her friend a quick smile. "My brain's mush at the moment."

"Maybe this will cheer you up." Yas brought in a small cardboard box with a return address from Montana printed on the label. "Appears that the Ghost of Christmas Past has a small present for you. I forgot about it until I looked over at the console table just a moment ago."

Cybil happily tore into the package and unfolded a short note inside a handmade Christmas card from their old college classmate. She smiled at the sight of a matching scrunchie to the one she commented on during their backstage tour. "Get a load of this! It has a hidden zipper that you use to store stuff inside."

"Neat." Yas smiled, and then walked away to give her friend some space to pack.

Cybil's duffel was filled in three minutes flat, before she met up with the officer checking in with dispatch on his radio. After a brief moment of chatter, he spoke to her with a serious level of concern in his voice. "I can't get ahold of either Detective Lawson or Officer Noel right now, so I can either place an officer outside, or I would highly suggest that you two stay somewhere else for the night."

"My father is going to put us up." Cybil pointed in his direction. "But I do thank you for the offer of having someone stand guard."

"Just doing my job." He snapped his notebook shut and placed it in his pants pocket. "Your roommate didn't have any idea as to why someone would throw a brick at the two of you. Do you have a guess? Is there anyone you aggravated lately? A neighbor or a disgruntled co-worker?"

Cybil caught herself in time to keep the laughter from escaping. *Who hasn't been irritated with me lately?* "No, haven't the foggiest clue."

"Okay." The officer didn't seem convinced, but he decided to drop the subject. Detective Lawson warned him that she was a stubborn one and it was futile to push back. Elsewise, the wall of silence would just become stronger.

"I have my things. Ready to go?" Yasmin collected Marjorie's journal from a drawer in the kitchen, where she stashed it whilst hiding from the flying brick. She zipped up the main section of her backpack as a thought suddenly occurred to her and she quickly dashed back into her bedroom. "Almost forgot my phone charger."

Her friend's head shook with a classic "good grief" look painted across her face. Yasmin's trademark was leaving the charging cord behind wherever she went. In fact, the most repetitive ding on her credit card was a replacement cord practically every month like clockwork. There was a running joke that a secret grave was filled with her forgotten ones, tangled in a big ball six-foot deep.

"I thought she was getting better?" David tapped on his daughter's shoulder and nodded to the painting resting on the space between the two bedrooms. It was the orange and blue landscape Betsy so carefully had framed. "Nice wintry scene. Is it one of yours?"

"No. It actually belonged to Marjorie Stonewell. But Raven was the one who painted it." Cybil gazed upon the artwork she had been meaning to give to the church. "I was going to contact Pastor Lawrence about giving it to the church with the rest of her stuff."

"What are you talking about?"

"That's who Marjorie left her earthly things too. The church gets everything."

"Huh. I never thought she would actually do that."

"Why not? She loved her job and would have done anything for Pastor Lawrence and the church."

"No. What I mean is…I had lunch with Rick Isles last month, and Marjorie saw us chatting in the café. She was on her way out, but stopped by our table to ask Rick for a later appointment due to an issue that popped up. Since Rick mainly does wills, I asked if she was going to leave her books to the small library in the community space at the church. That's when Marjorie told me, and I quote, 'I hope what I do will be for the good.'"

"Oddly worded."

"That's what I said to Rick."

"Okay. This time, I know I'm ready to go." Yasmin shut the door to her room with the backpack bouncing behind her shoulders. By where they were all standing, she ended up in front of the painting right before the lights in the canvas print simultaneously turned on.

Cybil's eyes squinted at the time being displayed across her phone's screen. "Ah, Yas. Weren't those lights supposed to go on a while back?"

"Yeah. I think there might be something broken with the timer mechanism. I have to check it out."

It was in that exact moment, that Cybil knew who the killer was. *Why was I so blinded? It was right there in front of my nose this whole time.* Her eyes lit up brighter than the sun on a clear morning rise, and she frantically typed away at her phone to connect one last dot out of alignment.

"Ah, Cybil?" Yas asked.

"I know who it is!" She raced outside to find the officer walking to his vehicle, and waved at him to grab his attention.

"Is something wrong?"

"I need to speak with Officer Noel immediately."

"I already told you that both he and Detective Lawson are unreachable at the moment."

Suddenly, the sound of a car pulling into the end of their drive caught both of their attentions, and Cybil wasn't surprised to find Marta Stonewell jumping down from the driver's side.

"Are you alright?" The hair salon owner seemed to be genuinely concerned.

"We're fine, but thanks for checking." Cybil swiftly changed her focus back onto the cop standing next to her. "Then get them on their cell phones."

"Ms. Lawson, I am not allowed to discuss with you…"

"Did they finally locate the car thief or something?" Her eyebrows rose with emphasis. "I'm not trying to be rude, it's imperative I speak with one of them now!"

"I'm not at liberty to say what they are doing, but if there is anything I can do…"

"Fine." Cybil opened her phone's lock screen and tapped on Officer Noel's number to place a call.

"What makes you think you will be able to…"

"Cybil, is everything alright?" Noel's voice came through loud and clear.

"It soon will be. Because I think I know who the killer is and we don't have a second to lose."

CHAPTER 62

"We're one step ahead of you this time, Cybil. We just arrested Jeffrey for the murder of his cousin, and we are fairly confident that he also did in Marjorie Stonewell."

Cybil felt the air being knocked from her lungs. "What?"

"Yep. That's why I couldn't check in when your emergency call was placed. Been staking out his house for a while and when he returned home, we found a couple of rosary beads rolling around in his car's cup holder. He might have even been the one who smashed your window, given the time he arrived back."

"I didn't know the fake nun's rosary beads were missing."

"We don't reveal all our secrets to the media, for obvious reasons."

"That's not exactly how I pictured it going down, but okay." She half spoke to herself and half to Officer Noel. "But you don't have Marjorie's killer."

A slight hesitation could be heard from the officer. "Come again?"

"Look, we're losing valuable time. If you could send some men over to Christine's house, I think we will be able to wrap everything up. And don't forget to check in on Melody's as well." Cybil waited for Noel's response before pressing the red button to end their conversation. "We have to get to Christine's as fast as possible." She shouted back at the front porch, where her confused father and roommate were locking up the house.

"Hop in the truck. I'm driving." David clicked on his key fob, unlocking the doors so as the other two could climb in from the cold.

"You should come with us, Marta." Cybil looked over at the weary hairdresser.

"Why…why are you going to Christine's?" She stammered her words with uncertainty, scared of what Cybil learned from the journal already.

"To eliminate where she isn't. Because you and I both know where she'll be."

Marta shared a look with Cybil, and once an unspoken understanding passed between them, the older woman silently nodded her head in agreement. She could tell the artist had cracked the code much faster than she had anticipated, and the extra time she thought she had, was no more than a mere illusion. There was no more sand in the hourglass and the time had come to fess up. But, the idea of having an outsider of the family know what the pages said about her specifically, felt more intrusive than she thought it would have. "I didn't think you would have figured it out so soon. I underestimated you."

"You can follow us in your car, or jump in the back seat with Yasmin. It's your choice."

"I'll follow the truck." Marta started up her vehicle and pulled out of the way for Cybil's father to drive onto the main road. Within minutes, the heater in the pick-up was roasting their feet while they made great time along the barren streets of town.

"You're going to have to give me directions on getting there." Cybil's father sped up by pressing further down on the gas pedal.

"Make a left up here." Yasmin instructed from the back bench seat. "Then make a right two intersections after this one." She looked through the truck's windows at the empty sidewalks and closed stores, looking more deserted than filled with holiday cheer. "Should have asked that officer back there for a police escort."

"We'll be fine." Cybil pulled out her phone and scrolled through her contacts in search of a name she ended up not having. "Great." She sarcastically remarked aloud. "I thought for sure I had Pastor Lawrence's number."

"What do you want to call him for?" Her father asked, at the same moment cop lights illuminated the dark and the siren wailed out for all to hear. "You want to dial Officer Noel?" He whispered out the corner of his mouth.

It didn't take long for the cop to reach the driver's side door and knock on the window for Mr. Lawson to put it down. Once the man's face could be clearly seen without snow slush in the way, all three of them were relieved to see the officer who responded to their emergency call earlier.

David's face cracked into a sheepish smile. "Did I do something wrong?"

"Normally, yes. Going nearly twenty over the speed limit in inclement weather conditions is pretty hazardous. But that's not why I stopped you. I have been instructed to accompany you to the Heighner house. If you would allow me to return to my vehicle, I'll take the lead."

"Certainly." David turned to see his daughter and Yasmin staring at him with shocked faces. "What? An older guy isn't allowed to get excited to catch the bad guy? Not as though I know who he or she is, but it's still fun none-theless."

"And you complain about my heavy foot on the gas?"

"This is under different circumstances."

"Sure thing, Dad." Cybil mustered all she could to keep her inner laughter to herself. It was amusing to see her father finding all of this rather enjoyable, especially after he was the one worried about her safety for the night.

As the police car pulled ahead of the pickup, Mr. Lawson shifted his vehicle into gear and followed him down the darkened street like a sorry-looking parade. Fifteen min-utes later, Cybil barely managed to stay in her seat when they noticed Christine's vehicle missing from the drive-way of the two-story house. Officer Noel was standing at the front porch with another policeman when her father stopped the truck by the sidewalk.

"Cybil!" Yas called from the back bench, trying to untangle herself from a twisted seat belt. Her foot stepped on the slippery concrete just as Cybil made it up the three steps to join the others at the front door.

"They aren't here. We've knocked three times and there isn't a light on in any of the rooms." Officer Noel informed her.

"Have you called Melody?"

"I had two men on their way over right after you called. They phoned in just as you got out of the vehicle. Appar-ently, she was already dressed in her winter garb and ready to leave with her husband when they answered the door. He shut her down trying to spout off a fabricated excuse and informed us that one of their relatives was missing." Noel shook his head. "You're certain of this?"

"More so than ever. If there is no one here, then that means my hunch is right, and we need to get to Marjorie's house as quick as possible."

"Wait, hold on there." Noel caught Cybil by the arm of her winter coat. "Just what do you plan on doing once *we* get there? Do I really have to remind you that this isn't your job?"

"Consider myself warned." Cybil halted at the topmost step, forcing herself to turn back around and apologized for her attitude. "I'm sorry. You're right. But I think she is going to respond to me better than she will with you."

"Like I said on the phone with you, Cybil, Jeffrey is the prime suspect for both murders. So, I'm not quite sure what you're driving at." He pointed a cautionary finger in her direction. "You better have some convincing evidence as to why we're doing this. Elsewise, it's not just my butt that's going to be in trouble."

"Trust me. Jeffrey doesn't fit when you realize that the motive wasn't about gaining something. It was about losing everything."

CHAPTER 63

Marjorie's house appeared deserted from the outside. There wasn't a soul around, and the ground was undisturbed from the front. Cybil allowed a small seed of doubt to plant itself in her mind. All of the neighboring houses were quiet as though nothing was out of the ordinary, adding to the sinking suspicion that she was actually wrong about where the murderer would be. Her thoughts looped in an endless cycle within her head, trying to convince herself that she was indeed right.

"Who are we looking for, Cybil?" Yas quietly asked.

She didn't respond, still scanning the darkened landscape with her eyes and peering into the windows of the building. It wasn't until she saw a small flicker of a flashlight, coming from the living room area that she suddenly spoke up. "There!"

Her father pulled the truck up the closest he possibly could to the door and watched the others file in behind him, by looking at his side mirrors. "Be careful!" David called after his daughter, already plowing her way up to the porch with Yas in pursuit. Officer Noel and Marta were soon to follow as they all waited for the key to unlock the house.

"My sister gave me a copy." Marta flipped it out from a key holder on a split ring and ushered the rest of them in. "RAVEN?!"

Loud footsteps could be heard descending the stairs into the basement, causing them all to charge down with Officer Noel at the helm. Cybil's heart was pounding from the excitement and dread of what was about to happen, and the tense nature of it all only increased when they reached the bottom.

What was left of the boxes Ms. Drake and her brother had taken, were soaked in a clear alcohol that not only continued onto the floor, but extended to the various curtains draped over the sub-ground windows and skeletal furniture. In the teenager's left hand, was a half-filled glass bottle with a rag shoved in as a wick, and she turned around to face them with a lighter flicked on in the other hand, primed to set the whole level ablaze.

"Whoa, Raven." Officer Noel held his own hands out in surrender, taking up the role of negotiator on the spot. "You don't want to take us all down, do you?"

"You weren't supposed to be here!" Raven grunted through clenched teeth. "None of you were. The house just needed to be burned. That's all."

"And why should the house be burned, Raven?"

"To eliminate the problem."

"Help me to understand your problem. And then maybe we can go upstairs to find a different solution."

"No!" She brought the lighter closer to the towel in a threatening warning. "Now, get back. Get back! I don't want to hurt you, but I will if I have to."

"And what about you, Raven?"

"Like you care. But I suppose you will try to convince me otherwise. But I'm done believing in all of that garbage."

Raven squinted her eyes at them. "If you move any closer…"

"You can still save him." Cybil interjected over the officer's shoulder. "Raven, you can still save your brother. He doesn't have to go down with you for Marjorie's death."

"I don't know what you're talking about."

"But you do." Cybil sidestepped Officer Noel to stand right beside him. "It started to click into place for me, when your great-uncle held me at knife point. I'm just sorry it took so long for me to see it."

"What great-uncle?"

"Martin Stonewell, remember? After he was incarcerated, the rest of the family dropped all contact with him. All except for Marjorie that is. She wrote to her brother every week, and they talked back and forth about a variety of things. One of them being about you." She paused to see the young girl's reaction, and managed to catch a note of curiosity in her eyes. "When his parole came around, Marjorie encouraged him to return to Robbyr's Cove, with the hope that the family could be reunited once again. She didn't see herself as the cause of everyone's pain exactly, but that of her brother's arrest. His conviction divided the family more than most realize. But Martin was unsure about how Melody and Marta would react to seeing him after fifteen years."

"And that has to do with Rex and me, how?"

"Marjorie wrote to her brother that you might help her reintroduce him to the others. Afraid to say hi to her, Martin followed his sister from a distance and saw Marjorie give *me* a hug. He knew his sister didn't do that for just anyone, and considering we have the same hair color and a shared interest in art, he mistook me for you."

"I don't understand. First, you accuse me of killing my great-aunt, and now, you are telling me a tale of mistaken identity."

Undeterred, Cybil continued on. "He felt sorry for you, and wanted to give you a meaningful gift. So, thinking I was you, he left a gold fish on my front porch, along with a handwritten note." Her hands brought a picture of the letter up on her phone to read from. "I am sorry that this comes late to you, as I would have preferred dropping this little guy off yesterday. However, my job did not allow me to do as such, though I do not think that Norris is worse for wear. I remember how Marjorie said you had a fondness for goldfish, as they are the only pets your mother allows you to have. My hope is for him to bring you some level of comfort during this difficult time in your life. Perhaps at some point, I will have the courage for us to meet face to face, but until that time, just know that there is a guardian angel watching over you."

"NO!" Raven shouted out, her eyes on the verge of tears gushing from her lashes. "She didn't care about me, or anyone else in this so-called family!"

"That's not true, Raven. Not true at all." Cybil went to step toward the young girl, now becoming panicked and schized. "She loved you very much."

"Yeah, right. She had a funny way of showing it then."

"She did to, love you Raven." Marta walked out from the darkened stairs, startling her great-niece. "I was the one who was wrong."

"No. You told me that she was only good at doing one thing. Hurting others, just like what she did to you and Great-Grandma Melody."

"Oh, my dear child, I am so very sorry for what I have done." Sorrow and guilt plagued the older woman's face. "I thought Marjorie was only visiting me more often to dig up more dirt on my life, just as she had done before. I blamed her for the death of my husband, and for what our parents did by stealing my future in order to pay for her new car. And when she handed that journal to me, I thought it was just another way of her mocking me that she thought I couldn't decipher it; even though she simply asked for me to keep it safe for her. Like a true sister would have done. But I was so bent on…that is when I decided to destroy the one thing she deeply cared about; your friendship."

The teen shook her head, determined not to listen any longer. "I talked to her, and asked about the cookie recipe, just like you said. You know what she told me? Huh? You know what she said to my face? Marjorie told me that none of us deserved that recipe. That she already had it being taken care of and that none of us were going to see it ever again." Raven was practically sobbing at this rate, still holding the lighter frightfully close to the alcohol-stained goods. "After all that we had been through, and the fact that I looked up to her closer than I was to my own mother. Closer than I had been to anyone except for Rex. But no, she still saw me as only an adopted member of the family. And I was never going to be anything more."

"Raven, listen to me. I knew about your trust issues, and used them to my advantage. Marjorie had nothing to do with any of that." Marta continued.

"Then why did she say what she did, huh? I hadn't had it all worked out, but when that nun showed up and said she was the winner with the recipe that no one else was good enough to make, then I snapped into action."

"I'm sorry, Raven. That can't be right." Cybil cut back into the conversation. "Because you already had it planned to happen on the night of the dinner. Your scrunchie, the one that you were wearing with the dress at the church? You had your hair up in a bun before Marjorie died, and then outside, your hair was down and it was missing." She held up the one her friend had mailed her for Christmas. "It's because you had a small bottle of the wood alcohol hidden in the zippered pouch. After lacing one of Yas's drinks, you let your great aunt die in the middle of the street, probably knowing full well what she intended on doing with her brother that evening. Rex laid in wait in his car, with sleigh-like tracks on the back of it, like many do in the wintertime. All you had to do was disguise what happened, by using an old bootlegger's trick called cow shoes. Or in this case, reindeer shoes."

"What better way to get revenge, then to mock the person in death?" Raven sneered. "I could have used the money from the sale of that recipe to go to art school. You know that my own mother won't help me? It was my mistake for going to ask the one person I actually trusted."

"Because the cookie recipe was not hers to give." Cybil announced. "Marjorie kept a journal, and made sure to write certain details in code, just in case it got into the wrong hands. In one of her entries, she documented learning about the original creator of the cookie recipe, and discovered the letters that her great-great-grandmother had written to a friend. She later learned that it was stolen after the friend died and there were no apparent relatives to lay claim. If Marjorie would have sold the recipe, her plan was to donate all the profits to the church. That way, everyone could taste the wonderful cookies the woman had created, and it was a way of repenting for her ancestor's sin."

"Why didn't she just tell me…." Raven stood there like a statue as she tried processing it all. "She could have just said…"

"Marjorie didn't like to share her own dirty laundry with everyone. She would have rather spread someone else's than have her family, whom she loved, be left out in the open." Cybil glanced over at Marta, urging her to say something more.

"Raven, my sister would not have wanted you to do this."

"I killed her, don't you understand!" The girl exclaimed. "I killed her because of what YOU told me. She wasn't going to give us the recipe that would have meant college for me, or an artist internship. That money could have helped Grandma get a new wheelchair, it could have…it could have…"

"Raven, put the lighter down." Marta politely asked.

"Why? Jail is the only other outcome for me, so what have I got to lose?"

"Think about your brother, Rex. It's bad enough that you had him help you in carrying out your deed, but if you die now, then he will be charged as an accessory to murder. You can still save him from going to prison by confessing to everyone and saying that he had nothing to do with any of it." Cybil could see the wheels turning in the girl's mind.

"You're lying!"

"No, I'm not. Tell her, Officer Noel." Cybil motioned her head in his direction.

"That's right, Raven. As of now, we have enough to put your brother away for being an accessory to premeditated murder. So, if you lower her hands, and surrender yourself, you can say that it was all you, and he is in the clear. You can still do some good in the midst of this mess."

Raven shifted her gaze between the three of them, weighing out her options, and if they were truly telling the truth or not. Her mind felt so confused. It was a swirling jumble of guilt, shame, and memories of what she had done. But her brother was also involved now, and it was one thing for her to be in trouble, and a different matter entirely when his life was on the line too. "Alright. I'll do it to save my brother." She dropped the lighter on the ground, and lifted her palms into the air to visibly show that she was surrendering.

Officer Noel pulled her hands behind her back and handcuffed her wrists. "Raven Hieghner, you have the right to remain silent. Anything you say, can and will, be used against you in a court of law. You have the right…" He continued to read her the Miranda Rights whilst walking her up the stairs and out to the squad car.

CHAPTER 64

More flashing lights filled the small driveway to Marjorie's house, causing the neighbors to stir and stand around to gawk at the scene before them. Marta was in full-blown tears, upset at all of the ruckus she felt responsible for creating, and looked to Cybil through her watery sight. "How did this happen?"

"I think you can answer that question on your own." Walking passed Marjorie's sister, Cybil had no inclination to peer over her shoulder at the woman who was sobbing in the doorway. She simply headed over to her father's truck and opened the door, when Officer Noel called her to halt.

"I have to take her in and get her processed, but afterwards, I have a few questions to ask you."

"You want to know how I connected all the dots?"

"Yeah. I mean…apparently I missed something in the case, and I would like to know where."

"For starters, Pastor Lawrence said that when Raven went to check up on Gabriel, the night Marjorie died, that the lights on the canvas print were on in the living room. But when I visited her at the gallery, she told me the timer was set for 5 pm to 10:50 pm, and since she wasn't released from the scene until much later, she couldn't have seen them on; so either she was outright lying, or she had visited her aunt earlier in the day. Considering how many times she has been able to escape from her mother's house undetected, she had ample amount of opportunities to lace Marjorie's jars of skin cream."

"And without a key, she used the window to get in and out. I thought it was weird that they were supposed to be so close and yet, Raven didn't have a spare copy to get in and out. When we asked her, she said that Marjorie was going to change the locks and had to turn her old one in." Officer Noel shook his head.

"It's also because of a piece of information I had, and you didn't. See, when we confirmed that the goldfish was intended for Raven, I thought back to when Melody told me how Marjorie would take her great-niece down to the basement and pretend they were in the 1920s. Since it was her favorite time period, and Martin named the fish Norris, I did a little online searching and came up with a man by the name of Charles Norris."

"He was the first Chief Medical Examiner of New York." Cybil's eyes widened.

"What? You don't think I know a thing or two about history?"

"Well, one of his bigger stances was against the government poisoning manufactured alcohol that was often times stolen by bootleggers and given to people in lieu of actual drinking liquor. In their opinion, by poisoning the stuff that was bound to be highjacked, it would teach the public a lesson."

"And she would have learned about wood alcohol and its lethal toxicity from studying him." Noel smirked. "Pretty neat deducing, if I do say so myself."

"I also realized that while everyone else was in search of the cookie recipe card, Raven never asked about it; meaning that she must have known what happened to it. She kept looking for the items that were stolen, in search of the journal in the hopes that Marjorie copied it down in the book. But Marjorie was ahead of her, by giving it to Marta for safe keeping." Cybil shrugged her shoulders. "Hey, I can't take all the credit though, when you handed me the clincher to seal the deal by telling me about Marjorie's journal in the first place."

"That was more of a twofer, really. I had a feeling Marta was lying about it being stolen and I knew she wasn't going to open up to me about it. So I sent you instead."

"Figures. You have me do all your work for you." She gave him a playful smile and climbed into the back of the pickup.

"One last thing," Officer Noel paused, "How did you figure out the scrunchie?"

"I had a little help from the Ghost of Christmas Past."

CHAPTER 65

Cybil knocked on the door to her uncle's office, next to his title as "Detective" painted on the glass. She waited until he glanced up from the paperwork on his desk. "We have an extra seat at the table for you. Christmas dinner, at 4:30 pm sharp."

"I already arranged to be on duty that day, so thanks, but I'm good."

"Yeah…about that. I had a few strings pulled so that your shift was removed from the schedule."

Detective Lawson gave his niece a perturbed look of puzzlement. "What are you trying to do? Isn't one murder this month enough for you?"

"Thought maybe an explanation was long overdue to my father."

"What are you talking about?" His head fell back as it dawned on him. "Marjorie's journal."

"It was pretty enlightening in many different ways. Including why you sold the farm after you promised your father, and mine, that you would never do that. Very coincidental that the Stonewells ended up with a large, and anonymous donation, right after the sale of the land."

"Everyone saw their family as being rich because that's the image they gave off. But they really weren't. Especially after Marjorie had her fatal car accident up in New York. That's why they had to tap into Marta's college fund. Mr. Stonewell was cash poor, as most of his wealth was tied up in assets."

"Ralph told me that you used to date Marjorie back in high school. Were you the distraction that caused her to look away when her sister fell? I would understand if you felt guilty for what happened, and so would my father."

"You haven't told him about any of this, right?"

"No. Thought it should come from you."

"Cybil, there are more factors at play here, then you realize. Just leave it alone."

"Don't you think it's time to put the past behind you two and repair the bridge?"

"Look, I already have plans to eat with Officer Noel that evening. It's his first Christmas away from his home town."

Cybil pulled her phone from her jacket's pocket, and primed her fingers at the ready to send her mother a text. "Should I tell her to expect you?"

CHAPTER 66

Cybil sat in her fleece pajamas, snug and warm with her feet underneath a green and red blanket by the end of her bed. It had been crocheted by her grandmother, a Christmas present from years past, and she smiled as the memory of peppermint-scented candies wafted into her nose. Snow fell peacefully against the window, coating the landscape in a softness unmatched by any artist she had ever seen. The serenity of a cold winter's night, cuddled up in blankets, and cradling a warm mug in the palms of her hands, was all she wanted in that wonderful, blissful moment. *This is perfect.*

She watched little Norris swimming around his tank in glee, catching all of the food she had just given him, and thought back to how everything truly did seem to work out for everyone in the end. Mrs. Norman's husband didn't leave her for good, and came back on Christmas Eve, when he explained that his friend was going to sell the beach house and it would be the last time they could hang out by the waves. The church obtained legal ownership of Marjorie's estate, and allowed her relatives to grab whatever heirlooms they wanted, before they were going to use it to help a less fortunate family get back on their feet. Pastor Lawrence decided not to press charges against Ms. Drake and her brother, and allowed for the items to be on display at the Historical Society as long as there was a plaque mentioning they were on loan. Rudolph had been discovered at the old treehouse marked on the bootlegger's map, safe and sound. John had enough time to get him dressed up for the Christmas Party at the hospital, after Rex "pretended" to find him wandering out there by myself. Apparently, that was what they were arguing about outside the gallery the day Cybil went to visit Raven. The reindeer had gotten lose, and he was meant to be blamed for the death of her great aunt.

Yasmin's family arrived on time from the airport, miraculously, and she told them all about her and Cybil's murder investigation, minus her being the main suspect. At the end of the tale, she introduced Martin Stonewell, who was seeking forgiveness for not having prevented Ezra's death. Not only did it work out well for him and the Manahans, but both his sisters were reaching out to him and invited him to Christmas dinner. Jeffrey confessed to killing his cousin when he discovered she was going to double-cross him to get her old job back, and had also used the same wood alcohol when he found Raven's and Rex's still at an old hideout in the woods.

The ironic thing was that Marjorie never did lie about the cookies she made. Being allergic to almonds, her mother would make her a slightly altered version of the recipe, and since she made it from memory, it was the true recipe as she had known it always to be. As for the recipe card, it was burned, along with letters. It came down to the point where Marjorie didn't feel right about selling the recipe regardless, and wanted it to die with her. And while Detective Lawson declined her offer of clearing the air by coming to her parents' for dinner, she hadn't given up hope on him yet.

Cybil stabbed at a piece of the warmed up leftovers she was thoroughly enjoying. Chicken, cooked in a parmesan cheese sauce, and sprinkled with crumbling cornbread muffins, looked better than gold, and was far tastier too. This was her; neither imported tea from England, nor fanciful coffee from specially prepared beans, nor rich European hot chocolate, was needed to complete her perfect night. Real food that had been cooked from the heart, and savored in a rare minute of peaceful bliss, was what she treasured; and valued above all presents wrapped in bows and beautiful paper. The feeling of happiness that engulfed her insides in warmth, seeing her friends and family have genuine smiles painted across their lips, as childhood Christmas shows played on the television.

A feeling such as that, deep and profound, that was what she had wished for Christmas, and Cybil Lawson finally got it; even though she would never find out that the last living relative, of the woman who created the cookie recipe, was Mr. Jeffrey.

The End

Cybil Lawson will be back in...
In Plein Air Sight

RESEARCH QUESTIONS

1. Did bootleggers really use cow shoes to avoid the police?
Yes, they did. Bootleggers used blocks of wood, carved to look like hooves, in order to throw police off their trails. According to an article from 1922, a newspaper in St. Petersburg Florida described how a shoe was discovered near Tampa, and it consisted of a metal strip with wooden hooves attached. This unique invention made it so that the individual would be able to slip them onto their shoes when coming to and from the still, keeping the location hidden from the authorities. You can search this topic online to see a rare photo of a policeman demonstrating how it worked.

2. What is banketstaaf?
Banketstaaf, also known as a Dutch Christmas Log, is a puff pastry that is served around Christmas time and is a tradtional Dutch holiday dessert. It is filled with almond paste and baked in the oven until golden brown. Its can also be shaped into an "O" for a wreath, or into the letters "M" and "S."

3. What are classic Pennsylvania Dutch foods?
Many of what are considered to be staples in the Commonwealth of Pennsvlvania, are specific to the region. Just like what Officer Noel gets introduced to at The Nickel of Time resturaunt, here is a list of menu items that are Pennsylvania Dutch through and through.

* Lebanon Bologna
* Shoofly Pie
* Scrapple
* Chicken Pot Pie (Pennsylvania Dutch Style)
* Chicken Corn Rivel Soup
* Apple Butter
* Whoopie Pie

CYBIL'S CHRISTMAS GNOME CRAFT

My Supply List:

- one tomato cage
- non-wired green garland
- zip ties
- diagonal cutters (pliers)
- duct tape
- styrofoam block
- Christmas tablecloth/ fabric
- something round for the hat's tip
- a collapsible dog's water bowl
- green crafting wire
- safety pins
- newspaper to protect crafting surfaces

Optional: upholstery foam or outdoor foam for cushions can be used inside the hat to bulk up the form. Pre-lit garland can also be used for this project instead of regular outdoor garland.

Step 1: To create the point where the top of the hat will be, first use some duct tape to join the three legs of the tomato cage together. Be careful while handling these ends, as they can be very sharp!

Step 2: Starting with the largest section of the tomato cage, which is also considered the "top" of the cage and the "bottom" of this project, take the garland and knot one end on either the bottom most rung or the top rung of the bottom section. From there, weave the garland from top to bottom, inside and out, in a repetitive fashion, until the bottom section is completely filled.

Please continue onto the next page ----->

<u>Step 3</u>: Keep weaving each section one at a time, moving around the "bottom" level and working your way up to the "middle" level, as described in the previous step. Do not go beyond the "middle" level, as this is where the hat will cover up the rest of the wire frame. (Try to maintain an even amount of space between the weaves.)

<u>Step 4</u>: Gather the rest of your supplies and make sure to have some protection for your surfaces, such as newspaper, because of the tomato cage's hard edges. Due to the height of your cage, it might be easier to work on the floor.

<u>Step 5</u>: Take a styrofoam block, or a square of floral foam, and shove it over the exposed ends that were taped earlier. Once it is in place, use the duct tape to secure it onto the wires. (You can use a retractable knife to shape the foam, but please remember the blade is sharp.)

<u>Step 6</u>: Take the collapsible dog bowl, which usually comes with a carabiner clip, and hook it onto the top of the "middle" section. The bowl can be used in either its popped-out form, as in the example image at the top of this post, or collapsed.

<u>Step 7</u>: Now is where the trickier part comes into play; trying to get the fabric, or tablecloth, to drape the way you would like. If you manage to get it right the first time, that's great! But don't get discouraged if it takes a few attempts to put it into place, like it did for me.

<u>Step 8</u>: Clipping on the ball tip of the hat is fairly simple if you have a plastic ball that can simply be attached to the material. If you don't have one, make do with what you have lying around! Be creative and have some fun with it. If you don't wish to add anything else, then you are done!

But if you want to add some fluffiness to the hat, bunch up a white tablecloth and use green crafting wire to attach it to the tomato cage underneath. (This also helps to hide any imperfections.)

For more detailed instructions, including some artist tips and additional images of the process, please visit my website. www.SarahIckesArt.com

About the Author:

Sarah Ickes has her Associates Degree in Art and Design. She has always held a passion for writing since her first publication of a poem in fifth grade. Not only does she pursue writing, but she also creates artwork that is available for purchasing; such as the illustrations and book cover of this novel. History is of a special interest to her, as she enjoys learning about the past. Please visit her website for more details or follow her on social media.

www.SarahIckesArt.com

Thank you for reading my book, and I hope
you enjoyed it!